Seph

The Reflection of Divinity

Writen By Ezra Sandborn

With artwork by Michael Brewster and Jacob Jessop

Written by: Ezra Sandborn

Published by: Sandpaper press 2021, P.O. Box 512 Monmouth, Oregon, 97361, USA.

ISBNs:

Paperback: 978-1-7371643-0-2

Ebook: 978-1-7371643-1-9

Hardcover: 978-1-7371643-2-6

Library of Congress Control Number: 2021938124

esandborn.com

sandpaperpress.com

Forward

This book has been a long time in the making, but honestly, I sort of wrote it on accident. While I have spent most of my life developing these characters and the world in which they live, publishing them into a book where other people could also experience them was never anything more than a vague fantasy. That was, of course, until I got to the lowest point in my life.

I had just been forced to close my first business, something I had been passionate about for a long time, if perhaps a little over eager. On the heels of trying to work through the debt and emotional roller coaster that went along with that, I was in a car accident in which I severely injured my leg, leaving me unable to walk properly, and perform many seemingly basic and simple tasks. All while living in a trailer in my in-laws back yard, (thank you by the way.)

It was in the middle of this that I stumbled across a writing prompt on the internet. It was simple, but it got something turning in my brain that wouldn't stop. "You climb into a taxi, it doesn't take you where you want to go, but where you need to go."

Ironically, while the scene that played out in my head did ultimately lead to the creation of our leading character James, it barely even got a passing reference in the final version of the book, not even making it into some of the early drafts at all.

It did, however, inspire me to write a short story

which, after a significant amount of prompting from my wife, and sister-in-law, would become the first draft of chapter one. Eventually what started out as a project to distract myself became more than seventy thousand words and almost four hundred pages worth of text.

Had I set out to write a book on purpose, this isn't the one I would have started with. I think if I were to have done it intentionally I would have started much earlier in the history of Ving with a very different cast, and a much more fantasy feel.

Since that isn't the book I wrote, there are a few things about this world you should know before you get into the story. If you are one of those people who skip the forward and dive straight in, you will probably be fine, if a little confused when something feels like it has been spelled wrong where it hasn't. Those of you skipping past the forward may not discover that you missed something but for the rest of us it will remain our little secret.

While the book is written in English, the language the characters within it are primarily speaking is significantly different. There are several key places within the text I have tried to represent this. Primarily with the predominant language spoken within the Alliance known as Truic. Truic is heavily based on the Spanish language. There is a reason for this, for now suffice it to say that many of the names and spellings of things throughout the book deliberately show this influence.

In places where numbers are represented as digits, or letters are set apart by themselves it would be appropriate to use the Spanish pronunciation of them. However, doing so or not doing so shouldn't change your experience with the book too much. Additionally there are specific words such as 'sumiller' that are written in the Spanish form instead of the traditional French 'sommelier' we are used to seeing.

With that in mind, it is my pleasure to share the products of my imagination. I hope you have as much fun reading it as I did when I wrote it, and that there will be many more adventures for us to share together in the future.

Pronunciation Guide

In "Seph: The Reflection of Divinity" we encounter many strange and unfamiliar words. Some are taken directly from earth languages, primarily spanish, but others are totally alien. This guide should be a helpful tool to help you navigate all those tricky pronunciations and become more immersed in the universe of Vinge.

Seph (sɛ f)

Drak'or ('drak 'or)

Fingal ('fɪn gaḷ)

Vyanna (vi 'ɑnɑ)

Dressick (drɛ 'sɪk)

Xious (zī 'os)

Meghnah ('mɛg 'nə)

Re'akke ('ri 'æk)

Zaeith ('zä Ith)

Aiunys ('ai unIs)

Andarin (an 'da ɾIn)

Jomar ('ho maɾ)

Fetu Gaielin ('fä tu / 'gä lIn)

Atlione ('at lio nä)

Maylis ('mä lIs)

Vyrant ('vi rInt)

Vinge (vI nǰ)

Sphiya ('sfi ə)

Vhast ('va st)

Theyes ('thä Is)

Arah'a'el (ara a ɛl)

Zymo (zi mo)

Dreku (drɛ ku)

Zhemarah ('zɛm ara)

Nevarian (nɛv ar iɛn)

Jasvlin (jæs vlIn)

Trepidor (trɛ pI dor)

Dramia (dra mi ə)

Aundreus (an drɛ əs)

Reicue (wri kʸð)

Norf (norf)

Gashwar (gæ shwar)

Lalazaria (la la zaɾ ia)

Sumillier (su mi ʎr)
A wine waiter,
Spanish equivalent of
sommelier.

Sylvinn (sIl vIn)

Jeriell (jɛ ri ɛl)

Pryne (praIn)

Ulun'tess (yu lun tɛs)

Destune (dɛ stun)

Mio'nayo (mio näo)

Frehn (frɛn)

O'rah (o ra)

Rek'ah (rɛk a)

Darith (där Ith)

Dessika Ar'eack (dɛ sIkə /
aɾ iak)

Corah'harin (ko ɾa haɾ In)

Glayina (glä Inə)

A'un (a un)

Meku (mɛ ku)

Re'kah (rɛ ka)

Fo'el (fo ɛl)

Ty'ell (taI ɛl)

Euinda (iun də)

Erindite (ɛ rIn daIt)

Vhen (vɛn)

Lavay (la vä)

A'el (a ɛl)

Laiem (la ɛm)

Aphiss (ä fIs)

Chellis (chɛ lIs)

Izarrius (aI za riəs)

Lameres (la mɛ Rɛs)

Buru (bu ɾu)

Cress (kR ɛs)

Zek (zɛk)

Ve'o (vɛ o)

Tru'all (tRu al)

Ah'trell (a tRɛl)

Seph

Prologue

Streaks of light danced across the projected surface of the Shade's hologram as the Andarin system populated the view field.

"Envelope closed." Meghnah, the ship's navigator confirmed.

"Thanks sis, land us on Jomar." Re'akke pressed the intercom button on the side of the command chair. "Captain, we have arrived."

The com chirped followed by a brief crackle of static. "Thank you, I shall join you shortly." another chirp before falling silent.

Inhaling, Re'akke pushed himself out of the command chair, moving to his position at the tactical station, and turning on the projected display.

The Andarin system was newly excavated, and terraforming efforts had only recently begun on its most ideal worlds for life. As such, huge harvesters blasted across the space between its other worlds, carrying mined resources back to Andarin Prime. Jomar, the only established civilian space port in the system, would have plenty of antimatter on hand to refuel the ship's archaic engine.

"Okay Meg, I got clearance for pad three." Said Chloe, who was manning the communications terminal.

"Got it."

The air in the room got colder as the door to the captain's private quarters opened without a sound. A sensation which accompanied the man wherever he went, leaving the tips of your fingers and toes numb.

His bright red eyes, highlighted like tiny flames against his obsidian skin, watched the holographic projection of the ships as Meghnah carefully brought it down to the landing platform. On Re'akke's display, visible waves could be seen spreading across as the bay's artificial gravity activated.

"Re'akke, I want you to come along this time. Go get Fetu and meet me at the hatch."

A smile twisted the corner of his lip upward. "On it."

The primary purpose of this stop was to refuel. Something that they did not need to do very often. However, on their last mission, they got into a nasty entanglement with a swarm of space dwelling monsters, which ate into a sizable chunk of their supply. But, it was also an opportunity to land a new client. In a system under active terraforming, there would be plenty of start-up corporation owners looking to make their mark on the galaxy, and willing to pay out to any mercenary able to help.

He dropped into the chute leading down to the crew deck skipping the last couple of rungs on the ladder. Fetu was already putting on his uniform in the cramped corridor of the crew's sleeping area, made to look even smaller by the man's hulking frame.

As Fetu slid into his undershirt, Re'akke found himself staring at the white scar-like streaks on his skin. Unlike Re'akke and his sister, Fetu was only half Drak'or and while their skin was lighter than the captains, Fetu's ash gray was almost pale in comparison. The mixing of Fingal blood left him caught somewhere between the two races, without fins, but with long ears and a bald head.

"I expected you would still be asleep." Re'akke said.

Fetu shrugged. "I felt the gravity turn on and figured The Captain would be calling on me soon."

Re'akke smiled. "You're not wrong. He sent me to get you, said to meet him at the hatch."

Fetu pulled on his uniform jacket, then slapped him on the shoulder. "It's about time he let you come along."

As promised, The Captain was waiting for them at the bottom of the ramp, arguing about refueling fees with a vaguely humanoid robot.

Re'akke descended the ramp, looking up at the stars through the open roof of the landing bay. As they reached the bottom, The Captain and the android came to an agreement, and the robot sped off disappearing into a hatch leading between bays. The captain turned to face them, tossing his head towards the port entrance, red eyes glowing under the shadow of his hood.

The inside of the station itself reminded Re'akke more of a bar than anything. The air was thick with smoke, and the stench of alcohol. Boisterous conversations and heated arguments drowned out the music being played in the background. An ideal atmosphere for whispered conversation in the darker corners of the room.

The noise died down as they entered, no doubt alerted to their presence by The Captain's strange aura. A quick glance was all he needed, and they returned to their own business. Soon the atmosphere returned to equilibrium.

"We are looking for anyone who-" the captain suddenly cut off. There was a new tension to his body, his shoulders tightening, lips pressed together in a tight line.

Fetu let out a long sigh. "Sorry kid, looks like you got robbed of your first negotiation."

"What do you mean?" He followed their eyes to the balcony level. His breath caught in the back of his throat. At a table near the guardrail sat the most extraordinary young women Re'akke supposed he had ever seen. How did he not notice her before? She stuck out like a quasar in the center of a fluorescent nebula.

She wore a plain white dress, and a purple shawl wrapped around her shoulders. With long silver hair which was tied in a simple partial braid. It was as though she existed in her own bubble which ignored the rules of the surrounding space.

"Go find a table, this might take a while."

Fetu tossed his head toward a table near the door. "Best get comfortable."

Re'akke, pulled up a chair, and ordered himself a drink. "Who is she?"

Fetu looked up from his data pad. "Her name is Guinevere, I don't know much beyond that. She just shows up sometimes and gives us a job."

"Does she pay well?"

Fetu shrugged. "Not sure, I never get to sit in on their negotiations."

A droid delivered an amber-filled mug, Re'akke took a sip of the liquid, the flavors of caramel and ash washing over his tongue.

"Is there anything else you know about her?"

The larger man let out a sigh, powering down his data pad and setting it on the table. "She always wears white. And The Captain always takes her job."

Re'akke lifted an eyebrow. "Always?"

He nodded "Always."

Re'akke sipped his drink, watching the woman's face. Had he seen her somewhere before? She appeared to be concerned, he got the distinct impression she was pleading with The Captain about something.

The Captain was difficult to read. He shook his head, then she reached her hand across the table, placing it on top of his. He relaxed, leaning back into his chair. She smiled softly and stood, placing her hand on his shoulder and pausing a moment as she passed.

Descending the stairs, she stopped before exiting, and turned to face Re'akke. For a moment they locked eyes, and he felt as if he could spend eternity in hers. They were a deep blue which left even the oceans of Atlione feeling dry by comparison.

"I'm sorry." She whispered, the words floated across the air between them like crystal chimes in a gentle breeze. Re'akke shook himself back to reality.

The captain's shadow fell across their table. "Come on, we are heading for DSI 5771."

"What's there?" Fetu asked

The captain did not look at either of them. "The son of a traitor."

Chapter 1

James rolled off the metal plank he called his bed, floating into the zero gravity corridor of the crew's bunk area. The ship-wide alarm still echoed in his eardrums. He reached into his foot locker for his discarded uniform from the night before, and pulled the black jacket on over his crimson undershirt. Years of military training made the motion automatic.

He glanced down the rows of beds. The sleeping area was divided into five sections, with six beds each, in stacks of three on either side. And a locker room at the far end. Even compared to alliance military ships, it was cramped.

Neither of the other two bridge officers on his shift were up yet. He pushed aside his worn blue jacket and handgun, grabbing a small sting blade and clipping it to the inside of his belt. He doubted there would be any need for it onboard the Shade, but carrying one had become a habit, one that had saved his life more than once.

He took hold of the guide rail, and used it to shove off towards the front of the ship. The alarm most likely meant they had been pulled out of hyperspace early. Out here in the blurred lines between the ring and the outer colonies, interdiction zones weren't exactly rare. Mercenaries were often hired to escort ships across it in case of a pirate ambush.

The intercom crackled, and a voice James didn't recognize began to speak. "You have entered restricted space, disable your engines and prepare to turn over your ship immediately."

He let out a sigh, not pirates. They must have accidentally crossed into a quarantine zone being patrolled by the Order of the Descendants. A fanatic paramilitary-pseudo-government passing themselves off as a religion. They were the only group he was aware of with the necessary tech to slice into the Shade's intercom like that. And the idea that a group of pirates could have stolen some of their tech was... well, unthinkable.

It would be strange for Meghnah to make that kind of a mistake though. Had the quarantine border shifted again? Ever since the Aberration began to spread in the outer colonies, stops like this had become almost routine. If the plague continued at its current rate, soon there would be no one left to inhabit the outer colonies.

James grabbed the ladder in the nearest lift chute, and propelled himself upward, catching himself on the railing at the command deck. He keyed the switch. The iris closed beneath his feet, activating the artificial gravity below him as the door slid silently open. A small chill traced the inside of his shoulder blades, and even after four months as a member of its crew, the impossible grace of everything onboard, made the Shade hauntingly ethereal.

Taking a breath, James stepped through the threshold onto the bridge. A holographic image of a Descendant Wyvern-class battleship hovered in the view field, massive wing-like structures protruding from either side, and wrapping around its central core.

Fetu, the ship's first officer and chief engineer, acknowledged him with a nod as he entered the deck. He slid into the tactical station to the starboard side of the captain's chair, and switched on his projected display.

A moment later Meghnah entered the room, relieving the SK01 model android from the navigation terminal located below his own. As droids went, Scot was a decent navigator, but if things got messy, nothing could replace a real pilot, and Meghnah was the best he had ever worked with.

Chloe entered right behind Meghnah and sat at the communication terminal across from her. James caught himself staring for a moment. She was certainly attractive, appearing mostly human, with platinum blond hair and bright blue eyes hinting at a mixed fingalin heritage. But she also exuded energy in a way that made her uncomfortable to be around.

James began running the tactical data over the top of the view fields projection on his own display. The temperature in the room dropped a few degrees, the tips of James's fingers growing cold. Turning his head slightly, he caught the figure of The Captain entering from the central chute, bringing with him his unmistakable aura which felt as if it drained the life force out of you.

Captain Zaeith and his ship had become somewhat of a legend among mercenaries, taking on missions considered impossible, or too dangerous for anyone else. Many people believed he didn't even exist, that he was an unattainable ideal all mercenaries were striving for.

It wasn't clear if Zaeith was even his real name, or if it was more like a title adopted by the Shade's captains from one generation to the next.

James stood and saluted, placing his thumb against his temple with his hand extended vertically parallel to the side of his head.

The Captain gave him a quick nod.

Fetu stood, stepping to the port side of the command chair. "We appear to have been pulled out of hyperspace by a Descendant blockade barrier. They are requesting we turn over the ship."

The captain's lips pulled into a smirk. "Are they now?" He pulled back his cloak as he sat in the command chair. "Let me talk to them."

"Channel open." Chloe said at the same moment the view field switched to a projection of a tall fingalin wearing a crisp white Descendant uniform, with the customary lavender accents. He had a single silver strip over his left breast, and two white gold clips on his collar.

"I see you are prepared to surrender your ship." His voice had the cool, pompous tone only a Descendant officer could be capable of.

The Captain shook his head. "No Colonel, but I am curious why you decided it was alright to pull it out of hyperspace."

The Colonel's ears flattened out to the sides, and his eye twitched almost imperceptibly. It was notoriously difficult to determine the rank of a Descendant. An intentional sleight of hand so outsiders would always assume they were in charge.

"This space is under a quarantine order, put in place by the Divine Council in the name of The Lady Vyanna."

The Captain's face softened a little. "I do not recognize the authority of your Vyanna."

The colonel's eyes narrowed. "You would defy the Divine Council?"

Zaeith sat forward in his chair, the lines in his face becoming tight. "The Divine Council has no authority here; this is free space, and if we are not allowed to continue our mission, the colony on DSI 3122 will die a needless death. Their blood will be added to the body count of your order."

James pulled up the Descendant ship's registration ID:

Classification: Battleship
Subclass: Defender
Registration: The Order of the Descendants
Internal Classification: Wyvern
Specific designation: Vyrant
Crew approximation: 300
Commanding officer: Gillian Maylis

James ignored the rest, except to confirm what the Shade's sensors had already told him.

The Wyvern-class ships were nowhere near as powerful as the Drake-class Dreadnought, or the legendary Dragon-class carrier ships.

Still, James had never heard of anyone defeating one before. This should have concerned him more than it did. But the Shade did have a reputation; having looked over the specs several times, the odds were not that one-sided.

The Shade's defensive and offensive capabilities far exceeded anything you would expect to see on a ship of its size. There were weapons systems onboard James had never seen anywhere else. Most of which were under the exclusive purview of The Captain.

The Descendant officer's eyes flicked to the side. He gave a quick nod. "You leave me no choice," he said flatly.

A warning light flashed on the tactical display. "Their forward plasma canons are charging." James adjusted the dimensional phase shift to match the projected output.

He didn't understand how it worked; the Phase Shift Modulator was something the captain had designed himself, but from what he understood, it warped space around the ship, causing it to exist in a different phase of reality. By tuning it to specific frequencies, the ship could be made to pass through some things as if they weren't even there.

Zaeith gave a quick nod. The eye piece unfolded from behind his head, clicking itself into place around his right eye. Part of a neural link system which allowed him to interface the ship's systems directly with his brain.

A second light began flashing on the tactical display, indicating that the Descendant cannons had launched their volley against them.

"No damage, all systems functional," James reported.

The shield was not impenetrable, it required precise calibration to a given energy blast, the Colonel had not dedicated himself to destroying them yet and that round had been predictable.

The Descendant officers eyes narrowed. "Who are

you?" his voice was low and suspicious.

The Captain rose from his chair, his hood slid up over his head, connecting the final circuits in the neural link. "I am Captain Zaeith of the Shade, and my name shall hunt you to your grave."

The channel cut off. The view field reverting to its projection of the Wyvern. There was a bright flash, the orange sphere of the infamous Descendant plasma shield erupting into existence.

James rushed to keep up with the influx of information. He adjusted the phase modulator, calling up an algorithm that would help modulate it based on inputs from the main deflector shield. He activated the built-in cloaking device. His display flashed, indicating the captain had armed one of the solid-state missile arrays.

* * *

The name rang through Colonel Gillian Maylis's mind. Zaeith of the Shade. The name was a direct reference to the Descendants' most sacred text, the Words of Eclipse; Zaeith of the Shade, the Lord of Death. It wasn't possible. It was a myth, a legend.

A chill ran down his spine. The ship had barely registered on any of their sensors. If it weren't for the hyperspace signature they wouldn't have even noticed it, combined with the fact that they got almost no information upon scanning the ship. Then there was that face, those glowing red eyes able to see straight through him.

"Shields up, weapons to maximum!" Gillian commanded. "I want that ship turned to dust!" He watched out the view screen as the plasma shield sprang up around them. The familiar orange glow faded as the computer filtered it from the sensor data. Nothing could penetrate the plasma shield. It was Vyanna's last and greatest gift: absolute protection. But if the stories were true…

No, he couldn't think about that now, he had to focus.

The Shade vanished, reappearing a moment later as if it had teleported. He glanced at the display in front of him, no indication they had opened a hyperspace sleeve. A second ship appeared identical to the Shade, followed by a third and fourth. Had the ship cloned itself?

The Vyrant's cannon fire tore through space, the plasma passed through the insubstantial clones becoming bright stars in the distance.

A fresh wave of terror welled up in Gillian's stomach, as a sense of inevitability began to set in. "Sir, I think we have it." one of the tactical officers shouted.

"Good, destroy it," Gillian let out a breath and grinned. So, it was just a clever trick, nothing more.

The clones coalesced into a single ship. The Vyrant's shots flew wide of its location, as it rolled around the spheres of glowing plasma being hurled in its direction. Gillian's face fell; what was happening? Thin blue lights erupted from the small ship, hurtling towards the Vyrant in long arcs. Missiles? What good did they think solid-state missiles would do against the omnipotent plasma shield?

The instant before contact the missiles vanished, leaving behind a burst of electricity scattering outward. Gillian collapsed in his chair as the tiny hyperspace envelopes vanished.

Alarms erupted across the bridge, first

communication went out, then propulsion, weapons, alarms cascaded over each other as systems began shutting down. The lights went out. Emergency power kicked in, red light illuminating the deck. That was it; Zaeith had won.

Slowly Gillian rose, people shouted all around him, error signs flashed on every screen, only the shields and life support remained active. Gillian stumbled off the bridge, ignoring the chaos around him.

* * *

The Captain's neural link disengaged. James stared at his display, the warship was almost invisible behind its plasma shield but it was obvious it wasn't going anywhere soon.

The ease of the Shade's victory was difficult enough to believe on its own. But what had James dumbfounded was the method that had gotten them there.

James scanned through the data once again, but there was no doubting it. Hyperspace theorists had ruled out the possibility of ever weaponizing hyperspace sleeves. They were too unstable and unpredictable at a small enough size to be useful. The Captain had done it, simultaneously, with sixteen separate warheads.

The Captain turned to leave. "Fetu, the bridge is yours." His voice was calm and steady.

He disappeared through the door to the rear of the bridge.

James had asked The Captain about the Shade's equipment when he first took over as tactical officer, to which he had only smirked and said. "Some new tools, with a few old tricks."

Chapter 2

James picked idly at his food. Travis, the ship's cook, had prepared an omelet stuffed with sweet vegetables and grilled meats. "How do they even get fresh eggs out here?" James asked half to himself.

"Well you know The Captain; he always has some kind of trick up his sleeve." Fetu's booming voice interrupted his thoughts. "Mind if I join?"

"Go ahead, but aren't you supposed to be watching the bridge?"

Fetu shrugged. "The Captain relieved me early. What about you? There is still fifteen minutes before the bell, why aren't you in bed?" he dropped into a nearby chair. "That little scuffle earlier got you shaken up?"

James smiled. "No. There is just no way I am getting anymore sleep on that chunk of metal you call a bed."

Fetu laughed before digging into his food.

"Hey, Fetu," James asked. "What can you tell me

about the warheads we used against the Descendants?"

Fetu's large pointed ears twisted forward quizzically. "Oh right, that was your first fight with the Descendants, wasn't it?" His ears pulled back as he thought. "Those were Hyper Sleeve Warheads."

James blinked, "No seriously, what were they?"

Fetu wiped off his chin with a napkin. "I am being serious."

James sat down his fork, leaning over the table. "But that's impossible."

Fetu chuckled. "You're right, but that's never stopped The Captain from doing anything before."

He slid his tray underneath James's. "Look, I don't know how he does it, he just does. It's like some kind of magic."

He stood to leave. "Well g'dnight." he laughed.

A small hand appeared on Fetu's shoulder and shoved him back into his chair. "Hang out a minute, I want to hear more of your theories about The Captain." A young female voice said as Chloe squeezed into the chair between them.

Great, she had always rubbed him the wrong way, so thus far he had avoided extended conversations with the girl.

"Yeah, spill." Meghnah sat down as well. She was straightforward, easy to read, with a grounded attitude that James found easy to tolerate. Why she was always following Chloe around was anyone's guess.

Fetu's ears drooped a little in confusion "Wait, what do you think I know about the Captain that you don't? If you have questions, ask him yourself."

Meghnah snorted. "Are you kidding? Has The Captain ever given us a straight answer?" Meghnah did an exaggerated head shake. "Aside from Nevarian, you've known him the longest, at least give us your best guess."

Fetu had been the Shade's first officer for nearly eight years. Even before that, he had been the chief engineer. Comparatively, Meghnah had been on board for almost two years, and Chloe was almost as new as James, who had only been an official member of the crew for three months. If anyone could sort through the mystery around The Captain, it was Fetu. It was possible Nevarian knew more about the captain than anyone, but the doctor kept to himself, and only interacted with the others when it was absolutely necessary.

Fetu sighed. "Alright, but I won't make any promises, The Captain keeps a lot to himself. What do you want to know?"

Meghnah sat back in her chair, a satisfied smirk on her face. "Well, where do you think he is from?"

Chloe blinked. "Wait a second, I always assumed he was from the outer colonies. What makes you think he isn't?"

Meghnah let out a short sigh as she sipped from her mug of tea. "The outer colonies cover a lot of space, which colony could make a big difference, but, he doesn't act like he grew up in the colonies. I mean sure, he's Drak'or, but he doesn't practice the Vhast religion like anyone else I know. And people in the colonies don't like to be tied down, but our captain is loyal to a fault."

James nodded. "More likely he grew up somewhere in the ring, more structured than the colonies but not quite as polarized as the core worlds. He would have been a minority, but not an outcast."

Fetu attempted to leave again. "Looks like you guys

got it figured out, don't know what you need me for."

"Hold on, we still want your input." Chloe protested.

Fetu sat his tray back down and looked her dead in the eyes. "You really want to know what I think?"

Chloe hesitated under his gaze then gave a small nod.

Fetu grinned mischievously "I think he is from Vinge."

"Wait, Vinge?" James asked. Vinge was the planet of origin. According to legend, all three races had come from Vinge. A war between them had ultimately led to its destruction, leaving behind little more than an uninhabitable shell. That had been over three thousand years ago, and while the alliance still held its capital there, unless you were a politician, there was no reason to even visit.

Fetu nodded slowly. "Do you know how the planet was destroyed?"

Everyone stared uneasily. That was one of the greatest controversies in the story, every religion and race had their own versions.

James spoke up first. "Well the general belief is it was caused by the use of powerful weapons developed before space colonization. The planet would have been destroyed if not for the Descendants' intervention."

This was the most prevalent version. Though the religion was not officially part of the treaty, which constituted the founding document for The Alliance of Powers. The order had facilitated the agreement, finally abandoning much of their own technology as well. Leaving only a few things such as the Plasma shield in place, to serve as both a monument to their history, and as a reminder to future generations.

Seph

"Right, as if three thousand years ago they had something stronger than planetary cannons," Meghnah interjected.

Chloe looked to her friend. "You have a different theory?"

"Magic," Meghnah replied cynically.

This theory was popular among practitioners of the Drak'or religion of Vhast, which taught that in the time of Vinge, people had possessed the ability to bend reality. It was their belief that the planet collapsed as a consequence of their tampering with the world's balance. The Alliance was brought about by a mighty magi known as The Dark One.

If you believed in such things, the theory was valid enough. It didn't make a lot of sense to think they hadn't rediscovered, or even surpassed, the technology of more than three millennia ago. Though James didn't bother pointing out that, interplanetary cannons could, in fact, destroy a planet, or at least make it uninhabitable. The problem with the story was the idea of magic itself, a concept kept alive only by the whispers of travelers outside the boundaries of colonized space, which most regarded as fiction at best.

Fetu shrugged. "The Descendants have a different story. Have any of you ever read the Words of Eclipse?"

James shook his head.

"No, why?" Chloe asked.

Meghnah shifted uncomfortably, "What does this have to do with The Captain?"

"Well," Fetu sat back in his chair, "the name The Captain uses, Zaeith, it comes from the Words of Eclipse."

"Really?" James leaned forward, elbows on the table.

Fetu nodded. "The ship's name too. Zaeith is said to

have been a shade, a shadow servant to the old gods. The Words of Eclipse say he wanted the gods' power for himself, so he murdered them, becoming a demon. As punishment for his sin, Vyanna sealed Zaeith away deep beneath the planet's crust, where he was to remain for all eternity."

"So what happened?" Chloe asked.

"Hate." Fetu said flatly. "It was not the war itself that caused the planet's collapse, but rather the hatred that fueled it. The blood-lust was so intense that it broke the seal. Zaeith awakened from his cursed sleep, drawing on their animosity and hatred he became the Lord of Death. Using the power he had stolen from the gods, he consumed the planet itself.

Meghnah looked skeptical. "Are you trying to tell us that our Captain is an ancient death god? Seriously, he isn't *that* scary."

Fetu laughed. "I wouldn't go that far, but I have never met anyone, outside of the Descendants themselves, who knew as much as The Captain does about their theology. If you consider that, along with his race and mannerisms, then the only place in the galaxy he could have come from is Vinge. I don't know, maybe he was the kid of a Drak'or lord who sold out to the Empire and had nowhere else to go, but it's the only thing that makes sense."

"Well, it is thought-provoking anyway." James nodded, sitting back in his chair as an electronic bell chimed on the ship's intercom.

"Well, we better finish getting ready," Meghnah said, setting her tray on top of James's

"Right…" Chloe hesitated a moment before doing the same. For a moment James eyes locked with hers, something shifted beneath her bright blue irises, an emotion James couldn't quite identify. Guilt perhaps?

James stared after them as they left the mess hall. He let out a sigh. "I guess I am cleaning up after everyone."

"Good luck." Fetu laughed, giving James a solid slap on the shoulder as he left.

* * *

The air felt dry and heavy in Gillian's lungs, rancid with the toxins building throughout the ship. His gills had sealed themselves to the sides of his neck trying to retain what little moisture was left. Even the spines in his fins had become brittle from malnourishment.

The gaudy stateroom that served as his quarters mocked him. Once bright walls now sagged with layers of dust, great lavender tapestries hanging unkempt. A grandiose mirror, standard in officers' rooms reflected a cold reminder of his own failings. At least the sirens had stopped, nothing had been fixed, they had finally given up and shut them off. There wasn't anything left to fix, the attack from the Shade had crippled the Vyrant, the impossible hyperspace envelopes had opened within the ship itself, evaporating components into the void between the fabric of space and time.

This was a punishment, Gillian knew it. He had stopped wearing his pristine white uniform three days ago, it hung next to the massive bed, its elegant lavender accents highlighting his inferiority.

He had never wanted any of this. His whole life had been spent chasing after his father's ambitions. It was his duty to make up for the failings of his older brother. His father had believed wholeheartedly in the mission of the Descendants, sometimes even more so than the others on The Divine Council. It was as if he had been on a holy crusade. He had always said as members of the noble bloodline that it was their responsibility, their right, to bring the lower races out of their shadows to show them the glorious light of Vyanna.

Gillian had never believed that, he had never seen anything to convince him of the existence of any deity. Sure he had studied the texts, but they were only words, written by those with power to control others they felt were beneath them. That was before he has come face to face with the Lord of Death himself.

As time passed Gillian became more and more certain of it, he had engaged in direct combat with the devil, and lost. Zaeith's cruelty grew with every passing day, even now, two weeks after the battle, the demon was still mocking them.

At first, Gillian had been grateful for the plasma shield, that perhaps through an act of divine intervention they would not fall victim to the next passing band of pirates. Even this turned out to be one of Zaeith's cruel jokes. The shield began to drain power from life support, the only other fully functional system. Faced with the choice between starvation and asphyxiation, relying on the mercy of pirates started to look like a good idea; however, Zaeith robbed them of even that option.

One of the envelopes had intersected the suspension field, the engineers were not sure if it was from the time dilation or the energy surge, but the shield had been locked in a feedback loop, turning it off was now impossible. Vyanna's ultimate protection had been turned against them; it would be the cause of their deaths. As power drained from the Vyrant's husk, the shield would shrink into itself. Dissolving the ship, converting its matter into energy, fueling its own demise. Eventually it would collapse, forming a micro-singularity which would remain for a month or two, anything left of the Vyrant would be scattered as dust across the emptiness of space. They were doomed, and there wouldn't be anything left to mark their grave.

"Light and dark, reflect divine providence" Gillian whispered the familiar prayer as he stared into the massive mirror. He wasn't sure what he expected to happen, but if Vyanna really was out there, only she could save them now.

A chill ran down Gillian's spine as for a moment he could have sworn he saw Zaeith looking back at him, flesh as black as the void, and eyes that burned with the fires of the abyss.

Gillian shook his head holding it between his hands. When he looked again, the face was gone. Only a memory. "Light and dark, reflect divine providence," Gillian whispered again.

Chapter 3

James straightened his uniform as he stared into his reflection. The polished metal mirror was a reminder of how different the Shade was from other ships.

"Hey, James," Meghnah said, as she dropped out of the corridor onto the tile floor.

"Hey." James nodded.

Meghnah tossed the tank top she had been wearing carelessly towards the corner of the room.

At first Meghnah's casual approach to the co-ed locker had caught James off guard. Alliance military ships all had segregated quarters and this had been new to him. Among the Drak'or the practice was common.

"Chloe, you coming?" Meghnah shouted into the corridor, as she removed what was left of her casual wear.

"N-no I can wait," She sounded uneasy.

James couldn't help but grin a little, he didn't know

much about Chloe, but he was once again reminded of the sharp contrast in the two women's personalities. "It's okay," he said as he stepped into the zero-g corridor, "I was just leaving."

* * *

Chloe struggled to find her footing on the platform James had vacated only a moment before. He always made the transition seem so effortless, he just popped off the platform.

It frustrated her how easy everything was for him. She had been on the Shade almost twice as long as him, but he was far more at home here. She took a deep breath. He had spent half his life exploring the galaxy; this was her first experience away from home.

A strange knot formed in the pit of her stomach as she stared down the corridor after him. The feeling that was becoming too familiar in her opinion. She kept catching herself struggling for something to say, but desperately wanting to keep up a conversation.

"What was that look for?" Meg shouted over the sound of water echoing off the walls.

Chloe sighed as she looked around the room. As always, Meg hadn't even waited for James to leave before discarding her clothing. If she had even half of Meg's confidence... Then again, she also wished she could be half as beautiful. "What look?"

"Don't try to pretend, I know what I saw." Steam filled the room and Chloe could hear water splashing as Meg washed her long red hair. "Look, it's fine to be embarrassed, but you've got to speak up for yourself."

"It's not that, I- He is the first human I have really had the chance to get to know."

26

She was glad Meg couldn't see her blush. The orphanage she had grown up in had been operated by the Fingalin Empire. Though the Midway station itself did not belong to anyone, it did represent one of the clearest divides in the Alliance. Except for Vinge, almost everything within the circle was part of the Empire, while the vast majority of the worlds in the surrounding ring belonged to the Federation. The only humans she had known were the politicians and traders she had helped to con.

Chloe gathered Meg's discarded clothes and set them in her wash pile. She found comfort in their routine, which gave her a sense of belonging, always the same. Meg would drop into the locker room practically naked before she even hit the floor and make sure the coast was clear. Chloe would clean up after her and make sure they both had fresh uniforms.

Running a finger along the crimson trim, Chloe admired the stark black fabric. She didn't blame her parents for abandoning her. Bloodlines were important to the Fingal; they claimed a divine heritage. Though they accepted the Alliance, many of them believed in a future where the Fingal would claim their genetic birthright to rule over the other races.

Her father had likely been the human parent, politician or trader, it didn't matter; either way, he would have left long before her mother even knew of the pregnancy. Her mother probably thought it was safe, not knowing her own heritage assumed her child would be purer than she was, but a single generation was not enough to produce a child as human as Chloe. Rather than losing her standing in society, Chloe's mother abandoned her.

"Your turn." Meg tossed a wet towel at Chloe.

Seph

"Hand me one of those, would you."

Chloe handed Meg a uniform. "I'll never understand how you can be so comfortable Meg, I could never be naked around others like that." She took her own towel and uniform with her into one of the three stalls.

Meg laughed. "And I will never understand how you can be such a prude."

She smiled, she liked having Meg around, though she often found she was jealous of her. Meghnah was so graceful, with long legs and pointed ears, even with her dark skin she was absolutely stunning to look at. Because Chloe was human, she had always been considered ugly. She was too short, too tan, and her ears were too round.

She scrubbed at her skin as if to wash the pigment away; it didn't work, of course, it never worked. At least her hair was white. She rinsed the long strands under the running water. That was the only reason she had even had a home, most abandoned human children died on the streets. With her blue eyes and white-blond hair, Chloe was barely fingalin enough to stand out. Mistress Sphiya had taken her in and showed her how to live on the streets. But even among Sphiya's misfits, she was an outcast.

Turning the water off Chloe patted herself dry with the towel and slid into her crisp uniform. Being on the Shade was different, nobody cared what she looked like, or who her parents were. Zaeith's crew was like the family she had never had. Besides, now that James was here, she wasn't the only human anymore, even if he was deliberately ignoring her.

Stepping back into the changing room, Chloe adjusted her uniform in the mirror tying up her still damp hair.

"You look fine." Meg teased impatiently. "Though black isn't really your color, it makes you look too pale."

Chloe smiled to herself, maybe for once she could be something besides 'the ugly human.'

Chapter 4

Nausea began to build in the pit of James's stomach as the edges of his vision began to twist and warp. The familiar sensation of transitioning in and out of hyperspace. There was always turbulence, the small fractures at the edges of space created when solid matter passed through the subspace barrier. There were several ways of dealing with it; primarily, a bigger ship. The more massive a ship the more space it could bend. The more space it bent, the less space it had to tear. At least that was the idea.

For a ship its size, the Shade handled the transition remarkably well, a feat made even more impressive by the absence of a fusion core. The fusion core had been around for just over a decade but had quickly gained popularity as the number one form of power generation. Not only did the reactor act as a perpetual energy supply, but it also produced its own gravity well. Artificial gravity plates like those used on the Shade were considered obsolete.

"Envelope closed, location confirmed, Croy Nebula DSI 3122," Meghnah reported.

The view field projected the Deep Space Initiative Station, a standalone colony, orbiting neither planet nor star. The station drifted along with the rest of the galaxy, anchored by its own gravity well.

This station resembled a cone-shaped tower. With one central shaft rising from the spherical generator section, which housed the fusion core. Decks designed to match the curve of the gravity well branched off the central pillar forming the tower's cone. Occasional observation platforms, overlooking the nebula, jutted straight out from the center at irregular intervals.

"Thank you, establish an orbit," James responded. The Captain should have been on the bridge, but he hasn't been seen in the two weeks since they had encountered the Descendant warship. He hid away in his private quarters, sometimes for days on end. "Chloe let them know we are here."

"Okay." Chloe keyed in the communication codes. There was a brief pause. She tried again. "James, I'm not getting anything."

It used to bother him that Chloe was so casual about bridge operations, occasionally he had to remind himself that the Shade was registered as a civilian ship. James cloned Chloe's terminal to his own and ran the scan data. Nothing.

"That's odd, the station appears to be. . . Empty." James stared at the view field for a moment reworking the data. "Meghnah, maybe we can get a better reading if we drop to a closer orbit."

The bridge grew a few shades darker as The Captain's unmistakable presence filled the room.

"We're too late, you won't find anything." The Captain's neural link was engaged, he had already seen the data.

"Captain." James said rising to salute, Meghnah saluted as well.

Chloe hesitated a moment then stood to follow suit.

"Don't worry about it." The Captain waved the gesture off, giving her a soft smile.

"You don't think…" Meghnah began.

"I don't know what to think yet." The Captain interrupted again. "But, this is not a coincidence."

James scanned through the data, trying to catch up to what The Captain had no doubt already seen. "I don't understand, how does an entire colony disappear?"

The bridge was silent for a moment.

The Captain's head and shoulders drooped wearily. "It doesn't." His voice was flat and grim.

"Is this…" Chloe's voice was withdrawn, a hint of disillusion and fear creeping in. "A repeat of DSI 5771?"

The Captain pulled down his hood and ran a hand through his mess of tangled hair. The fire in his deep red eyes faded as the neural link folded back against his neck. "I don't want to jump to any conclusions," he let out a long sigh, heavy with fatigue.

The hair on the back of James's neck began to stand as his stomach tightened. The Shade had been to DSI 5771 only a few weeks before he had first come on board. According to the mission report the former tactical officer had taken a small crew over to the station. They had lost contact only moments before the station imploded, half the crew had been lost. "What happened on 5771?"

Chloe's eyes flicked over to Meghnah, who was

uncharacteristically tense, lips pulled back into a thin line, muscles tight, eyes dilated. "It was empty…" Chloe's voice was forced and distant.

Silence filled the bridge.

The skin around The Captain's face tightened as he clenched his jaw. "We lost a lot of good people." His eyes burned with fire and determination. "James, go wake Fetu, help him put a team together. I will meet you at the hatch in two hours."

The Captain held his gaze until James nodded. "Yes sir," He saluted out of habit.

The Captain acknowledged the gesture with a nod and flick of his hand. "Meghnah." He said turning to the view-field. "You are relieved of duty until morning bell."

* * *

Fetu's loud snore echoed through the corridor. James wondered, not for the first time, how anyone could sleep so well on what the Shade offered for bedding; half the time he thought he'd get better sleep on the training mats upstairs.

Fetu's bunk was under his own, James was once again grateful they slept on opposite ends of the day. "Fetu, get up," James shouted, floating to a stop next to the bunks. Fetu shifted and continued snoring. Not only was the man built like a rock, he slept like one too.

James opened his footlocker, he dug for his extra stunblade then tossed it in his hand. Though it was potentially lethal, the small fingalin knife wasn't what James would call a weapon. The mirrored metallic blade was only a quarter inch long, despite this James's found them to be incredibly useful. Even a small amount of pressure on the blade produced an electric shock, capable of rendering most people unconscious. He tapped the blade against the exposed metal of his own bunk.

A loud clap shattered the air as the blade discharged.

Fetu flew from his bed, spinning wildly in the Zero-G corridor. "What in the nine suns are you trying to do, man!" Fetu shouted as he tried to steady himself. "Can't you see it is the middle of the night?"

James grinned, and placed the stun-blade back in his locker. "Ship's day," he enjoyed that a little too much. "We are going over to DSI 3122, Captain's orders, wants us to put a team together and meet him at the hatch in less than two hours."

"Why, what's wrong" Fetu finally managed to straighten himself and was shaking off the sleep.

"The place is empty," His uneasiness grew as he returned his thoughts to the task at hand.

Fetu let out a long sigh. "Another one, huh. Okay, go talk to Travis, see if he's on board." Fetu pulled on a grubby uniform, " I'll talk to the engineers who came along with that hydro harvester, maybe a few of them will volunteer."

"Right." James grabbed his rifle from the locker before closing it again, "Good luck."

James made his way down the corridor towards the mess hall, Travis would likely be cooking, if he wasn't he would still be in the vicinity. Travis was one of the few members of the crew to have his own quarters, something Fetu had regularly complained about. But everyone knew you never mess with the guy who prepares your food, so it mostly went unchallenged.

"Hey Travis," James shouted as he entered the kitchen.

The scent of toasted spices and coconut washed over his senses. The U-shaped kitchen ran parallel to the corridor, turning at a sharp angle behind the mess hall and around the cooks quarters, then bending again to run into the refrigeration area, opposite the corridor. Two entrances led into the room, one off the hallway, the other connecting directly to the mess.

The fingalin's head poked out from around a corner. "Hmm, yes? Oh, James! What's up?" Travis was always like that, talking so fast your brain couldn't keep up, never mind getting a word in yourself. Not only was he the ship's cook, but he was involved in almost everything else onboard as well. He was a computer expert and had programmed many of the ship's systems.

"We are putting together a team, headed over to DSI 3122, we could use you if you're willing." he reached a finger towards a simmering pot.

Travis was instantly in front of James, "Don't you dare!" Despite the yellow freckles which littered his face and forearms, the fingalin's six-foot-four frame and extended fins made him incredibly intimidating.

James yanked his arm back. "Okay, not touching."

Travis visibly relaxed as his fins folded themselves around his shoulders and forearms. "A team you say, is there something strange going on?" he began washing his hands, "Another one like DSI 5771, perhaps?" Travis gazed off into the distance as he dried his hands absently.

"You in?" James asked.

Travis's ears perked upward, "Absolutely!" he

shouted. "I wouldn't miss it." The fingalin grabbed a data-pad off the counter. "Well come on, can't keep The Captain waiting, now can we." His fins fluttered as he almost skipped into the corridor.

James rolled his eyes, leave it to Travis to be excited about something like this.

* * *

Docking the Shade with a station was always an interesting endeavor. Because the top and bottom decks' gravity plates were inversely polarized, this tended to cause some obvious problems when interfacing in another gravity well. It was for this reason that, though it was generally kept at Zero-G, the cargo and loading bay was set perpendicular to the rest of the ship.

Stepping out of the med bay, the floor became a wall with a short ladder extending towards what was now the floor. At first, the transition had been disorienting to James, but a lifetime in space made him used to such things.

When Travis and James arrived, Fetu and the engineers were already waiting. Four of them had agreed to come. They looked like they had just had an already bad night's sleep interrupted. That was likely the case. The Shade ran on a flipped schedule. Unlike most ships, its clock was adjusted to keep itself running almost exactly opposite the station or planet it was docked at. Most of the engineers were on Fetu's shift.

James checked his weapon, a standard fingalin sting-rifle, primarily designed to be non-lethal, though it could be when necessary. The energy weapon was far from his favorite gun, but it was lightweight and highly effective in close quarters.

Travis had brought along his own fingalin war staff, which functioned somewhere between a stunblade and sting-rifle. Fetu carried two Drak'or blades with flame-like serrations along the edges. One was long and curved upwards from the handle, while the other was circular in design.

The engineers were less prepared, three of them carried standard combustion side arms, the fourth didn't look armed at all.

James exchanged a glance with Fetu, the two hours was nearly up, and in all his preparations James had not seen The Captain once. Fetu's ears tilted slightly back indicating he was experiencing the same concerns.

A loud hiss sounded from the docking hatch which began to slide with a harsh grinding noise. The smell of sterilization filled the cargo hold as cool air rushed into the room. The Captain's dark figure stood in the open doorway, shrouded in his long black cloak and hood.

"We don't have much time. Fetu, take those two with you to the core, I want you to make sure it doesn't have a meltdown while we are on board." The Captain indicted two of the engineers, all of whom exchanged a confused glance.

This was probably the first time any of them had seen The Captain. James looked to Fetu who shrugged as if to say, 'Just roll with it' acknowledging the order with a nod.

"Travis," The Captain continued, "I want you to take the remaining two and head down to the colony decks. I want any record that someone was here collected and sent to the Shade. I don't care if it is only the sound of a baby crying on a monitor, got it?"

"Got it, sir!" Travis chirped in his overeager way. He was practically skipping down the corridor before The Captain had even finished.

"James." The Captain met his gaze and a hard lump formed in his throat. "You and I will go up to the command deck." The Captain turned sharply and re-entered the corridor, cloak trailing ominously behind him.

"Yes sir." The confirmation was half-hearted, more of habit at this point than anything else. The Captain, as always, had not waited.

* * *

Meghnah knelt legs crossed on the traditional wooden mat in the center of the sanctuary. The deck was reserved for meditation during the early morning and late evening hours. It was quiet now, quiet and empty. Meghnah had learned to relish these moments of privacy, occasionally The Captain would join her for the ritual, but that was rarely the case these days.

Exotic incense emanated from the small altar in front of her. The room was reminiscent of temples that served as both monastery and armory for the Drak'or, weapons and religious relics hung side by side along both walls. Unlike the sanctuaries from her childhood, both Drak'or and Descendant imagery was represented in a bizarre fusion Meghnah was certain existed nowhere else in the universe.

Most peculiar was the five metal discs that hung on the wall behind the altar, one of which was missing today. It was not uncommon for the drak'or to inscribe passages from the teachings of Drektue' on disks like these, but Vhastian scripture was often written in the ancient language of the drak'or people. These were written in a language Meghnah had only ever seen in Descendant artifacts. Emblazoned with a dark crescent shape along the left perimeter of the disk. It was reminiscent of the final moments before an eclipse, the most recognizable symbol in Descendant iconography.

It was strange that two religions so different from each other could have so much in common. Both religions had their origins sometime before the great fracture and revolved heavily around the event of Vinge's collapse.

Meghnah had never considered herself to be very religious, that had always been her brother Re'akke's department. He was the reason Meghnah was on the Shade, having been the ship's last tactical officer; that was before the meltdown on DSI 5771. He had always been asking her to come to meditation with him, funny how it had never been important until he was gone.

The Shade was the first place that they had ever felt safe. Re'akke had rescued her from their father when she was barely more than a child. They had been planet hoppers ever since, never staying in one place long enough to get noticed. It was strange to think about now, that had been a different lifetime.

"Drektue' be with us," she whispered into her slow breathing. "Dark One, reflect in us your providence.'

The prayer invoked the spirit of The Dark One, the ancient hero who raised the Drak'or out of obscurity and united the races under the Alliance. For Meghnah, it was a prayer of comfort, and hope.

Chapter 5

Xious stood over the dying boy's body, the stench of decaying flesh clawing at the inside of his nostrils. The boy was pale, almost white, a harsh contrast to his once graphite skin. His lifeless pale pink eyes staring up at the makeshift medical tent above, haunted by the final nightmare that was to take his life. At least the tremors had stopped. The Missionaries that served as nurses for the Descendant medical unit on Theyes said that had happened late last night. They only gave him a few more hours at best.

The Director strode to the entrance of the tent and looked out over the camp. There were a dozen more tents like this, each filled with patients, every one of them inflicted with the Aberration. There wasn't enough room for all the plague's victims, families huddled together against the cold, hoping someone else might die and free up a bed for a loved one, only to slowly watch them come to the same fate. The illness was taking over every planet and station in the outer colonies. The quarantine hadn't even slowed it down.

Director Xious grinned, that was going to change today. After centuries of preparation, a new era was about to begin, and he, Xious Delgri'ek, Director of the Descendant's missionary service, would be its prophet.

"Bring me Vyanna's hand," he instructed.

"Yes my lord," the young missionary girl said. She had been assigned to be his aid on the planet. She couldn't have been more than ten. Only a few years older than the boy he was intending to save.

The girl bowed, sunset red hair covering the black freckles on her ash gray face. "Right away." she scurried off.

Xious followed the child with his gaze, as she wound through the camp. Taking in the hopeless faces all around her. He wondered if this was the same scene that Drektue' came across all those millennia ago. On the day he had first united the Drak'or. The legend said that the people were oppressed, rejected by their own societies and stricken with illness. Then from the ashes of war, The Dark One arose. With dragon's fire burning in his eyes, he stood against the armies of the Allied Kingdoms and Fingalin Empire and demanded a seat at their tables.

The young girl returned with two soldiers from the Zhemarah, Xious's personal ship, and the most powerful ship in The Descendant's fleet.

"Sir, the Arah'a'el," one of the soldiers presented him with an ornate wooden box.

Xious clicked open the silver latch, pulling open the lid to reveal the white glove inside. Reverently he removed it from its case. The Arah'a'el was the most sacred artifact the Descendants possessed. There was only a handful in existence, trusted to members of the Divine Council, and a select few of the children of the old elders. However, none of them understood how to use it.

He pulled the gauntlet on his hand. The five gems implanted in the white gold running along the forearm began to glow, the first a sickly yellow, the others becoming progressively more purple until the final gem glowed a brilliant lavender. Power emanated from the two silver rings on the index and middle fingers, each engraved with the strange symbols of the long forgotten Gods Tongue.

Xious tuned back to the young boy on the cot. "Take him out into the open, and shut off the quarantine field."

"But sir," the soldier began to protest.

"Do not question me!" Xious spat.

"Yes, sir."

A crowd began to gather as the boy's cot was set in the middle of the encampment. Perfect, the more witnesses the faster word would spread. Xious knelt beside the cot and lifted the boy's head close to his chest. "Hold him like this," he instructed the girl.

She nodded and did as she was told.

Xious laid his hand on the boy's forehead. "In the name of Lady Vyanna," he declared loudly as the quarantine field vanished, revealing the soft green sky beyond, "I heal you." Xious held his hand high into the air. "Light and darkness reflect divine providence." As he spoke the prayer a faint light began to glow in the palm of his hand. Xious pressed his hand against the boy's chest and a lavender aura appeared around him. The light faded and color returned to the boy's face, life sprang into the now vibrant red eyes, and he began to cough.

"Water," he croaked.

Wonder and amazement welled up in the young girl who held him. "You… saved him," she whispered then shouted. "You saved him!" Tears welled up in her eyes, reflecting the hopes of the eager onlookers. He felt a sort of kinship with the ancient hero. Now, after so many millennia, The Dark One had been reborn!

Chapter 6

Electrical components hung out of walls, laying strewn across the floor of the station's command deck. Remnants of the computer that had once served as the central nervous system for DSI 3122. The scent of ozone oxidation, the unmistakable sign of sting-rifle fire, drifted on the air. Scorch marks could be seen around the non-functioning doorway. Someone had tried to put up a fight, but it didn't look like it had lasted very long.

"Last I checked, diseases didn't tear out computer terminals." James mused into the air.

"No," the Captain said flatly. He knelt, examining what remained of the central command node, "Someone doesn't want us to find something."

"This is a civilian colony, owned by the Coalition no less, what could someone possibly want here?"

The Captain stood shaking his head as he stared out the view window which overlooked the station. "I don't know."

"It must be someone on board, there was never anything else here besides people, maybe a prominent political leader?"

"Perhaps, there is a growing movement in the colonies that is gaining a lot of momentum." The Captain rubbed his chin thoughtfully, "If the magistrate here leaned too heavily in one direction, I suppose…"

James took another glance around the deserted room. "Why would the Descendants be involving themselves in Coalition politics like this?"

The Captain gave him a sharp look that was difficult to read. Surprise, perhaps? "What makes you think it was the Descendants?"

"Well…" The evidence wasn't conclusive, but as he thought about it, this was the only solution that made any sense.

"It wasn't the Alliance, no way they would be this efficient. The Descendants are the only other faction with enough military presence. It could have been a rival magistrate, but this was done with sting-rifles. No Drak'or military is going to arm themselves with fingalin weapons. Besides, if it was rival members of the Coalition, it would be all over the nets. There is also the matter of the quarantine boundary."

The Captain nodded. "I think you are right, I just wish I knew what they were after," his gaze returned to the window. "Let's see if the others have anything."

* * *

Fetu found himself working down in the core room itself. The generator controls had been gutted, nothing of the nodes remained. Contained within a thick casing of plasma shielding, the fusion core was something like a small sun. Fed by a matter converter, any waste produced by the station was broken down into its most basic element, converted into energy for the station.

Five conduits ran up and away from the spherical core. Cooling lines coiled around the matter stream conduit and core housing and weaved in and out of the infrastructure at regular intervals. Without the automatic control node, the system would overheat and evaporate much of the coolant.

Working in the core room was a bit of a trick because it put you right in the center of the gravity well. Fetu ducked under one of the energy conduits and resecured his safety line, the life support module looked like the system had already been down for a while, causing a significant energy backup.

"Help me get these scrubbers back online, maybe if we work them overtime we can dump the excess power." It wasn't a long term solution, but it might buy them a few minutes. What they needed was a way to cool the core itself.

This was without a doubt the work of the Descendants. They were the only ones who understood the fusion cores well enough to engineer a meltdown like this. Not that it was particularly difficult to cause a core meltdown, but there was a certain elegance to the method only a Descendant engineer would truly appreciate.

Fusion core technology was largely based on the plasma shield. The tech was virtually the same, though the generator itself was a much cruder design lacking the sophistication of the more ancient tech.

The Descendants had invented it on accident, in an attempt to figure out how the shield worked. They could duplicate the shield, but they didn't understand it. The fusion core was the closest they had ever gotten.

Everybody knew that when a fusion core collapsed it could become a supernova, but only the Descendants knew how to do it on purpose.

Under most circumstances, as the system began to shut down, iron sediment would start leaking through the filter and build up in the fusion chamber. The iron, which could not be used as fuel, more often than not caused the core to rapidly cool and solidify. To generate a full-scale explosion, the iron had to be kept out of the core, which meant the filter had to be kept functional until the last moments.

Unfortunately, it was already too late to shut off the filter, the core was too hot. There were only two options. Either the core would destabilize and explode, or the core would shut down, overload the matter stream, and then explode.

"Hey, what if we reroute the water lines from life support into the coolant?" an engineer shouted over the sound of the engine; what was his name, Keven? No Kurt.

"That is a terrible idea. Do you want to guarantee we all die?" Dumping water into the core was the easiest way to make sure it went nova. The water would evaporate too quickly, causing massive ruptures in the casing. In and of itself, that was a problem. The real issue was the unregulated supply of hydrogen gas it brought to the core. Unlike iron hydrogen fused very easily, an unregulated supply meant rapid core expansion.

"No it'll work, I did it once on a mining barge. Sure

it was a lot smaller, but the physics work the same."

He had a point; it would guarantee the core exploded but that was going to happen anyway. It would take time for the core to reach critical mass. It might temporarily cool the core down though, possibly buying them an hour or two.

"Okay we'll do it." he shouted, "You go grab the water supply line and I'll get a port open." Careful to keep the conduit between him and the core, Fetu maneuvered himself to the primary shaft of the matter converter and isolated a cooling feed.

"Try this," the engineer said crawling up next to him on an adjacent conduit feed with a water line.

Fetu rigged the connection and created a makeshift seal. "Okay pull the valve," he yelled.

"Got it," the other engineer hollered back from across the room as she pulled the release valve.

"This is such a bad idea," Fetu muttered to himself.

There was a loud clap, like thunder in the middle of a hurricane. "There's the signature on our death certificates!" He shouted over the sound of expanding gas and warping metal.

The cacophony hushed to a gentle clattering with a comforting rhythmic tone. Fetu released the air he had been holding in his lungs. The high-pitched screeching was replaced by a muffled creaky warble like you might hear in an unshielded subaquatic craft. "Thank Vyanna," he said under his breath.

He had taken to using Vyanna's name as a curse after leaving the Descendants, at least when The Captain wasn't around. The Captain had some strange fondness for the make-believe goddess. He had adopted the name of the Descendent devil as an alias; obviously, he was not a practitioner of their religion.

"Captain," Fetu keyed his com, "I would say we only have about an hour left on this thing, from the sound it is making we have water leaking into the core, it's stable now but I wouldn't count on it holding out."

"Acknowledged."

"Pack up guys, we need to get out of here," Fetu ordered.

"Why are you so sure it is going to blow?" Kurt asked beginning to put tools back into his pack.

"Hear that noise? That's pressure bubbles inside the plasma shielding, your plan may have bought us some time but trust me, that core is going to explode."

Fetu had dealt with unregulated hydrogen in a fusion core once before. Initially, he hadn't known that was the problem, but he would never forget the sound again. That had been his last mission with the Descendants. They had evacuated the ship and turned on the plasma shield. The commanding officer rammed the doomed ship into the hull of the rebel craft they had been sent to intercept.

The plasma shield ate the fleeing vessel, swallowing it whole as it rapidly expanded, fueled by the fusion cores explosion. Both ships vanished into the resulting black hole.

Fetu had been awarded a promotion and a medal for coming up with the idea of using the plasma shield to contain the explosion. Disgusted by the devastation, he left the next day.

That's when The Captain had found him, he could still remember that stupid grin when he asked. "So, now that you have denounced God, want to join the Devil?"

Seph

* * *

The medical bay looked like everywhere else onboard. Stripped of its network access terminals, remnants of electrical equipment littered the room. The air here was particularly sterile, a result of the sanitizing agents used to clean the four medical pods, the only remaining evidence of the room's former function.

"Travis, what do you have for me?" The Captain's voice echoed off the bare metal walls as he entered the room.

"Captain!" there was a loud clang, "Ouch!" Travis attempted to extract himself from under a medical pod.

He jumped to his feet. His whole body bounced with energy, his long white ears flapped with excitement. "Well at first, I wasn't sure, I mean I didn't think anything, I had already moved on when I thought that maybe it was something, but then I wasn't sure so I thought well maybe. You see a lot of these stations don't have a lot of experienced medical staff on hand, mostly nurses and such, with only a few doctors, and without access to some of the more advanced diagnostic equipment you can find on core worlds, so some of these med pods are equipped with real-time data transfer so patients monitoring information can be transferred off station and evaluated by a specialist who can relay instructions back to the pod's operator."

James glanced skeptically at the Captain raising an eyebrow inquisitively. "So we can access a data line, but isn't it a closed loop?"

Travis paused, ears dropping. He stared at James

blankly as if the question had not quite been able to process through his brain.

The Captain rubbed his chin thoughtfully then chuckled to himself, "So what did you get?"

The Captain's question must have hit some kind of reset button on the fingalin because he perked up again, "Well, at first I wasn't sure I could get anything because it is only for data transfer, not for data storage, they took everything used to store data, so I think they must have thought that this wouldn't really do anyone any good because it only talks to the med-net." Travis paused, ears flicking rapidly.

"Oh, that's what you were talking about James!" His ears perked straight up like a bunny rabbit who had just discovered dandelion paradise.

"Yes I suppose you are right, it is a closed loop, that is probably why they didn't take it out, but you see they didn't actually have time to delete the station's whole database, just the database access equipment. I used my data-pad to hack the med-pod, I used the med pod to hack the med-net, then I opened up a computer on the net and used that to hack the station's database, and transfer it back over to the Shade."

The station shook violently, a loud moan reverberated through the walls. Lights flickered, a warning siren burst over the intercom. "Warning, core failure imminent, all personnel please report to their assigned evacuation terminal."

"Captain, I lost the core." Fetu's voice crackled over the comlink.

"How much time do we have?" The Captain's voice remained level and calm.

"I give it about fifteen." Fetu's breathing sounded heavy, he was running.

Seph

James did the math in his head, Fetu's team wouldn't make it back to the docking bay. He had studied the station's layout before coming on board, they would need at least twenty minutes but likely more, it was questionable if they would even be able to make it from the medical bay, the numbers were not in their favor.

The Captain's neural link clicked into place over his eye and there was a soft beep as he opened a com channel to the Shade, "Chloe, move the ship away from the station, make sure it is clear of the gravity well."

"I am not leaving you behind," Chloe's voice crackled back.

The Captain's complexion suddenly grew dark and serious as the gentle calm he had maintained thus far faded. "Do not question me, just do it," he ordered. Pulling his hood up, The Captain complexion softened again. "I need you to trust me, okay Chloe. Do you trust me?"

Silence hung in the air for a moment until Chloe's voice finally chirped back over the com. "Yes, I trust you. Okay, I'll do it."

"Thank you," the Captain acknowledged before switching his comlink back to Fetu. "You won't make it, take shelter on the aggro-deck."

"Acknowledged," Fetu chirped back.

"Let's go." The Captain strode from the room, his oversized black cloak catching the air behind him.

"He's killed us all," one of the engineers shouted.

"Shut up, and let's go." James motioned with his rifle, "We don't have time to stand around and debate."

James couldn't remember the last time he had run so hard, The Captain was walking at a swift pace, but it took everything James had just to keep up, how did he move so fast? Stumbling onto the agricultural deck, The Captain came to an abrupt stop. The deck itself was the closest thing to planetary conditions on board the station, occupying one of the lowest floors closest to the core. It was also the largest open deck onboard. Pasture grounds stretched out across the floor, intended as a grazing area for cattle, and other bovine mammal species, with three large domes situated in a sort of lopsided triangle towards the middle of the deck, reaching up to support the vast ceiling. Holo-projection panels imitated a natural celestial cycle. For a moment it was almost possible to believe they had left the station and arrived on an unfamiliar planet.

"Orders?" Sweat drenched Fetu's face and uniform.

"Get everyone inside that dome," The Captain commanded, indicating the closest of the three.

"Right," Fetu nodded. "Everybody in the agdome."

The "agdome" as it was called was a giant greenhouse of sorts. Each station had two or three. They were basically self-contained ecosystems. As far as emergency shelters went, it was their best option. The deck was relatively close to the core, and would compress less when the station collapsed. Since the dome used an energy field to maintain its unique atmosphere, it could in theory hold back the vacuum of space. The dome also was not dependent on life support for air or water, and provided readily available food sources.

"Go to the center of the dome and form a ring," The Captain instructed as he sealed the airlock.

"You should have left us, this is never going to work," one of the engineers said. "Once the core goes out, the energy field won't hold, and there is no way that the hull isn't going to rupture. If anything, this is only going to give us a few extra seconds to think about it before we die."

So she'd figured it out. James wasn't an expert on physics but his tactical training told him that this was a last ditch effort. An extension of meager hope before the inevitable end. Glancing at the faces of the engineers, it was obvious the exercise was futile. They were doing as they were told, but the look in their eyes was one of defeat. Anyone who might have believed the plan would work, had taken the time to run the numbers. James couldn't work them out himself but judging from the expressions of the others he didn't need to, he knew they weren't good.

"Relax and be glad he didn't," Fetu stepped into the forming ring next to her. He appeared calm despite the station's violent shaking, which was only getting worse. Fetu said they might have fifteen minutes left, it had only been nine, it was looking unlikely they would make it to eleven.

"Shut up and assume a fetal position," The Captain ordered as he tossed something on the floor. His voice was harsh and commanding. He gave Fetu a knowing look, was that amusement in his eye?

The object The Captain had thrown into the center of the ring appeared to be a metal disc. It was about the size of a dinner plate, it was tugging at the back of James's mind like he had seen it before. Was he missing something important?

The Captain knelt placing one hand on the disc, "Zymo dreku seph zhemarah."

The unfamiliar words lurched in James's mind as his stomach shot up through his chest. His lungs collapsed in on themselves, the ritual was all but forgotten as nausea overcame his senses. The world folded in half before turning inside out. Everything began to spin in all directions, it felt as if every molecule in his body were being pulled apart by their electrons. The world lurched as it came to a sudden stop.

* * *

Chloe watched in horror as DSI 3122 began to collapse. Small fires erupted sporadically from the outermost corridors, quickly snuffing out, deprived of oxygen. Contrary to popular belief, big stations didn't explode when their cores failed. Reality was far worse. Fetu explained it to her after they had lost Meg's brother to DSI 5771. During the initial core explosion, the structural integrity of the station was compromised. The station collapsed under its own mass, folding into the remaining gravity well.

The worst part was the silence. With no air to transmit the sound between them, watching the station's layers of nearly indestructible alloy crimp and collapse under their own weight, was like watching a giant invisible hand crush foil into a ball. The decks crinkled together around the center.

Chloe slammed her hand against the projector and screamed. She couldn't hold back the tears. This time was supposed to be different; Zaeith had gone with them. 'Trust me' he had said, and she did, she did trust him, more than anything. Now he was gone, this time Meg would never recover. She had let her guard down and allowed herself to believe, but the universe had played its cruel joke, and robbed her of the only family she had ever known.

Seph

James rolled to his back, the familiar wooden training mat pressing against him.

"You said the first time was the worst," Fetu moaned painfully from the other side of the room.

The Captain hung the metal disc on the wall with the others. "I lied."

Someone vomited.

"Get Travis up to see Nevarian, I am going to go check on Chloe." The Captain chuckled entering the lift tube.

***

Chloe felt a chill in the tips of her fingers as Zaeith's unmistakable presence filled the bridge. "Zaeith…?" she managed turning to face the lift door.

There he was, skin the color of obsidian and burning red eyes as deep as eternity itself.

"How… did… you…" she managed between her tears, refusing to believe her own eyes.

Zaeith descended the stairs and pulled her into his arms, holding her in a tight embrace. "It's going to be alright," he whispered.

Chloe hung there in his arms the way a child clings to a lost parent.

Chapter 7

Silence filled the Shade's empty corridors. James made his way gingerly along the guide rail. It was midway through the day and the ship's crew was either at their assigned workstations, or sleeping in the bunk room. Though like him, a good portion of them were still recovering from their return from DSI 3122.

After being confined to his bed for a couple of days, Nevarian had finally cleared him for duty starting on the second half of the shift. It felt good to move again, but James found himself uncommonly grateful for the lack of gravity. His entire body still ached, he finally understood how Fetu could sleep so well.

He would likely have to fend for himself for food. He had been in his own bed. With the number of people out, the medical bay was reserved for those in the most serious condition. This time around that meant Travis.

He lowered himself into the dining room, carefully

getting his feet under him as he made the transition into artificial gravity.

"James!" Chloe shouted.

"Ow." James winced as she threw her arms around his neck and hung her weight from his shoulders.

"I can't believe you're up, I've been so worried about you," She said squeezing him tight.

"Uh, thanks, but do you have to hug me so hard?"

"Sorry, I, well I thought you were dead, okay!" She pulled away a little too quickly and wiped her eyes trying to hide a tear.

"I wouldn't rule it out just yet," James smiled. "Half of me still thinks I might be." He chuckled lightly.

Chloe smiled softly, "Glad to see you found a sense of humor over there." She pulled out a chair from a nearby table and supported James by his elbow as he maneuvered into it.

"Let me grab you something to eat." She said hastily.

"Where's Meghnah?" James asked as Chloe set a hot plate of roasted potatoes and grilled meat in front of him, not at all the ration he had been expecting.

"She is on the bridge still." She said sitting across from him, "I am supposed to be too, but Nevarian said he was going to release you for duty and Fetu said I could come down and see you. We're in transition now, so it's not like there's much for me to be doing."

James took a bite of food then relaxed back into his chair, letting the soft warmth of it wash over him. "Is Travis feeling better?" he asked, the pounding in his head beginning to subside.

Chloe watched him for a moment. "Yeah, I mean, I guess so."

She drew back a little, "Listen, I should go back to

the bridge, but I am glad you are feeling better." She rose from the table.

"I'll see you later okay!?" She popped into the corridor without waiting for a reply.

What was that about? James took another bite of his food, it really was good.

* * *

Fetu rose from the command chair as James entered the bridge. "Good, you're here," the large man yawned as he slapped James on the back. "That means the bridge is yours, and I can go back to sleep. Bunch of weirdos staying up all night." He chuckled.

"Where's The Captain?" James asked, trying to steady himself after the impact.

"Quarters last I checked, he's been locked up in there all day."

James lowered himself into the command chair having given up on trying to remain standing. "Why?"

"Your guess is as good as mine," Fetu said, then disappeared into the shaft.

James keyed the command console and pulled up the current nav data. "Hey Meghnah?" He asked, looking at the destination coordinates. "Isn't this where we encountered the Descendants?"

"Yep," Meghnah said shortly. "Captain's orders." She added after a brief pause.

Casually, James looked through the ships logs, but there wasn't much to explain The Captain 's decision. He found a communication log with the engineering corps. They were scheduled to rendezvous with a deep space salvage crane. Maybe it was just a convenient place to offload the equipment and engineers.

Seph

The air grew colder, and James turned to see the captain enter from his private shaft.

"Captain," James said rising from the command chair and saluting.

The Captain nodded dismissively. "I want you to take a look at something. Meghnah, you have the bridge."

He led James through the center lift shaft to his quarters. James swallowed hard; no one, at least not that he was aware of, had ever been permitted into The Captain 's room.

The room itself felt... old, like something time had misplaced and forgotten. The air smelled of ash and smoke. Not dirty, it was more like embers, burning stubbornly under heavy rain. The smoke filled with the scent of wood from a thousand trees from a hundred worlds.

It was dark, the only light coming from the dozens of screens hanging from the perfectly circular wall. A single full mirror reflected strange unearthly shadows in every direction. Shadows that reflected back into themselves, like staring into a kaleidoscope of eternity.

James stared a moment taking it all in. The space was otherwise empty, adding to the mirror's illusion of infinity. He almost didn't notice the door sliding shut behind him.

The Captain walked to the center of the room, from somewhere in the ceiling a virtual console projected in front of him, the silver white light of the control panel softening the shadows around the edge of the room.

Refocusing, James examined the various monitors, Descendant soldiers appeared to be systematically working their way through familiar corridors taking prisoners and destroying equipment as they went.

"Is this DSI 3122?" James asked watching the commotion.

"Yes."

A held breath escaped from his lips, when Travis said he got everything he hadn't been kidding. Each screen rotated sequentially displaying footage from a different feed. As James watched, he realized each monitor was displaying at least two dozen different cameras grouped by sets of eight, each showing a different security sector. Every column displayed a separate deck. It *was* possible to view nearly the entire station at any given moment. There must have been millions of hours' worth of footage.

"What exactly am I looking for?" he asked after a moment.

"Anything unusual," the Captain said, not turning from the monitors.

"How much of this have you been through?" James ventured to ask.

"All of it."

James stared stunned. "Wait, you mean-"

"Twice." The Captain added, turning to face him, his red eyes seeming indifferent in the harsh light.

"Right." James said, more to himself than anything. He looked at the scene playing out on the monitors. It was only a few minutes, but it felt like an eternity before something caught his eye. "Strange to see a fingalin on board a drak'or colony ship." he said, pointing to a monitor in the left bank.

"Her name is Jasvlin Maylis." The Captain said.

James hoped the darkness would hide the skeptical look on his face, he knew better than to doubt The Captain, but it was still absurd to think that he had memorized the crew manifest.

Seph

He watched the girl as she was moved around the ship. Unlike male fingalins, the females grew hair behind each of their fins. Judging by her clothing and braids, she had at one point held noble status. Wait, wasn't Maylis the name of the Colonel onboard the Descendant warship? "May I?" he asked, stepping toward the projected terminal.

The Captain nodded stepping aside, watching with a note of curiosity on his otherwise stone face.

James adjusted the displays, his instinct told him this girl was important, but why? James followed as she was rushed through the identification check. He enhanced the video, moving it from the wall to the projection field and turning on the audio feed.

"This is the one."

"Hmm, I had expected it would be one of the drak'or."

"You can dispose of the rest."

The officer who had been escorting the girl saluted.

"And lieutenant." The second officer spoke.

"Yes, commander?"

"Make sure there isn't any evidence."

His chest tightened, cheeks growing cold as the Descendant soldiers began executing everyone else in the room. The girl screamed, rising from the floor she threw herself at the soldier who had given the order. He pressed a button and her body went rigid, then collapsed.

"Get this one in a cell, Trepidor wants her alive."

James felt a tension in The Captain he had never sensed before. "What aren't you telling me?" he asked only half to The Captain.

"Was she the target? Or is it a coincidence?" The Captain asked, his voice tight and even.

James hesitated then closed down the holo-projection. He matched the time stamp on each of the other feeds. Blood froze in his veins. Silently, effortlessly, efficiently the Descendants began their sweep. In minutes there was nothing left.

His voice caught in his throat. "Why?" He managed.

"We will soon find out." The Captain turned to face the monitors. The door slid open, a shaft of light appearing on the floor.

* * *

Gillian clawed his way out of sleep, fighting off the terror that had suddenly gripped his chest, heart pounding he attempted to draw in breath. The air caught in his throat. as if his lungs had collapsed. His gills spread open, an instinct, desperate for air, but there was no water to filter. The result was nearly as painful as using his lungs had been.

Had the life support given out finally? No, this was different. If the life support had stopped functioning, the result would be a slow build-up of carbon dioxide. He would have likely died in his sleep never knowing anything was wrong.

Forcing himself out of the bed, Gillian used the pounding in his head to focus his thoughts away from his burning lungs. The silence hung so thick in the empty chamber, it was as if it echoed off every wall. It took an eternity to get to the uniform stand and its emergency oxygen supply. Reaching for the mask, Gillian caught sight of the mirror.

His body stiffened, blood-curdling in his veins. Instead of his reflection, red eyes stared at him as if from the pits of hell itself.

Seph

Gillian backed away, stumbling over his own feet. He collapsed to the floor. "No, it can't be. You can't be here," he managed, a whisper as his lungs struggled to inhale. The pain from before was gone, replaced by a terror that reached through him grabbed his spine, thrusting shards of ice into every fiber of his body.

The room grew darker as unearthly shadows began to leak through the mirror, its surface twisted and bubbled. Gillian's heart stopped as the Devil stepped through the portal.

So Zaeith was not going to let him die in peace; he had come to personally escort him to the abyss.

Crossing the first half of the room in two impossible steps, Zaeith grabbed Gillian by the throat. He flew the remaining distance slamming his back into the far wall.

"Why did you destroy DSI 3122?" the demon's voice echoed in Gillian's mind, shadows stretching out from his body like the legs of a spider hunting its prey.

It felt as if his soul was being drawn into Zaeith's fiery eyes, beckoning him to surrender, demanding his obedience. "It was a quarantine mission." The words cut into his throat like hot sand, a fresh wave of anguish shot through his body.

"Why are you lying to me?" The disembodied voice demanded.

"I'm not, I swear," he gasped for air. "We were not permitted to make contact." His lungs heaved under the pressure of speaking. "It was too dangerous."

Zaeith released him, dropping his body to the ground like a rag doll, the shadows began to recede. The sweet taste of oxygen filled his lungs.

"So you have been lied to as well," Zaeith said, his voice flat as he turned his back on Gillian.

Life returned to his limbs. "Lied to? What are you talking about?" He pulled himself to his feet experimentally. "Everyone knows about the outbreak."

The Captain waved a hand in front of the mirror, its surface warping round itself, images dancing across its surface. Camp after camp of dying Drak'or, their faces flashed by, each with the same look of hopelessness. The images changed to display Director Xious talking with the sick. He wore a crisp Descendant uniform with a clean white cloak and silver white glove on his right hand.

"That's Director Xious." Gillian said words coming easy now. "He is healing them!" the figure placed his gloved hand on a dying child's chest, there was a flash of light, the sickness left their eyes, strength visibly returning.

"No he isn't." The Captain's voice was cold and flat.

"Then what do you call that?" Gillian demanded, regaining some of his courage.

The Captain eyed the colonel skeptically, then returned his gaze to the mirror. "Removing a curse."

Gillian looked at the man who, despite his black skin and burning eyes, seemed entirely too mortal now. "Why are you showing me this?"

The Captain waved his hand in front of the mirror again, the image became an open room, Drak'or lined one wall, Descendant soldiers checking IDs one at a time. "No don't, please, we have done nothing wrong!" a woman's voice screamed as a fingalin was thrown into the middle of the floor.

Gillian's stomach dropped, the last time he had seen his niece she had only been a child.

"This is the one." an unseen voice said.

"Hmm, I had expected it would be one of the

Seph

Drak'or. Very well, let's get this over with."

"NO!" the girl screamed, parents could be seen covering their children's eyes as weapons fire lit up the liquid surface.

As the light faded so did the effect, and Gillian found himself staring into his own reflection.

"Why?" he asked again, finding his voice.

The Captain looked into the mirror one eyebrow raised. "Who was she?"

His blood drained. "What do you mean who was she!" He demanded, grabbing at the demon, who casually sidestepped the attack. Gillian found himself clutching nothing but air.

"What do you want from me, demon!?"

"Answers." The Captain said sharply, "Who was she?"

Gillian slumped to the floor, his back against the wall. "She was my niece." He said finally.

The Captain stared for a moment, his gaze seeming to see straight through Gillian, it was like being put underneath an electron microscope. Every detail being put on display, like an open book for him to read.

Reaching into his coat, The Captain produced a small ion power cell, and handed it to him.

Gillian's voice was elusive. "Why are you doing this?"

The Captain turned back toward the mirror. "That should keep you alive until I return."

Waving a hand in front of the glass, it rippled and became liquid. "And Colonel." The Captain added before entering the portal. "Remember, Xious isn't helping anyone."

* * *

Fetu's voice echoed from the locker room, James smiled as he folded and tucked his uniform jacket into the foot locker at the end of his bunk. When Meghnah had first recruited him, she had promised that the Shade would be the most interesting ship he would ever serve on.

James smiled to himself again, as he made his way to the locker room. He should have taken her more seriously. Compared to the Shade, being an enforcer had been, well, ordinary.

Fresh steam from a running shower filled the locker room. James touched down on the platform, water vapor clinging to his skin and clothes. Fetu sat on the bench in the middle of the room pulling on his jacket. "James! You're out late." He laughed, his singing coming to an abrupt stop mid verse. He stood straightening the uniform, "Shouldn't you be getting ready for bed about now?"

James shrugged. "Normally I would be, but I hoped I could pick your brain for a few minutes this morning."

The sound of running water petered out, the splash of footsteps on wet tiles taking its place. Strange, whoever was in the shower had not bothered to hang out a new uniform. Fetu gathered up his discarded sleepwear and deposited it in the laundry basket at the bottom of his locker.

"Sure, but you'll have to follow me to breakfast."

"After you," James motioned, stepping aside to let the larger man into the corridor first. Something nagged at the back of his mind. He looked over his shoulder. The room was oddly empty. He shrugged then followed Fetu, was he being paranoid?

Seph

There were fewer crew on duty during night hours then on day shift, so finding a table wasn't a problem, Those that were there were content to eat in silence. The distinct absence of aroma from Travis's cooking added to their mornings already groggy start.

Fetu dropped a plate of rations on the table and pulled out the chair. The metal legs squeaking on the tile floor interrupting the silence.

"What's up?" Fetu asked, flopping his massive body ungracefully into the chair and tearing open the packaging of a meal bar.

James glanced around at the half asleep engineers preparing for their shifts. Each seemed lost or distracted by their own thoughts.

"How did we get off DSI 3122?" James asked leaning over the table.

Fetu shoved the remainder of his meal bar into his mouth. "Hyperspace." He said between bites.

"Come again? I swear you just said hyperspace."

Fetu swallowed and gave a nod. "Hyperspace."

James sat back and took a deep breath. "How? We were unshielded."

Fetu shrugged, popping the lid open on his prepacked hydration drink. "I don't understand it myself, but I have been through it twice now and it is the only explanation that makes any sense."

James let out a long sigh as he relaxed into his chair. In what universe did that explanation make any sense? He had studied hyperspace theory while in the academy, and it wasn't possible. He watched Fetu closely, he looked serious, though James was still skeptical.

"Say I believe you. How did he do it? I don't suppose you are going to try to convince me that those disks are fold generators."

Fetu snorted almost choking on the last sip of his drink. "Hardly." He said after catching his breath. "Look, I have run over the data at least a dozen times; it was a fold, but now you know as much as I do. That disk is from the training deck, and other than being written in a language I can't read, appears no different from any of the other Vhast scripture I have seen."

James nodded slowly, of course, that is where he had seen the object before. Remembering the five disks from the first time he had ever been to the ship's strange dojo-sanctuary hybrid. Meghnah had told him the arrangement was common among the Drak'or. James admitted it was rather practical, assuming everything else there had likewise tied into the Drak'or religion.

"Do you know what language it is?"

Fetu stuffed the wrapper from his meal bar into the box from his drink, then tossed it across the room into a disposal bin. "Some Descendant relics have similar symbols, but nobody really knows where they came from, not originally." Fetu pushed his tray across the table to James. "Take care of that for me, will you?" he paused rising from his chair. "If you really want to know more about it, you should get over yourself and ask Chloe. She is good with that stuff."

"Get over myself? What is that supposed to mean?" James shouted after the larger man who had made his way across the cafeteria.

"If you can't figure that much out, you are hopeless." With a wink he fell backwards into the corridor, as he picked something out of his teeth. "Man, I can't wait for Travis to get back."

"Wait, what!?" James shouted, launching out of his

chair, which caused a stir from the others. James hardly noticed. Of course Travis was back, he had made breakfast for him that afternoon. He stared down at the discarded packaging from his friend's meal. The events of that morning clicked, he let out a sigh. Travis hadn't prepared his breakfast.

* * *

Chloe's bunk was easy enough to identify, two compartments back from James and Fetu's beds. Chloe's was the top alcove on the right-hand side of the corridor, and the only one with a full privacy screen projected over the compartment. James hesitated, it was silly, this could wait until after the end of shift tomorrow, and she wouldn't appreciate being awakened now.

James let out a small sigh and pressed the com button on the screen projector. "Chloe?" a small lump formed in his throat, there was no way he was going to get any sleep tonight, maybe he could come up with an excuse.

A minute passed and there was no reply, James considered trying again.

"She isn't there," Meghnah said from the bunk below.

Meghnah stared into her data pad, otherwise ignoring him.

"Where is she?" Meghnah clearly didn't want to be disturbed, It was strange that she was here and Chloe wasn't, Chloe almost never went anywhere that Meghnah wasn't going first.

Meghnah let out a long exaggerated sigh. "Not here, obviously."

"Obviously," James repeated dryly, he didn't have the mental capacity for this tonight. Meghnah continued reading as if he wasn't there. The subtle warbles of the fold generator, and distant clanking of the ship's hull against hyperspace filled the gap in the conversation, like an ugly sofa in the middle of an otherwise empty room.

James ran a hand through his hair. "I could use her help with something, so if you could tell me where she is I would appreciate it."

Meghnah set the data pad on her lap and gave James a critical look, after a minute her eyes softened. "Honestly, I don't know. She said she had some stuff she needed to take care of when we left the bridge. Said she needed to be alone for a little while."

"Is she okay?"

"She will be," Meghnah said, picking up the tablet again and attempting to find her place. "If it means that much to you, just go look for her. It isn't that big of a ship, there aren't that many places to hide."

"Right, thanks."

James went to push off and head for his bunk, he should try to get some sleep. He could resume the investigation tomorrow, it was still his first day back on duty and he shouldn't push himself too hard.

He nearly collided with Chloe as she drifted from the other direction.

"James? What's up?" her white blonde hair was damp and hung long down her shoulders and back, leaving streaks on her loose fitting t-shirt. James realized it was the first time he had ever seen her with it completely down. There was more color in her face than normal as well, which brought out the blue of her eyes in a way he hadn't noticed before.

Seph

James blinked trying to clear his head. "Um, well, I was looking for you, actually."

"Me?" Her eyes widened a little, confusion? Surprise maybe? "Why?"

James let out a huff as he tried to focus, "I just, are you okay? I mean is now a bad time?" he caught a faint blush and a hint of redness in Chloe's cheeks.

She hesitated a moment before turning off the privacy projection over her alcove, no longer making eye contact with him. "Yeah, I just, I wasn't expecting to see you, here I mean."

James nodded. "Uh, right…"

Chloe had caught him off guard. He couldn't think straight, he had never seen her out of uniform before, there was something different about her now, first this morning and now… It was like some kind of invisible barrier had dissolved between them.

Meghnah scoffed. "Did you actually need something, or did you come to stare?"

James felt the blood rushing to his cheeks, had it been that obvious? "Chloe, I… wanted to talk to you about a project I am working on."

Chloe opened her footlocker and stored the fresh uniform she had been holding. "Sure, how can I help?"

"It will be easier if I show you, can you come up to the training room with me?"

Chloe bit the edge of her lower lip. "Yeah, sure. Can I meet you up there in like fifteen minutes?"

James nodded. "Of course." He turned and pushed off into the corridor, he could use a few minutes to collect his thoughts anyway.

* * *

James ran a finger along the gold letters engraved into the black disk. It was cold and hard against his fingers, like highly polished steel. A stark contrast to its soft matte appearance.

James lifted the disk from the wall. It was lighter than he expected. Thin like someone had shaved the curve from a pool of liquid. He hadn't given the plates much thought before, content to pass them off as just another piece of The Captain's cultural heritage. Now, holding one in his hand, James couldn't help but be mesmerized by their strange alien beauty.

"James?"

Chloe's voice broke into his thoughts like a rock through glass, shattering them across the deck.

"You're looking at that book as if it is the key to the entire universe," she giggled. Her voice was soft, absent of criticism, and held the kind of warmth that made you feel grounded again.

She took the plate and flipped it over in her hands.

He let out a sigh as he removed another plate from the wall, now that he thought about it, they bore a resemblance to holo-books used more commonly in the Ring and Inner Circle, but those were made of thin layers of polarized glass printed on top of each other. They were not used very often anymore, Datapads were far more versatile. It was possible that these plates were an early predecessor to them. It was certainly more permanent than the paper books which predominated literature in the outer colonies.

James looked up from his study of the characters, "Do you know what language it is written in?"

Chloe squinted at the letters, "It's an ancient Vinge dialect. It shows up sometimes on artifacts coming out of the Inner Circle. Family heirlooms and such, a lot of it's fake though."

James stared at the disk again, his sense of wonder being restored, as far as most people were concerned, Vinge might as well have been a fairy tale. Few outside of the very elite ever had any reason to go there. Even as a member of the Alliance military, James had never had a chance to visit.

"What do you mean most of it is fake?"

"Just that," Chloe shrugged. "Lots of high-level officials would carry bracelets and such. They are supposed to bring luck. Sphiya would give us double pay if we managed to snatch something with a few characters. Most of what we got were cheap replicas, there is a market for them on the midway stations, so it isn't hard to find someone willing to sell you a knock-off."

James hung the disk back on the wall. "Would you believe me if I told you it was a fold generator?"

Chloe laughed. "Not for a second. I may not know much about hyperspace, but I do know that a fold generator needs to be a lot bigger than this."

James smiled. "You're right, it does. Until a few days ago, I would have believed it was impossible."

Chloe looked confused. "So what has changed your mind?"

"That is how The Captain got us off the station," James said, pointing at the disk still in her hand.

Chloe raised an eyebrow. "I thought he used the jump-pod in the Agdome."

James shook his head. "That's what he is telling everyone."

"So why don't you buy it?"

"Chloe," James made eye contact with her. "A jump pod requires two active pads."

"Nevarian could have activated one." Chloe protested.

James nodded. "That isn't the problem. The Shade doesn't have a jump pad, and even if it did, we wouldn't have had time to establish a tether."

"Could it have been a blind jump?"

"Possibly," you could do a blind jump. launching a pod randomly into space using a single pad. Their situation had been that desperate, but James clearly remembered falling onto the mat here in the sanctuary. "Although it would probably have taken you guys hours, if not days to find us."

Chloe stared in silence for a moment as the implication sunk in. The primary fold generator was simply too powerful for the jump to have been initiated onboard the Shade. Chloe carefully hung the plate back on the wall above the altar.

"I am not sure I can be of anymore help with this," her voice was distant but honest.

A familiar dark presence filled the room and tips of his fingers began to grow cold.

The Captain was leaning in the doorway. Lines formed at the corner of his eyes. His shoulders slouched. He looked tired, not the kind of tired you get when you have been awake for too long. The kind of tired that comes from running a marathon, on a mud trail, in the freezing rain.

"Zaeith?" Chloe went to step towards him but stopped herself. "Are you alright?"

He gave Chloe a warm smile. "I'm fine, I just need a minute to pray, that's all." He pushed himself off the door frame standing upright and straightening his cloak. "You two should go to bed, day comes early tomorrow and I will not be excusing any tardiness."

"Right," James said following Chloe towards the lift tube.

The Captain caught his arm as he passed. James froze looking into his endless red eyes, a chill ran down his spine.

"James, there are some things in the universe better left unknown."

James nodded slowly unable to fully meet his gaze.

"I will not try to stop you." The Captain released his arm. "I knew from the moment I first met you that we would one day be having this conversation." He laughed, it was almost more of a chuckle, the kind that is filled with memories that are too painful to think about.

"Be careful."

The Captain continued across the vast empty room. James watched for a moment as he knelt by the small altar lighting incense and chanting to himself.

James turned back to the lift tube where Chloe was waiting.

They made their way back down the corridors in silence, for James, the investigation had brought more questions than it had answers. The more he learned about the man who they called Captain, the less he felt like he knew him.

James stopped in front of his own bunk, letting Chloe drift ahead before speaking. "Hey Chloe."

She stopped herself and turned to face him. "Yes, James?"

James hesitated. "Thanks for breakfast."

Chloe smiled softly. "Your welcome."

Chapter 8

The mess hall was crowded, people's normal routines getting mixed up as the ship's clock adjusted to match the salvage cranes. James wondered what planet they picked to align with. General practice was for each ship to align to a nearby planet to avoid accidentally misaligning during transit. Dramia or Aundreus were the obvious choices; however, salvage cranes tended to stay space born for long periods of time, not willing to be put out too much by the unusual circumstances. They may have requested a planet more suitable for their next destination.

"You two were out pretty late last night. This 'project' of yours must be pretty interesting, James." Meghnah winked as she took a bite of her nutrient bar.

Chloe sighed. "I already told you, we were just looking at the scriptures in the sanctuary."

Meghnah turned to face her friend, then glanced back at James. "Uh huh." It was obvious from her tone that she didn't entirely believe them. "Whatever, I don't really care, but it is a small ship. Keeping secrets isn't going to do any of us a whole lot of good."

James aimlessly picked chunks off his nutrient bar. "Meghnah, there is something strange going on with this ship."

Meghnah smiled with an amused look, "So, you finally noticed?"

James sighed. "Besides the normal strange, I mean. I feel like we are caught in the middle of something."

Meghnah finished her breakfast and slouched back in her chair. "The Shade is always caught in the middle of something, and the stakes are usually pretty high. I told you when you first came on board; this would be different than any other ship you would ever serve on. There isn't another ship in the galaxy that can do what the Shade can."

She was right, of course. Normally The Captain only took the most desperate jobs registered with the Coterie of Mercenaries, offering the highest prices. The Shade was equipped with the most streamlined and elegant fold generator James had ever seen, allowing it to slip in and out of subspace faster and smoother than any other ship in the galaxy. That, combined with the fact that it carried an entire armada's worth of firepower, well, there wasn't much it couldn't handle. The ship was a legend. This felt different though, even given the urgency of it. Transporting station equipment was not the kind of job The Captain usually took, add the Descendant involvement... No, things were definitely not quite normal onboard the Shade.

James shook his head and dropped the remainder of his crumbled nutrient bar back on his tray. "This is different. Last night, when I was leaving the training deck, the Captain told me to be careful, that there were some things better left unknown."

Chloe looked up from her own barely touched breakfast. "Wait, he said all of that?"

Meghnah looked from Chloe and back to James, studying his face carefully. "Then I suggest you listen," she said after a long pause. "I don't care what this project of yours is, I suggest you drop it."

James looked to Chloe who met his eyes, for a moment they stared at each other. Meghnah was right; if even The Captain, the man who had single-handedly disabled a Descendant War ship, said to stay away, it was best to stay away. But, James wasn't very good at just leaving things alone. Even in the Alliance he couldn't just drop things. No matter how hard he tried to ignore the questions nagging at his mind, there was always one more rock to turn over, or one more hornet's nest to poke.

"Don't you ever wonder?" James finally asked into the silence.

"Wonder what?" Meghnah replied.

"How The Captain does it all, why the Shade is the way it is?"

Meghnah shrugged. "Now you are starting to sound like my brother, he liked getting philosophical." She pushed her tray towards him and stood to leave. "No, I don't wonder, because I don't care. The Captain got me out of a pretty tough spot, that's all that matters."

Chloe added her tray to the pile. "Is it really that easy for you to dismiss everything, Meg?"

Meghnah let out a heavy sigh as she stood. "Honestly, yes. No matter what the answer is, the Shade will still be the closest thing I have to a home," she clenched her fist and looked away. "I can live with that. No reason to make it more complicated."

Chloe watched as her friend left the mess hall letting out a sigh of her own. "Maybe she is right James, even if you do find the answers you are looking for will it change anything?"

James shrugged as he gathered the discarded meal trays. In truth, he didn't know, something was going on, and he felt he was only seeing the tip of it, while underneath the surface lay an iceberg.

"I think the questions concern me more than the answers." He said rising from the table.

Chloe cocked her head to one side. "How so?"

"It's difficult to explain, I'll see you on the bridge."

* * *

James exhaled as the shaft doors slid soundlessly in the tracks, he wasn't sure when he first began holding his breath before entering the bridge, but it helped him feel grounded somehow.

"James." The Captain didn't turn to face him as he spoke. Something flashed in the air between them, instincts moved his body and he caught the thin band. A neural link, much simpler than the Captain's. This model was a simple headband which fit over the user's ears, and had a small display screen attached over the eye. Once activated, the electron array would lock into the user's prefrontal cortex, allowing them to control the connected system just by thinking about it.

More advanced systems like the one The Captain wore went even further, connecting to the optic nerve, temporal lobe, and cerebellum. With practice, the wearer could interpret sensor data as if it were a part of themselves. The performance of various functions could be programmed into muscle memory, making the system an extension of the user's own body.

As useful as a link could be, they were considered too dangerous for regular use. The flood of data could overload the brain and cause permanent damage. The more advanced the model, the higher the risk. It was amazing that The Captain could use his as much as he did. It wasn't uncommon, even for trained users to slip into a coma and never wake up again. If you were lucky you might get away with only varying degrees of sensory loss such as agnosia.

Neural links were part of the standard curriculum in the Alliance Military Academy, fighter pilots used a full transfer system. Instead of connecting to the brain in parallel with normal body function, the neural transfer supplanted them. The wearer's body was kept alive in stasis while their mind acted as the primary controller for a drone unit. There were less immediate risks with the transfer, most pilots only experienced an hour or two worth of disorientation afterwards. However experienced pilots also accepted that the build-up of trauma in the brain would eventually have serious consequences, often leading to an early death.

James had hated using the transfer in the academy and swore to never do so again, if at all possible. Now, looking at the link in his hand, James was grateful for the experience.

"You have three days." The Captain's voice was hard and distant, he didn't look away from his display as he spoke.

James inhaled, taking his seat at the tactical station. Three days wasn't enough time to map a neural interface, most pilots would spend several weeks getting to know a ship before trying to operate it. It could be done, of course, the less time you spent doing it, the greater the risk.

James fitted the band to his head, holding his index finger over the activation sensor. The familiar tingling sensation began, it was something like putting your head against a sound plate vibrating at a frequency too low to hear. Once the device had mapped out his neurons it began aligning his brainwaves, a small warmth began to develop in his temples, growing hotter and accumulating in a sharp pinching sensation.

The small screen which hovered less than a millimeter above his eye flashed. 'Link established.' James took a deep breath and thought the word, 'initiate.'

Data slammed into his brain like a brick wall coming out of hyperspace. James mapped the information to various parts of his brain, by assigning each system to a specific thought, phrase, or action. The most important thing in the first few seconds was getting the information out of the frontal lobe, and into less active parts of the brain. Data could always be re-sorted later, but damage to your cognitive function was usually permanent.

Presorting the data had been tried but an individual user's thought patterns were too unique, assigning the information ahead of time always resulted in not being able to find it later. Fortunately, once you had interfaced with a system the map was stored, unfortunately, the mind was a lot more elastic than the computer and without regular use, the pathways would eventually decay and need to be remapped before it could be interfaced again.

* * *

Chloe tried not to stumble as she transitioned into the gravity of the medical bay, the lights inordinately bright after the dark corridor. The air was clean compared to the rest of the ship. This section ran on a separately dedicated air scrubber.

Situated between the corridors to the bunk room and the mess hall, the medical bay was divided in two by a thin privacy wall. The first half of the room had a small desk and a fingalin sleep pod for Nevarian to use, while the other half served as an examination room. All medical equipment, including a small single bed, which could be adjusted to fit the needs of a given situation, were kept in this second room.

The whole setup was far more simplistic than the med pods found on most stations, which required very little skill or training to operate. But most stations also did not have the benefit of a skilled physician.

Nevarian held the distinction of having the longest tenure of any crew member. Apparently in a lifetime long forgotten, he had served as a chief surgeon for the fingalin imperial palace on Celaria. He never talked about that. He rarely talked to the rest of the crew about anything. Especially not Chloe.

"Miss Chloe, can I help you with something?" Nevarian turned from the datapad on his desk. Unlike Travis whose face was dotted with mustard yellow freckles, Nevarian's body was almost completely white with the deep sapphire eyes universal to his race. In his case, enhanced by the thin blue stripes in each corner. Nevarian's fins were the color of sea fog at the base and faded evenly to a brilliant blue towards the edges.

"Is Travis up?" Chloe peeked through the opening

into the adjoining room.

Nevarian's long ears stiffened. "Yes," he nodded. "However, it is extremely inappropriate for a young woman such as yourself to be visiting him now."

"Oh stop it Nev, Chloe can visit me whenever she wants." Travis sat up and swung his legs over the side of his small bed. He wore loose-fitting trousers but no shirt.

The doctor set down his datapad and let out a long sigh. "Travis, you are in no condition to be entertaining young women." He gave Chloe a long hard look. "Especially not a human woman."

Chloe looked away, absently, anxiously squeezing her hands together. She had been used to comments like that growing up, Sphiya has constantly reminded her that she wasn't good enough to hang out with the other kids. It stung more now though, since the rest of the crew had always made her feel so normal.

Nevarian sat back in his chair, his gaze softening. "Come now, I seem to have slipped into my old habits, some things are harder to unlearn than others I suppose. I do not mean to cast doubt on your intentions Miss Chloe, but it is a small ship and I would not wish to propagate any rumors that you might be attempting to take advantage of him."

Travis chuckled, pushing himself out of bed with far more energy than Chloe would have expected. "I suppose it is a good thing we have you around Nev, that way, if any such pesky rumors do come up, you can sterilize them before they have a chance to reproduce."

The doctor inhaled deeply, swiveling to face Travis through the opening. "Please, I do not wish to ask again, refrain from using that nickname. You should not be addressing the senior staff so casually."

Travis grinned then saluted stiffly. "Sir, I shall take your suggestion under advisement, sir." He released the salute in a sharp jerking motion. He grabbed his t-shirt from off the hook on the dividing wall and pulled it on. "However as the only cook on board, I outrank everyone, so I won't be making any promises, Nev."

Nevarian glared critically but didn't say anything.

Chloe smiled, Travis's energy was as contagious as ever. "You don't have to get up for me, I just wanted to check on you. James and Fetu explained the whole thing to me."

As Travis stretched his legs he flared and unflared his arm fins. "Actually, I'm feeling great. The Doc here was about to ship me out, weren't you Nev?"

Nevarian eyed him for a moment unamused, then let out a sigh. "By all rights, you ought to be dead, but you do seem to be able to move around alright on your own, so I don't suppose I can keep you here any longer. I expect you to check in again in twenty-four hours, and I want to know immediately if you experience any dizziness." The doctor swiveled around to his desk and made a note on his datapad.

"Great!" Travis grabbed the remainder of his gear. "Chloe, Let's go make some breakfast!"

* * *

Travis dropped a case of large black peppers on the counter in front of Chloe as she tied the black apron around her waist. Chloe recognized them as sweet peppers from Reicue 12. Travis used them almost exclusively, he said it was because they traveled well.

Seph

They had been bred for the moon's thin atmosphere and to withstand the harsh radiation from the system's enormous sun.

"I am thinking of doing a stuffed toast loaf with egg scramble and fresh salsa," Travis said as he set a slab of meat on his cutting board. "The Captain got me this pork belly and I have been waiting for a good excuse to use it!"

"Wait, real pork, like from an actual pig?" Chloe looked more closely at the meat now, anticipation bubbling up inside her. She had never tried real pork before, pigs were rare and expensive. The norf, a genetically modified version of the creature, had almost entirely replaced them because of their ability to handle consecutive hyperspace folds.

"You bet!" Travis handed her a knife, it was light with the dull wave pattern characteristic of the Drak'or forging process. The millennia old technique used by the Drak'or resulted in a knife that both felt more natural, and lasted longer. "Let's do the peppers in a small dice."

Chloe began peeling off the thick outer skin of the peppers revealing the bright red flesh underneath. She enjoyed her cooking lessons with Travis. She was getting to explore the galaxy through his dishes. Besides, his energy made him easy to talk to.

"Hey Travis." She set a peeled pepper aside as she began working on another one. "Can I ask you something?"

The grill came to life, sizzling, the sweet aroma of bacon and cracked pepper rising from its surface. Travis laid out thick strips of meat. "Of course, you can ask me anything."

"Why won't Nevarian accept me?" She began

cutting the peppers into thin strips before cutting them again on the cross-section.

Travis washed his hands after laying down the last strip of pork belly. "Somebody tied his fins in a knot a long time ago, don't pay any attention to him."

Chloe let out a sigh. "He just treats me like I'm so…" she paused moving to the next pepper. "So…"

"Human?" Travis offered trading out his cutting board for a fresh one.

Chloe nodded slowly, "And ugly," she added wiping her eyes with the back of her forearm.

"Ah," Travis said knowingly, setting two large onions on the counter next to her cutting board. "Dice those next." Fresh herbs joined the aroma of the grill. "Beauty is highly subjective you know, we can't all judge ourselves by someone else's standard."

Chloe was grateful she could blame her tears on the onions now. "Yeah, I mean I guess, but why do the Fingal hate humans so much?"

Travis took a long breath and let it out slowly. "Chloe, we grew up in two very different worlds," he set a case of gashwar eggs on the counter. "You were raised by a fingalin who could never show you the love that you deserved. And I was loved by human parents who had never been given a reason to. I cannot say for certain why the Fingal think so highly of themselves, but trust me when I tell you that Humans are far more beautiful than you think." Travis placed a hand on her shoulder. His eyes kind, filled with the sincerity of a father comforting his daughter. "You are not ugly, child. James would be lucky to have you."

Chloe felt the blood rushing to her cheeks. "You know about that?"

Travis smiled and winked. "No, but I do now." He

removed the pork from the grill and began slicing it into chunks. "I had heard that you made him breakfast the other day, I filled in the rest."

Her face grew even warmer as she began cracking the multi-colored eggs into a bowl. The eggs came from a species of flightless bird, native to the islands on Atlione. The birds were adapted to living in limited space and ideal for agriculture onboard stations. Their eggs came with shells in every color of the rainbow and yolks ranging from bright orange to deep reds, and on occasion even purple.

"Hey, Travis." Chloe wiped her eyes. "Why are you so good at this?"

The knife against the cutting board paused. "I was married once." The chopping resumed, slower now, there was a distant sadness in his voice. "My wife was a lot like you actually."

Chloe handed Travis the mixed onion and peppers. "What happened?"

Travis smiled softly taking the container and adding the pork belly and herbs. "We had been expecting a child, but things got complicated," he stared absently as he chopped and mixed the ingredients for his salsa. "We had a good doctor, but in the end, I lost them both."

Chloe leaned against the counter tugging on her apron. "I'm sorry, I had no idea," she managed after a long moment.

Travis inhaled letting his breath out slowly. "That was a long time ago."

The silence went on for an eternity. "What was her name?" Chloe eventually asked.

Travis pulled a tray of mini bread loaves out of the oven and set them on the counter. "Hannah," he said, the energy returning to his eyes as he hollowed out each loaf.

"She sounds beautiful." Chloe said softly folding her hands together against her lap.

"She was the most beautiful creature in all the galaxy." Travis smiled as he began filling bread, "Lady Vyanna herself couldn't even compare," he chuckled at the memory. "Her hair was dark and thick, with curls that would fly wild if she did not keep it up."

Mixing the eggs he poured them over the stuffing. "She had dark skin, the color of toasted walnuts, and deep brown eyes that made you feel like you were sitting next to a fire with a warm cup of cocoa. And when she laughed it was as if you were jumping in a pile of leaves." He smiled, sliding the tray back into the oven.

Chloe watched him adjust the temperature. "She sounds beautiful," she said again watching the memories dance across his face. Imagining Hannah in her mind did not conjure the images Chloe had come to think of as pretty, but that look in Travis's eye told her she had been.

Chapter 9

Kurt exhaled as the hot tea warmed his chest. It was nice to have the cook working in the kitchen again, it felt like ages since he had eaten a proper meal. This mission had not turned out to be what he had expected.

The Engineering Corps had received an urgent contract from Coalition representatives, for the DSI project. The life support on Station 3122 was in need of urgent repairs. They saw it as an opportunity to gain a political foothold in the outer colonies, where neither the Mining Guild nor the Trade Commission had been able to.

The mission was assigned to Kurt and his team, stationed on Aundreus, the closest Federation controlled world to the station. It was both conveniently located, and a hotbed for Coterie activity. Kurt had listed the job with the Coterie of Mercenaries. At first, it had been a simple request for an escort, he didn't want to risk losing the payload to pirates. With the continued spread of the Aberration, and time running out, the situation had looked hopeless. His superiors had started pushing him to get it done, even if it was at a loss.

That's why when Commander Fetu Gaielin, First Officer of the Shade, approached him, Kurt thought it was a joke. The Shade was a legend. Impossibly fast, with more firepower than an Alliance Enforcer. The Shade represented the ultimate realization of a mercenary's dreams. A ship that only ever did the jobs it wanted, and could charge whatever it wanted to do. Never taking orders from anyone but yourself; absolute freedom. Placing a bid as the Shade was a mercenary's way of telling you that your job was impossible.

The bids were always placed anonymously on the net, requesting a ridiculous upfront payment... Fetu had approached him in person, given him the ship's verification codes, and offered to do it for over half of the next lowest bid. He had even promised to get them there two weeks before the requested deadline, if they could fill in the gaps in his crew during the trip.

It had been too good an offer, experience had told him not to trust it. But, after he looked up the codes everything checked out. In hindsight, the fact that most of the mission logs had either been redacted or classified should have been a red flag. At the time it had served only to confirm the superstition surrounding the vessel.

If the offer had surprised him, the ship itself had been even more of a shock. It looked like it had been created from the carcasses of over a dozen different ships, repurposed cargo hold and bunk bays fused together so elegantly into a single vessel, that the untrained eye would never have noticed they were not designed that way. It was as if someone had hand-picked each component, from over a century's worth of ships to serve their specific purpose.

The most interesting feature had been the antimatter generator and ion drive. Most ships, even small ones, used some form of a fusion core and gravity drive for sublight propulsion. Not only did it offer the advantage of providing real gravity to the ship, but it also meant not having to deal with an antimatter containment breach. Not that a collapsing fusion core was a lot better, but they were easier to shut down in an emergency.

Kurt hadn't had time to ask himself why the Shade was bothering with their mission. No, he had wondered that, the problem was no matter what the answer was, he wasn't in a position to refuse. It met all the criteria he needed, and the job needed to get done. If only things had remained that simple.

The first sign of trouble was when the Descendants showed up, the strange plague which was devastating the outer colonies had spread to the station. It seemed that The Captain was of the opinion that it was worth the risk, and was unwilling to condemn the residents on DSI 3122 to death by asphyxiation.

Kurt hadn't been too thrilled about the idea of boarding a station under active quarantine, but compared to finding it empty, it would have been preferable. That hadn't been the only thing wrong on DSI 3122; the fusion core had been deliberately sabotaged. As soon as he saw it, Kurt knew he was going to die on board. But, he hadn't somehow, though it was impossible. They had all survived.

It was difficult to remember clearly what had

happened, what Kurt did remember was the day he had spent in bed with hyperspace fatigue. Fetu had told him that The Captain had gotten them off using the agdome's jump pod, but there hadn't been enough time to establish a tether. It could have been a blind jump, that was plausible, the others bought it at least. But if they had been in a jump pod, why did he have this memory of a Vhastian shrine?

The last puzzle piece had come when Kurt checked the nets two days later. DSI 3122 was being reported as a forced self-destruct, a decision made as a last effort to prevent the plague from spreading into the ring. It was the second time in the last six months. But it wasn't a programmed self-destruct, and if it had been designed to prevent the spread of infection, where had all the residents gone? More importantly, why hadn't the crew of the Shade been more surprised? It was as if the Captain had been expecting it.

The clanging of a meal tray against the table brought Kurt back to the present. It was Jaks. He was a tall lanky guy, new to the team. Talia was with him, she had been stationed with the Aundreus crew for as long as anyone could remember.

"What's with the eyes?" Talia asked as she pulled out the chair next to Kurt.

Kurt rubbed his eye's forcing his thoughts back into the mess hall, "What eyes?"

Talia nudged his shoulder, "You got the look of someone who's forgotten where they are going, and can't remember where they've been." She dug eagerly into the panini on her plate. "Man, why can't we get food like this back home, eh?"

Kurt chuckled. "Because it's too hard to grow anything and too expensive to ship it."

Seph

Jaks sat his mug down hard on the table. "You give any thought to the offer to stay on board?" He asked, wiping the residue from his drink off his upper lip.

They had all been offered a commission to stay on board, it would be a two-month tour, the pay was pretty good. It would require three day shifts a week in the engine room and a shift on bridge duty. They were promised three days' shore leave at the next planet and a shuttle to anywhere in the quadrant when the job was up. It was a formality more than anything though, most mercenary ships made similar offers at the end of a job because it benefited everybody. It provided a way for freelancers to move around the galaxy without having to pay out-of-pocket and provided the extra hands mercenaries almost always needed.

Talia gasped. "Wait, that's not what you were thinking about just now, is it? We're about to start on that new Solar Harvester, you can't leave now!"

Kurt gave Talia a friendly slap on the shoulder, "No, I wasn't planning on staying on board."

"Well, I might do it." Jaks said between bites. "My internship is almost up anyway, and I think I can convince the corps to give me two months education leave for not having to pay to bring me back into the ring. Besides, you never know when a little experience with one of the older engines will come in handy, ya know?"

There was a brief crackle of static before the first officer's voice echoed over the ship wide intercom. "We have paired with the crane, all personnel on duty please report to the cargo bay for assignment."

"That's our cue," Kurt said, gathering his tray.

* * *

Kurt stared out the cargo cranes' observation window, the massive ship dwarfed almost anything in the Alliance, or any other fleet for that matter, except for stations and carrier-class ships. Designed to rescue and tow stranded ships back to safety, though they occasionally hauled pieces of a station or pre-terraforming settlement structures.

Outside, the glowing orange orb of the Descendant plasma shield could only be observed through the most intense solar filters. It was something like being parked in orbit right outside the corona of a sun. He had been told that this was part of a rescue mission, he had never guessed that they would be attempting to do it, through an active plasma shield.

The Shade's main crew had gathered in the crane's largest jump pod. They planned on using it to jump through the plasma shield. In theory it was possible, except there was no way to communicate with the pad on the other ship. No way to establish a tether, something which should have taken days if you didn't want to suffer from hyperspace fatigue, and if you weren't connecting to a station.

An electric hum began to build in the room, the kind that vibrates deep in your bones. Space around the jump pod began to ripple and twist as electricity arced across its hull plating in brilliant colors. The noise swelled into a hushed whine followed by a loud crack as bolts of lightning leaped from the pod, caching on the invisible resonance field. The pitch of the sound continued to climb as more electricity jumped from the ship dancing in a sphere around the pad. The air grew hot and dry. His hairs stood as the static electricity began to build in his body, like gravity had stopped working. Everything slowed as if time were attached to an analog clock with a dying power cell. In one bright flash, the energy collapsed in on itself sucking space into the emptiness behind it. Reality snapped like someone letting the slack out of a vast sheet then pulling it tight again.

Kurt let out a breath. He was certain the Shade's crew had teleported to their death. Everything he knew about hyperspace told him that it could not be done. Except, he had met the Shade's Captain, and he was no fool. That man would not needlessly sacrifice his crew. He didn't know how, but his instinct told him that he had witnessed the impossible. And if this trip had taught him anything, it was to trust his instincts.

Chapter 10

The image of the decaying plasma shield flickered in the view field. James stared absently at the hologram, not really paying any attention to it. It was mostly a distraction for his eyes, while his brain operated the ship via his neural link. The plasma shield resembled a small sun from a visual standpoint, but to the Shade's sensor array, it appeared very different.

Stars showed up as chaotic masses of energy jetting incredible amounts of radiation across vast reaches of space. Dozens of magnetic fields twisting and distorting as flares erupted from their surfaces, with space-time dilation caused by their gravity wells.

The plasma shield was a perfectly contained spherical body, one stable magnetic field suspended with perfect layers of radiation evenly dispersed across its surface.

The shield had shrunk considerably since they had left the Wyvern stranded here. It was impossible to tell for sure since the sensors couldn't penetrate the shield, but James guessed that it had already started absorbing the ship it was protecting.

The Captain had led Fetu, Meghnah, and Chloe to evacuate the crew, leaving James Nevarian and Scot, to control the bridge. With Travis operating the jump pod from the Engineering Corps's cargo crane.

Scot was an SK01 android AI unit. His primary function was as the second engineer, his small limbs and metallic body were ideal for working around the antimatter and fold generators as well as the ion drive. Having multi-spectral eyes allowed him to detect anomalies long before any of the biological crew members could. He could run millions of computations per second and was considered self-aware enough to operate independently of direct command inputs. He could be an efficient navigator. Though, using an AI for that could be difficult. They tended to over-optimize. Their algorithm's struggled to balance the need of finding the quickest route, and the safest route. Asking for one or the other could often elicit a polarized response, which could lead to a disaster. Normally, Scot only maintained the navigation calculations Meghnah provided.

James accessed the droids subroutine via his link, Scot was running several sub-processes directly interfaced with the ship's system via an entanglement transmitter. He tried probing the data stream to decipher their purpose but found he was locked out. It was unusual for an android to run an encrypted link, but not necessarily unheard of, keeping a constant data flow meant that Scot maintained a permanent full neural link with the Shade. Having a built-in entanglement transmitter meant instant communication from anywhere.

James filed the information away for later use, before deciding to run an experiment. Accessing the ship's tactical data, James overlaid battle scenarios into a rudimentary simulation. He passed the program over to the android. At first Scot was confused as its AI tried to figure out what to do with the new information.

The first round ended in a spectacular disaster. Scot initiated a battle strategy and was unable to respond to the simulator's adaptations. He quickly realized that the puzzle required a dynamic approach and applied a processing algorithm. The next two tries went better, except for Scot's entire crew being either sucked into space, or suffocated. Scot was focused only on the objective and failed to account for the necessity of maintaining an atmosphere. By the fourth try, it had managed to successfully beat the simulator.

The robot turned to face James. "That was fun, Sir. Do you have another?"

James grinned. "I'll see what I can put together, Scot." Teaching artificial intelligence how to conduct combat operations was not the best idea he had ever come up with. But, if he was successful, the ability to operate the Shade via remote may prove invaluable. James inhaled slowly; only time would tell.

* * *

The jump pod was more like a simple metal box than anything else. Their only real purpose was to provide shielding from the hyperspace turbulence during a jump. The pod itself didn't play any part in the process of opening the envelope. It did have some life support capabilities, but in the end, it was just a box with armor plating and an electromagnetic shield.

Meghnah strapped herself into one of the five-point harnesses on the pod's outside wall. This was one of the largest pods on the crane, with two dozen of the bucket seats available. With the help of the engineering crew, they had installed two extra sets in the middle of the compartment, bringing the pod's total crew capacity to thirty-four. Bringing over the Vyrant's entire crew would require nine trips. The odds of even being able to manage one were so stacked against them. What was on the Vyrant that The Captain felt was worth the trouble?

Chloe strapped herself into the chair next to her. "This is going to work, right?"

Meghnah shrugged but didn't say anything.

Fetu flopped down in the chair across from them and pulled the harness over his shoulder. "It'll be fine."

His voice lacked the confidence his words implied, still they helped a little. The Captain had gotten them out of more impossible spots than this before. . . Hadn't he?

Meghnah took a deep breath and held it. The tingling sensation of excited electrons began to build as the air filled with the acrid scent of oxidation. The humming noise began to climb in pitch to a whistle as electricity jumped from the pod's outer shell in explosive pops and cracks. Her vision began to twist and the world folded inward on itself then turned inside out. Her gut lurched. Everything stopped.

An eternity passed, the void of nothingness filling with a cascade of more nothingness as sensation and feeling became so removed. Meghnah began to wonder if they had ever been anything more than an illusion. Reluctantly, she began to fade into the emptiness.

With a loud bang, reality snapped back into existence. Meghnah exhaled, her breath turning to fog in the cold air. The pod doors clicked and hissed as they slid open, spilling light into the darkened room beyond. Somehow, they had made it.

The Captain's hooded form rose onto the ramp like a shadow out of the darkness, his neural link engaged over his right eye, the left reflected light from the pod like a glowing ember. Ionized particles caught on the hem of his cloak causing it to drift about his ankles as water droplets returned to vapor.

For a moment The Captain reminded her of the ghost stories from her childhood, tales of witches and demons who roamed the far reaches of space beyond the edge of the star cluster, inside of nebulae where starlight couldn't penetrate and quasar maps became useless. The kind of stories that parents tell their children to keep them in bed at night.

The Captain removed a small bundle from his waist pouch. "Fetu. I need one of these welded to the hull of every pod in this room." He tossed it to the first officer. "There is a circuit line on each of the pods, connect them there."

Fetu caught the pouch out of the air and dumped its contents into his other hand. There were about a dozen small disks. "Right…" there was a hint of amusement in his voice as he examined each of the coins.

"Meghnah, I want every pod's emergency locator lights activated, then see if you can't get the power to the jump pad working again, Fetu will help when he is finished. Chloe, you come with me." The Captain turned in the doorway and vanished back into the cargo hold.

Meghnah inhaled deeply, she dropped her pack from her shoulder and removed the drone light. Synchronizing the spherical robot to her datapad, she set it on flood mode. The droid came to life, leading about a foot over her right shoulder and illuminating the area. "Right." She whispered to herself as she stepped onto the ramp.

* * *

Fetu examined the small discs The Captain had tossed him. They looked like tiny hyperspace focusing lenses. Made of a ceramic composite about an inch in diameter each. The back face was perfectly smooth. A glass meniscus was set into the opposite face with a silver circuit inlaid between the layers. Each circuit appeared unique to the coin it was printed into.

He returned the lenses to the pouch before activating his light and following Meghnah down the ramp. Fetu let out a gasp as the drones lit up the floor around the jump pad. The cargo hold itself, though only a fraction of the size of the cargo cranes, was still expansive enough to fit four ships the size of The Shade inside. Thirteen jump pods sat in a ring about ten meters from the pad.

Having served on an identical ship once, Fetu had been expecting this. What he had not been prepared for was the floor itself. Hundreds of lines made of fiber optics and conduit etched into the plating. They formed an intricate pattern moving outward from the jump pad towards the pods in a giant ring. It was a perfect recreation of a two-dimensional schematic for a hyperspace fold generator. Normally the circuitry for a fold generator would be layered on top of each other in a cylinder, or sometimes wrapped around each other in a sphere with a single focusing lens at its center.

This configuration looked more likely to function as a hyperspace bomb. Sure, it could tear a hole into subspace, but that was a lot different from hitting a hyperspace sleeve and opening an envelope.

Fetu shook his head. Then again, this was The Captain of the Shade; his ability to predict, and manipulate the flow of hyperspace more than anything, was the reason for the ship's reputation. Still, Fetu found it difficult to put aside his doubts.

* * *

Chloe followed Zaeith down the ramp, losing him in the cast darkness of the cargo hold. She turned on her datapad, pulling up the interface for the drone control. Red light spilled into the room through a doorway at the far side. Zaeith's shadow hung in the opening where he waited.

The hallway was far grander than anything Chloe had ever seen before. It curved out in each direction from the door like a giant ring. The white walls stretched upward for almost four meters. Glass runners lined the edges where the wall met the ceiling, the progress of a solar eclipse etched in silver along their length. The floor appeared to be covered in a single sheet of curved marble stone as if it had been melted and poured there. Small flecks of crystal glimmered red from the emergency light above.

The whole thing was so awe-inspiring that Chloe almost didn't notice the thick scent of dust in the heavy air, or the echoing throb from the dying life support system. Collecting her presence of mind, Chloe caught up with Zaeith as he approached an ornate door on the hallway's inner wall. A thin cloth drape hung from either side of the door's carved wooden frame. The door itself was inlaid with glass and silver in a pattern that reminded her of planetary orbits.

Without warning the door swung open. The lift beyond was as elaborate as the hallway. Perfectly round, the floors and ceiling matched the corridor outside. A mirror filled the wall opposite the doors. Strange shadows distorted their reflections in a way that rendered them unrecognizable. Chloe felt herself drawn to the glass, an ethereal voice seemed to whisper her name in the back of her mind.

Zaeith paused for a minute studying the twisted image. "Officer's quarters." His clear voice shattered the room's strange spell. The large wooden door closed, and darkness surrounded them.

Chloe shifted her weight, leaning closer to Zaeith. In this new environment, his familiar presence somehow comforted her. "If the lift works, why are the lights out?" That had been bothering her since they arrived. All the lights in the cargo hold were out, but the corridor was still lit. The lift clearly had some power because it was operating, however, not even the dim emergency lights came on.

There was a long silence before Zaeith answered. "The price of greed is paid slowly." Chloe sighed, knowing that was all she would get from him. Then again, what had she really been expecting? She couldn't say that she had known The Captain very long. Even at that, the more she learned, the less she understood.

The door swung open to reveal another grand

corridor, identical to the first. A massive hallway extended out from the lift shaft towards an even more impressive set of double doors. Carved out of the wood of an Empress tree, streaks of silver and gold grew out of the wood's natural grains. The wood itself appeared almost crimson, the red light canceling out the tones of blue in the otherwise purple-gray wood. On the face of the door hung a large black circle, with a crescent-shaped mirror on the left side. In the center of the doors, nine stars with silver tails chasing it in an intricate spiral.

Chloe followed Zaeith as he drifted down the hall, the shadows cast by the strange light seemed to pull off the walls and coalesce around him. Voices whispered in her mind, distant as if calling out from across both time and space. She tried to focus on them, but the words evaded her. Chanting in the rhythm of what she could only assume was a forgotten prayer.

The two majestic doors opened inward as they approached, revealing a stateroom lit by a series of dim sconce lights around its perimeter, their white glow leaving a strange purple haze at the edge of her vision. Lavender tapestries hung from the ceiling, coming within millimeters of touching the stone floor. The voices concentrated around a gigantic mirror that filled the back wall, framed in the same intricate patterns found in the corridors.

The frail figure of a fingalin pulled himself out of the bed against the right wall, only a shadow of the proud figure who had appeared in the view field a few weeks ago.

"Greetings Captain. I must admit, I was beginning to doubt you had ever been anything more than a figment of my deranged imagination."

Seph

He rose to his feet, standing at attention pride returning to his features, dispelling the image of fragility he had displayed a moment before. With perfect white skin, and eyes that, even dimmed with fatigue, still exuded dignity. His fins clung tight to his forearms ending in lavender strips at their edges. Chloe felt a tinge of admiration, she had seen statues less perfect. He was the pinnacle of what the fingalin considered masculine beauty.

Chloe could feel the Colonel's gaze scrutinize her. "Who is your friend?" His head tilted to one side as one of his ears twisted forward in a classic look of fingalin curiosity.

She swallowed, a lump forming in her throat as she tried to push the voices to the back of her mind. "Chloe, I'm... Chloe," her voice was something between a stutter and a whisper, the words seemed to come out backward. She shrunk into herself, feeling small, like a child in the two men's herculean presence.

Zaeith looked at her, his face was firm, like a stone wall. He studied her for a moment, but his gaze did not communicate anger or hostility. More like curiosity or maybe, amusement?

Gillian bowed at the shoulders. "Colonel Gillian Maylis, Commander of the holy Descendant vessel Vyrant under Lady Vyanna. A pleasure, Chloe."

She shifted her weight uncomfortably, Chloe had never been formally addressed before, something about being spoken to as an equal made her feel even smaller.

Gillian met Zaeith's eyes again. "Now then captain, seeing as you have decided to spare us, the Vyrant is yours," he gave Zaeith a deep nod, "Do as you please."

The mirror pulled her back towards it, beckoning her with its intoxicating calls.

Zaeith studied the Colonel for a moment. "Take Chloe to the armory, I need uniforms for my team. Once everyone is changed, begin gathering your crew to the forward cargo hold." He put a hand on Chloe's shoulder and gave her a light squeeze. His glowing red eyes stared into hers for a brief moment. The voices fled like shadows from the morning sun.

She watched him disappear back into the lift. Uneasiness welled up in the pit of her stomach. Wishing for his presence again as the ship seemed to expand, growing even more massive compared to her shrinking frame.

Gillian broke the silence. "You are new to this, aren't you." His voice soft carrying sympathy.

"Is it that obvious?"

Gillian chuckled with a half-smile. "Let's just say I have been on your end of this a few more times than I am ready to admit."

It was half comforting, she was unqualified for this mission. Maybe, when she got a chance, she could ask James for some training. Right now, she was more in the way then she was useful. If the Colonel had any inclination to fight back, he could use her as a hostage. At least if she knew how to handle a gun, she might be able to defend herself.

Gillian motioned to the door. "Please follow me."

* * *

The Armory looked more like a museum than anything, with white walls the grandeur of which was equal to the rest of the ships. A row of flat benches carved from empress wood floated over the stone floor on glass supports. Opposite the doorway, the wall sloped outward, glass displays held a variety of weapons ranging from handguns to warstaffs.

Adjacent to the door, square alcoves lined with two rows of what Chloe could only assume were personal lockers. Each one plated with frosted glass, a name etched in silver on its surface. The end caps were plated in gold with the black and silver eclipse symbol embossed on the face.

Most impressive was the wall furthest from the entrance. Five sets of white gold breast plates hung displayed on glass poles, with helmets which resembled a dragon's head, two long prongs protruding backward from the temples. Two additional plates covered in white gold appeared to be able to fold forward, providing protection for the larger ears of a fingalin.

Attached to the breastplates were white gold shoulder guards which secured a long lavender cloak to the back. Chloe's eyes drew to the armor, the intricate details calling to her as the mirror had before, pulling her closer. The center set included a gauntlet which sat on a raised pedestal in front of the display.

Chloe's breath caught in her lungs. The glove's fabric was bright white, with white gold plating along the back of the forearm and hand. Glass rings wrapped around each of the first two fingers. Five small purple stones were embedded into the arm plate, energy ebbed and flowed beneath their surfaces like gentle waves in an ocean. The artifact was alive somehow, it drew her in like stars falling from the night sky.

Gingerly, Chloe reached out and touched it, the voices becoming clearer in her mind. It was cool and surprisingly soft against her finger tips. Characters were engraved into the surface, printed in a thin layer of glass almost invisible to the eye. Her heart stopped, these were the same letters used in the books of the Shade's sanctuary. What were they doing here?

"Beautiful, isn't it?"

She pulled her hand back from the glove as if it had burned her, the whispers pulling back from her like tar reluctant to release a captured animal. She had forgotten Gillian was even there. The fingalin's eyes grew distant as if drifting in a dream..

"May I?" She reached for the gauntlet once more. The ethereal voices urging her to take it.

He regarded her for a moment saying nothing, his eyes carving her face and features out of stone.

"I suppose it doesn't matter now." He took a long deep breath then let it out slowly, as he stared at the distant wall. "I am already a traitor. I will not likely be needing it again." His head tilted, his gaze returned a look of curious amusement playing at the corner of his mouth. "Besides, it would be a shame if we left it behind."

She lifted the artifact from its pedestal, careful not to smudge the polished metal with her fingerprints. The voice growing more intimate as if the glove itself were speaking to her. "What is it?"

Gillian removed a long lavender wrap from the base of the pedestal. "It is called the Arah'a'el Zymo, which translates as, 'protecting touch of light.' Though it has been argued that it is more correct to translate it as 'divine hand of influence.

"Though I suspect that is not really what you were asking." He handed her the cloth, "That will protect it in your pack."

It was a little embarrassing how easily he could read her thoughts, she had never considered herself predictable. Had she always been this soft?

"It is an ancient artifact, it and others like it have been handed down by the Descendants for generations. It is ceremonial, but does have practical uses. It's somewhat of a predecessor to the neural link, which operates some of our more... unique technologies."

As she wrapped the glove in the cloth, its voice quieted to a gentle pressure on the back of her mind.

Unique technologies. That sounded ominous, but that was what set the Descendants apart from the rest of the galaxy, which had only begun to catch up over the last few centuries. Chloe laid the wrapped package softly in the bottom of her pack, "Something like a key?"

"Precisely." He gave a deep nod. "Now then, I believe your Captain requested uniforms?"

* * *

The milky glass door slid open as Meg stepped back through. It was strange to see her in a Descendant uniform, though Chloe had to admit she wore it well. Her graphite skin contrasted the white leggings which clung evenly, but comfortably to her body, emphasizing her natural figure. She had refused the white coat. A breach of uniform which may have been a problem, except, so far most of the crew had stopped caring a long time ago. Those who were still alive anyway.

Meg exhaled, "This one is dead too."

"That's almost a third of the crew, isn't it?" Chloe didn't really need Meg to answer. They had spent the better part of the last two hours going room to room. Zaeith had ordered them to get as much of the crew as they could on the jump pods. Gillian had taken to gathering the higher ranking crew members, and enlisting them to help, while Chloe and Meg started with the civilian crew. Their numbers had been somewhat better here, where people still believed that this was a test, and Vyanna would eventually deliver them. But most of the informed crew had already committed suicide.

"Yes, and the last one on this deck." She keyed it into the datapad. It wasn't clear if Meg found the whole thing revolting, or if she simply didn't care, but it was apparent she did not share any sympathy for them.

Chloe keyed the Descendant communications device connected behind her ear. "We have cleared the civilian decks, what's next?"

The Colonel's voice echoed back, lacking the electronic crackle of a traditional comm-link, it sounded more like a crystal bell. "Return to the cargo bay, all personnel have been accounted for."

The lights in the lift were working again. The plasma shield was drawing too much power, and the computer had shut down anything considered non-essential to maintain it. Meg and Fetu started working on it as soon as they arrived. Over an hour after Chloe and Meg left the cargo bay, Fetu got the lights on.

Chloe's reflection in the mirror looked small next to Meg's. Ever since she had wrapped the glove, the voices had stopped. The white coat of the uniform she wore, with its lavender cuffs and silver edging, making her feel even more out of place. She suspected that was why Meg had refused it, neither of them ever worn anything so elaborate.

"Meg?" Chloe ventured her thoughts into the empty

air. "Do you believe in magic?"

Meg laughed, small but sweet. "Magic is everywhere, Chloe. Fold generators, hyperspace sleeves, fusion cores, what's the difference? It's all magic in a way. As a child, I was taught it was all evil. That the exploitation of it was witchcraft and would lead to corruption and destruction."

"So you guys didn't use any technology?" Growing up on a space station, it was difficult to imagine a world vacant of modern automation.

"Not completely. Technology at some level is always necessary. The trick is only ever using what you need."

"How do you know if you are using too much?"

She shrugged "I suppose if it ever stops being magic. I think magic is a word we created to describe things that seem impossible. Once we begin to use something every day, it loses its sparkle and becomes mundane. Witchcraft is when you get so absorbed by it, that you don't even see it anymore. You must always be able to look out at the world and contemplate its wonder, otherwise, you risk losing yourself."

The more she thought about it, the more profound the Drak'or philosophy seemed. Technology was so interwoven into her life, most of the time she didn't even recognize it. In the quiet hours of the night, she had caught herself cursing the lack of comforts on board the Shade. Its sparse artificial gravity, the absence of any proper mirrors. She didn't want to be ungrateful and usually rejected these thoughts. She smiled to herself, James was always complaining about the beds. It was easy to forget the magic of such simple things.

The corridor went on for an eternity now, the lights highlighting the vastness of the Vyrant with its emptiness. It was one thing to imagine the absence of life in some unknown blackness, The light made it tangible.

"Hey, Meg… does it ever scare you?"

Meg's eyes grew soft, a small crack in her hard exterior, like a furry animal poking its head out of the ground for its first look at spring. It was a look Chloe hadn't seen very often but it helped.

"I don't think it ever, doesn't scare me." The words came out heavy, they seemed to draw a vacuum behind them like a rock sinking in a lake.

Meg never appeared to be afraid of anything, Always so strong, so determined, like she could take on the universe and laugh about it afterward.

"Why do you keep going then?"

Meg paused in front of the cargo bay door. "There isn't really another option. You keep moving forward, or you stop. And if you stop, you die." Her voice grew distant as if lost in some forgotten corner of the world. "Sometimes, you just keep walking, because no matter how hard that next step is, it is always easier than turning back."

The words resonated like a fire breathing in the wind. That described her whole life up until now, every day dragged into the next by the wheels of an incomprehensible machine called Time. It didn't care if you ate or slept, it kept rolling forward, endless in its pursuit of the future. She had never considered that strength, it felt like weakness, always letting everyone or everything tell you what to do.

The lift door opened, and they stepped into the corridor.

Chloe's stomach dropped as she entered the cargo bay. For a moment she swore she saw the letters from ancient Vinge engraved in the floor.

She pushed down the wave of nausea trying to ignore the tingling sensation in her fingers, then looked again. A network of glass and metal was laced intricately around the jump-pad, overlapping each other. It was impossible to tell if any of them could have been a replication of one of Zaeith's books.

* * *

Hours had passed since the Shade's crew had been teleported into the void between the layers of reality. No one had heard from them, not even Travis, the technician operating the jump pad.

The fingalin had tweaked the resonance field. He had made the field more oblong with a bulge on one end. It wasn't clear why, when asked he had said it was The Captain's orders, and he didn't really know the reason. Kurt could only guess at what the result would be. Most of his speculation led him to suspect it would end up working more like a cannon than a net.

Most of the time however, they sat around doing nothing. How long would it be before The Captain of the engineering crane gave up and left without them?

A high-pitched hum erupted into the room, a blue haze appeared around the jump-pad igniting the air with electricity. The hair on his arms stood on end, catching in the waves of static. For a moment time stood still. A thin crack appeared in space at the narrow end of the resonance field. It was hard to tell if it was bright white or absolutely black. The crack appeared hazy, like something stuck at the corner of your vision that disappears every time you try to look. It exploded into a blinding flash, as hot waves of energy surged through his body.

Space sucked back into itself, like a collapsing vortex in a thick liquid. The air was cold, droplets of water beaded on his skin.

Behind the jump-pad thirteen pods, still glowing with remnants of ionized particles sat in a perfect ring. Kurt stared in disbelief as the Shade's technician deactivated the pad and entered a note into his tablet.

A snap-hiss signaled each door before it opened. The Shade's first officer descended the ramp and inhaled deeply. "Let's get these guys to see a doctor." His voice boomed with the amusement of someone who has just finished an impossible task. He tossed a datapad to Travis. "You handle this from here, I'm going to go take a shower."

Others began emerging from the vessels. Some still wore the Descendant uniforms, others had discarded theirs. All looked hungry and exhausted. Despite their appearance, an air of hope hung around them.

Kurt smiled to himself, somehow the Captain had done it. The Shade and its Captain had lived up to their impossible reputation. Maybe there was more to this man then he had previously thought.

Chapter 11

Grand Admiral Trepidor pressed firmly on his forehead and temple, elbows resting on the long stone table. This debate had gone on for an hour, and still they had gotten nowhere. The Vyrant had disappeared, and like that, the most powerful governing body in the galaxy was reduced to a group of bickering children.

The High Council Chamber of the Lady Vyanna may have looked impressive, with its impossibly high ceiling, elegant lavender tapestries, and colossal mirrors. All twenty members of the council sitting on their own glass throne, adorned with white gold and lavender cushions. But at this exact moment, Trepidor felt as if it were an elaborate facade.

"Tell me again, General. How exactly did the Vyrant… 'disappear,' was it?"

The High General stiffened with a huff. Like Trepidor, he was in command of approximately one-third of the order's military strength. The Vyrant had been part of his division.

"It didn't disappear. All evidence suggests it was a plasma shield malfunction. It was a feedback overload, nothing more. This is not the first time this has happened."

Plasma shield failures had become more frequent since the advent of the fusion core. However, of all the ships in the galaxy, why this one, and why now? There was too much risk to pass it off as a coincidence.

The Counselor who served as the primary liaison to the Engineering corps, spoke from the far end of the table. "All reports lead me to believe that the quarantine was, in fact, a success. Even if someone had breached the perimeter, there is no way they could have made it to the station before it collapsed."

A protest erupted from about half of the participants around the table. It didn't help matters that the reports from the rescued crew were unreliable. The report from the Engineering crew was a little more cohesive, but it was missing too many details to make for a strong argument. That was probably for the best. They were having a hard enough time handling the survivors already.

A clear crystal bell chimed from the head of the table and the arguments began to settle down.

Governor Sylvinn was the head of the council. Her primary function was to direct discussion. Because council decisions had to be unanimous, her practical authority did not extend outside of this room. However, within its walls, her power was absolute.

"Arguing with ourselves will get us nowhere. We cannot afford any doubt on this matter. Director Xious, what is your opinion?"

Xious was quite possibly the most powerful man in

the order. As the director of missionary efforts, he was not only in command of the remaining third of the cumulative military power, he was also considered the final authority on disputes of doctrine. A responsibility he had inherited when the last of the elders had passed away.

The director's dark red eyes scanned the others in the room. "We cannot afford to ignore the possibility that the infection has spread beyond the station. The surviving crew must be quarantined until we can be sure. If this plague spreads into the ring, we will never be able to contain it."

Sylvinn tapped her long white fingers on the table. "I understand you have made some progress in that area, Director."

Xious shrunk back into his chair, not quite making eye contact with the others. "Well, yes… I suppose we have made some progress, but it would be foolish to become too optimistic at this point. A handful of resolved cases is hardly a victory."

"An entire world cured in a single day is hardly a handful, Director." One of four correspondents with the Drak'or Coalition said.

Xious glared at the counselor. "I do not know what rumors you have heard Councilor, but I can assure you they have been greatly exaggerated."

Trepidor clenched his teeth. Something had to be done to stop this line of questioning, if their plans were revealed now it would unravel centuries worth of preparation.

"Governor, if I may. I have a vessel in the vicinity, it would not be a significant drain on our resources to have them investigate the matter further. Maybe then we can get a clearer picture of what happened, and put this matter behind us."

Involving the Vyrant had been risky enough, but the others had felt it was necessary to divert suspicion. At least this time the commanding officers would report directly to him. If he couldn't go in person, it was best to keep the investigation limited. If the truth of the DSI 3122 quarantine ever got out, his future on the council would be... uncertain.

The Governor nodded. "I would very much like that. Are there any objections to allowing Grand Admiral Trepidor to investigate?"

The room fell silent, nobody else wanted to take on the responsibility themselves. That was good, none of them were suspicious, at least that is what Trepidor hoped.

Sylvinn rose from her seat, "It is unanimous. This meeting is adjourned, I await your report Grand Admiral."

Xious followed Trepidor to his office. "I should not have to tell you the consequences if you screw this up again." The Drak'or's features were hard as stone.

"Me? If you had let me handle the quarantine from the beginning, we would not be in this position."

Xious loomed into the room, an ominous presence building around him as he jabbed a finger into the admiral's chest. "We would not be in this situation if you had not allowed that girl to escape on DSI 5771."

He exhaled, regaining his composure. "In any case, the survivors need to disappear, I trust you can at least handle that."

Trepidor nodded, swallowing hard. "Yes sir, I will take care of it."

The Director turned to leave, then stopped in the doorway. The darkness in the room seemed to concentrate into his voice. "And Grand Admiral." The words dripped off his tongue like poison. "If Maylis lives, I will deliver your head to Cathrin personally."

Trepidor let out a long aggravated sigh as Xious left. Soon enough, theirs would be the only version of events left to tell. The Director need not concern himself. The Dressick was far more powerful than anything General Chellis had at his disposal, and, unlike Gillian Maylis, Captain Darith was loyal to the enlightened.

Chapter 12

James exhaled, keeping his heart rate down. Two pirates waited for him at the end of the corridor. So far, they hadn't noticed him. Crouched as he was in a custodial droid's hibernation hutch. He couldn't hide here long though, and he was running out of options.

Scot had been getting better at predicting his movements. Ever since he had given him the first space battle simulation, he had been using the android to run training scenarios. During his shifts on the bridge he would program space sequences for Scot to puzzle through. When James was off duty, Scot would take the place of the simulator AI in various combat scenarios.

Unlike a traditional simulation, Scot was not limited to a predictable set of pre-programmed variables, designed to emulate real behavior. Scot was able to learn and adapt to him in real time. The android was also capable of operating his units like a hive mind, adding even more of a challenge.

This particular simulation took place on an Alliance citadel class ship, E series. The ships were mostly automated. They carried huge compliments of fighters, and served as a mobile staging station for the smaller enforcer-class ships. They patrolled the galaxy on regular routes; which in theory helped maintain order within the Alliance of Powers.

In this case, a band of pirate raiders had managed to infiltrate the ship and take the bridge. James was playing in the role of a petty officer trying to retake control. Each time Scot won they would switch roles, however in the last dozen rounds that had only happened twice.

James had started in the mess hall. When the ransom call was made, all he had to defend himself were his spoon and a metal meal tray. In real life this would never be a problem, he made sure to always carry a small fingalin stun-blade just in case. However, that was part of what kept this interesting. The first few rounds, the tray had been a decently effective shield. But Scot had one fingalin sting-rifle at his disposal. Ever since the third round, the tray had been obsolete.

The first challenge had been to secure a proper weapon. Scot made accessing the weapons room through traditional means almost impossible. The kitchen had yielded access to a knife and a blowtorch. The blowtorch had subsequently lent access to a maintenance tunnel, via an improvised access hatch. He was careful to only use walls located in relatively obscure locations, such as private quarters or bathroom stalls, which thus far had kept Scot oblivious.

Scot had placed two guards in the armory itself.

Using the torch as a makeshift grenade had solved that problem.

Selecting the right weapons became its own challenge. Combustion weapons drew too much attention to themselves. While lasers were bulky and required too much time to charge. James found the rail rifle to be the best option for most things, silent with superior range and accuracy to combustion rifles. There was a drawback though, since the pirates almost always used combustion weapons, he would not be able to steal their ammo. With planning, and a few extra grenades, it wouldn't make a difference.

Next James had cut off access to the pirate's ship, this was easily accomplished by convincing the maintenance droid there was an airlock malfunction. In real combat it would serve to incite panic. Taking away the exit is a good way to get a little chaos going. In this case he used it to confuse Scot and keep him guessing at his location. The android had rarely made any serious move to stop him and judging by the two pirates he now faced, this round Scot had ignored it all together.

James launched himself into the hallway, then exhaled. It wasn't even a thought, his body glided through the motions, practice and training turning him into a machine whose only purpose was to eliminate his enemy.

He squeezed the trigger, two shots in rapid succession, between heart beats. Both pirates dropped before they even had time to lift their guns.

He kept his gun ready, eyes on the door just beyond. It led to the primary cargo hold, and was the quickest way to the bridge from this deck. Of course, Scot knew that, and would be waiting. No guards came out this time, Scot had learned his lesson about wasting crew last round.

James positioned himself to the side of the door, keeping his back to the wall. He pressed the keypad and it slid open with a hiss.

Bullets whizzed into the open corridor, followed less than a thought away by the concussive bang of the combustion weapons that had fired them.

He pulled the small spoon from his pocket and tossed it into the room. It clanked loudly on the floor.

"Grenade!"

He spun and dropped on one knee. Exhale, squeeze the trigger. Both bodies dropped, but he hardly noticed, his focus had already moved to the additional guards in the room.

Two more on the floor, and four on the upper walkway. The sniper already had him in his sights; James was at a disadvantage. Quickly he fired off a shot, he didn't have time to sight. It missed. The bullet ricocheted off the rail with a spark, causing the sniper to flinch.

It was enough. James rolled off his knee and over his shoulder, coming to a stop behind a larger crate. The space where he had just been erupted as electricity from a sting-rifle crashed into the floor, scattering sparks and filling the air with the scent of oxidizing hydrocarbons.

That's where it had been waiting. James removed his small datapad from his belt and pulled up the cargo manifest. It was mostly harmless, fuels and such would all be stored in the hangar bays.

One crate on the far wall held spare acetylene canisters. He removed one of the two grenades from his belt and pulled the pin before rolling it across the floor.

James inhaled, filling his lungs and covering his eyes. The explosion reverberated off the walls, flames licking out into the room as the compressed gas rapidly combusted.

The ship's fire suppression came on, doors slammed shut as life support kicked into reverse, sucking oxygen from the room.

The pirate guards gasped for air. In the confusion, James stepped out into the middle of the room. His first target was the sting-rifle, one shot. He didn't even wait for the man's body to slump before grabbing the closer of the two guards left standing on the floor.

He spun the man around holding him by his neck, placing his rifle near his hip, then shot the remaining guard.

James shifted, a bullet from the sniper caught his hostage in the head.

James dropped the body, bringing his rifle up in one fluid motion. He felt his heartbeat behind his ears. Exhale, squeeze the trigger. The man he had been holding hit the floor with a thud. Heartbeat, Step, Target and Fire. The sniper was still preparing his second shot. Heartbeat, Step, Trigger.

He inhaled as he cleared the room through his sights; silence, everything was still. He was the last one standing in the hold.

James smiled to himself, he now had a clear shot to the upper deck. Scot would be sure he was coming this way, and have guards waiting for him at the hatch.

He lowered his gun and walked back into the hallway. Normally taking one of the central lifts would be suicide. There is no cover once you are in the car, and someone would almost always be guarding it on the bridge deck.

But, most pirates didn't have a hive mind, and every member of Scot's crew was already aware of the massacre in the cargo hold. They would all be guarding that exit. A mistake the Android would not make again.

James stopped the lift one floor before the bridge, it wasn't good to give away too many secrets.

With a hiss, the doors opened.

"James?"

He spun around, pulling his rifle into his shoulder. The voice had come from... behind him?

"James?" It was Chloe's voice.

He breathed a sigh of relief and powered down his Augmented Virtual Reality Gear. "Scot, we are going to have to pick this up later." He said into the com link.

"Alright sir, but I should warn you, this time you will not escape. I would be happy to accept your surrender now, and spare you the embarrassment." The androids' mechanical voice echoed back.

"Thanks Scot, I'll keep that in mind."

"Sorry, I didn't mean to startle you." Chloe's voice was soft, hands tucked behind her back, and she wasn't really looking at him. Her hair was done up in tight intricate braids which trailed down around her shoulders.

"It's fine." He hung his AVRG on the wall rack. "What's up?"

"I... Well, I wanted to show you something." She brought her arm out from behind her back to reveal a small lavender bundle, "I sort of smuggled it off the Vyrant."

James chuckled. "You what?" He reached for the

package.

"Don't laugh, I thought it might be important."

"What is it?" He undid the cloth wrapping, unveiling a white glove with white gold plating along its back. Five purple gems set in the forearm.

"The colonel said it was like a predecessor to the neural link."

"Really?" He pulled it onto his arm. It was beautiful, the same strange characters on the mysterious disks ran along the inside edge, etched in glass they reflected brilliantly in the training room's light.

He opened and closed his hand experimentally. It was soft like cotton, and formed to his hand. There was a slight pinching sensation near the base of his palm. "Ouch."

"Are you okay?" There was genuine concern in her eyes.

"Fine, it just pinched me, that's all." There was a new hum at the edge of his consciousness, like a thought you can't quite grasp.

"Really?" She stepped closer, leaning in for a better look.

Something like the neural link? He reached for the new sensation, like an emptiness waiting for an instruction.

James tried flexing it like a muscle. Warmth built in the palm of his hand, swirls of green appearing in the flowing pattern of the top gemstones.

A bright lavender flash lit the room, followed by an explosive force that threw them both to the ground.

"What was that?" He heard Chloe shout over the ringing in his ears.

"I don't know." His head pounded. He yanked the glove from his hand, the pain began to subside.

"Maybe we should learn more about it before we try anything else."

Chloe pulled her hair back out of her face with a child-like grin. They both laughed

"James?"

"What's up?" He returned the glove to its wrapping.

"Could you teach me how to use a gun?"

* * *

She felt the weight of the gun in her hands, it felt so real. A second ago she had been standing in the sanctuary on board the Shade. Now she found herself looking down the range of a military training facility. It wasn't her first time using AVRG, but it was still difficult to believe it was an illusion.

James materialized beside her. "Are you ready?"

Chloe nodded. "I think so."

"Good, that's your target then," he pointed down range at the black circle against the far wall. "Remember to keep your weapon pointed down range at all times. It is not a toy, never point it at anything you do not intend to kill. And keep your finger away from the trigger until you're ready to shoot."

Chloe nodded slowly, it was a lot to take in, but she felt like she had a good handle on it. James was watching her carefully.

"It looks like you are right-eye dominant, so you are going to want to steady the gun with your left hand. Remember to keep your back straight, and your shoulders square with your feet."

He pulled his own gun up to his shoulder demonstrating the posture. "Make sure the butt of the gun is in your shoulder pocket. Remember these are combustion rifles, even though they are low caliber they'll still kick."

He moved fluidly and confidently as he demonstrated. A loud bang rattled the air. She jumped a little, before she could catch herself. Even muffled, the explosion was louder than she had imagined.

Raising her gun, Chloe tried to duplicate James. The butt of the gun rested comfortably in her shoulder. Bringing the sights together over the target, Chloe squeezed the trigger.

The concussion was even louder than it had been before, echoing in her ear drum as the rifle was shoved back into her shoulder.

"How was that?"

"Good, but next time, don't drop your barrel down until after you have hit the target."

She pulled the gun back up into position and exhaled. Trying to focus on the black circle which wouldn't stop bouncing.

"Keep your shoulders square and you back straight." James walked over to her and tapped the side of her foot with his toe, he grabbed her shoulders and positioned them over her feet. "Try to fire between breaths."

Chloe nodded, it took extra attention not to lose the stance, but finally the target came into focus, "Why aren't you going to put your hand on my hip, and press up against me?"

"This is weapons training, not a romance novel. If you want that, let me take you to dinner when we get planetside. Otherwise, stay focused on your target."

Blood rushed to her face, she hoped the virtual reality would not let him see her blushing. "Right, I mean, I would like that."

Seph

It took a moment to regain her composure. Exhale, the target came into focus, her heart pounded rapidly in her ear and it felt like it was going to beat out of her chest. She squeezed the trigger. This time she was prepared, an eternity passed before she heard the clear ring of the bullet hitting the target.

James clapped beside her. "Nice shot, shall we see what you hit?"

He pressed a button on his glove and suddenly two targets appeared in front of them. Orange spots glowed where they had hit. James had a single spot in the center of his, while Chloe had one on the bottom left, and one up and left of center.

The simulation disappeared, and she found herself back in the shrine on board the ship.

"Keep practicing." James said as he hung his gear. "We can get some more time in tomorrow, but you are picking this up fast."

Chloe removed her own helmet, he was watching her again. "Thanks… I guess." She avoided making eye contact.

"Tomorrow then?" He asked.

"Right, tomorrow, I'll see you."

He nodded then ran a hand through his hair, a sweet smile played at the corner of his lips. A strange knot formed in her stomach as he leapt into the chute.

Chapter 13

Reality and memory blended together in Gillian's mind, mingling with strange dreams. Images of glass palaces and lavender tapestries drifted in and out of his consciousness. They merged with his brief moments of awareness in the Shade's medical bay.

The young women, Chloe, drifted seamlessly from one realm to the next.

"Gillian. Gillian, it is time for you to wake up. I need you to answer some questions."

Except when he opened his eyes, it wasn't Chloe speaking to him. It was a young man, someone he had never seen before.

Gillian tried to force himself to consciousness. It felt something like trying to swim through concrete as glass shards tore through his gills. His numb limbs refused to move.

"You only have about five minutes, sir." The voice belonged to the doctor, Gillian recognized it through the haze of deranged dreams.

"That will have to be enough." The young man again. "Commander Maylis. What exactly was your mission?"

"It was a quarantine mission." Words tasted bitter in his mouth and his throat cracked as he spoke. "The plague, it got on board somehow, no one was to go near it. It is too dangerous to risk spreading infection into the Ring."

The man sat back in his chair. "Do you know what happened on board the station?"

Gillian tried to shake his head, but his body didn't respond. "No. Your captain, said the station was destroyed, but I don't know how or why it was sabotaged."

"We think they were looking for someone, a fingalin girl, do you know anything about that?"

Jasvlin, she had been on board DSI 3122, but why? His brother had disappeared after their father had died. Gillian had attempted to find him six months ago after receiving a cryptic letter, but had been unsuccessful.

"She was…" he was struggling to get words out now. "My brother's oldest daughter."

"Do you know why someone would be hunting them?"

Hunting them? The words hurt like someone had stabbed a knife between his ribs. "No, they just wanted to be left alone."

The man leaned forward elbows on his knees. "What do you mean?"

"My brother. He left the order, he didn't want anything to do with it after our father died."

"Why did he leave?"

"Because our father was a fanatic, he did not want to be a part of his legacy." He had considered himself to be one of the enlightened, the ones who would help to usher in a new era of prosperity to the galaxy.

"His legacy?"

Gillian coughed, suppressing an inward laugh. Some legacy it had turned out to be. "My Father was the last of the Elders. His eldest child should have succeeded him."

Darkness overtook him, fading into visions of glass palaces and impossible blue eyes. . .

The next time he awoke, the pain was gone, and he could breathe easier.

Someone must have placed him in a sleep pod. The mattress under him was damp. And his gills no longer felt as if they had turned to sand paper. They still ached, but his body was moist again, and he could breathe easily.

It was dark now, the medical bays lights had been shut off and the only sound was the gentle humming of the antimatter engine overhead.

He closed his eyes, sleep would come easily now, real sleep this time. Not the restless drug induced haze he had been trapped in before.

As he drifted towards unconsciousness, a darkness settled over him, like a cold talon reaching for his heart.

"Welcome Captain, you will excuse me if I do not get up to greet you properly."

Silence followed, like thick oil it crawled through the room and deposited its film on the air.

The shadow hung ominously on the far wall, betrayed only by his unmistakable aura. This man who had taken the name of a demon, what was his stake in this.

"Why are you wasting your time here?" Gillian eventually asked.

The figure shifted, stepping closer to the bed, his fiery red eyes becoming visible.

"It was a favor... to an old friend."

"You have those?" Gillian scoffed, he couldn't help it, he was too tired to hold back, and besides, it was difficult to imagine the kind of person this man would consider a friend.

The silence returned dragging on to the end of space. Not the empty kind of silence, the kind of quiet that speaks when words stop meaning anything.

"Xious took Jeriell's place, didn't he?"

Icicles formed on the inside of Gillian's rib cage. Questions slammed into him like a tidal wave, how had this man distilled so much from the void? "You knew my brother?"

Silence again.

Gillian exhaled into the darkness. "So, what happens now?"

"Why was Jeriell hiding?" There was no emotion in his voice.

It had been nearly eight years since they had spoken. After their father died, Jeriell had severed all ties with the order. He believed they had overstepped their bounds and defied the will of Vyanna, but the council would not listen. "I don't know."

"But he did reach out to you."

He stared for a moment into The Captain's eyes, was there a limit to his perceptiveness? "Yes, six months ago, I received a message."

The Captain's body stiffened. "What did it say?"

Gillian shook his head, closing his eyes as he

inhaled deeply, it wasn't much to go on, but if anyone alive could decipher its meaning it was this man. "He sent me a note. All it said was, 'Remember the cave.' It was a reference to our childhood. There was a cave on Atlione we used as a secret hideout long ago."

The Captain turned to leave, then paused in the doorway. "Get some rest."

"What are you going to do now, captain?"

It was impossible to see his features in the darkness, the air grew colder as he spoke. "I am going to find the secret Jeriell died for."

Chapter 14

James closed his overnight pack and swung it over his shoulder. More than a month had passed since he had slept in a real bed. Now that they had made it to Dramia, he was not spending any more time with his metal plank than he needed to.

He pushed himself off the bed, into the Zero-G hallway.

"James, wait up."

Chloe drifted toward him, from the back of the crew area. Her own overnight bag on her back.

He caught himself on the hand rail. She had not changed out of her uniform yet. His shoulders tightened, conscious of his T-shirt and work pants.

When he told her he was going to book a room on the orbital, she was eager to book one herself, so they agreed to go over together.

Locked in geosynchronous orbit around their planets, orbital stations were the gateways between space and land, with docks for anything not running on a fusion core. Larger ships, with gravity wells too deep to maintain low planetary orbits, relied on shuttles to ferry crew and passengers.

While their original purpose had been a place to park ships, the Trade Union had not missed any opportunities to capitalize them. The result was that most stations resembled massive space resorts, more than anything else. With rooms, restaurants, and spas, all dedicated to selling you on the tourism of the planet below.

Chloe caught up to him, her eyes glittered with excitement as she took a quick breath. "I'm ready." Her voice was eager and confident like a kitten ready to pounce at a new toy.

"Too bad The Captain is only giving us a few days, huh? It will be nice to have a real bed for a change."

"And my own shower." There was a giggle in her voice, James held back a smile. She had mellowed out over the week they had spent training together. He appreciated this new side of her, comfortable and free.

He laughed, "Don't get too attached, we're going to be stuck back here for the next two months before we reach Atlione."

"Atlione?" She smiled wistfully as if about to fall into a field of wildflowers.

"Ever been there before?" He asked. Atlione was one of the crown jewels of the Fingalin Empire, and one of the few planets that had not required any terraforming before it was settled.

"No, but I have always dreamed of it." Her shoulders slouched a little as she got lost in the day dream. "It's supposed to be magical."

"Maybe so, but how about for now we enjoy

Dramia while we can." James smiled, drifting down the corridor again.

The station's docking tunnel opened up into a spacious foyer. Automated custodial droids swarmed the floor and walls, in a continuous battle to polish away the evidence of several centuries worth of foot traffic, wearing away at the once involuted mosaic pattern over time.

Various agencies with multi-colored stalls heckled passersby with promotional brochures, adding the air of a market from a romanticized past which had probably never existed to begin with. People flowed through hallways either going or coming from their rooms, restaurants, or the planet via the ion lift.

The commotion was a stark contrast to the reception desk, which stood out like a quasar in the center of the room. Station employees made an attempt to look busy, behind the pristine white counter which gently curved into a thick black band around the perimeter.

Chloe paused in the doorway, the chaos danced in her eyes, casting shadows of childhood memories across her face. It wasn't clear if they were good memories or not, but for a moment James thought he had caught a glimpse of the girl she had been before The Captain and the Shade turned the world upside down.

"It's smaller than I expected."

James couldn't help but laugh. "I suppose if you have spent most of your life on a midway station, that is a reasonable response."

Chloe considered him for a moment, conflicting emotions flitting across her complexion. She smiled, the solitary girl from the sanctuary disappearing behind her effervescent facade.

"Maybe we should check in." James continued. "Most of the stuff worth seeing is on the planet anyway."

Chloe giggled with a slight smile, it was soft, and a little forced. "I can't wait to see it, Meghnah is going to show me around first thing in the morning." Excitement bubbled out of her.

"The view from the ion lift here is pretty good." James offered as they approached the reception desk.

Chloe's eyes grew wide. "You can see the planet from the lift?"

James paused, again caught off guard by the wonder in her eyes. It was the same sort of wonder he had felt the first time he had visited a midway station. A new kind of world he had never experienced before. It had all been like magic back then.

He smiled, letting himself get caught up in her excitement. "Just remember to take a minute to savor it all." he said with a laugh.

"Are we checking in today?" A hostess behind the giant white desk interjected into their conversation. She smiled in that way only an experienced service worker can. A smile which said 'thank you for staying with us,' and, 'can't you tell I am too busy to be dealing with this?' all at the same time.

"Yes we just came in on the Shade. Docking ID B126-37."

"Ah yes, I have a single bed for a…" She squinted at the screen for a moment, "James Ayunis. And Chloe…" she looked up from the screen, the silent judgment evident behind her practiced mask of courtesy. "Just Chloe?"

Chloe's shoulders dropped a little as the tips of her ears started to turn pink. "Is, that a problem?" Her voice was quiet and broken.

She shrugged and pressed something on the screen. "No not really, It is none of my business. Here you are, room B-126-3-1736," she handed Chloe a card, "And you will be in B-126-3-1735. Right across the hall."

Next she handed each of them a brochure. "We have some excellent dining options on board the station, you will find them listed here, along with other station amenities such as our selection of spas. The ion lift schedule is on the back, and underneath that you will find instructions for scheduling with the jump pad.

"Your room keys will allow you to charge any expenses both here on the station and on the planet directly to your room account. Your rooms include access to a planetside room, should you need to use it. Space planetside is limited, so if you do need to stay on the surface, please let us know as soon as possible as they are filled on a first come first serve basis. Please enjoy your stay on Dramia."

The lift to the rooms was plain, metal walls, with a screen at the back flashing ads for Dramian businesses.

"Are you planning on going to the planet tomorrow?" Chloe asked breaking up the awkward silence that had followed them from the lobby.

James nodded with a yawn. "Fetu asked me to help him find some parts for the fold generator. We really pushed it with those last two jumps I guess, and The Captain wants to push even harder with this next one. We might need to put a new buffer on the shielding as well."

Normally they would not need to do maintenance like that for another few years, but the last few sleeves they used would have been considered impassable by most navigators. Meghnah had admitted that she would have never even considered them in any ship other than the Shade.

"I never realized hyperspace travel was so complicated, and so hard on ships."

"Depends on the ship. The Shade handles it better than most, but The Captain finds a way to push even that." He laughed.

The lifts came to a stop and the doors slid open with a snapping hiss. The hallway was rather plain. With a carpeted floor in an uncompelling blue-green, an unobtrusive pattern of swirling lines imprinted in the texture. Walls painted in a sandy tan, with specks of shell-white and various grays and browns.

No visible doors, the rooms marked only by tan-gray numbers written on the walls. The whole thing was designed to be as visually boring as possible, without appearing bland.

As they approached the section of the wall with their room numbers, the holographic projection vanished revealing sleek metal doors.

"What are you and Meghnah planning on doing tomorrow?" An odd sense of dread formed in the pit of his stomach, as if the answer to such a simple question was bearing the bulk of the whole universe.

She shrugged pausing in front of her open door. "I don't know," she laughed to herself. "I don't even know where to start. I have only ever been on Aundreus before, and there was not a lot of sightseeing to be done. I guess I will have to see what Meg comes up with."

James inhaled, bracing himself against the torrent raging in his abdomen. "How about dinner tomorrow night?"

Chloe broke eye contact, the ridges under her eyes

changing shades. "I… would like that." She said as she tapped the toe of her foot on the carpet.

The storm in his gut broke, shattering into wildflower seeds, blowing in a light summer breeze. "I will meet you back here at six then?"

She nodded, and when she met his eyes again a bright smile tugged at her cheeks. "I'll be here."

Once in his room, James dropped his bags on the floor. Old habits and routine drills yanked on his mind to do something with them, other than just leaving them in the middle of the room, but his fatigue won out. Dropping his body on the large mattress, he felt the tension melt out of his muscles. Tomorrow night he thought wistfully. There would be time for that later though, now he needed to get some sleep. Some real sleep, for the first time since he couldn't even remember anymore. Then there was the ship, it had to be ready, and there was not much time.

"Three days" The Captain had said, and the first was nearly over already. That deep fire glowing in The Captain's eyes tugged on his consciousness. They wanted to be in Atlione in less than two months. It was almost an impossible trip. They would be traveling across the ring, and most of the way across the circle. The midway station itself usually took over a week.

Meghnah would no doubt have them skim around the inner edge of the ring, using the galactic drift to their advantage. But that would make it significantly more likely for them to run into Alliance patrols. Which was never a good thing in a hurry.

Pirates and mercenaries alike tended to take up bases in the area as well, anyone who spent too much time hugging the boundary had a tendency to draw a lot of attention.

Chloe's smile drifted back into his mind, the haze of sleep enveloping his consciousness. His cheeks grew warm as his thoughts became more distant. She faded into the darkness. The darkness grew and morphed until it became a field of glowing embers and ash amidst his dreamscape.

* * *

He stood on a long empty beach, white sand filling in the spaces between his toes, warm against the arches of his feet. A massive object, larger than the moon, with wings swiping out as if a menacing beast across the horizon, casting a shadow in the deep reds of sunset.

The ocean began to pull back, until the rocky floor was exposed for more than eighty feet. The wall of water hung suspended in the air, a great wave waiting for a release that would never come.

Light from the sun grew more intense, burning his exposed skin. The air became dry and brittle in his lungs, like sheets of ash blown from a fire. Breathing was painful.

"We have to find shelter." He could not identify the owner of the voice, it was distant, indistinct.

A bright flash lit up the sky, drowning out the shadow cast by the ship, growing brighter as it hurtled across the expanse of space. He looked on in horror as four seconds later the plasma beam struck the atmosphere. Flames crawled through the sky as the beam racked from one horizon to the other, spreading outwards until the entire world was engulfed in an inferno. Molten rock spayed upwards from the impact, spraying lava thousands of feet into the sky.

Seph

Screams filled the air as one after another streaks of plasma rocketed to the planet, followed by explosions of liquefied earth.

He spun around to gaze upon the demonic ship which had summoned such destruction. But met only blackness. Red eyes glowed like embers out of the emptiness. The scent of ash heavy in the air.

A sound, barely a whisper, like an echo drifting in the nothingness, "Zymo."

"Dreku," the voice was ethereal, it felt fuzzy in his ears, like an illusion you can't make sense of.

"Seph," electricity wrapped around his nerves and crawled through his body, something ancient and powerful awakening inside him.

"Zhemarah." The word exploded in his mind, like a large rock being dropped into a still pool, consumed by the silence that followed.

Chapter 15

Consciousness did not come easy; the abyss of sleep wrapped itself around his mind. It was like clawing his way out of earth and clay.

James fought to gain control, forcing his body to sit upright, and blinking in the reality of the world around him. Beige walls, dark wood floors, and deep blue blankets now tied in knots from his tossing and turning during the night.

So much for a good night's sleep. The holographic window mocked him, displaying a serene sunrise, recorded somewhere on Dramia rotating peacefully below.

A tiny clock flashed the station time at 6:03 a.m., the first lift was leaving in less than an hour.

He cast off the blankets, leaving them strewn about the floor.

"Good morning, master James, would you like me to begin the shower for you?" The disembodied voice of the room's AI asked in a soothing feminine tone.

"Yes, and get me a quick breakfast as well." He pulled open the bag he had discarded on the floor the night before, pulling out a nondescript t-shirt, and an old off-duty uniform jacket from his days with the Alliance.

"I will have one of the service bots bring you something right away. Would you like to specify any preferences?"

"No, just get me something I can travel with." The shower was already running when he stepped in, the warm water washing away the dregs left over from his strange dreams. They melted away like fog dissolved in the sunlight.

He took a moment to go over his check list for the day. He was supposed to be meeting Fetu at the ion lift in a few minutes. Finding parts for the fold generator would take up most of the morning, and Fetu would already have something planned for lunch planetside.

James could make a dinner reservation from the station desk. He had hoped to do so early this morning, but there wasn't time now. He would have to try to squeeze it in after lunch, which meant his options might be limited.

He let out a long sigh as he washed the water from his hair. It would all work out, Chloe would be satisfied with almost anything. It wasn't like there was a lot of competition, but still…

James dried off with one of the warm towels hanging by the shower door. More of a luxury than anything, since technology had existed for centuries which could dry you instantaneously. For that matter, showers as a whole were sort of an archaic nicety.

There was something strangely comforting about

it though; it reminded you that you were alive. And James found that he enjoyed the sensation of slipping into his clothes slightly damp, and letting the water evaporate on his skin.

He stepped back into the bedroom, as he pulled on the faded blue jacket. The colony of nanotech living inside the fibers adjusted to fit around his shoulders, like greeting an old friend.

James removed the stun-blade from his bag and clipped into the jacket's sleeve. The nanites went to work absorbing it into the cloth. A dull yellow ring appeared on the inside of his forearm, indicating the weapon's presence within the fibers. A dead giveaway for anyone who knew what to look for, which not many outside of the military did.

Jackets like these were standard issue in special ops units. Everyone always joked that it was the Alliance's way of protecting their investment. Though they paled in comparison to combat gear, the civilian uniform provided some substantial benefits.

Besides the limited storage capacity for concealing small items, it also offered significant protection from low grade energy weapons. As well as being impossible to cut with any sort of blade.

It was possible to adjust the color, but for now, the default blue was inconspicuous enough, and it was a good idea to conserve the nanotech's energy reserves. While they did recharge over time, putting too much strain on the colony was a good way to get them to stop listening to you.

He grabbed the breakfast wrap waiting for him on the table as he stepped out into the hall. A rice shell stuffed with eggs and seasoned ground meat, all of it synthetic. Even luxury hotels had their limits. Though, he had not been very specific, and the computer had decided that efficiency was more important this morning than quality. Which, to be fair, was true.

Once in the lobby, finding Fetu was not difficult. He had traded his uniform for an orange tank top, which combined with his hulking figure, made him stick out like a volcano.

"I was starting to think you weren't going to make it," he called waving one of his massive arms. "We can talk on the lift."

The ion lift was less elevator and more ferry. A large shaft filled the center of the circular room, surrounded by convenience stations where snacks could be purchased and prepared, as well as other essential facilities.

Chairs were arranged in groups to create lounging areas around squat tables throughout the space. All facing outward toward the large windows which made up the outside wall.

Fetu led the way to where Meghnah and Chloe sat. Meghnah was still wearing the tight gray undershirt from the Descendant uniforms, over the top of black cargo pants and fingerless gloves.

Chloe was dressed in a fingalin style tunic with a halter neckline, and sleeve cuffs hanging loosely from her upper arms, leaving her back and shoulders exposed. The jewel blue fabric accented her eyes, but made her skin appear pale in comparison.

Her hair was tied in double braids pinned to the sides above her ears. They came together at the back, a single line of red weaving its way along one side.

Meghnah grinned with one corner of her mouth, her eyes staring criticizing daggers into his skin. Was she scrutinizing him or threatening him?

"Looks like you made it." There was a hint of amusement in her voice, the kind of mocking you get from an older sibling.

James shrugged and sat down in the seat beside her. At least he had made it, and he did not have to settle for whatever was stocked in the machines for breakfast. As bad as printed eggs were, they were still more substantial than convenience foods. And tasted better than nutrition rations. Some planets had cafes on board their ion lifts, but Dramia was not *that* luxurious.

"Give him a break Meg, it was the first decent sleep any of us have gotten in weeks. I'm just jealous he got to enjoy it longer." Chloe gave James a soft smile that betrayed no actual envy.

"Maybe if he hadn't been enjoying it so much, he would have been around to help with the diagnostic on the fold generator."

Fetu dropped himself into the chair across from James, it was something like watching a meteor crash into the moon, and James could swear the floor bounced at the impact. "Settle down already. You're more qualified than he is Meghnah, and besides with Scot around he would have been dead weight. Let the boy enjoy his beauty rest."

James caught the datapad as Fetu slid it across the table, largely ignoring the banter at his expense. It wasn't that it didn't bug him, just that Fetu was right. James liked to think he was competent enough, but he was not an engineer. And while Meghnah wasn't either, when you are planet hopping as a navigator you are often the only one on board who knew which end of the fold generator was which. James was a tactician, and in a pinch, a decent navigator. He could tell a faulty generator from a bad one, and perform most routine maintenance tasks on a drive. But he never had to hold an envelope together from the inside of a hyperspace sleeve. Sure he knew the theory, but knowing why a tool works, and knowing how to use it, isn't the same thing.

Glancing through the data on the pad, he studied Fetu's notes. It didn't look too bad, the fold pin needed to be realigned, and the field stabilizer was due for a refitting. The ion drive needed some attention too. Pulling out of DSI 3122's gravity well must have been more difficult than the ship had let on.

"There's nothing wrong with a little beauty rest." Chloe was saying as she brushed her braided hair back over her shoulder. They were in public again and her defenses had come up.

"Protective are we?" Meghnah asked with a wink towards James.

Chloe turned red, her white makeup not quite covering the blush. Maybe not all her defenses.

James pulled up a map of Lalazarja, the city directly below this orbital. Of the four of them, James was the only one who had ever been to the city before.

"I think we can get everything we need here." He passed the tablet back across the table. "We will want to grab a green line tram from the lift terminal, get off at the east plaza station, and from there we'll have to walk. It is a little off the beaten path, but he does good refurbishment work, and it's a clean business."

Fetu took the datapad and nodded as he looked it over. "I think that will work, what about you girls, what are you working on today?"

There was a deep whine from somewhere in the center of the room, artificially generated, so that passengers felt like they could hear the lift mechanism. In a moment the lifts dropped out of the station and the planet could be seen stretching out below in a giant sphere. The sun was already well above the horizon for the city below, and hidden beyond the edge of the lift's ceiling, causing the atmosphere to glow in a slight halo around the edges of the horizon, and reflecting brilliantly off the artificial oceans.

Chloe gasped as she slowly rose from her chair and walked to the window. "It's so… green."

Fetu laughed. "What were you expecting?"

She smiled, the hint of a giggle in her voice. "To be surprised, I guess."

Meghnah pushed herself out of the oversized seat and joined her friend by the window. "I heard it took longer than most to terraform, but this is incredible. If I didn't know better I would think it was Theyes or Galrik."

James played idly with the seam of his arm cushion. "Dramia was developed to demonstrate that it was possible for the presence of civilization to not only exist in harmony with its environment, but to enhance it as well. It is the most expensive terraforming project to date, and took more than two decades to complete. But that's why it has proper oceans and forests instead of the networks of concrete waterways and manicured gardens you see on most ring worlds."

He knew they didn't care. That for them it was more of a point of fascination than legitimate curiosity, but it just sort of came out. Like Chloe, he was starting to feel comfortable around the others, and his guard was slipping.

"Wait, they aren't all like this?" Chloe spun to face him, the thrill in her voice was infectious.

Seph

James laughed, sitting forward in his chair. "No planets are pretty unique, a lot of the worlds the Alliance had colonized started out like a blank slate, especially here in the ring."

In reality, Dramia was one of the most natural looking planets in the ring. It looked like Theyes and Galrik, because it was modeled after Galrik. Natural planets, planets capable of supporting life, specifically planets whose ecosystems were favorable towards the three races, were hard to come by. Within the inner circle there were a few, but most of them had high water to land ratios, and when picking a model for Dramia, the designers wanted something with more cross compatibility.

Not being able to use Vinge for obvious reasons, Galrik was the next best thing. With a thirty percent water to land ratio it meant small shallow oceans, which were easier to manufacture and maintain, yet still provided enough usable space for possible underwater cities. It also produced sufficient land mass to showcase flora and fauna from around the galaxy, interspersed with sprawling cityscapes connecting the world back to the galaxy at large.

However, most planets in the ring were homogenized. It was simpler, and more economic to pour giant aquifers in a giant lattice around the usable portions of the planet, and encase them in a single city. Green spaces could be manufactured as parks providing the atmospheric stabilization necessary for the colonies, and manicured like sculptures so that everything could blend seamlessly together.

Planet design had become a true art form, and not very many artists were interested in duplicating someone else's work.

But that's what made Dramia special.

Meghnah shrugged, continuing to watch the descent. "I think colony worlds are way more unique than ring words; here almost every plant looks like a generic recolor of the one next to it."

Fetu laughed and for a moment, James thought it might have been the only sound on the lift, as everyone else stopped to wonder what was so funny. "That's because no one is interested in terraforming the outer colonies."

The outer colonies had been abandoned by the larger colonization efforts. That was a little backward. The Coalition had formed to get away from the industrialization and modernization predominant throughout the ring and inner circle. They had expanded out beyond the ring in an effort to gain independence from the other races' reliance on technology.

As a result, there was no money to be made in expensive terraforming projects. What money was being poured into colonizing the perimeter of the Alliance territory was going to the DSI projects, which was little more than a thinly veiled effort to re-integrate the Coalition into the main body of the Alliance.

Most terraformed planets in the outer colonies were in a state best described as half finished. Bio domes for incubating plant life. Moisture harvesters and weather controllers to stabilize the atmosphere. In a strange twist of fate, their rejection of technology had made many of the planets more reliant on it than ever before.

Meghnah clenched her jaw and shrugged, the muscles in her biceps tensed. It lasted only a moment, but James was sure she had been about to rip Fetu's arms off, and to be honest, she might have been able to.

"What do you have planned for the day?" James tried to break through the hostilities.

The tension vanished from her body in an instant as Meg turned to face him and leaned her back against the window. "We're going shopping!"

James sat up a little straighter, letting his back fall into the chair. Shopping? Something was off, that wasn't something he would have expected Meghnah to get so excited about.

"Really? I wouldn't have thought you were into that sort of thing."

"Oh, I'm not." Meghnah laughed. "Normally I detest the idea, but today is different."

"Oh?"

"Chloe has never been before." She nodded her head in Chloe's direction. "And tonight she has a hot date," she winked.

James's cheeks grew warmer as his abdomen began to sink.

Fetu laughed again. "Chloe has a date? With who?"

James pushed himself lower into his seat.

Chloe managed to unstick her eyes from the surface of the planet as the tops of the city's tallest building reached up to catch them.

"With James, who else?" Her eyes were blank, head cocked.

Fetu looked between the two of them a huge grin spreading across his face, causing his ears to perk up. "Seriously, you finally asked her?"

He leaned forward on the edge of his chair. He slapped James on the shoulder with an enormous hand. It felt like getting hit by a twenty pound cotton ball.

Sure it was soft, but it could still crush you.

"It's about time!"

James had never been so grateful for the descending whine of touchdown, and the chime that indicated the boarding ramp was in place.

"I know, why don't we all meet up for lunch, I'll send you the location!" Fetu shouted, punching something into his datapad.

"Sure." Meghnah smiled giving James a mischievous grin, something told him she was enjoying this a lot more than he was.

"That settles it. Com'on James, let's get this over with, I wouldn't want to be the reason you were late for your date."

"Right." James tried to hold in a groan. At least they weren't at each other's throats.

Chapter 16

James once again felt the odd contagious wonder that followed Chloe around like a fog behind someone who put on too much perfume. Meghnah tried, with limited success, to drag her across the open square of the ion lift's landing dock.

Eight small waterfalls sprang from the fountain which served as the landing platform, and flowed down three tiers of a huge sandstone block, until they reached the city floor. From the edge of the square, buildings reached upward in layered steps to create 'the cradle' which housed the landing site. A single row of towers more than five miles high made up the edge of the bowl, beyond it the city would gradually slope back down, creating the effect of a mountain which plateaued at its peak. Not terribly different from models used when teaching children about natural geological formations and volcanoes.

Magnetic rails caught the sunlight, glowing like a

network of interconnected spider webs in the early morning dew. They ran between and around the buildings, guiding civilian traffic in an intricate dance through the city.

The larger tram rails cut outward, along the radial vectors of the city, in eight straight lines, sloping on the tangent of the skyline. Though they were invisible from the square, each one would run through several junction points, allowing passengers the opportunity to board additional trams traveling along the tangential lines.

Chloe stumbled along behind Meghnah, stopping repeatedly as she tried to take in the glittering city around her.

James smiled, he had been that way once he thought, it was a lifetime ago now. But he too had stared at the marvel each new planet presented. Space continuing its endless call to his young imagination.

"Alright dream boat, at this rate they will have finished with lunch long before you get that stupid grin off your face." Fetu laughed, not even looking up from his datapad.

"I got us a spot reserved on the jump pad, so we are up against a deadline now."

James shoved down the nostalgia. What exactly did he mean by stupid grin? It didn't matter. He had not been this excited about anything since his first day in spec-ops training. So what if it showed a little?

"We're taking the green line east?" James pointed at the green banners hanging beside the tram station on the squares east side.

"Right!" Fetu said, his booming voice echoing across the square.

Fetu dropped his pack on the ground waiting for

the tram to return to the station.

James watched him, realizing this was the first time they had been able to talk for a while. There had been something he had wanted to ask him about. James thought back on the last several weeks he had spent training with Chloe.

"Hey, Fetu. you ever see anything like an armored glove when you were with the Descendants?"

Fetu's ears flicked, like a cat hearing a strange noise in the next room. "You talking about the Hand of Vyanna?"

"I don't know. Is that a glove?"

"White with shiny stuff in it?"

James laughed, that almost described the glove Chloe had shown him. "I guess you could say that."

"What of it?"

There was a caution to his voice that James was not accustomed to. "I think Chloe might have found one of these 'Hands of Vyanna' or whatever."

Fetu turned to face him, one ear twisting forward in curiosity. "Where in Vinge's core did she find something like that?"

James shrugged. "I think she got it from the Colonel we rescued."

Fetu's shoulders relaxed. "That guy had one?" He turned to look back at the ion lift, following its trail towards the station invisibly orbiting above them. "Who in Vyanna's name is he?"

Following Fetu's gaze, James noticed someone staring at him from across the terminal. Probably a vagrant who had picked them out as easy targets. Chloe's wanderlust, and Fetu's near shouting tended to draw that kind of attention.

They made eye contact and the man pulled his hood

up and turned a little too quickly. Alarm bells started ringing in his mind. Vagrants didn't care if you caught them, they would just choose a different mark.

"Is it strange that he would?" James turned casually back to face the tram pulling into the station, trying not to draw any additional attention to himself.

Fetu lifted his bag back over his shoulder and started toward the tram. "It's supposed to be able to allow the wearer to manifest the will of Vyanna." He laughed, a little too loudly for James's comfort.

"I think it's connected to the Captain somehow." He had to get a message to Fetu and let him know they were being followed. But he had to be discrete about it. Someone had put a tail on them, and James wanted to know why.

Fetu paused before getting into the car. "Really, how?"

"Keep moving," James said, trying to force a little humor into his voice. "I think it is connected to that fold generator he used back at the DSI station."

The tram was about what you would expect: clean, but only in that way an illusion hides reality below the surface. Narrow and cramped, with barely enough room for a few people to stand between the rows of seats on each side.

Fetu flopped himself into a chair near the door they had entered at. The stranger boarded the same car, only at the opposite end.

"You on that hyperspace stuff again?"

James gave a quick nod, trying to point with his eyes to the other end of the car and nudging Fetu with his elbow. "I just feel like there is something else going on here."

Fetu cocked his head both ears twisting in opposite

directions in a look that was as comical as it was confused. "Of course there is something going on, I already told you though, it's not worth digging into."

Okay, maybe that was too tactful. "I feel like I need to keep looking over my shoulder, you know like I need to watch my back."

Fetu's eyes went wide, his pupils pressing the light red of his irises to the edge of his whites, his ears went flat. "You mean now?"

James did a mental facepalm. Fetu might have been a brilliant engineer, but a tactician, he was not.

"I think maybe we should keep quiet about it for now, you never know who might be listing, you know what I mean?"

It was somewhat of a crude trap, but it should work. James was sure that whoever it was knew they were on to them. Maybe he could still convince them it was worth their time to stick around. That was of course, if Fetu could manage not to screw things up too much.

Fetu leaned back, his spine straight against his chair, hands braced on his knee caps in the worst 'keep it casual' posture James had ever seen, and started whistling.

Great, well the damage had been done. "Look, if someone is watching us, we can just ditch them in the crowd at the next station."

"Well, you know me." Fetu said, barely not shouting. "I don't want to get mixed up in none of your shenanigans, you hear me?"

Fetu leaned sideways keeping his back perfectly straight, then whispered in that scratchy voice you could still hear on the other side of a room. "How was that?"

"Great" James groaned, giving him a thumbs up.

"Absolutely brilliant."

As the tram pulled into the station James nudged Fetu, standing he let the crowd brush him out the door. Fetu was not so dexterous and it took him a minute to catch on, though he did manage to shove his way into the crowd.

"James, where'd you go?" Fetu was whispering over the hustle.

If James had been alone and trying to ditch the tail, that trick alone might have worked. As it was, it would be difficult to lose someone with Fetu's insistence on acting like a traffic control beacon.

James stepped out of the flow of traffic, melding into the passengers waiting to board until he could rejoin Fetu.

"I'm right here," he whispered, folding himself back into the flow of traffic.

He needed to find somewhere he could hide the walking orange wall. Whoever was following them must know by now that they had been caught. Which meant James only had a few minutes now to convince them otherwise, or risk losing any information they might be able to give him. Which meant convincing Fetu as well.

There was a mag-car rental yard just outside of the terminal; that could work.

"This way, we can double back through there, and lose them before we get on the next line." James pointed at a small gap between two of the vehicles.

They ducked under the guard rail, between the two cars, then dodged over to the next row. Instinct told James to exit the lot through the same way he had come in. Anyone who had seen them enter would be looking for them to come out on the other side. But he wasn't trying to lose them, he was just trying to make them think he was.

"Okay, lie low for a minute, and can you ditch that shirt? It kind of makes you stand out."

Fetu glance down at himself. "It's all I got," he whispered, "and I don't think your jackets' going to fit."

James considered this for a moment. It might, the nanotech would allow him to resize it, but it was not a task he normally required of it so it might take longer than they had to produce the extra material. Besides it might work a little too well, and James would lose his trump card.

He shrugged. "Maybe not, you okay going topless?"

Fetu sighed, but dropped his pack and pulled off the shirt. His torso was littered with scars, not only from the fins he never had, but the kind you get from too many tours in combat.

"Here give me that." James grabbed the shirt from Fetu before he could stuff it into his bag, then reached up under the frame of a mag-car and rolled it through the electromagnetic guidance rail, before stuffing it into a coat pocket.

"Don't worry, you can put it back on as soon as we are on the tram again." James led Fetu on a perpendicular line from where they came in, leading directly back into the junction terminal. Everyone would notice, which would make them look like amateurs. Depending on how much the tail knew that might scare them off. There was nothing to be done about that now.

They stepped out into the loading area just as their connecting tram arrived, James brushed some dust off his clothes, drawing a few stray looks from the crowd.

"That should keep them guessing for a little

while." James glanced around the crowd trying to get eyes on their pursuer again. He hoped he had not overestimated them.

"You sure we lost them?" Fetu asked, falling in step beside him.

"Sure we did." James tried to keep the smirk out of his voice. "There is no way they're following us now."

"Right." Fetu hesitated as he stepped onto the tram.

"Here," James pulled the orange tank top from his bulging pocket. And shoved it into Fetu's chest. "Trust me okay?"

* * *

"None of these are working for me," Chloe said tossing the bundle of pastel-colored dresses back over the top of the changing room door.

"They would all look so good on you though." Meghnah took the clothing and tossed it into the bin for resorting.

"You know I can't wear pastels!" Chloe's voice was something between a four-year-old demanding a second ice cream, and royalty turning down an aperitif before dinner.

"How about this one?" Chloe stepped out and did a spin, causing the hem of her bright ruby dress to twirl around her calves.

"Absolutely not," Meghnah pushed her gently back into the changing stall.

"Why not?" She adjusted the dress watching herself in the mirror. "I like what it does for my skin color."

"No pockets," Meghnah said closing the door behind her friend and turning back to the clothing racks. She couldn't tell Chloe the dress made her look like a ghost, the girl did things like that on purpose.

A man on the other side of the room was keeping the attendant busy with questions. Nodding too frequently, repeating the phrase "Ah , I see." As if he weren't interested in any of the answers.

"Why do I need pockets?"

Meghnah had sworn she had seen the same man in the landing square. And a chill ran up her spine. Had they been followed?

"Here, try this one," Meghnah tossed a short black dress over the door. "It has a pocket hidden under the right arm, and one in the hem."

"Yes, but why do I need them?"

The man on the other side of the room was staring at them. He claimed he was looking for a surprise for his girlfriend. He pulled something off the rack without even looking at it. "What about this one?"

"What if you need to carry something?" Meghnah scrambled for an answer, avoiding eye contact with the stranger.

"It doesn't fit right, besides, what could I possibly need to carry that won't fit in a handbag. Or at least that I couldn't ask James to carry?"

Meghnah selected a pale dress with a light green skirt. "Try this one." She passed it through the door in exchange for the black one. "What if you want to be discreet? Besides, you don't want to be dependent on James for everything."

The attendant was now trying desperately to convince the man that the dress he had picked out would be perfect. Meghnah could see him wearing on her patience. He brushed it off. "I don't know, can you look in the back to see if it comes in a different color?"

Meghnah kept an eye on him as she thumbed

through the dress racks. He pretended to look as well, had he noticed her watching?

"What do you think?" Chloe stepped out of the dressing room.

Meghnah gave her a glance. It was cute, but the green combined with her makeup had an almost seasick effect. "It isn't quite right, try this one." She handed Chloe a plain white dress, with a pocket hidden in the waistband.

"Really, white?" Chloe wrinkled her nose as if the idea was somehow repulsive.

"Just try it for me, will you?" Meghnah spun her back, closing the door in a single motion.

The dress would be perfect, but Chloe was right, if she insisted on wearing the same make up she usually did, it would make her look something like a snow sculpture. Something dark, but with color could help break up the lines.

Chloe stepped back out of the stall. "I don't know, it's not exactly my style." She was studying herself in a full length mirror as if she had gotten lost in her own reflection.

Meghnah selected a dark blue shawl and clipped it over Chloe's shoulders. "James will love it, you look stunning."

She shook as if startled, and took in a sharp breath "You think so?"

"Absolutely, let's buy it and get out of here, we have a spa appointment waiting for us that, you, do not want to miss."

The man followed them with his eyes as they walked to the door. He handed the dress back to the attendant. "You know what, never mind, I don't think you have anything in her style."

Seph

* * *

The shop they were looking for was near the edge of the city on the lowest level. There was not nearly as much traffic here, as this was where the designers had chosen to hide the more utilitarian sectors.

Fetu pushed open one of the large double freight doors, stepping inside. James followed, it was almost exactly as he remembered it. A small room with a vertical garage door for a back wall. A small desk sat off to one side where rows of small shelves held a variety of small tools and components.

"Can I help you two boys with something?" A large man came out from between the shelves wiping grease from his fingers with an old rag, a friendly smile spreading on his cheeks.

"Trying to find a few things for our ship." Fetu said, offering him the datapad. "You think you can help?"

"Let's see." The mechanic took the datapad from Fetu and sat down at the computer, powering up the monitor with a touch of his fingers.

"What are you guys flying in that needs this stuff? I haven't seen a parts list like this in years."

"It's a custom model. There isn't much like it around." Fetu laughed.

"Not anymore there ain't!" The man laughed too. "You're seriously going between worlds on antimatter and an ion drive?"

"Our Captain likes antique things, besides it's nice to be able to bring the whole ship all the way in sometimes."

"Alright, it looks like I got everything you boys are looking for, not a lot of demand, and a lot of salvage out there to pick from. It will take me a couple of days to get a spot on the pod though." He handed Fetu the datapad.

"We already got a jump slot. I'll forward you the credentials." Fetu taped the screen, then returned the pad to his pack.

"You guys run a pretty clean operation, huh?" It was more of a statement than a question. "I'll tell you what. If you can promise me this kind of preparation, next time you need anything else, no matter where in the galaxy you are, shoot me a message. If you have time that is. I know a whole bunch of people with parts to these old drives lying around. Not much use for them since the fusion core came out."

The man entered a few things into his computer. "Speaking of salvaging and fusion cores, you two hear about that crane they found a few days ago?"

James and Fetu looked at each other. A familiar tingling sensation developed behind his ears, something wasn't right. "What of it?"

"Well, 'found' might not be the right word for it, it had done a good job of broadcasting itself. It had disappeared though, just over a week ago. Engineering Corps was blaming pirates, probably the Knights Pryne. Anyway, it seems they did something wrong because they ended up ejecting their core over Ulun'tess."

He finished entering data into the computer and leaned back in his chair "All set, you boys take care now."

"Is the planet alright?" Fetu asked.

The man shrugged. "I'm not too sure, I can't imagine it was painless though, that's a pretty big object to be in an uncalculated orbit if you know what I mean."

Seph

"There is no way that was an accident," Fetu began to say.

James inhaled through his nose, then cut him off. "Did the Knights Pryne claim it?"

"No, not that I heard of, you think it might have been terrorism?"

"Of course it was!" Fetu began again. "You can't just-"

James held out a hand effectively cutting him off again. He shrugged "No one is suggesting that." He turned to leave motioning Fetu to follow. "Thanks for the info, we'll be sure to forward you a tip."

* * *

Chloe stared into the small changing rooms mirror, still wearing the soft linen wrap provided by the spa when she had refused to go naked into the heated pool. Refused wasn't really the right word. Meg had encouraged her, but the staff had been very understanding and not pushed her into anything she was uncomfortable with.

She touched the tips of her ears, fingers brushing against the almost invisible feather-like hairs nobody else even knew were there. The spa experience had left her skin softer than ever before. And there was almost a faint glow about her. Warmth rushed to her cheeks, even though Meg was the only other person in the room.

She imagined what she would look like in the white dress. She never wore white, preferring jewel tones which did not conspire with her hair to make her skin seem too tan. No matter what Meg said about it. Everyone couldn't have her perfect graphite skin. And Chloe's wasn't the warm butterscotch color of most other humans. She was stuck with this pale pink nonsense that just made her look sick, no matter which race you compared her to.

In her mind, the reflection changed to match her imagination, the contrasting white and dark blues of the illusionary outfit bringing out the depth in her eyes, while both contrasting and complimenting her hair.

The room vanished away, replaced by a long marble corridor, rows of mirror framed on each wall. She approached the nearest mirror, but the reflection looking back at her was not her own. Hidden in shadow, and indistinct, it moved in strange ways and seemed to whisper back at her in a language she almost understood.

She moved from mirror to mirror, each one showing an image more complete than the last. Like pictures moving through glass, they each depicted the same young women at a different age. A girl who was at the same time Chloe, and something more. The way she carried herself was smooth and regal like a queen.

Wandering forward into the fantasy, music wafted down the corridor, carrying with it the scent of apple blossoms. The melody beckoned her onward like threads of silk pulling her, urging her to discover whatever lay hidden beyond the illusion.

The gentle weight of Meg's hands on her shoulders dragged her back to reality. Taking in a sharp breath of air, she released her palm from the mirror which felt as if it had been tied there by an invisible cord.

"You okay?" Meg asked, running her fingers through Chloe's hair as she began to tie it back into its braids.

Seph

Meg's bare skin pressed into her back, a warm sensation rising in her chest and cheeks. "Yeah, I'm fine, just daydreaming, that's all."

Meg smiled, pushing back a strand of her own hair, darkened by the water becoming a rich mahogany with dark almost black highlights. "You seem to be getting lost like that a lot lately."

"I guess my imagination is just fleeing the present."

Tying off Chloe's braid in an elastic band, Meg pulled her own hair into a loose ponytail. "Well don't let it go too far, or James might not be able to catch up."

Chloe watched herself turn bright red as blood rushed into her face. Meg stepped away, grabbing her bra and pulling it on over her head.

Taking a few deliberate breaths, Chloe calmed the conflicting emotions wrestling in her body. "That isn't what it was about."

Meg cocked an eyebrow with a skeptical smile on her lips. "No? What are you so infatuated with that you keep wandering off?"

She shrank into herself, unsure of how to respond. "I'm- not sure…" She looked back into the mirror, ephemeral voices echoing in the back of her mind

Chapter 17

The cafe was small, open air, with a fenced in dining area, which James was grateful for. He was not sure if he could handle the scent of the obligatory drak'or incense right now. Fetu had spent most of the morning sorting through reviews on the net, and according to his research this was "the best, most authentic, drak'or dining experience on Dramia." James couldn't vouch for its authenticity, but at least it wasn't in a fake shrine designed to create an experience of "culture."

There was another advantage to the open layout: it had finally exposed the tail they had all but lost outside the tram station. James had seen a glimpse or two of the man after leaving the warehouse. However, he had become much more cautious, and until now James had been unable to confirm if it was the same man or not.

They had already ordered by the time Meghnah and Chloe joined them.

"Having fun yet?" Meghnah pulled out the chair

and sat down. Chloe sitting across from her.

Something was different about the girls. Meghnah's features were somehow softer, and her hair was almost glowing, the way smoke on the horizon glows after sunset.

Chloe could only be described as stunning. The white makeup was gone, and her skin took on a warm glow in the afternoon sun. The blues and golds in her tunic highlighted the color of her eyes and hair. She didn't look at him, and James had to stop himself from staring.

"What happened to you two?" Fetu laughed.

"Is it that bad?" Chloe asked, trying to cover her shoulders with her hands, while not drawing attention to herself.

"Ignore him." Meghnah jabbed Fetu with her elbow. "He doesn't appreciate any aesthetic that isn't capable of interstellar travel."

This elicited an almost invisible chuckle from Chloe.

Fetu leaned back in his chair, "Hey now, you don't have to be mean about it. I was just asking."

"We went to a spa." Chloe offered, she relaxed a little, now that everyone was settled.

"Come on! Now what did you go and do that for?" Fetu threw his hands up in a mock gesture of exasperation. "Now I'm going to feel guilty for making you crawl into the engine later."

"Good, maybe you will let Scot do his job." Meghnah laughed.

"You guys do anything exciting?" Chloe asked, attempting to change the subject.

"We had to ditch some crook after getting off the ion lift." Fetu shrugged. "Otherwise, not really."

Meghnah locked eyes with James for a moment.

James shook his head in a half negative. Meghnah nodded in the direction of their tail, who James noted had been joined by a second man. So they had all been followed. James nodded the affirmative.

The server returned with Fetu and James's food. Fetu had ordered a beef variant stewed in sauce, with vegetables over rice. James had ordered the same meat, fried with rice noodles and ground nuts.

The young woman bowed to Meghnah and then to Chloe. "Can I get you anything?"

"Give me what he is having." Meghnah motioned to James with her chin.

Chloe took a moment to look over the menu. "The steamed fish, I guess." There was a slight hesitation in her voice.

The girl bowed again before leaving.

"Are you guys alright?" Chloe asked after the server left.

Fetu shrugged. "It was probably a petty thief looking for an easy mark." He shoved a fork full of food into his mouth and leaned back in his chair. Closing his eyes he let out a deep satisfied sigh. "That is almost as good as Momma used to make." He chuckled.

"Right..." Chloe's chin dropped a fraction of an inch as she drew back into her seat.

James pulled the memory of their conversation that first night in the sanctuary, and the pieces began to click together.

"You know, it is not always their fault, sometimes you do what you have to in order to survive." Meghnah's voice was soft with an edge of hostility, which served to comfort Chloe, and chastise Fetu.

The server returned with the girls orders, as well as the usual bows. "Here is your order, is there anything else I can get you four?"

"All good here." Fetu bellowed with a half-wave of his hand. "Thanks."

The girl bowed once more before leaving.

A bubble of silence formed around the table as they each began to eat. Chloe pulled back the leaf wrapper her fish had been steamed in, filling the air with the provocative scent of spices.

James sampled his meal, layers of savory flavor unfolding themselves on his tongue. One major positive to Drak'or food, it was never synthetic.

"I don't think I have ever heard you mention your family before, Fetu." Chloe broke the silence, picking at the edge of her fish.

Fetu shrugged. "I guess there just isn't a whole lot to talk about." An awkward half-smile tugged at his cheeks, and his ears perked up. "They own a small farming operation on Destune. Last I heard several of my younger siblings still live there."

James paused between bites. "Do you still talk to them?"

Fetu stuffed another fork full into his mouth, chewed, then swallowed. "I try and take a day or so to stop by if we are in the area. Every now and then I'll get a communication from someone. Things have been a little tense ever since I left the Order. It was bad for the first couple of years. Dad wouldn't talk to me. But things have evened out since then."

"That's true." Meghnah chimed in. "A couple of years ago, he took me out to meet them. It was… nice." Her sentence trailed off at the end, leaving some uncertainty in its conclusion.

"Nice, huh?" Chloe giggled to herself before tasting her fish. Meghnah and Fetu stared.   "Well?"

Meghnah asked when Chloe hesitated to respond.

Chloe laughed covering her mouth as she tried to swallow. "It's really good."

"I told you it would be." Meghnah grinned returning to her own dish.

Fetu laughed one of his deep belly laughs. "First time I take it? Don't worry Chloe, we wouldn't feed you anything too poisonous. Anyway, your reaction was a lot like Meghnah's when she met my family."

Meghnah smiled and laughed. "It definitely was a lot different than I was expecting, but in a good way."

"What about you Chloe, any family?" Fetu finished what was on his plate and pushed back in his chair relaxing.

An ache grew in the pit of James's stomach. It wasn't as if Fetu meant to be dense, he just was sometimes.

Meghnah placed a hand on her knee, but didn't say anything.

Chloe gave a half-smile, practiced, fake, like the receptionist in the station lobby. It was a facade designed to hide any real emotions. The irritating trait that had at first caused James to avoid her, and which he now admired as a hidden strength.

"Not unless you count yourselves." Chloe forced a giggle. "Zaeith is the closest thing to a father I have ever had."

"Really?" That caught James off guard. Of all the people he had ever met, the Captain was not one he ever expected to be called fatherly.

"Is that strange?"

Fetu shrugged. "I wouldn't say that care and compassion are among our captain's finer points, but he does seem to have a soft spot for you."

Chloe shrugged. "Or maybe he goes easier on me

because I am still new to this, and you guys are all experts."

"Maybe," Meghnah acknowledged with a conceding nod as she sat back from her now finished meal. "But give yourself some credit, it's only been what, six months? And I bet you could already outperform most of the crewmen in the galaxy."

Meghnah wasn't far off, Chloe could pass most of the military's competency tests, and she was way ahead of all but the best communications officers he had worked with, none of whom were even half decent navigators. There was no questioning it; Chloe was a prodigy.

She laughed. "I don't know about that, but I'll take the compliment."

The server returned with a small datapad. "I hope you enjoyed everything." She bowed before placing it on the table near the center. "And please enjoy your stay on Dramia," she smiled, it was a sweet genuine smile.

James nodded and took the datapad. "Thank you." He entered his payment credentials, then handed it to Fetu. Nodding to Meghnah in the direction of their tails.

Meghnah nodded back. "You guys headed back up to the station?"

"Well, I am," Fetu stretched as he stood. "There is a lot of work to get done tonight."

"We will go with you to the lift. We're headed that way anyway."

"Sounds great." James stood and straightened his jacket. "What is the quickest way to the terminal from here?"

"The map says to follow the main walk back towards

the center, but Chloe and I found a shortcut, if we go to the next line over."

The cafe sat on a sort of rooftop on the outward slope of the city, which served as a sort of ground floor for the district. Sky bridges and balconies connected it to other rooftops, each with its own area of shops, restaurants, and living areas like self-contained villages within the massive metropolis.

James followed Meghnah along the walkways, careful to position himself so that Fetu always remained behind him. If he did this right, Fetu's presence would keep anyone from noticing if he disappeared from a moment.

Meghnah turned down a narrow street leading between two taller buildings rising off their level moving in towards the city's bowl. James stepped into a doorway, motioning for Fetu and Chloe to continue.

Fetu paused. James's heart stopped for a second, this entire plan depended on everyone's ability to work together without tipping off their pursuers.

"Just keep walking," Chloe whispered giving James a nod, and pressing on Fetu's arm.

"Right." Fetu's ears twisted in confusion, but he resumed walking.

James accessed the control system hidden in the forearm of his jacket, shifting its color from blue to red and beginning the materialization process of the small stunblade. In a moment, the weapon appeared in the palm of his hand.

James stepped back out into the alleyway falling into step beside someone coming from the other direction, and headed back towards the plaza they had just left.

"Busy streets today, huh?"

The stranger looked at James, obvious confusion,

then frustration forming behind his eyes. "Look, I don't want to buy anything today, okay?"

"I guess it's a good thing I'm not interested in selling." James stepped away from the man waving and reaching out to an imaginary person in the larger crowd. People pushed past him, ignoring his gesture, he slipped into the flow of traffic headed in the direction of the cafe.

He spotted the two men watching the alley from a nearby bench. It appeared they didn't want to get caught in such a narrow space, and with Fetu wearing his bright orange shirt, finding him on the other side would not be a challenge.

James stepped out of the crowd to read an informational posting and waited.

As soon as Meghnah, Chloe, and Fetu had disappeared from the alleyway, the tails began to move again.

James ducked back into the crowd coming up from behind them. He rounded the corner into the ally and in one fluid motion brought the stunblade up under the back of the first man's rib.

He let out a scream as his muscles went tight, and he collapsed to the ground. The second man was fast. He was already coming in with a right hook by the time the first one dropped. James pivoted around his left leg, sweeping his right leg back, narrowly evading the punch. Tossing the knife from his right hand, and in the same motion, grabbed the man above the wrist and twisted outward into an extended lock.

Catching the knife in his left hand, he brought it down hard between the man's shoulder blades. The force of the impact knocked the air from his lungs, eyes going wide. A moment later, he was on the ground beside his friend.

James dragged both men off to the side of the path, making an effort to conceal the bodies until the others returned.

Fetu was the first to re-enter the ally.

"How did they find us again?"

Meghnah followed behind and searched the men, "You never lost them." She handed Fetu a small single-shot handgun.

Fetu took the weapon turning it over in his hands. "But James said…"

James clipped the stunblade back into his jacket, letting the nanotech re-absorb it, "It was a trap, I needed them to think we didn't know they were following us; otherwise we wouldn't have been able to catch them."

Fetu stuffed the gun, along with two knives Meghnah found into his pack. "But why did we need to capture them?"

"Because these are not petty thieves." Chloe stood over the unconscious men. "They were looking for us for a reason."

"Right. And now we need to get them somewhere more private. It won't do us any good to draw attention to ourselves. Maybe that parts vendor can hook us up with an empty warehouse."

* * *

"Good morning, sleepy head." James said as the last of the cold water poured out of the bucket. He tossed the bucket against the far wall, causing a loud clang which echoed and reverberated in the small room.

Fetu had told the mechanic they had picked up

some new cargo, which they needed to store planetside for a few days while they prepared a space for it on board their ship. What Fetu lacked in elegance he made up for in diplomacy. The mechanic didn't have anything that met their requirements open, but he knew a guy, who knew a guy, and found them two abandoned storage sheds on the ground level of the city.

The stranger inhaled deeply, gasping for air and sputtering, struggling against the ropes Meghnah had used to tie him to the old metal chair.

"What the core!" He blinked against the flickering of the room's single unstable light. "Where am I?" he spat.

"I am the one asking the questions here." James kept his voice even and his jaw set, crouching down to look the restrained man in the eyes. "You and I have a problem. I am willing to let you resolve it for me."

"What the core are you on about?"

James stood, every motion slow and deliberate, taking two steps to the side and facing away from the prisoner, while keeping him in his peripheral. "I am talking about your ability to fix our present predicament of asymmetric information. You tell me what you know, I keep my friends outside from killing you." James feigned at brushing dust off his shoulder. "Who knows, they might even let you keep your tongue."

"I've got no idea what you're talking about."

James grabbed the second bucket of ice water Chloe had prepared and dumped it over the man's head.

The prisoner closed his eyes and held his breath against the freezing water. "What the core!" He yelled, trying to shake it from his hair and eyes.

"You were obviously not awake." James set the bucket beside the chair, then leaned over and placed his hand on the man's shoulder. He applied just enough pressure to keep him from struggling. "Let's try this again. Who hired you?"

The man inhaled trying to regain some composure. "I think you've made a mistake, I ain't working for no one. I was just looking for an easy mark."

There was a light knock on the door. The old tracks screeched as it slid open spilling light from the floodlights outside into the room.

"Alright commander, I got the bomb set like you asked, we have two hours." Fetu's voice boomed from the alleyway.

James half glanced over his shoulder, letting just enough light slip past for the prisoner to catch a glimpse of Fetu's silhouette. "Good, send Meghnah in would you? I think I am done with this one."

"R-right," Fetu said, dropping the door with a loud crash.

"It's too bad you got yourself mixed up in this. If you had been paid, we might be able to work out a deal. But as a witness, you are useless to me."

James stood and began walking towards the door.

"Wait!" the man screamed, fighting against his bindings once again. "I don't know anything, I promise! I won't tell nobody about you, I wouldn't even have anything to tell, I swear!" He was struggling so hard he knocked himself over, landing with a loud crash on the floor.

James paused not looking back. "Who hired you?"

"Okay, okay." The man inhaled. "I don't know his name. This doesn't work like that. It's all cloak and dagger and stuff." He began trying to roll his chair onto its back.

James resumed walking.

"Alright!" the man spat. "I'm not stupid, I did do a little digging, good business not getting into these thing blind, you know. And the pay was just too good. He was with the Descendants, that's all I know. They have a ship, it is supposed to be here in two days, that's when we were supposed to check back in."

James pulled open the garage door. "Meghnah, he is ready for you?"

The man's screams could be heard as Meghnah closed the door behind her.

"How did it go?" Chloe sat on the ground across the alley leg bouncing impatiently.

"Good, I think. Now we hope the other one is as cooperative."

James pulled a chair into the room with him spinning it around and sitting on it backwards to face the prisoner. The muted sounds of the first man struggling could be heard in the next room.

"Wh-what's going on over there?" the other man asked.

It looked like the intimidation tactic was doing its job. Meghnah had been instructed to make sure this man was awake. She was to stare at him from the corner, until he sent Fetu to get her.

"Your friend was not very helpful." James set his jaw and stared hard into the man's eyes.

He swallowed, trying desperately to break eye contact. "What are you doing to him?"

James shrugged holding his gaze. "Honestly, I don't know what she does to them, and frankly, I don't care as long as it gets cleaned up afterwards."

"I don't know anything, I promise."

James sighed and looked away. "Don't give me that." He tapped his palms against the back of his chair. "I already know you were hired by the Descendants, your friend tried to deny it though." He nodded towards the wall.

The blood drained from the prisoner's face. "How do you know that?"

James leaned forward arms crossed over the chair back, bringing his face close to the prisoner's. "You know what?" He whispered. "I am feeling courteous today, so I'll go first. Next time the Descendants ask you to do a job, ask yourself, what kind of person are they too afraid of to deal with themselves?"

The man's resolve broke as any remnant of ego he was still holding onto dissolved. As his shoulders slumped, his eyes dropped unwilling to even look at James's face.

There was a long moment of silence.

James stood turning the chair as he did so, metal scraping against concrete. "Looks like you can't help me." He turned to leave. "Unfortunate, I was hoping to only have one body to deal with tonight."

"I'll tell you anything." The man's voice was cracked and hoarse.

James turned back to face him. "That's better." He pulled the chair forward and sat down facing the man, sitting in the chair properly this time he kept his posture relaxed and open. "What were you looking for?"

"We're looking for a fingalin. The Descendants think he was one of their officers turned rogue."

"What makes you think he is with us?"

The man shrugged as his muscles visibly relaxed. "I'm not sure, it had something to do with the cargo crane that disappeared, apparently its last known location was a deep space salvage. According to the Engineering Corps's logs, your ship was the one that called it in. Also, your last registered location was DSI 3122. That puts the rendezvous not too far off your projected route."

James nodded slowly. "You're resourceful, I'll give you that." He stood and walked towards the door.

"Wait, aren't you going to let me go?"

James pulled the door open and met the man's eyes. "Meghnah, I'm done here."

Chapter 18

James waited on the ion lift, absently clicking his fingernails against each other as he stared out the windows. There wasn't much to see while it was docked in the belly of the station, not that James was really looking. His mind was preoccupied with the information he had gathered earlier.

"Anything interesting out there?" Chloe brushed out her skirt sitting in the seat beside him,

James stared a moment, not quite registering what she had asked. "Huh? Oh, no not really."

She smiled softly, it was delicate, and drew him back to the present. She was beautiful, in an elegant sort of way that made her more like something out of some ancient tale of magic and goddesses, than anything out of reality. The plain white dress hanging loosely from her hips and shoulders, accented by the deep blue shawl which appeared as if it had been torn from the evening sky in the first moments after twilight.

Seph

"You sure you still want to do this? I mean, with everything else going on." She leaned over her chair not quite making eye contact.

James shrugged. "If the information we have is any good, we have at least another full day before they catch up to us." He looked out the window again, not focusing on anything, "Fetu needs to get the fold generator reassembled, so it's not like we could go anywhere even if we wanted to. Also, The Captain isn't back yet, we can't very well leave without him."

The artificial sounds of electric motors began to rise. James pressed his hands against his knees and stood. "No, I think at this point we would be in the way up here." He held out his hand. "Come on, I want to show you something."

James led Chloe to the center of the lift, where a doorway set into the central shaft opened to a spiral staircase wrapping around the drive motors. The stairs lead out into a large glass dish, allowing for a full unobstructed view overlooking Dramia.

Throughout the day the room would have been filled with tourists, most with young children, exploring the wonders of the planet from low orbit. However, most of the passengers now were older, jaded from the experience by too many trips to and from the various planets they had visited.

The edge of the atmosphere caught the sunlight as it began to set over the horizon, casting a glowing blue halo around the planet as the ion lift fell into its shadow.

Chloe gasped as she stared at the display of dancing lights below. The lift broke through the upper levels of the atmosphere, the halo erupted into a brilliant display of yellow and orange drifting over a sea of red, reflecting off the clouds below. The peaks of Lalazarja's tallest buildings reaching up like the spires of an ancient temple.

"It's beautiful." Chloe whispered, the vibrant light caught in her long blonde hair, cascading down her shoulders like dim flames licking at the night sky. Red and gold dancing in her blue eyes like koi.

"Yes." James realized he had been watching her, more than he had been watching the sunset.

"I suppose you have seen this hundreds of times." She said meeting his eyes.

He shrugged, staring out at the rising cloud line. " Most habitable planets have a similar atmospheric composition, especially the terraformed ones. The light diffraction is fairly consistent, though there is a certain amount of luck and planning that goes into this particular view."

Chloe laughed stepping up the side of the dish and sitting down where she could lean back on the up-slope. "You are a very interesting man, James." She giggled and brushed out her skirt.

"Oh? Did I miss something?"

Chloe shook her head and smiled softly tilting her head to the side. "You're just refreshing, that's all."

James sat down beside her, watching the clouds below as they erupted around them and engulfed them. "How so?"

"Well." She turned to look at him, sitting forward and craning her neck to look into his eyes. "Here we are, miles above the planet, with this amazing sunset, and the thing you chose to talk about is light refraction and atmospheric composition."

She leaned back cradled in the soft curve of the glass, as the clouds broke, revealing the towering city.

Seph

She closed her eyes, listening to the soft inaudible humming of the lift drive. "It's sweet."

She looked so serene, like she had somehow captured the reflection of the moon, from the surface of a lake. "Is that really so strange?"

She shrugged. "Maybe, I am not the best one to say. But it seems that all my life, the only thing anyone ever cared about was how perfect I was. I could never look at anything beautiful without someone reminding me that I was not." She sat up and pulled her hair back. "But with you it's different; you make everything seem so... normal, like even the most amazing things in the universe have some logical explanation waiting for you to find it."

They stared at each other for a long moment. How was he supposed to respond to that? The artificial whine of the motor began to build indicating the lift was about to touchdown. The ground came up to greet them in a great stone bolster.

James stood and straightened his clothing. "Let's go, our ride is waiting." He held out his hand helping Chloe to her feet.

The mag-car waiting for them at the bottom of the stone stairs was a common design, four doors with smooth curving edges around the cab and magnetic guides, giving it the look of luxury. The driver held the door waiting at attention for them. He bowed as they approached, letting them slide in and closing the door without a sound.

Chloe watched the city lights fly by as they climbed higher towards the top of the bowl. "We never had anything like this on the station. The lights were always on, there was never any proper night there."

"I guess I had never thought about that." James

leaned back into his seat. "What was it like? Growing up the way you did, I mean."

Chloe sat back, her lips twitched in an almost smile. "You know, you are very blunt."

He inhaled sharply. "I'm sorry." He exhaled. "I don't mean to be, I understand if you don't want to talk about it."

She shook her head and laughed. "It's not that. I think I am just scared you might actually care."

James studied her soft features. "Why would that scare you?"

Chloe shrugged looking back out her window. "I guess, because you make me feel like I might be worth caring about. And I am not sure I know how to care about myself."

James rested his arm on his window, leaning his head against his hand as he watched her. "I don't know if I can really answer that."

She turned to look at him again. "I don't think I expect you to."

They were silent for a moment.

Chloe folded her hands into her lap. "Thank you, James."

"For?"

"Listening."

James smiled, "Any time."

Silence again.

"Who was Sphiya?"

Chloe started off into the distance, not quite looking at him. "She was the woman who raised me."

"What was she like?"

"Awful." Chloe laughed, it was forced, the kind of sarcastic laugh that hides pain behind indifference. "I was never grateful enough for her liking. The simple fact that she had been willing to take me in. 'A human child'." She twisted the word making it sound like an insult. "I was always the last to eat. No matter what, I could never be as good as the fingalin children." She shook her head. "No, I didn't deserve to be as good as the fingalin children."

James hesitated, then placed a hand on her knee, trying to comfort her, she glanced at him for a second but didn't flinch or protest. "Is that why you became a thief?"

She wiped her eyes, clearing away what was not quite a tear. "Yes, that is how we paid our rent, she had a particular fondness for anything with the ancient language from Vinge."

She shrugged. "I don't know, I guess I never cared. I always assumed she had a buyer who was willing to pay for them."

The mag-car coasted to a smooth stop alongside a protruding balcony. The door opened automatically. James slid out, then offered his hand to Chloe. She took it stepping from the vehicle up to the platform.

The restaurant was open, facing outwards from the city two hundred stories above the planet's surface. The spacious terrace was covered by a glass canopy, which echoed melodically as tiny raindrops beat against it, like a steel drum in the distance. Water collected in intricate grooves draining out into waterfalls, strategically placed to enhance the view.

An android, modeled after a female humanoid, approached them. Her skin appeared pale compared to most humans, with tints of soft greens and muted pinks, iridescent speckles shimmered around her eyes and cheek bones.

"Greetings." It bowed spreading its arms open from

the elbow. "Do you have a reservation?"

James returned the gesture "Ayunis for two."

The android's luminescent green eyes went vacant for a moment, while it retrieved the reservation file. It blinked then motioned with its hand. "This way Commander Ayunis, your table is waiting."

They sat on the edge of the balcony, sheets of silver metal delineated the border where an invisible force field protected the interior space from more extreme weather patterns, while allowing patrons to enjoy the scents, and feel of a fresh breeze.

The hostess pulled the two chairs back from the table. It folded its hands across its lap and bowed in a deep nod. "Your servers will be with you shortly."

"I have never seen anything like this, James." Chloe pulled her chair forward as she sat, eye mesmerized by the horizon. "I am having such a hard time accepting the idea that it isn't just an illusion, and there isn't a wall out there."

A smile started to form in his cheeks. He had picked this location for the view. Good food and atmosphere could be found anywhere. But a true view of the horizon, could only be found on a planet.

"I think everybody feels that way a little after spending too much time in space." James allowed his eyes to follow hers out across the end of the world.

Chloe reached across the table placing her hand on his. "Thank you, James."

James glanced at her hand, a strange feeling not unlike nausea, in all the most pleasant ways, began to build inside his stomach. "For?"

"This." She sat back in her chair, pulling her hand away and indicating with her eyes. James tried not to flinch as something inside him ached to have her touching him again.

Two servers appeared, producing tall thin glasses seemingly out of nowhere and setting them on the table.

The one who had served James clasped his hands together in front of his chest and bowed slightly. "Sir, My lady. I hope you are enjoying yourselves this evening." He paused for a moment. And the other server began to pour their water. "Tonight, we have a menu for you, which has been prepared to showcase the variety and versatility of Dramia. Each dish will be accompanied by a drink pairing chosen by our sumiller. Similarly, each dish will require its own utensils which will be given to you as part of the presentation."

Each of the servers bowed, folding their arms over their laps before departing.

"That was impressive." Chloe said with a light chuckle in her voice. "How did you find this place?"

"Travis recommended it to me." Travis had approached James, with a list of recommendations… before they had even arrived on Dramia. James wasn't sure how the chef had discovered his intentions, but Travis had been discreet, so he didn't mind.

Chloe laughed. "He is full of surprises, isn't he?"

James nodded. "Like everyone else on the Shade." He laughed.

The servers returned with a serving cart that hovered silently a few inches above the floor. Each of the servers removed a bowl from the cart and placed it in front of James and Chloe.

A soft nutty scent drifted up from the thin broth. James inhaled, breathing in the aroma which sat warm on the back of his tongue.

"This broth is made from the bones of a mio'nayo,

though the meat is inedible, you will find that the broth produced from it is rich and nutty. Today's soup was prepared by first smoking the bones before simmering."

The second server placed the appropriate soup spoons next to the bowls, before presenting them with two new glasses, and beginning to fill them with a light amber liquid.

"The drink pairing with this dish started its life as a chilled tea, which has been enhanced with the essence of various nuts. The beverage was then carbonated to add an appropriate lightness to match the accompanying dish."

Both servers bowed and left.

Chloe dipped her spoon into the orange liquid, tasting a small sample. Her eyes lit up and an almost inaudible squeal escaped from somewhere in the back of her throat.

James tasted his own. It melted on his taste buds, starting in the front with the warm flavor of toasted nuts, and the deep dark flavors of smoke.

"This is really good." Chloe said sitting back and savoring the flavor.

James nodded his agreement.

Chloe took a second taste, pulling her bowl a little closer to the edge of the table. "You know James, you are not what I was expecting when you first came on board."

"Oh? How so?"

"You came off as cold, calculating, and indifferent. You seemed to keep your distance from the rest of us. I never would have guessed that you were so... kind."

James paused for a moment, before finishing his soup and setting his spoon aside. He had always thought about himself as a decent person, but there was something different about the way she had said it.

"I guess I'm glad I was able to change your mind." he laughed.

Chloe pushed her own bowl forward. "I guess, I mean, it's just nice to feel like someone is listening."

He watched her for a moment, it was easy to get lost in her delicate features.

The servers returned and cleared the table settings, quickly replacing them with a plated salad.

"Our next course is a salad, the greens come from lettuce originally from Frehn. It requires high altitudes with low atmospheric pressure, which gives it a light crisp flavor. It is accented by fresh fruits and a sweet vinegar dressing."

After pouring and explaining the drink accompaniment, the servers bowed and left.

The flavors of the salad were bright and fresh, a complete contrast to the deep flavors from the broth before. Small fruits reminiscent of blueberries exploded with flavors of light citrus.

Chloe picked at the salad, tasting each of the elements by themselves. "I guess I never imagined feeling like it was okay to have a real relationship."

James shrugged, trying to incorporate all the flavors into a single bite. "I guess I never cared before."

"You can't tell me no one else was ever interested." There was a hint of challenge in her voice.

James shook his head. "It's not that there haven't been other girls, I guess I was too cold and calculating to make it last. It was always too much of a distraction, I think." That, and he had always had a hard time staying in one place for very long. That had been one of the primary advantages of going into special operations, as well as what had drawn him to the Shade.

He finished his salad and set his fork on his plate. "I guess I was too dedicated to my job to pay attention to anyone else."

"Why did you leave the military?"

James leaned back in his chair resting his arm on the table. "I guess I just got bored."

The servers returned, trading out their plates for a small dish with a roasted root vegetable which very closely resembled a potato, covered in a crispy layer of baked cheese.

"Border patrol between the Ring and the Circle not quite as exciting as you expected?"

James shrugged. "I didn't spend a lot of time on the border. I was recruited for spec-ops not long after I left the academy. I had already broken most of the records in the training simulators, and I had been in the field for less than two years when I made Lieutenant Commander. I was given command of my own squad as part of an enforcer unit. We were basically a covert strike force. We spent a lot of time trying to dismantle pirate outposts around the outer colonies. Their smuggling operations keep a lot of the Alliance resources tied up in the Ring, so a lot of them hideout in the colonies where they feel like no one is watching."

"So, what happened?"

"Well after that, it stopped mattering how good I was. I couldn't move up, and I started to feel trapped by my missions."

Chloe tilted her head, brushing her hair back. "Why couldn't you move up anymore?"

"After a certain point, tenure is more important

than anything else. Well, other than having the right connections. I had a hard time taking orders from people who I did not feel were qualified to be in their positions. So when I was given the opportunity to, I resigned."

The truth was, he had been ordered to seize what they had been led to believe was a stronghold for the Knights of Pryne. His gut had told him it was a trap, so he intentionally delayed the mission. After weeks of watching, the ambush that had been prepared for them got impatient and revealed themselves.

Once their original plan had fallen through, James had allowed himself to be captured. After several weeks he escaped, having gathered incriminating evidence against several of their major investors, and sabotaging their database. In the end it led to the arrest of several prominent members of the Trade Union, dealing a heavy blow to both the funding and the manpower of the organization.

His commanding officer wanted to have James court-martialed for not following orders, but the Overseer had decided instead to recommend him for advancement, and commendation for valor in the face of insurmountable odds. His commanding officer was less than pleased and decided instead to offer him an early release.

The servers returned to change out the course once again. This time it was a small scoop-like cup, a small ice cream ball sat in its center. The cream was smooth and rich with the flavors of toasted cinnamon.

Chloe pulled her spoon slowly between her lips, "So, how did you end up on the Shade?"

James watched her, enjoying the cold sensation on his tongue contrasting with the warmth of the dish before. Everyone knew that Meghnah had recruited him; they had met in a bar on Frehn, but he had never told any of them how he ended up at that bar.

"It was an accident." He tapped the tip of his spoon against his bottom lip before taking another bite. "I was picked up by a taxi. I asked to go to the landing square."

The memory flashed through his mind. A mag-car filled with the scent of apple blossoms. A young girl in a white dress, with silver hair and pointed ears.

He shook his head, repressing the haunting images. "Instead, she dropped me off at some bar. She was insistent it was the right place."

Chloe let slip a little giggle, a couple strands of hair falling into her face as she tried to hide it. "And that's where you met Meg?"

James nodded. "The driver told me that 'I didn't know what I was looking for,' then drove off." He let out a sigh. "Meghnah was waiting for someone else, at first she mistook me for him. But when that guy never showed up she introduced me to Fetu, and they offered me the job."

Chloe brushed her hair back again, trying discreetly to tuck it back into its clip. "Why did you stay?"

"I guess it was what I had been looking for all along. Ironic, that cab driver was right."

The memory returned, deep blue eyes like oceans of eternity threatening to drown him in their depths.

Chloe's laugh brought him back to reality. The servers returned and changed out their dishes.

The lead server described the entree as tenderloin steak grilled over a fire, and served with drak'or rice noodles. Fried and served with an emulsified egg sauce made from gashwar eggs, and butter made with real cow's milk. The dish had been paired with a beverage of sweetened fermented ginger.

"What about you, why do you stay?" James asked after they had both tried the dish.

"Where would I go?" Chloe asked sampling the sauce on the tines of her fork.

"Anywhere you wanted. Do you really see yourself as remaining a mercenary your whole life?"

She looked down at her dish, gently nudging it with her fork. "I'm not sure what I see myself doing with the rest of my life. Before Zaeith rescued me, I never imagined I would ever become anything."

He sat back watching her for a long moment, the layers beginning to fall away. He felt once again like he was seeing her for the first time. "Wait, rescued you? Not hired you?"

Chloe looked up meeting his eyes, squinting in contemplation. "You thought I had a commission?"

He laughed. "I had always assumed, it never even occurred to me to ask, and the Captain obviously didn't feel the need to say anything."

"Obviously not," She laughed. "I do get an allowance though. I've never felt like I belonged anywhere as much as I do on the Shade, and besides, I don't even have full citizenship anywhere else... After Zaeith took me in, he started training me on all the systems. Meg kind of adopted me as her little sister. The whole crew, except for Nevarian, sort of just embraced me. Maybe someday I will want to do something different, but for now... it's nice to feel safe."

Silence passed, and James felt that he could somehow fit an eternity into the space it occupied. The mysteries of the Shade, its captain and crew. It was like trying to put together pieces of a million piece puzzle, with no edges, and no idea what it was supposed to look like.

Every member of the crew appeared as if they had been hand-picked for their skill and ability. But the more he learned, the more he got the impression the Captain simply had a peculiar habit of being in the right place at the right time, and an unfathomable amount of luck.

"I asked him why he did it once." Chloe interjected into his thoughts. "He said I reminded him of someone he had lost a long time ago."

James realized he had finished his dish several minutes ago, and set down his fork. "That's not cryptic or anything."

Chloe shrugged. "It was good enough though… at least I never asked again."

"Well whether or not he ever chooses to reveal any of his reasoning to us, I for one am grateful you're here." James tried to put as much sincerity into his smile as he could.

"Thanks James. I don't know if anyone has ever told me they were grateful I was around before. It means a lot."

He fell silent again as the servers changed out their entrees for desserts, custard piped into a chocolate shell.

"What do you think is going to happen now?" Chloe asked after finishing her first bite of the cream.

That was a good question. There were so many things going on and so few of them made any real sense; with Descendant war ships showing up in places they had no obvious reason for being; the complete disappearance of the population of not one, but two

DSI stations; and the pirate ambush and raid on the
Engineering Corps's crane; add to that the subsequent
massacre of the crew, and possibly the innocent
population of Ulun'tess as collateral damage; on top of
that there was the Captain 's decision to move into the
Circle and arrive at Atlione in such a short time frame.

"I don't know. I feel like the discord within the
Alliance is coming to a head, and we have somehow
found ourselves in the middle of it."

"Did you hear about the crane?"

James sat forward in his chair. "You guys heard
about it too?"

She nodded. "It was sort of the only thing people
were talking about. Is it that unheard-of?"

"It shows either an extreme lack of competency,
or an extreme act of desperation. It is incredibly
dangerous to put a fusion core into orbit around
a planet. The added gravitational mass would be
something like introducing an enormous moon to the
system. It would be very hard to predict the kind of
damage that would do."

Chloe placed her silverware and napkin on the table
"Why would you do it then?"

He could come up with a hand full of plausible
explanations, none of them incredibly reasonable, but
plausible. The most obvious; someone running from
something and not having time to calculate a new
orbital path. If the Knights of Pryne got too ambitious,
it was possible the Alliance had sent an enforcer after
them. The ambush would have likely been composed
of a small fleet of ion drive crafts, which would have
been easier to get in close and board with. Meaning
that their combat ability would have been limited.

By opening a hyperspace sleeve close to a known

orbital path, they would make it difficult for the Alliance to pursue them. It was risky, but it was a risk James might take in a similar situation.

The other, more disturbing, possibility was that it had been done with the intent of causing chaos among the already dissonant government factions; demonstrating just how incapable of protecting the population the Alliance was.

Many of the pirate organizations, especially the larger ones, had already set up pseudo-governments unto themselves, declaring themselves outside of the government's influence. It was possible this was a new war tactic, one which would have devastating results, undermining what little authority the Alliance had to begin with.

"There are a few possibilities, none of which I particularly like. Like I said, incompetent or desperate."

The servers returned, clearing the table onto the hovering cart. "We hope you enjoyed our dinner presentation this evening." They both folded their hands over their laps and bowed. "Feel free to stay as long as you would like, and enjoy our spectacular view. As well as the music provided this evening by the rain."

"Well, do you have anything else planned for us this evening?" Chloe asked.

"One last thing. Come on, I'll show you."

James stood from his chair and held out a hand to his date, she took it with a bright smile spreading across her face. He pulled her through the restaurant, towards an unassuming lift tucked in the back of the room.

"Where are we going?" She took several quick steps

running up beside him.

James waved his hand over the call sensor. "You will see."

The lift doors slid open with a faint hiss drowned out by the room's ambiance.

The lift descended several stories before opening up to a generous courtyard. James led Chloe out of the lift, and tiny drops of rain fell on their skin. Chloe flinched at first, then gasped, mouth hanging open and eyes dancing in the city lights.

"The water, it's falling from the sky!"

She released his hand and ran off into the rain giggling and squealing.

He smiled to himself, checking the weather had paid off. You might not be able to control it, but with a little planning, it was definitely possible to take advantage of it.

The mag-car was waiting for them across the courtyard, James made his way over to it, watching as Chloe was filled with the wonder of a child. She pulled the loose braid from her hair, letting it fall unkempt all over her back and shoulders. Beads of water formed and dripped from the edges of her dark blue shawl and white dress, which began sticking to her skin as she spun laughing in the gentle drizzle.

After several minutes of what James thought looked like pure joy, she joined him at the car. "Thank you!" She laughed.

James let her slide in first. "I figured, growing up on the station, you had probably never experienced rain before."

She sidled up beside him laying her head against his shoulder. "You are a very interesting man, James."

His heart began beating a little faster in his chest, as

the unfamiliar feeling returned to his stomach. "How so?"

She inhaled, relaxing against him. "Not once this evening have you given me any superficial compliments, or tried to seduce me in any way."

"Is that a good thing?"

Chloe let out an amused huff. "What I mean to say is, even without that, you still made me feel like a princess."

Chapter 19

Once out of the rain and on the ion lift, James took Chloe's wet shawl and traded her his jacket. The nanites went to work collecting the water and converting it into energy. A process that also produced a gentle warming effect in the clothing. She lay next to him in the dark and silence of the observation dish, now well into the planet's shadow, cast by the faint glow of Dramia's atmosphere as it refracted the light of the unseen sun.

Images from his dreams flashed through his mind. The screams of mothers and children echoing in the emptiness. He tried to ground himself, feeling the warmth of Chloe's body pressed up against him. Water from her cool damp hair soaking into his t-shirt. Her heartbeat, slow and steady like a drum welcoming him home.

"You alright?" She asked.

"Fine, I was just thinking."

She sat up turning her legs so she was facing him. Her blond hair the color of white beach sand in the faint light. "Anything in particular?"

He shrugged, not quite looking at her. "Just a dream I had last night, nothing important."

She smiled softly then laid her head back down on his lap stretching her body perpendicular to his own. "A good dream?"

He shook his head. "A strange dream. I was on a planet, I don't know which one. It looked like it was being attacked."

"By who?"

He stared for a moment into her blue eyes, soft and compassionate like the ocean waves. "I'm not sure, I feel like the Captain was there with me, like he was watching me, waiting for me to do something."

The whine from the drive began to build, indicating that they were slowing down in preparation to dock with the station.

Chloe sat up again. "Maybe there is something he wants to show you."

He pushed himself up, tugging on his shirt where water from Chloe's hair had stuck it to his skin. "Do you put a lot of stock in dreams?"

She pulled her knees up to her chest. "I don't know, Meg says they are a bridge between our O'rah and our Rek'ah."

He held out a hand to help her up. "What is that supposed to mean?" He chuckled.

She smiled, letting out a puff of air, "I don't really know." Taking his hand. She pulled herself to her feet using James as a counter balance. "Something about balancing your substance with your essence. Body and mind, I guess."

Seph

"Have you started practicing Vhast?" They walked slowly to the staircase.

She shook her head. "No, not really. Meg talks about it a lot though. I guess I feel like I am already too far behind for it to make much of a difference."

James held the door for her. "How so?"

"There is a lot more to it than believing in something. It's a whole lifestyle."

"Not ready to give up on synthesized food?" James laughed.

She giggled following him out into the lift room. The lights were bright compared to the observation dish, he squinted while his vision cleared.

They both stopped; two men in white uniforms with lavender embellishments waited for them.

"This way, please," One of the Descendant officers motioned stiffly. Other officers escorted passengers from around the lift to the station.

Moving on instincts, James stepped in front of Chloe. "What is going on here?"

The officer exhaled in a huff. "We have received information that the party responsible for the massacre of Ulun'tess may be somewhere on this station or within the city. Now please come with us. It is for your own protection," he motioned again.

"James, isn't that something the Alliance should be handling?"

The second man rolled his eyes, accompanied by an exaggerated head motion. "The Alliance is handling it. We are only here to help move things along. Now let's get moving along," he motioned with his head, unclipping a stunblade at his waist.

The first man held out his hand to stop his junior officer, "Calm down lieutenant, this is as much an inconvenience for them as it is for us. Now then, shall we?" He turned his palm upward, expertly changing the gesture to an invitation, including a shallow bow for good measure.

Their escorts led them to the merchant stalls, which had been commandeered for the purpose of questioning passengers as they came off the ion lift. Judging by the people in the lobby, most of the station had been questioned before the lift arrived, then been diverted to less public areas.

A single Alliance captain stood at the reception desk with a large Descendant officer. The Alliance man looked like a puppy dog who had lost its owner in a crowd, compared with the Drak'or. "You said you were only going to question them, you said nothing about taking any prisoners."

The Descendant placed a hand on the captain 's shoulder. "Come now Captain, everything is going to be fine. As soon as the rest of your team gets here, we will turn everything over to you. For now, let's focus on keeping these very dangerous criminals from doing anymore damage than they have already done. Alright?"

The Alliance officer hesitated. "You are going to turn everything over, including the ship?"

The large man patted the officer's shoulder. "I told you, everything is going to work out, now stop worrying so much."

He turned to face James and Chloe as the soldiers brought them to the desk. "Ah welcome, I hope you have not been treated too poorly now." He flashed a broad grin nodding his head to both of them.

James nodded cautiously. "Who is it we are supposed to be protected from?"

Seph

The Descendant blinked, shaking his head in feigned shock. "Why, Lieutenant Commander James Ayunis. From yourself, of course."

The muscles in his abdomen clenched, a buzzing sensation building in the back of his skull.

The Alliance officer glanced at James and Chloe. "Wait, this is the man you have been looking for?"

The Descendant turned his head in the direction of the officer. "Captain, would you please give me a minute, I would like the opportunity to speak to the commander here in private."

"If these are the last ones, there is no longer a need for you to be here, turn them over to me and I will escort them back to the enforcer. You may turn over the others, and the ship; as promised."

The larger man's face stiffened his lips compressing into a tight line. "I said in private," he jerked his head in the direction of the Alliance captain. The two escorts moved around the desk taking positions on either side of the man.

The Alliance officer began to nod, chuckling to himself. "Alright Captain, I get the message." He shook his head. "I trust you will let us know should you discover anything relevant?" His voice was hollow with defeat. He turned towards the shuttle bays and left.

The large man turned back to James and Chloe, the grin returning to his face. "Now then, where were we?"

James studied his face, a perfect mask of deception hiding anything that might be useful behind artificial smiles and exaggerated expressions. "I believe you were explaining how you are here to protect me from myself?"

The man clapped his hands together, "Ah yes. You

know Captain, you are an extremely dangerous man."
He waived both of his hands pointing with his index
fingers, "In fact, at the moment, many consider you to
be the most dangerous man in the history of our fair
Alliance."

James inhaled against the surge of adrenaline in his
system. Now was not the time to be losing his head.
"You are going to have to catch me up."

"Come now , let us not play anymore games. I
know it was you who detonated that fusion core over
Ulun'tess." He puffed out his cheeks releasing a huff of
air. "I'm not sure what surprises me more though. Your
willingness to slaughter billions of people, or the fact
that you convinced one of our own to help you do it."

James went to speak, but the man cut him off before
he could. "Don't try to deny it. Unfortunately for you,
there were some survivors from both ships; we have
witnesses."

Chloe stepped up beside James slipping her hand
into his, and pressing herself against his side.

James tried to reassure her, giving her hand a gentle
squeeze. The set up was well planned. They had been
quick and thorough. "What happens now?"

The man's grin grew in size, to match his apparent
ego, spreading his arms in a welcoming gesture.
"Now, that wasn't so hard, was it? We are cooperating
already." He nodded to the escorts. "Join me on my
ship. You are a military man, so I am sure we can come
to... an arrangement." He folded his hands over his lap
and bowed.

*　*　*

It took several hours to reach the Descendant ship

by shuttle, a result of the wide orbit a ship of its scale required. Either the captain was stalling, or he was in a hurry. Using the shuttle meant James and Chloe would have plenty of time to think about their situation. It was an intimidation tactic that James was well acquainted with.

He suspected however, that the captain was trying to make use of a bad situation. They didn't use the jump pod because they couldn't use the jump pod. There had been no sign of the Descendant presence when he and Chloe left the station for dinner. Judging by the amount of time it took them to get to the station, that meant they could not have been in orbit very long. Also, if the men they had questioned this afternoon could be trusted, getting here today already put them significantly ahead of schedule.

Even skilled navigators would need several hours or more to establish a tether for their jump pad. They had dropped out of hyperspace only to realize their informants had been discovered. The captain rushed to the station with as many men as he could find to lock it down and secure it. Which explained the lack of an Alliance presence as well.

The station contacted the most local citadel-class ship as soon as the Descendants started throwing their weight around. The quickest response the Alliance could throw together was a single ranking officer.

For all his posturing, the Descendant Captain was desperate. An idea started to form in James's mind. Maybe there was still a way out of this.

The battle cruiser loomed into view outside the shuttle windows as they approached on a deep orbit. The ship wrapped around its central core like the jaws of a great beast swallowing a planet, dwarfing the wyvern-class escorts which orbited on the edge of its gravity well.

The shuttle turned, orienting itself with the downward direction of the ship's gravitational pull, facing the glass canopy out towards the stars, the ship's hull stretching out underneath them like the surface of a small comet.

Slowly the shuttle descended into the landing bay. A steady vibration which was barely audible, indicated the presence of the bay's landing mechanism taking over for the pilot and guiding the shuttle into place.

The shuttle door opened into a ramp, and two new Descendant soldiers boarded. "Captain," the second soldier spread his arms in a welcoming gesture and bowed to James. "We have been expecting you. Please, come this way."

James took Chloe's hand squeezing it comfortingly. They followed the guard, while the other soldier took up the rear. Neither of the men appeared armed, though James suspected each had at least one stunblade.

The shuttle bay let out into a round corridor twenty feet in diameter. The walls were made of curved marble, with dark almost black wood floors. Bands of intricately woven glass ran along the center of each wall, which were not only visually appealing but also muted the surfaces, reducing the amount of echo in the cavernous space.

Two guards joined them in the hallway. Both armed with rifles. From the looks of it, dual function sting guns with thirty-two rounds of rail ammunition. The message was clear: they were prisoners, this was not a negotiation, and while they did not want to use lethal force, they would not hesitate to do so.

Seph

Waiting to reveal the guard until after they reached the corridor gave James another insight into the captain's state of mind. It was designed as an intimidation ploy. Designed to turn a false sense of security into panic.

To James, however, it indicated that the Descendant Captain was suffering from a lack of confidence. If he truly felt that he was in control of the situation, he would not need to use such tactics. He was showing off. Also, it indicated the possibility that not everyone on the ship knew what was going on, it avoided parading James and Chloe in front of crew members who might start rumors. Rumors which could make it back to the Alliance.

A smile tugged on his lips, quickly he clenched the back of his jaw, and flexed his cheek muscles.

Chloe clenched his hand pressing herself close to him. "Do you have a plan?" She whispered.

James wrapped his arm around her hand and pulled her against himself. "Everything is going to be fine. Be patient and do what you have been told, we can get through this together."

He intentionally kept his voice loud enough to be overheard, and hoped Chloe would pick up on the message intended. And put to rest any fears the guards might have of a conspiracy forming.

Their escort led them through a set of double glass doors, leading to an open room. A mirror, which filled the entire wall, hung on the far side, opposite the door. To the left was a monitor, running the length of the room. Across from that, the room opened up into a private courtyard garden. The path appeared to be intricately carved white gold hovering less than an inch over the groomed ground. The curved walls emulated the sky, tracking the passage of time.

The large descendant officer rose from a lavender sofa as they entered, arms spread almost as wide as his smile. He bowed gesturing to the sofa across the glass and white gold coffee table. "Captain, it is good to see you again. You took longer than I expected, I hope my men didn't give you any trouble."

"None at all." James kept his face rigid, refusing to return the bow.

"Right." The large man said, his eyes drew back into themselves, almost imperceptibly. "Well then," he motioned to the couch again, "James, have a seat. We have much to discuss." He gave a quick nod to two of the soldiers.

Each of them grabbed one of Chloe's arms and began to pull her away.

"James!" her voice was high and cracked, as if there hadn't been enough air to form the word.

James swiped his hand from his belt line outward, finger parallel to the floor in a clear 'cease' command. "She stays or we have nothing to discuss."

The large man rolled his head and shoulder into an exaggerated come over here motion. "Of course, Chloe can stay. I was just about to protest myself." He sat down tugging on his uniform jacket at the waist. "I wouldn't want you to be so preoccupied with worrying about her well-being that we're unable to make our arrangement." He winked, then grinned with the same side of his face. "Now then, would you please have a seat? I would hate for you to think we had been anything if not hospitable."

James allowed Chloe to sit down first, he sat beside her placing his hand protectively on her knee .

"You there," the Descendant Captain pointed at one

of the escorts, "bring us some drinks. Would you like anything specific, either of you?" He paused looking between them. "No? Well then tea for all of us, and bring the sugar and cream so our guests can serve themselves."

He returned his gaze to James. "Now then, shall we begin?"

"I am afraid you have me at a disadvantage, Captain, you seem to know a great deal about me. But, I know almost nothing about you."

The man smiled, accepting a teacup as it was presented to him. "Well then," he sipped the drink. He smacked his lips and exhaled, setting the cup on the glass table. "A gesture of good faith. I," he pressed his finger against his chest, "am Captain Darith of Vyanna's High Navy," he motioned at their surroundings, "and this is the Dressick." He let the last syllable of the name drift in the air as if the mere mention of it should inspire awe.

He took another sip of his tea. "Now then James, tell me, where is the traitor who helped you overthrow the Vyrant?"

James leaned forward, elbows rested on his knees. So, Gillian had somehow evaded them. James set his jaw focusing on Darith's pupils. "First, I need to know what is in it for me, you don't expect me to simply turn him over," James sat back, placing his hand firmly over Chloe's forearm, and pressing it into her lap, "without any protection. Do you?"

Darith chuckled as he sipped his tea. "You are a clever one C, I had been warned you were quick, but I had my doubts. Seems you are every bit as impressive as they say."

He set the cup down and placed one fist on his hip

while shaking a finger at James. "I'll tell you what, you turn the traitor over to me, and I'll make sure you are pardoned of all crimes, Core, I might even give you a position as an officer on this ship."

"And Chloe?" James tightened his grip on her wrist.

Darith grinned sipping his tea. "What about her?"

James took a spoonful of sugar and tapped it into his cup. "I want her released. Immediately." He added a touch of cream and began to stir, "Once I know she is safe, we can talk."

The large man's face fell into a tight line, He gave a direct nod to the escorts. "Take the girl some place more… private, the commander and I have some things to discuss."

The guards grabbed Chloe from behind, lifting her over the back of the couch. "James, don't let them do this!" She screamed, struggling against them.

James took a sip of his tea, "Hurt her and I don't talk." He said, bleaching his voice of any signs of emotion.

Darith lounged back in his chair, his grin exposing his teeth from ear to ear. "A long as you cooperate, Chloe will be just fine."

* * *

Chloe continued struggling until after the glass doors clicked shut. She had resigned herself to being carried out of the room, there was not much that could be done about it at this point. But something instinctive told her she needed to make a show of trying. Judging by the hot tears on her cheeks she had been successful.

She took a deep breath and more calmly allowed

the guards to lead her down the hallway. James and Darith played some complex game she could not even pretend to understand. She had tried to keep up with the conversation, pick up on the subtle hints and clues that would give away the enemy's weakness.

James was always able to extract the information he needed as if the walls themselves talked to him. "Knowledge is your most powerful weapon." He had repeated that to her almost every day for the last two weeks, and now, she couldn't make sense of it.

She took another deep breath in through her nose, and exhaled out her mouth. James had a plan, she had to trust that.

Her escorts continued to hold her arms until they had boarded a lift, or was it a tram? It was elliptical with no clear front or back. The domed ceiling was plated with silver and etched with colored glass, in what appeared to be a map of the galaxy, that seemed to whisper a half remembered melody in the back of her mind. The vessel moved around the perimeter of the ship, creating a sensation not unlike falling uphill.

The soldiers must have decided she had given up on escape, because they relaxed, releasing her arms and taking up a position opposite her on the car. At the moment though, she had nowhere to go, and besides, even if she tried to run now, both men still kept their guns ready. Not pointed at her per se, but she knew from the simulations that if she tried something now either one of them would have plenty of time to shoot her.

Something cold and hard pressed into the palm of her hand. Almost as if it had simply appeared there. The shape felt somehow familiar. She used the heel of her palm wrapped in the sleeve of James's jacket to wipe a tear off her cheek. She let her hand fall into her lap trying to get a good look at the object.

Her heart began beating faster, as if Vyanna herself had granted her a miracle, a small stunblade had materialized out of thin air. No Vyanna was their god, maybe some other god then? It didn't matter, whoever it was, she was grateful.

The lift coasted to a stop, then began to ascend. It was only a moment before it stopped again and the doors clicked, and opened with a hiss.

One of the guards waved the tip of his gun at her. "Com'on, it's not much further."

Chloe stood slowly keeping her hands folded in her lap. A plan all her own was starting to form in her mind, she only needed to wait for the right opportunity.

This corridor looked identical to the last, doors carved from empress wood appeared every thirty feet or so, reminding her of the crew decks on the Vyrant. She felt a twinge of déjà vu as they approached the end of the hallway. Now, in the proper lighting, she could see the grandeur Gillian's door had been meant to display.

As they approached the door, the guard to her right broke from formation, stepping towards the control panel.

With her next step, Chloe planted her left foot putting her body in line with the remaining soldier. She brought her right leg across her new line of direction. In a single motion stepping out in front of the soldier, she jabbed the stunblade into his left arm just below the shoulder.

"Hey!" The second soldier turned to level his gun.

The first guard's body went stiff. She grabbed his

gun with her free hand and took another quick step. Rotating around on the momentum of her attack, and positioning the body between her and the remaining guard.

There was a loud cracking sound as the soldier fired, in the same moment Chloe kicked the falling body of the unconscious guard. The force yanked the gun from his hand and placed him in front of the energy blast.

The guard's body twisted back again before collapsing on the ground.

Chloe pulled the trigger. A burst of light erupted from her rifle as the scent of the oxidizing atmosphere filled her nose.

Chloe inhaled, drawing in breath against the pounding in her chest. Her whole body was shaking from the surge of adrenaline.

The rifle clattered on the floor as she tried to rub feeling back into her arms. She took a deep breath focusing her mind. She needed to think clearly now. They had been through simulations like this several dozen times in the last few weeks. What she needed now was information.

She searched the unconscious soldiers, but found nothing useful. She had to get out of the hallway. She keyed the control panel and the door clicked then swung open. She dragged the bodies into the state room.

Familiar lavender tapestries and mirrors greeted her in an almost identical reproduction of Gillian's room from the Vyrant. She avoided looking directly at them, afraid she might get sucked in and forget herself the way she had on Dramia.

She began searching through drawers in the desk until she found a datapad. Darith must not have been concerned about others gaining access to the device, and it wasn't difficult for her to find a map of the ship.

The crew areas were contained to the north hemisphere of the ship, with most of the engineering and utility sections on the smaller south side. Huge fleet hangers ran along both the port and starboard sides, lined with tactical and weapons stations. Inset up a level were the five shuttle hangers. Two on each side and one at the stern.

The atrium lounge Darith had taken them to appeared to be on the same level as all five docks. The lift they had taken to the state room, traveled north from the corridor parallel to the core until it had reached the officers' decks running the length of the northernmost point. From there they had then traveled upwards to the highest deck.

It would not do her a lot of good to go back there now, she would only be recaptured. Chloe swiped her fingers across the screen, bringing the map in a layer towards the core. Directly below the officers' section was the crew and civilian areas. There was an armory on each side, directly in from the fleet bays. Inside of that were the quarters and living areas for military personnel. Placing the civilian living areas at the ship's most central point above the core room. The bridge sat on a level between the civilian area and the officer decks.

One of the armories was tempting, but even fully armed she would not make it very far on her own. And carrying a weapon just served to make her stick out more. If she could get to the civilian sections she would be fine the way she was, but first she would have to get down there. And once there, there was not a lot she could do for the others. She would need a disguise to get around the military sections.

Neither of the uniforms her escorts wore would fit her, and the armory was too risky. If she could find the Shade and make it on board however; she still had the uniform she had taken from the Vyrant.

The Shade was significantly larger than any of the small shuttles, it was unlikely for it to be held in one of those bays, which left the fleet hangers. She checked the log for the starboard hanger first. Their shuttle had come in on the port side, if this had been one of James's strategies, he would have taken the precaution of keeping them as far away from the ship as possible. There was no indication that the Shade was on the starboard side, though several of the pads looked like they had been doubled up.

She checked the port side hanger. A cluster of pads showed as "temporarily reassigned," the command log indicated a ship having been brought in for holding just under three hours earlier.

It was not a lot to go on, but it was the best clue she had. Now she needed a plan to get herself there. She looked at the map of her section, studying the corridors. She tried for a second to look at the maintenance tunnels, but they were complicated, and navigating them would be far too difficult.

The officers' dining area caught her eye. The dining areas connected to each other by a shared lift running along the radius line towards the fusion core. If this ship ran on a similar schedule to the one Travis used, it would be late for anyone to still be eating dinner, and too early for the night shift to be going to lunch. So, those areas should be relatively vacant.

She pulled up the maintenance map again. There was a tunnel right outside of the state room which led straight to the officers' kitchen. It ran between this corridor, and the one beneath, with a junction coming up behind the prep area to a vent in the staff locker room.

"Prefect." She memorized the junction code, then shut down the datapad before putting it in the pocket of James's jacket.

She took both of the soldiers' communication devices, sticking one behind her ear. It made a quiet sound somewhere between a chirp and a beep when it activated. At the moment the line was silent. She hopped that meant no one was missing her yet.

The hatch to the maintenance tunnel was difficult to find. It had been hidden by a projection barrier which blended it with the wall. By feeling along the stone, she theorized she might be able to find it. The texture changed from marble to metal. Chloe pressed on the hidden plate and the illusion vanished. With a click the hatch pushed back, then slid open with a hiss.

Chloe tied the skirt of her dress up over her knees, then climbed down the ladder into the tunnel.

The light came on automatically. It was just barely large enough for a regular-sized person to stand in, and as wide as the corridor above. The air was heavier here, the fresh quality replaced by the scents of dust and metal. She hoped the automated life support would not give away her escape.

The echo of her footsteps chased her heartbeat. She paused, inhaling through her nose and counting to five before exhaling. Focus; that's what she needed now. She began walking again, pushing the echo out of her mind. She focused only on the junction number she was looking for, worried that if she stopped counting them she would lose track and miss it.

Seph

She began to wonder if she had misremembered, and pulled out the datapad to check when she saw it almost directly in front of her. She took another deep breath trying to quiet the tingling under her skin.

The ladder led upwards about fifteen feet, then came to an end. A small crawl space came off the side near the top, which ran along a life support conduit.

Chloe squeezed into the space, crawling with her elbows until she came alongside the vent assembly. Her heart stopped, like time freezing in the moment a glass slips out of your hand and it is too late to catch it.

To access the locker room from here, she would need to remove the assembly from the life support, which would surely trigger an alarm. "Okay Chloe, just think about this. What would James do?"

She exhaled, "Maintenance mode, it must have a maintenance mode." She started looking for an access panel. She pressed on a thin metal plate which slid open and projected a holo-interface.

"Right." She scrolled through the menu of technical terms, most of which meant nothing to her, until she found it. She pressed the glowing indicator. The menu changed to display a list of procedures.

Chloe let out a sigh, letting her head drop to rest in her arms. Hot tears pooled on her skin.

She wiped her eyes. "You can do this." She whispered to herself scrolling through the list. Her heart jumped, almost skipping a beat when she found the option, "Assembly head removal."

The display vanished and the cover plate slid back into place. There was a click and the whole assembly cover swung upwards, revealing the manual release clips. She turned all eight into the open position.

There was a hiss, and the assembly separated

a fraction of an inch from the life support duct.
Chloe grabbed the inside edge and pulled it free.
The assembly slid out on its glide track, creating an
opening barely big enough for her to squeeze herself
through.

She pulled out the stunblade, turned it off, and used
it to pry open the vent guard.

Cursing her choice to wear a dress, she pulled
herself up against the assembly. Propping herself on
top of it and using the extra space, it gained her to
twist her body so she could drop down legs first.

She fell to the floor, her legs buckling out from
underneath her. She caught herself with her forearms,
and rolled onto her back. She laid there, breathing in
the fresh air. Sweat and dust caked on her skin.

A small single occupancy bathroom facility
attached to the locker room. A shower was not ideal, it
would be obvious she had recently washed, but better
than the grime of the maintenance tunnel.

Rolling to her stomach, she pushed herself up on
her knees. The world was still spinning a little from the
fall; it took a moment to regain her bearings.

Once on her feet, she began looking for a spare
kitchen uniform. Dark gray pants and a lavender coat,
designed to be worn over more civilian clothing. Her
dress would need to be discarded, but she had been
expecting that. James's jacket would be harder to give
up.

She gathered up the uniform parts and carried them
into the bath area. It wasn't a proper shower, like she
had become accustomed to on the Shade. This type of
shower cleaned using ultraviolet, and ultrasonic waves
calibrated to remove bacteria and other particulates.

In hindsight, she wasn't surprised; proper showers

with running water were somewhat of a luxury, which encouraged long soaking. This was a professional setting, and the more efficient, more effective UVUS system made sense. Which was good for her, it would not be so obvious she had just washed.

She removed the datapad and stunblade from the jacket, setting them on the counter next to the stolen uniform. She started to take off the jacket, remembering the way it had warmed her body after dancing in the rain.

She paused. Why had she not thought about this sooner? The jacket must be made with nanotech. She had never used it before, but it was certainly a hot topic of conversation among the other children. Every one of them had dreamed of getting their hands on some of the stuff. Nanotech could solve any problem; it made you immortal.

Chloe doubted it was everything her and the other children believed it to be. But now that she knew what it was, maybe she could make use of it. Feeling the inside of the sleeve where the stunblade had appeared, she found the small ridge, she slid the small knife against it and it clicked into place.

A yellow ring appeared on the underside of the arm. She took a slow breath. That had been easy enough. She swiped two fingers along the length of her arm. The fabric shimmered, a control panel dissolved into the fabric, not unlike watching a drop of die falling into a cup of water.

Using the interface felt something like running your fingers through microscopic grains of sand laced with static electricity. It moved like a thick liquid around her fingers.

The first menu was straightforward, with easy

to read labels. The inventory tag indicated that in addition to the sleeve clip which hid the stunblade, there was one in the pocket she had been using to store the datapad, and one in a pocket hidden in the chest. James had all except the sleeve clip disabled at the moment.

Most of the other menus were far more complicated than Chloe was ready to deal with. Color options had 5 sliding scales, none of which gave any indication of what they did, and the fit adjustment was not any more user-friendly.

Several modes presented themselves. In moisture collection, there were charge modes for solar collection, thermal collection, charge collection, and auto variable.

Outside of the energy collection modes it had an inert, an active defense, and… a clone?

Chloe swiped her finger across the clone selection. The interface vanished, like a million glowing bugs flying off into the night.

Nothing happened. Maybe it needed some kind of catalyst? It's not like she had told it anything to 'clone' yet.

She laid the jacket on top of the uniform coat she had stolen, careful to line up the seams and edges..

Nothing happened.

"Strange," she mumbled to herself. It had been worth a try though.

She peeled the remainder of her clothing off her sweat-drenched body, the cool air feeling amazing against her bare skin. Climbing in the body cleanser, she flipped the switch. An odd tingling sensation scattered across the surface of her skin, like laying in the sun after getting soaking wet.

Seph

The cleansing process lasted exactly two and a half minutes, and left her skin matte and clingy, like a balloon that's been rubbed on carpet.

She stepped out of the cleanser, turning back to the desk where she left the new outfit. James's jacket was gone.

Chloe rifled through the clothing, even checking under her discarded dress. She left them together, hadn't she?

She paused, carefully lifting the lavender chef's uniform from the counter. It tingled under her fingers.

She turned over the sleeve of the right arm. The dull yellow indicator stared back at her. No, it wasn't James's jacket that had disappeared, it was the chef's coat that was missing. The nanotech jacket had become an almost perfect replica.

Shaking herself from the new-found wonder, she quickly slid herself into the outfit. Taking out the datapad, she pulled up the kitchen staff roster. She needed a name to throw around that would get people's attention, but not draw too much suspicion. And someone who would not be working in this kitchen.

The Sue Chef for the officers' mess had just gotten off duty. He would likely have some authority over the cooks in the main mess, but would not be as intimidating as the executive chef, so she would still be able to keep her head low.

Stashing her discarded dress and shawl into laundry, she exited the locker room and made her way to the staff lift. Only a few people worked in the officers' kitchen, all too busy with their cleaning tasks to give her more than a passing glance.

It was only a few seconds before the lift let her off

again in the back of the main kitchen. She hesitated, then stepped onto the prep floor.

A tall man across the room looked up from something he had been staring at on the prep station in front of him, it appeared to be a note of some sort. His hair was a mess, fatigue obvious under his eyes where bags had begun to form.

"Can I help you?" His tone was sharp, lacking patience.

Chloe inhaled, and prayed to anyone who would listen that this would work. "Um, well, I'm new upstairs." She stammered.

The man raised an eyebrow. "And?" it was more a demand then a question.

"Well, Christoph," she used the Sue Chef's name, "said I needed to come down here and get some practice before I clocked out."

"Did he now?" He picked up the note card and moved around the table walking toward her. "Why would he do something like that?"

Chloe shrugged, averting her eyes. "Something about… Not being a team player," she hoped her fear of getting caught was coming across as embarrassment.

"Zaeith's prison." He muttered. "Christoph would do something like that." He waved the note card pointing it at her. "You know I taught him everything he knows, and what do I get for it?" He sighed exasperated. "He passes me his rejects and expects me to do all the work for him."

Chloe tucked her head down trying to look small. "I'm sorry, I am just trying to do what I was told."

The Chef glanced over and his features softened, clearly he did not have the energy to be mad, and if she was lucky, maybe he even pitied her.

"Here take this, it's tomorrow's menu for the buffet, memorize it and report back to me." He held out the note card.

"Right." Chloe said hesitating before, reaching for the card.

The Chef handed it to her and walked off to his office, a cloud of gloom following behind him. Chloe hoped he was not going to call Christoph to complain about passing off his work to him.

She became aware of the other eyes staring at her, some with amusement, other jealousy, and still others who did seem to feel sorry for her. Even if it was just their own gratitude for not being in her position.

She ducked her head, again, not making eye contact she made her way across the room, disappearing into the mess hall. It was mostly empty, service had ended, and only those who were looking for a late snack, or had missed out on their meal were still toiling around. She hoped the kitchen staff would think she was looking for a chair to sit in while she studied, and the crew members here would think she was getting off her shift.

Best case scenario, she had one hour to report in, or set off an alarm. That was if the guards she left upstairs didn't wake up and report her, or someone didn't find her dress in the laundry.

She stepped into the corridor inhaling to calm her nerves.

"Attention all units." A voice chimed over the intercom system. "Report to your command center immediately. Repeat, all military personnel are to report for duty."

Chapter 20

Meghnah sat back against the wall, knees tucked up against her chest on the prison bed. She was attempting to look shy, vulnerable, the way she imagined Chloe might look about now.

The cell floor had fallen silent. The guards left almost an hour ago. The air was clean, too clean, like freshly washed laundry scented with exotic flowers. A smell not at all fitting for a detention block.

This whole place was different from any prison she had ever been in before. For one, her cell used a force field in place of bars. Something people in the outer colonies couldn't afford to waste energy on. And while the gray stone which made up the walls of the corridor might have been the plainest of the stones used onboard, the elaborate carvings depicting images of battles fought, and victories won dispelled any delusions of humility they otherwise might have induced.

Seph

She had not been prepared for the efficiency with which the Descendants had captured them. She had been running the calculation to get from Dramia to Atlione when the drake had appeared in high orbit. Space was a big place, but still, it was difficult to hide something that displaced as much of it as this battlecruiser did.

She tried to communicate it to the rest of the crew, to warn them, but it had been too late. By the time the Dressick arrived, they had already jammed all communication signals on the station, which meant they already had someone there ahead of time.

It really shouldn't have been a surprise, followers of the faith were everywhere. The religion had even begun to spread its plague in the outer colonies, setting up schools and hospitals, bringing with them technologies that were like magic, promising enlightenment and freedom from oppression.

They promised to bring the people of the Coalition out of obscurity and raise them to stand as equals in the Alliance. Recently, they had even twisted Vhast back on itself, claiming that The Dark One had been sent by Vyanna to prepare them to receive the full truth of her doctrine.

A chill ran down Meghnah's spine at the thought of it. Hypocrites, that's what they were, every single one of them. Maybe if they followed their own teachings it wouldn't be so bad. The connections were almost plausible. The Dark One had instilled in his followers the ideals of harmony. He taught that the path to enlightenment was achieved through perfect balance within oneself.

The Descendants taught that the enlightenment was achieved through total peace. While peace and harmony might not sound that different, if the Descendants wanted peace, they would not be populating the galaxy with warships.

After the Dressick had appeared, she still had time to find the crew that had been on board the station. But all outgoing traffic had been blocked. No one was allowed on the ion lift, and jump pod activity was brought to a halt, even shuttles were grounded.

Gillian, Nevarian, Chloe and James were all still down on the planet, which, unless they decided to come home early, was a much safer place to be. Scot claimed to have communicated to the Captain via a subspace link, though he hadn't offered any details before retreating to the engine room, where he promptly shut himself off.

The soldiers arrived, accompanied by an officer from the Alliance, and an arrest warrant. They could have ran, but that would make them fugitives, and it meant abandoning the others.

Meghnah couldn't help it, she laughed a little, the tiniest hint of a smile pulling at her lips. There had been a time when she wouldn't have given it a second thought. She had abandoned many crews over the years to save her own neck.

But the Shade was different; it wasn't just a ship, it was a home. So she had surrendered along with the others. Willingly turned herself in, trusting her fate to a system that had failed her and her people time and time again. Today had not been any different. Once they had been taken into custody, the Descendant Captain made it very clear who was in charge to the Alliance officer, and that justice was not on the agenda.

Once on board the warship they had begun the interrogations. Not once did they ask if they were associated with any of the known pirate bands; she was never asked when was the last time she was at Ulun'tess. They didn't care about any of the pretenses under which they had been arrested. All they wanted to know was where they could find Gillian Maylis.

She had tried to act too terrified to answer, tried to pretend she was a poor Drak'or stowaway lost in a big galaxy she didn't understand.

It hadn't worked, the interrogator knew too much, too much about the Shade, and too much about her. The soldiers who had been escorting her around the ship however did not seem to be so well-informed. They treated her like a porcelain doll, one wrong glance away from erupting into tears.

She didn't like playing weak, it went against everything in her nature. But sometimes, when backed into a corner, the best option left was to play dead.

Footsteps echoed down the corridor. She pulled her knees closer to her chest, forcing tears back into her eyes.

The low hum of the force field stopped, and the air pressure changed as her cell opened to the corridor.

"Hey now, nobody is going to hurt you."

The soldier stepped into the room using the softest voice he could manage, he placed a hand on her shoulder patting her gently. For a moment she considered breaking his arm, overpowering him here and making a run for it. She would have nowhere to go though, and she would be recaptured before she even made it off this deck.

"We just have a few more questions we want to ask you." The man was kneeling now, placing himself at eye level with her. She fought down the urge to reward his carelessness. She would get her chance soon enough.

He took her hand, handling her as if he pressed too hard she might break. "Come on, this will all be over soon."

Meghnah slid herself off the bed, wrapping her arms across her chest and gripping her sides. She wiped tears from her eyes nodding. " Okay," she let her voice crack.

The guard led her into the corridor, only the echo of their footsteps for company. He made no move to restrain her, he hardly even checked over his shoulder to make sure she was still following him.

When they arrived at the lift, he allowed her to enter first, punching in his authorization code without taking any precautions to guard it. Meghnah forced herself not to laugh. The Descendants might have superior technology, but superior soldiers they were not. She rubbed at imagined tears, memorizing the code for future use.

The lift opened back to one of the pristine marble tubes which served as this ship's predominant corridors. Other crew members ignored them as they made their way to the office where she had been interrogated once before.

The wooden door slid open as they approached and her escort motioned for her to enter first. The room was exactly as she remembered. Holographic windows to an imaginary outside world on the walls, a larger wooden desk at its center with a single datapad.

The Drak'or officer in her flawless Descendant uniform stared, scrutinizing her with a gaze that could have competed with the Captain's.

"Why is she out of her restraints?" She demanded as Meghnah stepped into the door.

Seph

The blood drained from the soldier's face. "I didn't think she needed them. Look at her, there is no way she is dangerous."

The officer rose from her desk tossing a pair of cuffs at the guard. "I don't care what you think. I expect you to follow protocol."

"Yes Ma'am." He hesitated, pulling Meghnah's hands behind her back and engaging the magnetic restraints around her wrists.

"Now stand guard outside the door," the officer said sitting down again.

The escort left and the door slid closed. The officer pressed something on the bottom of her desk and there was a click as the door's lock engaged.

"Sit." She ordered, not breaking her gaze from Meghnah.

Meghnah did as she was told, edging around the chair on her side of the desk.

"Now then. Are you ready to talk?"

"I already told you I don't know anything." Meghnah spat, all traces of the pathetic girl from the cell vanishing, that facade wouldn't do her any good here.

The interrogator let out a sigh and activated the data pad. An image of Chloe and James being escorted by Descendant soldiers appeared on the screen. "It is no use fighting us anymore, we have the rest of your crew, all we need now is the traitor. Give him up and it will make your life a lot easier."

Meghnah leaned forward in her chair, wiggling her hands underneath her body as much as the restraints would allow. "Look, if you think there is that much loyalty on that ship you have another thing coming. Trust me, if I knew anything I would tell you."

The interrogator brushed back a strand of bright red hair that had fallen out of her bun, leaning over the desk attempting to intimidate Meghnah with her gaze. "That does appear to be your track record, miss…" she spun the data pad around and entered something, "Te'kell, is it?"

Meghnah flinched at her last name. It had been years since she had heard it spoken aloud, longer still since she had last used it.

The women grinned. "You were all but nonexistent until about two years ago." She continued, scrolling through the datapad. "Something must have happened to bring you out of the shadows. If it isn't loyalty, what is it?"

Meghnah inhaled slowly, then exhaled. "Light and darkness reflect in us your providence." She thought the ancient chant in her mind, bracing against the pain. She twisted her torso to the side, using the weight of her body against the chair as leverage, her left shoulder pulled out of its socket. "The pay was good, and until now, we had never been caught."

The officer watched her, a blank expression masking her face. "What are you doing?"

She brought her legs up, placing her feet against the underside of the desk. "What does it look like?"

The Descendants' eyes widened but it was too late, Meghnah straightened her body, kicking out with both legs. The heavy desk rolled backwards pinning the officer behind it against the floor. Meghnah hit hard as her own chair fell, landing with her back to the ground, she pulled her hands underneath her, and rolled off the chair. Pain shot through her arm, reminding her of the dislocated joint.

"Help!" The women screamed.

Seph

Meghnah jumped to her feet, it took the guard a second to override the lock which gave her time to get into position, and pop her shoulder back into place. There was a click, and the door slid open.

"What's going on in here?"

Meghnah clasped her hands together, she stepped in front of him, bracing herself, she swung her arms hitting him with the heavy restraints across the temple. The man spun as he fell, flying several feet from the force of the impact.

He struggled to stand, Meghnah lunged through the air, landing on top of him, she pressed him against the floor, then wrapping one arm around his neck and leaning back squeezed his windpipe until he went limp.

She rolled off him springing to her feet as the officer managed to extract herself from underneath the desk.

"You will never get off this ship alive!"

Meghnah exhaled the remainder of her breath, then inhaled slowly, leveling her gaze at the women she turned her shoulder to her like the blade of a knife. "I think I will take my chances."

The interrogator kicked high. Calmly, Meghnah brought her forward leg back shifting her body out of the kick's range. It fell short by less than two inches, but left her attacker horribly off balance. Meghnah grabbed the Descendant woman's ankle and twisted hard, there was a loud snap and the officer cried out in pain, her body contorted as bone and ligaments snapped under the pressure. Meghnah released her foot as she fell to the floor.

Searching the guard's body, she found the controller for her restraints and released the cuffs. The officer attempted to use the desk to pull herself to her feet, but was unable to put any weight on her broken ankle and collapsed again.

Removing the guard's stunblade, Meghnah stood over her.

The woman froze, panting from the exertion, "What are you going to do now?"

"Well," she said, kneeling down beside her. "If this is going to work, I will need your uniform." She pressed the blunt side of the blade against the woman's collarbone, and activated it. Her muscles went stiff before falling limp.

Meghnah pushed the desk upright, then found the datapad. Fortunately it was still open, it didn't take her long to find the layout for the ship.

She was somewhere near the back, it was difficult to tell exactly where, but it appeared to be near the equatorial layer, behind the military section on the starboard side. The detention block appeared to be one level below her current location.

It didn't make sense to attempt to free the others yet. For one it was predictable, and there was no guarantee that she would be able to set them free once she got there. Without weapons, each new person was a liability.

One of the armories would be the first priority. With the new uniform she could sneak in alright, she might even be able to make it before anyone noticed she was missing. But if someone found this room her disguise would be useless.

Meghnah undid the officer's jacket, pulling it on over the Descendant undershirt she was already wearing, then slid herself into the uniform pants. She would need a diversion, something to keep suspicion off the interrogator.

Seph

Carefully she returned to the unconscious guard; for good measure, she placed the stunblade against his spine and gave him a quick zap. His body jumped from the shock. She removed the communicator from behind his ear. It stung for a second as its tiny spikes sank into her skin. Taking the officers comm, she dropped it into her pocket.

The comlink chimed as she activated it. "The prisoner has escaped, she overpowered me during my interrogation, she is to be considered armed and dangerous, current location is unknown."

Chatter erupted on the speaker. After a minute it calmed down, a distinct voice could be heard. "Lieutenant, why are you not on your own comm?"

Meghnah grinned, "The prisoner stole it from me, assume she is monitoring our communications."

"Understood." The voice cut out.

The shipwide intercom system chimed. "Attention all units. Report to your command center immediately. Repeat, all military personnel are to report for duty."

Stepping into the corridor Meghnah locked the door, then slipped the extra com unit into the pocket of a passing soldier. That ought to keep everybody busy for a while. At least it gave her a reason to go to the armory without suspicion, and to check the detention cells.

It took longer than she expected to reach the armory. It was difficult to comprehend the immense size of the ship, even things right next to each other had more hallway between them than the Shade had in its entirety. She found herself continuously rechecking her position, worried she had missed it somehow, her sense of space being overwhelmed by the scope of everything around her.

She had opted not to take the tram, to avoid leaving a trail to follow; now she wondered if that had been a good idea. Soldiers arrived from all over the ship, reporting for duty, and needing to change into their uniforms, before receiving orders.

Meghnah froze as she entered the enormous room, what had she been expecting? She couldn't remember anymore. The room was separated into a grid of locker blocks, each section appeared to be designed for units of thirty or so soldiers. She didn't bother to count how many there were in total. Lifts could be seen along either wall, indicating that this may not even be the sections only floor.

Every surface was decorated glass, white gold, or carved from empress wood. A long desk ran the length of the back wall, droids dispensed weapons to soldiers as they checked in, the robots reminded her somewhat of Scot, except these were plated in polished silver.

A chill ran down her spine as the blood drained from her cheeks. So far removed was it from the sanctuaries of her childhood, no incense to calm the soul, no priest to guide your preparation. This was cold, heartless, like a wind-driven wave preparing to devour everything in its path.

"Are you lost, lieutenant?" A harsh voice interrupted her thoughts.

Meghnah turned to see a fingalin man. How long had he been watching her? His face betrayed little emotion; his eyes, hard like polished river stones, scrutinized her, judging her every move.

"Yes." She nodded quickly, she had to think fast, she hoped this uniform did not give away too much about its proper owner. "I just transferred here, I can't seem to remember where my locker is."

Seph

The man's lips twitched in a slight curl at the edges, a hint of amusement creeping into his voice. "A lieutenant who can't find her own locker?"

Meghnah bowed her head, breaking eye contact. "The promotion came with the transfer, I have never served on a ship this size before."

She could feel his gaze soften, "What unit are you with?"

"Well…" she hesitated.

The Fingalin held out his hand, "Let me see your badge."

Panic began to build in her chest, did she even have a badge? She felt her pockets, there was a single card in the inside pocket over her left breast. Mustering what confidence she could she handed it to him, and prayed to every deity she knew it was what he was looking for.

He plucked it from her hand with more force than she had been expecting, then glanced at it. "'Lieutenant Dessika Ar'eack, unit A13-0B.' You are on the wrong floor." He handed her the card. "Try not to forget it next time, Lieutenant."

She slid the card back into her pocket, not taking the time to look at it herself. "I'm sorry." She bowed. "I guess the suddenness of the call has me a little disoriented."

"Right, don't let it happen again," he extended his left arm pointing towards the lifts. "Take the second lift, three floors up. It shouldn't be too hard to find after that, look for the unit plates at each block."

Meghnah bowed again, then turned on her heels, walking in the direction indicated. She exhaled, releasing a breath she hadn't realized she had been holding. That had been too close, every nerve in her body felt hot with electricity. She was not very good at subterfuge. She preferred a more direct approach. While that might get her out, it would not do any good for the others…

Once she was on the proper floor, it was not too difficult to find the locker reserved for Lieutenant Dessika Ar'eack, now that she knew her designation number. The units were organized first by floor, A in her case. She walked down the columns until she found section 13, from there it was easy to locate row 0B.

As she approached she saw several other soldiers in the block, soldiers who would without question be able to recognize Lieutenant Ar'eack, so she kept walking, until she reached the weapons desk. Pulling out her ID, she handed it to one of the droids. The droid scanned it, then disappeared into the next room, returning with a single fingalin sting-rifle.

Meghnah let out a sigh, Dessika would prefer a sting-rifle, it was one of the few weapons she had never trained with. Oh well, if everything went well, she wouldn't need it.

"Your communicator, please." The metallic voice requested in a strange monotone she had not been expecting. If these droids did share a common ancestry with Scot, Scot's personality had obviously been modified to make him more palatable.

"You need to see my comm?" She asked skeptically, trying to not make her search for the rifle's safety mechanism look too obvious. They had handed her a gun! They couldn't have caught on to her right?

"Your communications device must be updated with the new encryption code." The mechanical voice responded with an emotionlessness which was somehow harsher then if it had been angry.

"Oh right," Meghnah removed the device from behind her ear. Her skull felt like it could breathe again with the pressure, and persistent humming removed. Of course they would be re-encrypting everyone's comms, according to her own story the communications network had been compromised. Simply instructing everyone to change channels wouldn't do any good, "the prisoner" would simply switch channels alongside them. This was quick, and effective. A cold tingle started between her shoulder blades; had she been trying to escape, it would have worked.

The robot took the device from her unapologetically, and plugged it into a socket near the heel of its hand. A moment later it handed the unit back to her. "Thank you, Lieutenant," the Droid folded its hands over its waist and bowed.

Meghnah did not bother returning the gesture, making her way back towards the lift, she let out a long sigh. The hardest part should be over, if she could keep this up long enough to find the others, they could get out of this mess.

Chapter 21

Fetu grimaced, he was elbow deep in a wall section where he had removed the paneling to gain access to the phase modulator, which controlled the force field on his cell. The general alert had gone out only a moment ago calling all military personnel to report for duty. Most likely one of the other crew members had broken free and gained access to a comm unit.

They were likely going to add a new encryption code, that was standard procedure whenever the system was compromised. If Meghnah was the one free, the tactic might work; if it were Travis, well, no encryption in the galaxy was going to save them.

Fetu couldn't help but smile at the thought of the eccentric fingalin playing havoc on the ship's computer. If Travis was not already free, that would certainly be Fetu's first stop once he got himself out.

"Hey you get away from that!" Someone shouted from behind him.

Seph

Fetu had considered trying to put the wall panel back together, but he figured he would not have had enough time before a guard showed up, the one shouting at him now confirmed that. Besides, he was so close to finishing now that it wouldn't matter. "Get away from what?"

"From that wall!" His voice indicated he did not appreciate the joke. "Stop doing, whatever it is that you are doing."

"Oh this?" Fetu pulled a small screw off the field modulator and held it out for the guard to see, twisting his body to the side to get a look at him. "I ain't doing nothin, I promise." He dropped the screw to the floor where it made a sharp ping sound which echoed off the ground and stone walls.

"What do you mean you're not up to anything? I just watched you pull that out of there." The soldier was pointing with his rifle as he spoke.

"Oh this?" Fetu adjusted the modulator and the force field's pitch fell into the audible range. Fetu extracted himself from the wall, hopping off the bed he had been using as a stool onto the floor. "I didn't say I wasn't up to something, I said I was not doing nothing. The double negative is an important difference." He wiped his hands on his shirt as he spoke.

The purple haze of the field flashed, becoming solid and vanishing, the only evidence of it the loud hum from its emitters.

The soldier raised his rifle and fired, blue sparks from the fingalin weapon dancing across the force field dissipating near the cell walls. "What in the nine suns did you do?" He dropped his rifle to his hip and reached out to touch the invisible barrier.

"I wouldn't do that." Fetu cautioned.

The man hesitated for a second, then ignoring his advice reached forward, his body seized, muscles growing stiff, eyes opening wide. A moment later he fell unconscious on the floor.

"Why do they always touch it?" Fetu shook his head and returned to dismantling the field emitter.

It only took a minute more to detach the power supply from the emitter control. The hum fizzled out as a few sparks leapt across the opening, then silence.

Fresh air from the corridor rushed into the cell. Fetu leaned his head out, checking to see if the guard had any backup coming. There was no evidence of anyone in the corridor, which likely meant their forces were spread thin looking for whoever had escaped.

Fetu drug the soldier's body into the cell, then searched him. The uniform was too small to be useful, he didn't bother giving it a second glance. Instead, he took the stunblade, ID card, comm unit, and datapad.

The comm unit pinched at the back of his skull, it erupted with chatter, as units reported in from around the ship.

The datapad was locked, capillary recognition was required for access. He took the soldiers hand and rubbed along his thumb a few times, attempting to get enough blood into the appendage to work. He pressed the man's thumb against the sensor. The lock display vanished, replaced by the standard Descendant background, the symbol of the dark moon with its thin crescent on one side overlaid on lavender.

He pulled up the ship's information files, then scrolled until he found the personnel manifest for the detention block. None of the Shade's crew were logged as in custody. Fetu checked the manifest for prisoners by cell number, looking up his own. The cell had been marked as unavailable with no name attached to it. Someone wanted to keep them a secret.

Slinging the sting-rifle over his shoulder, Fetu made his way down the corridor towards the command node for the deck, keeping his eye out for the cells he had noted as being "unavailable." Chatter over the comm indicated they were looking for a female prisoner, from what he could tell, they suspected she would be looking for a way off the ship and most of the search efforts were targeted towards the main hangers.

The detention block itself was not garnering as much attention, with only basic security reporting from either end of a long hallway, which stretched around the lower waist of the ship. Looking at it from the top, it would have appeared as a giant horseshoe, with the command node hanging like a bell from the top of the arch. However, since the floor followed the gravitational line of the core, from the perspective of anyone inside the corridor, it was more like perpetually falling, uphill, on a flat surface.

It was an optical illusion, which while disconcerting, was a constant when working on decks close to the center of a gravity well. And not as bad as the reverse polarized decks on the Shade.

Most of the cells were empty, which was to be expected. Descendant ship prisons were more for show then for functionality. The ability to remove rogue elements from the community was usually enough of a deterrent in Descendant society, to prevent most of them from even showing up. Like Fetu, almost everyone who did not want to follow the rules and play along, just waited for an opportunity and left. The organization was too big, too powerful to fight against. It was better to keep your head low, and not draw unnecessary attention to yourself.

Of course a few people always felt like they had something to prove by making a spectacle of themselves, especially young officers who felt they knew better than their superiors. But that was a cardinal sin among the Descendants; you could never know better, not than your commanding officers, and especially not than the council. They were ordained of God. Their words were written into the very fabric of reality. At least that's how Fetu remembered it.

As he started around the arc in the corridor, movement caught his eye in one of the cells off to the right. A lanky fingalin man with yellow freckles and a human style graphic t-shirt, depicting what Fetu assumed could only be the logo for a band, paced eagerly back and forth.

"I was hoping I would find you before I got too far." Fetu laughed, removing the stolen ID card from his pocket.

"Fetu!?" Travis stopped his pacing, turning to face him, his ears twitching with excitement. "I cannot express how delighted I am to see a friendly face, I trust you are doing well? I mean relatively so, obviously not so well as we have been captured, but you seem to be moving about freely so things are improving, no? In the very least I hope things are about to become considerably more exciting, thus far being a prisoner has been painfully more boring than I had previously anticipated it would be."

"Hacking into the control computer, and stirring things up a little exciting enough for you?" Fetu slid the ID card through the keypad, then entered the force fields shutdown command.

"Indeed that would be, in fact that sounds like a

most entertaining way to dispel the monotony around here." There was a bounce in the fingalin's step as he moved from the cell. "Where might we be heading to cause this commotion?"

Fetu smiled and pointed down the corridor with his gun. "This way, there is a command node just ahead, its computer is a sub system to the primary control network, but I am sure that will not be too much of a problem for you?"

"Not at all my friend." Rocking up on his toes and eyeing the sting-rifle. "Only, you would not happen to have another one of those, would you?" he asked pointing.

Fetu removed the stunblade from where he had stuck it in his belt and handed it to Travis. "Sorry, this is the best I got at the moment, so stay behind me. Hopefully we won't be needing it."

"Well then, hopefully isn't terribly reassuring, now is it?" He said taking the small knife with a grin. "Lead the way I suppose, and try not to let me get shot, okay?"

"Right" Fetu laughed. "Follow my lead, and try to keep it down from now on, okay?"

"Oh right!" Travis nodded.

They crept as they approached the apex of the corridor's curve.

"Did you hear something?" a voice echoed down the hall.

Fetu held out his hand to stop Travis and took a short step back.

"No. Did you?" The other asked.

"I thought I heard footsteps."

"It is probably just the other patrol. If she had come this way, she would have been caught at the lift."

"I'm going to check it out."

"Suit yourself man, but I am telling you it's the other patrol."

Travis inhaled sharply. "Now what?" He whispered.

"I got this." Fetu whispered back. "Hold here." Fetu let the rifle drop to his hip then started walking, more deliberately this time, trying to make sure his footsteps created the desired echo.

"Who goes there?" The guard asked as his head appeared over the arching floor.

"It's just me," Fetu waved.

"Why are you out of uniform?" The soldier called as he approached.

"I couldn't find one that fits." Fetu shouted back, lengthening his stride.

"You couldn't…" The guard paused a look of obvious confusion twisting his face. "Wait, aren't you the prisoner they put in cell 1093?" The soldier reached for his gun, the confusion Fetu had generated causing him to hesitate for the briefest of moments but it was enough.

Fetu grabbed his own rifle, ducking into a roll as light flashed over his head accompanied by the unmistakable scent of sting-rifle fire. Rising to one knee he stood, and squeezed the trigger, blue light leapt from the barrel of his gun accompanied by a small rush of air bursting outward.

Not waiting for his vision to clear, Fetu spun into a nearby cell pressing his back against the wall.

"What in the Core?" The second soldier's voice came echoing down the hall.

Rapid footsteps raced towards him, Fetu inhaled deeply then held his breath. Counting each step as it got closer and timing it in his mind.

Seph

"Hey, hands out! Where is your weapon!?" He shouted, he must have spotted Travis.

"This is all I got." Travis's voice echoed back, Fetu could not see him past the cell wall.

"I saw the blast, what happened to your rifle?" More footsteps.

The man stepped past the edge of the opening to the cell where Fetu stood hidden from view. Fetu leveled his rifle, then squeezed the trigger. A flash of light, a rush of air.

"What in the nine suns was that?" Travis shouted. "You could have gotten me killed!"

Fetu laughed, dropping the rifle back to his hip and meeting his friend in the corridor. "It all worked out in the end, didn't it?"

"That was rash, and you know it!" Travis retorted, laughing as well.

"But at least it wasn't boring, right?" Fetu slapped him on the back, forcing him to catch his balance.

"I'll give you that." Travis said with a grin, stopping to grab both soldiers sting-rifles. "Now then, I believe you said there was a computer you wanted to introduce me to?"

"Right through here." Fetu scanned the ID card on the lift control pad. The doors slid open after a moment.

The sensation of gravity increased as the lift descended half a dozen meters or so to the command node. This close to the core every couple of feet started to make a difference.

Fetu pushed himself into one of the back corners of the lift. Bringing his rifle into the ready position. "There will be at least two soldiers waiting for us. Aim carefully, we don't want to damage any of the equipment unnecessarily."

"Right, got it; shoot people, not computers." Travis grinned to himself taking up a position opposite Fetu.

The doors clicked, then slid open with a hiss. Silence.

The room beyond was round with the lift sitting in the center, computer terminals ran around its perimeter with large display screens flicking through security footage from across the ship.

"Is someone there?" A voice called from somewhere beyond the lift door.

Fetu gave Travis a quick nod.

Travis smiled his ears perking up in delight. "Just some concerned citizens taking it upon ourselves to check in."

"How did you get in here?" The confused soldier stepped around the edge of the lift door. His eyes went wide as he reached for his weapon, a flash of blue light lit up the lift as Travis fired.

Fetu dashed off the lift, rotating his body to maximize his field of vision around the curved room.

"What in the nine suns?" The second soldier was almost on the opposite side of the lift tube. As he lifted his weapon, Fetu fired. The shot was rushed, but it caught the man on the shoulder, twisting him in the air as he collapsed to the floor. Fetu exhaled, scanning the rest of the room.

Travis met him at the back having cleared the other side. "Looks like it was just the two of them, so that takes care of that, now which of these computers has the most access?"

Fetu dropped his rifle to his hip and pointed to the terminal directly behind the lift shaft. "That would be this one, it talks with the control AI and acts as a relay to the others.

"Right!" Travis nodded repeatedly. "And what about this one?" He asked, pointing to a security display adjacent to the command terminal.

"That's a monitoring station, it doesn't even have a proper input interface."

"So you are saying all it does is rotate through security footage?"

Fetu nodded. "Pretty much."

"Right." Travis clapped his hands together, facing the monitoring station, "We will use this one then. I'll need a datapad, and some cables." He pulled open the terminal's casing and removed the stunblade from his belt. "Don't mind me little fella, I'm just going to give you a few upgrades."

Chapter 22

The blood drained from Chloe's face. The order given over the ship wide intercom surely meant she had been discovered. Had the guards she left outside the captain state room come around and reported in? Possibly, had the chef decided to follow up on her story and discovered her fraud? Also possible, in fact, now that she thought about it. This whole venture was absurd, she was such an idiot for ever thinking she could pull this off. These were not some glutinous politicians looking to get a little extra-curricular entertainment. These were the Descendants.

She inhaled through her nose, then pressed the air out between her lips. No, she had not been caught yet, even if they were on to her, she had not been captured, so there was still a chance.

She needed a new plan; the Shade would be out of reach. No, they would expect her to go there. There would be extra security all over both of the main hangar bays. She would have to create a diversion, something to make them think she was somewhere she wasn't.

Breathing more steadily, she began walking down the corridor. When she felt confident no one was looking, she ducked into a side room. It was a garden area filled with exotic plants with peculiar leaves and delicate flowers. It was larger than the one attached to the conference room, where Darith had taken them when they first arrived. A stone path wound its way around the room, images of suns and planets carved into the surface. Matching benches were scattered sporadically along the pathway which looped around the room ending back at the door where it started.

A meditation room most likely, but whatever it was used for, it would work perfectly for her needs. If someone were to walk in on her here, it was unlikely she would be disturbed without cause for suspicion.

Sitting on one of the benches, Chloe removed the datapad from the side pocket of her coat, and called up the map. Her best option was to make it look like she was using the maintenance tunnels to make her way around the ship. Even better if she could make it look like she was lost, and didn't know where she was going.

She located the nearest access hatch and followed the tunnel to the nearest life support vent. Now that she knew what she was doing, it should be a lot easier to get it open. She then found another access hatch, further away this time, and followed the maintenance tunnel in the opposite direction locating a vent and making a mental note of it.

She repeated this process, making note of the location of six vents, backtracking up a floor or two occasionally. This would allow her to get ahead of herself by not following the imaginary trail she was making in her mind, but by exiting back into the corridor.

By making her selections at random she decreased the odds of them predicting which tunnel she would be in ahead of her, or which direction she would be moving within the ship.

She took a deep breath and exhaled. "You can do this." She shut down the datapad, tucking it back into the coat.

The doors slid open as she approached. She leaned out into the corridor. The hall was silent, absent of any echoing footsteps or signs of traffic, which was almost as disconcerting as if there had been a guard waiting for her.

It was easy to find the first access hatch, get to the vent and disable it. Leaving it in the open position, she returned to the corridor. Again it was empty, free of both pedestrian and military traffic, the uneasiness in her stomach began to grow. It shouldn't be this simple.

Breathing deeply, she forced the thought out of her mind. It didn't matter. Until something changed it, she needed to stick to her plan.

She took the lift down a floor, then found her second access hatch, quickly disabled the vent, leaving it once again in the open position. Once again, the corridor was empty. Maybe that meant the plan was working? That would explain the lack of any military presence, but where had all the civilians gone?

She stepped off the lift trying not to let the thought distract her. If she spent too much time worrying about it she might let her guard down; the most important thing was staying focused on the objective.

"There you are, I have been looking everywhere for

you."

Chloe's heart stopped, and for a moment it was all she could do to force herself to keep breathing.

"When you didn't report in, I got worried." It was the chef from the main mess.

Chloe closed her eyes, letting her lungs expand as she forced herself to relax, he was not showing any signs of being hostile, but that did not mean this was not a trap to get her to lower her guard.

Ducking her head and avoiding eye contact she slipped into the role of an embarrassed junior officer. Rubbing her right forearm she pressed the yellow indicator to summon the stunblade.

"I'm sorry, I got lost." She looked up giving him a crooked smile and trying to force blood into her cheeks.

"Obviously. Come on, it isn't safe here." He reached out to grab her shoulder.

She felt for the stunblade, but it wasn't there, it hadn't rematerialized, a cold chill ran down her spine.

"Hey now, it's okay, I'm not going to hurt you." The chef paused.

The panic must have been evident on her face. Without the stunblade she had no way to overpower him, trap or not, she was just going to have to play along.

"Right, sorry." She broke eye contact looking away. "I guess when I couldn't find anyone for directions I got scared, and my nerves are still a little on edge."

The chef smiled, knowingly patting her on the shoulder and pushing her down the hall in front of him. "I know the feeling; it's a big ship, but don't worry, you will figure it out eventually."

"What's going on anyway?" Chloe kept her voice

soft, trying to sound hesitant, and forcing as much uncertainty into the question as possible. It was a risky question, and the answer was probably something she should already know, but if she was walking into a trap, she needed as much information as possible.

"They're running a military drill. They do it periodically to keep everyone in shape, there are not many people who would be stupid enough to attack one of our ships, but it has happened. All the crew members are supposed to report into a security station as part of the drill, didn't you learn any of this in your orientation?"

"I think I remember something about that, I guess I was just caught off guard, and since I was already lost I wasn't thinking, you know?"

He chuckled, releasing her shoulder and walking beside her. "I understand. Here, the security station is through this door."

The automatic doors slid open. He motioned for her to enter first. She hesitated a moment before stepping into the room. It was small and circular with a desk running across its diameter, two silver androids worked on computer screens behind it.

"Name and position." The android on the right demanded.

"Flin Hernayis, Head Chef, main mess. And Erica Galia line cook, officers mess."

The droid on the right stared at each of them for a moment. "Unable to verify identity Erica Galia, no DNA record on file, subordinate identification is required."

The blood drained from her face; so this was it, the end of the line. All her work up to this point was going to end right here. She took a step back, preparing to run, praying the doors would open for her again, trying desperately to call up as much information about this deck as she could remember from the map, there had to be somewhere she could go somewhere to hide. She couldn't over power them, but maybe she could outrun them.

"I will vouch for her." Flin said, placing a hand on her shoulder once again.

"Subordinate identification accepted, please proceed to Civilian Area G34 and await further instructions."

The android on the right produced two small cards and handed one to each of them. Then both robots silently returned to their work.

Civilian Area G34 was basically a giant warehouse for people, it was dressed up of course, lavender curtains draped from the ceiling along the side walls, concealing small private sleeping rooms and restroom facilities. Along the back wall hung an impressive mural of white gold which appeared to have been poured in a continuous eighty-foot sheet around details of colored glass. It depicted an image of the expanding universe suspended between two hands which were more implied than visible.

The ceiling itself was plated in warped mirrors which reflected the dark wood floor and the people there like abstract stars dancing across the night sky.

It was mesmerizing, stunning in fact, more perfect illusions had probably never been created by even the most sophisticated holographic generator. Chloe found herself sitting on one of the many dull gray couches, which served only to accentuate the grandeur of the room, drawn into the image as if it were calling to her from another world.

The room went dark, the magnificence of it

vanishing. The myriad of conversation coming to a halt.

Flin shifted on the couch next to her. "Don't worry, the emergency system will kick on shortly, and then we will have lights again."

"Is this normally a part of the drill?"

Flin inhaled. "No, but it isn't unheard of either. Occasionally, the system needs to be tested, just in case."

"Right." Chloe sank back into the cushion. As far as she could tell, Flin believed this was a drill, and Darith would be presenting it that way. How was Flin supposed to know that this whole thing was an elaborate plot to capture the girl sitting next to him. Though it had been a stroke of luck that this Erika existed, eventually the real Erika would show up, so her time was limited.

A deep hum began to build in the wall behind her, she wondered if she would even have noticed it if her nerves were not so on edge. The lights flicked back on and the hum dissipated.

"I think I am going to walk around a little." Chloe said standing and straightening her jacket.

"Okay, but don't wander too far."

She gave him a double nod. "Of course, I just can't keep sitting around like this, it's making me all agitated."

Flin laughed at that. "I noticed, I promise it gets easier."

She allowed a smile to peek from the corner of her lip. At least he was trying; possibly under different circumstances they could have been friends. She caught herself for a moment wondering what the real Erika might have been like. "Thanks, I'll try to remember that."

She wandered through the crowd, swaying back and forth between tables, letting herself get lost in the mesmerizing dance up above. All the while aware of Flin's eyes watching her, she waited until someone else approached him for a conversation. No one else knew who she was, or would notice if she went missing, but she had to be sure Flin did not see her leave.

Once she was convinced he was no longer paying attention to her, she made her way to the door. Unlike before, it did not open on its own. She took a deep breath and pressed the manual release, with a hiss it slid to the side.

Unlike the civilian room, the lights in the corridor had not all come back on, instead everything was now bathed in the same ominous red the Vyrant had been when they had first boarded.

A tall fingalin guard stepped in front of her, blocking her path with his sting-rifle. "I'm sorry miss, but you will have to remain here until the drill is over."

The door hissed shut behind her.

Chloe let her face fall, trying to force desperation into her eyes. "I know, it's just that… well, it's really embarrassing, but I forgot something that's kind of important."

"Whatever it is, I am sure you can find it in there." He waved his gun barrel in the direction of the door.

"Well…" She tossed her head side to side as if trying to decide something. "It's a little more delicate than that."

The guard glared at her squinting with one eye skeptically, letting his rifle drop back down to his hip.

Chloe let out a frustrated sigh, emphasizing it with as much exasperation as she could muster. "I just started… you know, it's a little early, so I wasn't prepared, but I'm really sensitive you see… so I can only use certain kinds of products…"

The fingalin stared at her blankly, confused; it was the reaction Chloe had been expecting. Fingalin women did not have the same issue as human women did, at least not in the same way, and as a result fingalin men were almost unaware of the reality of menstruation. She was hoping that on a mixed species ship, he would have at least heard of it from his coworkers.

His eyes grew wider as he dropped his rifle letting it dangle from the shoulder strap, then folded his hands over his waist and bowed. "Yes of course, I am sorry, but make sure you have your security card on you and come right back as quickly as possible."

She let out a sigh of relief. "Thank you so much, you have no idea how much I appreciate this." She placed her fingertips gently on his arm as she passed. "You're a lifesaver."

Now all she had to do was find the Shade. The primary power being cut could only mean one thing, and Flin had unknowingly confirmed it; if the lights had not been shut off to reinforce the idea it was a routine drill, that meant someone else had escaped, and the Descendants had their hands full.

Using the datapad she reoriented herself with the ship, and began making her way towards the hanger she suspected was holding the Shade. Following a network of interchanging corridors to move along the ship's latitude and longitude lines.

There was a maintenance tunnel up ahead that would allow her to move up a floor without using one of the lifts, which might give away her location.

Seph

As Chloe approached the hatch, she felt her cheeks growing cold. The maintenance tunnel was already open and the sound of boots echoed off the tunnel's metal walls. Had they predicted she would come this way? No, if that had been the case, and they were laying a trap for her; they likely would not have left the door open. Of course there was always the possibility they were just bad at setting traps.

Leaning close, Chloe tried to gauge the distance from the sound of the echoes. There were at least two of them, and they were moving closer. At least as far as she could tell. This was a lot more difficult than James had made it sound.

Holding down a fresh wave of panic, she began looking for an exit. There was a lift nearby but no rooms to speak of. The hallway was long and open. Even if she ran at full strength, she doubted she could get far enough that they would not see her. She stared for a moment at the lift door, it would only serve to delay her capture, she might escape this patrol, but if she alerted the whole ship to her location, they would eventually catch up to her.

She flicked through the map on the datapad. There had to be something, anything. There was a custodial droid hutch a few feet away, it was probably occupied, and she doubted she would fit in it with the droid. Leaving it out would be a dead giveaway; once they found it, they would know exactly where she was.

A sly smile pulled at the corner of her lip as an idea began to take shape. Maybe that is exactly what she needed. "Knowledge is your most powerful weapon." James's words echoed in her mind. "The knowledge you give your enemy is just as valuable, and just as dangerous, as the knowledge you have about them."

He had demonstrated it multiple times in the training simulation. Providing Scot with an endless trickle of just enough information and misdirection to keep himself a few steps ahead.

She didn't have a lot of time, she could hear voices in the maintenance tunnel now. Slamming her hand against the manual release for the hutch, she pressed on her thumbs, impatiently fidgeting, and glanced over her shoulder at the tunnel entrance, half expecting a full platoon of soldiers to emerge at any moment.

The hutch door slid open, revealing the lone custodial robot collapsed in its hibernation position. It looked like a small upside down trash receptacle, its various arms and utility instruments hidden under a smooth, white, cylindrical shell.

Chloe unfastened the metal clips, locking it into the small hibernation compartment. It moved easily, floating less than an inch above the ground.

The voices grew louder, but the distortion from the hallway kept her from being able to make them out.

She pushed the robot over to the lift door, which opened once she was close enough to trigger the hidden sensor. Giving the droid a final shove, she sent it careening into the far wall. Reaching through the door, she felt along the inside wall until she found the controller, and swiped for a random floor.

The door was patient and waited until her arm was fully clear before closing. She did not wait for it. Running as fast as she could, Chloe dove toward the hibernation hutch, hunching down and squeezing herself into the space only half her size. Keying the manual release once more, she held her breath. The door began to close and a pristine white uniform appeared in the entry to the maintenance tunnel.

Seph

Before she could react, the hatch door sealed itself around her. The silence was deafening, threatening to choke her with its grip around her lungs. Her heartbeat counted out the time like the hands on a great analog clock ticking away the seconds into eternity, pressure pounding in her temples like being trapped inside a giant leather drum.

She inhaled the darkness, sweat drenching her hair and arms. The silence stretched on, like falling into the endless abyss of space. She waited, forcing herself to breathe steadily. The door remained sealed around her.

A new form of panic formed behind her breast bone and under her cheeks. She had been in such a hurry to get into the custodial droid's hutch, she had never even considered how she would get back out of it. When she assumed she would be discovered, that hadn't mattered. But now that the plan had worked, the fact that there was no release mechanism on the inside of the hutch, was a serious problem.

The space was hardly even big enough for her to fit in, even with her knees tucked firmly against her chest, the variety of charging ports and metal sockets still stabbed uncomfortably into her arms, shoulders and back. When she had first gotten into it, she had been hyperventilating; there likely was not much air left.

She pressed against the inside of the door; nothing happened. There had to be an answer here somewhere, she had come too far to die of asphyxiation because she could not open one stupid door.

She gave up trying to use strength, all she was doing was burning through her oxygen supply. Somehow she had to get the computer to open the door for her. But she did not know much about droids, or computers for that matter. She was getting good at working with the

Shade's pilot AI, but working with a program to do what it was supposed to do was different from making it do something just because you wanted it to.

No, it didn't matter what she didn't know, focusing on that would only make things worse. She needed to focus on what she did know, and figure out how to use that to her advantage.

This hutch belonged to a custodial droid, while custodial droids varied widely from model to model, and there were hundreds if not thousands of manufacturers. They all worked about the same. They were designed to clean messes, and perform minor repairs in their designated area through routine patrols, then return to their hutch and charge.

That did not do her a lot of good, while it meant the door might open on its own eventually, she didn't have time to bank on that possibility.

If there was a major mess though, sometimes multiple droids may be called on to cleanup, a neighboring droid would need to leave its designated area to assist. Of course, there was the possibility that each area had multiple droids monitoring a single area, providing continuous monitoring even when most of the droids were in hibernation. It was a start thought. On the midway station, it was possible, though rarely necessary, for someone to report an issue of concern for a droid to investigate. If she made a report significant enough, it might send this droid into action and open the hutch.

It was unlikely, but it was all she had at the moment. Chloe wrestled the datapad out of her pocket. Keeping her breathing as shallow as possible, she keyed through the various command screens. It wasn't too difficult to figure out, having gained a considerable amount of experience with Descendant computer layouts since she left her room this morning.

She couldn't report anything close to herself, at least not a first. Once a droid got to the site it would be confirmed as false, and could give away her location, which meant it had to be big. She decided to code it as an unknown, possible biohazard to raise the priority tag, and spread it across as many areas on the deck below her as she could. For good measure, she tagged several of the vents she had sabotaged earlier. If it was a biohazard, and it got into the life support, that should really get things moving.

She finished the report, holding her breath, she pressed submit. Time passed in silence. It was difficult to track now, between her heart racing and the air thinning, either real or imagined, her head was beginning to hurt.

There was a hiss, as fresh air from the corridor flooded into the small alcove. The door slid open and red light flooded her vision.

Her muscles protested against her as she unwedged herself from her tiny prison. Everything was starting to ache now, as fatigue worked its way into every joint in her body.

Forcing past the pain, Chloe made herself get back on her feet. She had to get to the Shade.

Several custodial droids darted past her as she made her way along the corridor, using the wall every few feet to keep balance. Her report must have spooked something in the AI for so many to be active now.

Small doorways had opened up to ramps leading between floors. The cylindrical droids popped out of them in regular intervals, heading for the apparent spill site. By now the spill should have been identified as fabricated though, so why were they still coming? It was like every droid on the ship had been mobilized to deal with the issue.

Chloe held a hand over one eye and shook her head, fighting against the headache; it didn't matter, that was the Descendants problem. Besides, the new tunnels were exactly what she needed to move between floors.

Avoiding the lifts, it took an hour longer to get to the hanger bay. Somewhere along the way she became vaguely aware of an alarm sounding. She ignored it; it didn't matter, not now. She was staying so far off the main path. And even if it did, she was spent. She couldn't think about it, even if she had wanted to.

She emerged from the custodial droids network. And stopped. The corridor was filled with Descendants, not the armed uniformed kind, but the civilian kind. They pushed and shoved each other, trying to be the first to get into the hanger bay. Two guards stood by the doors trying in vain to control the fevered crowd.

What in all the worlds of the Alliance had happened?

Chloe found herself swept up by the mob, who all but ignored the fact that she had just climbed out of a droid tunnel. They tossed her helplessly in the current and swept her into the hanger right along with them. She avoided eye contact with the guards, though the looks on their faces said they were too overwhelmed to recognize her.

Once in the hanger, the crowd dissipated like a firework into the night sky. Chloe was thrown to the ground, catching herself on her palms, she managed to narrowly avoid being trampled in the stampede.

Pulling herself away from the chaos, she took

Seph

a moment to catch her breath and take in her surroundings. Soldiers stood by the shuttles and other ships in the hanger, trying to maintain order as civilians pushed their way into any open seat they could find. Was the entire ship being evacuated?

There was no way her false biohazard caused all this, was there? The reality she was seeing was too absurd to make sense of. But she found it hard to argue with the results.

Getting on board the Shade was easy; no one was paying attention, no one cared. The only thing on any of their minds was getting off the ship.

The Shade had been put in landing mode, which meant the Sanctuary had been flipped to align with the rest of the ship, creating a sort of bubble on top of the hull, and the cargo hold rotated down to form the loading dock.

She climbed the ladder from the cargo hold to the crew deck, then made her way to James's foot locker. There she found a fresh uniform, his sting-rifle, a stunblade and his neural link. Tossing the uniform on the bed, Chloe pocketed the stunblade and strapped the sting-rifle over her shoulder. She left the link.

The sting-rifle was an improvement over nothing, but it was far too conspicuous. Though she wondered how much any of that mattered now. Still, she had been training with mostly combustion weapons. James said they were the most difficult to master, therefore the best to start with. She was more comfortable with one of them than the more bulky energy weapon.

Looking again she found his handgun; once again, she had practiced mostly with rifles, and his belt was nowhere to be found.

Holding the gun in one hand, she made her way

to the locker room and checked his locker. Uniforms hung neatly in a row, pressed and ready to be worn. Chloe could not help but smile to herself, compared to Meg's locker, James kept his immaculate.

She pushed the uniforms aside to reveal two rifles: A combination railgun, and a semi-automatic low caliber combustion rifle, as well as several belts and straps along with the appropriate magazines.

Chloe strapped his belt around her waist, then holstered the handgun, and grabbed the rifle and all the available ammunition.

She took a deep breath, her first objective was complete, now she needed to figure out how to get out of the hanger, and make her way to the detention block.

Chapter 23

Meghnah slipped into a side room, not far from the armory. The space was small, less than ten feet from floor to ceiling, and only as wide as it was high. Crates and boxes were stacked on sleek metal shelves along the walls.

Chatter chimed over her comlink. Unit commanders reported in and received their orders. The captain seemed to think that the primary life support hub was going to be targeted. It was a silly target, anyone but an amateur would know that if the life support was disabled it would simply switch to the backup system.

It did make for a nice diversion, with the crew focused on life support, the fold generator would be left vulnerable. If they jumped now, it could take days for her to recalculate their position once they managed to escape, meaning they would likely be recaptured before she could even open an envelope.

Meghnah stepped back into the corridor and found

the nearest lift. Several soldiers waited patiently, they watched curiously as she emerged from the storage room.

"Lieutenant." A somewhat short human man bowed holding his rifle across his waist.

Meghnah braced herself internally, wishing she had a better grasp of Descendant ranks. "I will be joining you on this lift, special orders."

"Right." Another soldier nodded. "After you, ma'am," he motioned with his rifle as the doors slid open.

Meghnah half bowed at the waist and moved to the back of the lift, watching the others as they filed in after her.

"Any idea what this is all about?" One of the soldiers asked, seemingly to the group as a whole more than to anyone specific.

"I'm not convinced this is just some elaborate drill ol' Darith's cooked up to remind us who's in charge." Someone answered.

The man who had first spoken to her shrugged. "I don't know, I heard that the ship we brought on board belongs to the pirates responsible for the Vyrant."

"Seriously? You think one of them is really loose on the ship?"

"What do you think, Lieutenant?"

Meghnah set her jaw and gave her best scowl. "Just follow your orders and keep you head down."

The men straightened a little in response to the command in her voice. No one said anything after that.

The doors slid open with a hiss, Meghnah waited until the last of the soldiers disappeared beneath the curvature of the floor. She steadied her breathing slipping into the familiar rhythm of inhales and exhales. Her heart rate slowed as her senses sharpened.

A loud crack echoed down the corridor like a heavy switch sliding into place. One at a time the lights in the hallway burned out, darkness engulfed the space. Fifty-seven seconds passed. A hum began to build somewhere behind the walls, and the red emergency lights illuminated the passageway.

Meghnah concentrated on her breathing, maintaining the pattern and pushing her senses outward. Maybe she wouldn't need to worry about the hyperdrive.

"Report, what's going on down there?" The comm unit in her ear chimed.

" I don't know, it's like, everything just shut itself off." Came the hesitant reply.

"Computers don't just 'shut themselves off.' The prisoner must be there somewhere."

"I'm looking right at the life support controller, I'm telling you, it shut itself off."

"Then check the sub controller, you idiot, and get life support back online, or Vyanna help me, I will drag you down to Vinge's core myself."

The comm chimed again, "Sorry to interrupt your little whatever this is," a new voice chimed in, "but it looks like the system may have triggered a failsafe. I have multiple units registering as having been tampered with across decks ninety-four through one-o-one, along sectors G through K."

Meghnah paused; that was an impressive amount of sabotage, up until now she had assumed the crew was chasing a ghost, based off her own report, but there was no way their imaginations could have invented something on this scale, was there?

Had she gotten lucky and there was someone else on board trying to hijack the ship? Not likely, it was a Descendant war vessel. None of the pirate organizations large enough to pull it off were stupid enough to try, and none of the ones stupid enough to try had the resources it would require.

Someone else from the Shade? Maybe, Fetu had the knowledge and skill necessary, and it certainly felt like a plan James would have come up with.

Meghnah activated her comm. "I'm in that area now, I will check it out."

She held her breath, not sure what she would do if the orchestrater on the other end of the comlink decided to protest.

There was a long pause before the comm chimed again. "Go ahead, Lieutenant. I am updating you datapad with the new information."

The comm chirped, and was silent a second before other units began reporting in again.

Using the datapad, Meghnah located the first of the flagged life support units, if she could meet the other saboteur they might be able to secure their escape, and rescue the others at the same time.

The hatch to the maintenance tunnel opened easily. It was dark inside, the emergency power system must not include lighting for non-essential areas, if there was lighting in these tunnels at all. It occurred to Meghnah that few organic beings had ever been in these tunnels, likely they were maintained by droids of one form or another, with complicated sensor arrays which all but negated the necessity of amenities such as lighting.

She dropped down into the tunnel, ignoring the ladder. Even with her heightened senses, Meghnah could barely make out the shape of the walls. She closed her eyes and began to subtly change her breathing pattern, focusing her energy outward towards her skin and past her finger tips.

It would be easier to use a light; she hadn't checked but there was probably one built into her gun, and more than likely a drone tool built into her datapad. If, however, she did encounter anyone while she was here, she wanted to have the advantage.

The sensation of her heightened senses began to fade, leaving her ears feeling dull and heavy, the smell of the air becoming muted. The air began to buzz with electricity, subtle changes in currents tracing along her skin like projections of light, leaving behind impressions of her surroundings.

The comm unit continued to chime with reports from around the ship, but they sounded more like someone beating a drum underwater. It was difficult to make out exactly what was being said. Her mind translated the information less in words and more in vague ideas floating just out of reach.

One report stood out as significant, something about taking a suspect into custody, though it lacked any real context.

Meghnah pushed it out of her mind, keeping her eyes closed and focusing on her immediate surroundings. She navigated her way to the life support node. From what she could tell it had been disconnected from the rest of the unit somehow. Unfortunately, she was not familiar enough with the design to be able to tell much else just by sensing it.

Releasing her breath and returning her pattern to normal, a wave of nausea washed over her as the familiar muscle ache which accompanied this particular technique set into her joints. Resigning herself, she powered up her datapad and found the small light drone.

The droid detached itself from the side of the pad, hovering only a few feet in front of her to partly illuminate the area.

The life support unit had in fact been disconnected, though as far as she could see, there was no other tampering. Whoever had done this, it did not appear true sabotage was their intention. It was possible they had used the vent in the unit to move discreetly between floors, though the fact that the vent itself was closed suggested otherwise, a diversionary tactic maybe? But from what?

Meghnah pushed down her own curiosity, at the moment, it didn't matter. Whatever the culprit's intention, she had her own agenda and for the moment at least, they appeared to be working to her advantage.

Meghnah activated her comm link. "I have located one of the compromised units, it appears to have some kind of additional canister feeding into the system. No safe way to detach, further analysis required. Strongly advise against restoring the system until the contaminant can be removed."

There was a brief pause before the comm chimed again. "Confirmed, do not reactivate the unit, the contaminant is suspected to be a nerve agent, exercise extreme caution."

A nerve agent? Where were they getting this information, had she somehow found the one unit that had not been compromised? Her ghost was taking on a life of its own, and she didn't like it.

She recalled the light drone and steadied herself

against the wall, taking a few minutes to breath and recenter her energy.

The chiming of her comm unit interrupted her meditation. "All units prepare for immediate evacuation, report to the nearest civilian station and act as escort. Repeat all units, begin the evacuation procedure."

Her head made a thud against the wall behind her as she leaned back, inhaling deeply. "Cursed suns, what is happening around here?" She forced herself to her feet, and began taking deliberate breaths falling into the pattern that would sharpen her senses. She did not have the physical capacity at the moment to use the same technique she used to get here, so she would have to settle for this. Besides, she had been able to make a clear enough mental map of the place on her way in, navigating it blind shouldn't be too hard... right?

Retracing her steps from memory, she occasionally checked her location by reaching out and touching the wall, feeling for landmarks she had sensed earlier, eventually grasping the ladder which led up to the corridor.

Lifting the hatch from underneath, the sound of an alarm erupted in her ears, she gasped as the air was forced from her lungs, her heightened senses causing the sound to reverberate in her head like a high-pitched ringing inside of a glass bell.

A fresh wave of dizziness washed over her as her vision blurred, and she struggled to remain standing.

Meghnah took a moment to steady herself, before pulling her body out of the hole in the floor. She was vaguely aware of the footsteps running past her.

Someone's hands reached under her shoulder and began to lift her up, setting her against the wall. "Hey, are you alright?"

Panic erupted around them, the fleeing civilians began giving her ample berth as they passed by. Her vision began to clear as whoever had helped her up shined a light into her eyes.

"It looks like she has been exposed. Get that hatch closed, and seal off this corridor."

Meghnah fought back the rising headache, placing the heel of her hand on her temple. "What's going on?"

The man with the light appeared to be checking her for other signs of injury. "The whole ship is being evacuated. What happened down there?"

Meghnah blinked through the pain, pulling her knees in close to her body, how much should she say? How much would he already know about her, or her supposed identity? As she regained her bearing, she realized almost everyone around her was a civilian, with only a handful of soldiers mixed in, making a vain attempt at maintaining order. The man kneeling next to her was not wearing any kind of uniform, at least not as far as she could tell.

"I was investigating a report, there was some tampering with the life support system."

The man nodded a few times then grabbed her arm and attempted to help her up. "I'll say, come on, we've got to get moving, or it will only get worse."

Meghnah slapped his hand away, rising unsteady to her feet under her own power. "Thank you, but I will be fine."

"I'm not just going to leave you here, whatever this thing is, you have clearly been infected. Let me help you."

Meghnah focused her breathing, and looked him

dead in the eyes, forcing as much of her Drak'or heritage into her gaze as she could muster. "And the longer you stay here, the more likely it is you will also be infected. Go on, save yourself, I have work to do."

He took a step back, his confidence melting. "In the state you're in, you won't be much use to anyone."

Meghnah grabbed the handle of her gun, bringing it parallel to her body. "I will not tell you again, get to your shuttle or hope someone drags you there."

The man hesitated for a moment. With a nod, he rejoined the crowd bustling towards the hangar bays.

The haze began to clear, Meghnah unclipped the comlink from the side of her head, letting out a sigh of relief as the pressure it created on her mind was released. She tossed the device on the floor. Now was her chance to get to the detention block, with everyone else fleeing the ship no one would be paying any attention to a few prisoners.

Chapter 24

The mass of wires lay spread out across the floor and wall of the command node, each one meticulously labeled and laid neatly in rows. The metal casings of the computers and terminals lay discarded in a haphazard pile in the corner, but that did little to distract from the beauty which was Travis's art.

Fetu had taken apart and rebuilt his share of computers, and he was familiar with the idea of using a dummy machine. What Travis had done however was something different. What had started out as three separate machines had been fused together seamlessly into a single unit, eliminating any latency which might be caused by passing commands from one machine to another.

That in and of itself was impressive, but Travis had taken it a step further by maintaining the original identification codes of the command terminal, while moving all the command functions to the monitoring screen, which he was controlling from a basic datapad, then using the third computer to create a second ID set which would overwrite the original access commands, making it appear that it had originated somewhere else on the ship.

The amount of code required was absurd, and the layers of security he had to get through before he could even start on the reprogramming even more so. It would have taken Fetu weeks, if not months, to get it all worked out, and it would not look this tidy afterwards. Yet Travis had accomplished it in under an hour.

"Okay, what kind of mischief should we cause first? Maybe a sensor error, drive malfunction, fire on all decks?" The grin on the fingalin's face was almost as wide as his ears.

"How about shutting off the life support?"

Travis's ears twisted. "I don't know, that seems awfully mundane, don't you think? Also predictable, why not do something with a little more flair?"

Fetu nodded, he made some good points. "You're right, but I have been monitoring the comm lines, it seems like somehow they got it in their heads that someone is already going after life support. There is something to be said for minimum effort, with maximum effect."

Travis nodded keying a command into his datapad. "Alright then, let's see where that gets us."

Briefly the lights flickered, then came back on.

"Well that was slightly less dramatic than I was hoping for." The fingalin's face twisted his nose wrinkled, ears sticking out at strange angles.

"What did you do?"

He shrugged. "I shut off power to the whole ship,

then slipped a bug into the life support so that when it tried to reset it would trigger a series of cascading failures throughout the system, nothing major, just a small hitch here, and a little bump there, but they all add up to a pretty big mess."

Fetu turned his attention back to the comm unit. Not a lot of radio traffic had been sent in their direction, so he had needed to build a patch to tap into the other frequencies, with Travis working on the computer terminals, who had time to work out the algorithms. Unfortunately the signal was less than perfect, which made it difficult to distinguish who was who at times.

"It's like everything just shut itself off."

"Computers don't just 'shut themselves off.' The prisoner must be there somewhere."

"I'm looking right at the life support controller, I'm telling you, it shut itself off."

"Check the sub controller, you idiot, and get life support back online, or Vyanna help me, I will drag you down to Vinge's core myself."

Fetu nodded to Travis. "It definitely sounds like you caused some chaos out there, "

The comm crackled, "Sorry to interrupt your little whatever this is, but it looks like the system may have triggered a failsafe. I have multiple units registering as having been tampered with across decks ninety-four through one-o-one, along sectors G through K."

Fetu twisted his ears. "Travis, what is going on with the vents along here?" Fetu pulled up the section of the ship on one of the untouched monitoring terminals.

Travis leaned in close, eyes darting around the mapped decks before returning to his datapad. "Let's see, hmm… I got it! Well that's interesting; many of the vents seem to have been set into maintenance mode for some reason."

"Something you did?" Fetu raised an eyebrow.

Travis shrugged, "Possibly, but probably not, at least not with so many in such an isolated area. My bug should have affected things more randomly across the whole ship."

Fetu watched the flickering image on the screen in front of him. What was going on here? Had Meghnah been tampering with the life support already? Comm chatter suggested she was loose in the ship somewhere, and it would certainly explain why they had been so sure that someone was going after the life support. Something about it felt off though.

The comm crackled as overlapping channels exploded with communications data, and Fetu was forced to shut it off.

"Hmm, this is interesting," Travis interrupted his thoughts. "It appears a small biohazard leak had been detected not far from that area."

"Really?" Fetu pulled the datapad over where he could see what Travis was looking at.

Travis began entering commands into his datapad.

"Now what are you doing?"

Travis grinned. "I am linking the disassembled vent module to the biohazard, and having one of the custodial droids report it as a nerve gas which is spreading through the rest of the system. That ought to give them something to talk about, don't you think?"

Fetu stared at his friend, it was amazing how fast he could come up with these things and put them into action.

The alarm sounded, and an automated voice began playing over the room's internal intercom. "All units prepare for immediate evacuation, report to the nearest civilian station and act as escort. Repeat all units, begin the evacuation procedure."

Fetu and Travis exchanged glances both twisting their ears.

Fetu grinned, "Well, it looks like it got them talking alright." He laughed.

"Well, they will be busy for a while at least; maybe adding in the unrelated area reports was taking it too far, you think? In any case, shall we see if we can find the others?"

Fetu burst into a deep belly laugh. "I think you have performed brilliantly, my friend." He turned to the computer terminal. "If my suspicion is correct, we should be able to find Meghnah not far from those vents."

* * *

Finding her way out of the hanger had been easier than Chloe had imagined it would be. Everyone still on board was so focused on either getting off the ship, or attending to whatever task they had been assigned; most didn't even notice her, those that did barely even took the time to give her a concerned look, let alone make any attempt at questioning her.

Her footsteps echoed back at her down the corridor of the detention block. Once again, she found herself overwhelmed by the audaciousness of the task she had undertaken; what if this wasn't even the right block? What if in all the chaos they had already been moved off the ship. Or worse yet, what if they had already figured out ways to get themselves free, and now they were searching for each other in separate parts of the ship. She hadn't thought to consider it before, the stress and the adrenalin of the situation had flooded her mind. She had become so focused on moving from one task to another, it had not occurred to her that each of the other members of the crew were independently capable of getting themselves off this ship.

Chloe found herself wishing she had just sat still and waited in the state room to begin with, what had she been thinking?

"Chloe."

She jumped, swinging her gun around and bringing it up into the fire position before the word even fully registered in her mind.

Meg was standing over her; before she could even finish processing, she had pushed the gun out of the way with her forearm, grabbed Chloe's wrist and expertly disarmed her. "Watch where you are pointing that thing." She whispered. "Com'on, Travis and Fetu have been searching the ship for you." Meg held out the gun, offering it back to Chloe.

"R-right…" Chloe managed to take the gun and strapped it over her shoulder once more. She followed Meghnah into the lift leading down to the command node.

Travis and Fetu both looked at her in bewilderment as she exited the lift, examining the small arsenal she was carrying.

"Remind me never to cross you." Fetu laughed. "Looks like we had nothing to be worried about. Where is James?"

Chloe shrugged, taking in the sight of disassembled computer pieces strewn about the room. "We got separated, as far as I know Darith is still interrogating him."

The four all exchanged glances. The pit of Chloe's stomach sank as the implication of everything that had transpired in the last few hours formed into perspective.

"Maybe we should catch each other up on what has been happening," Fetu suggested.

Meg nodded. "I freed myself from an interrogation cell, and managed to disguise myself as an officer; my goal had been to shut down the hyperdrive, but before I got there life support went down, and I was sent to investigate tampering with the vents."

Fetu's face twisted in confusion, "Wait, so you weren't the one tampering with the life support?"

Meg shook her head. "No, by the time I got that far, most of the systems on the deck had already been opened.

"Then who…"

Blood rushed to her face as she shrank back into herself, trying to be as small as possible.

"Wait, that was you?" Meg and Fetu asked in unison.

Travis let out a high-pitched whoop sound and began to laugh.

"Yeah… I did that." She admitted.

"That's amazing. But what, might I ask, was your intention?" Travis asked.

"I found it to be an effective way to move between decks, but I realized it might make me too easy to track… So I opened up a few extra to create a false trail."

"So what was the biohazard report?" Meg asked.

Chloe avoided eye contact, "That was me as well. I got trapped in a custodial droid hutch, and was trying to get the computer to open it for me."

Fetu broke out into a huge grin. "Travis may have helped with that a little."

"Oh?"

Travis nodded. "I used a custodial droid to confirm your report, I also may have expanded the area a bit, and duplicated it in several other sectors of the ship."

Chloe let a smile slip out. "That explains the sudden escalation of everything."

Meg leaned back against the computer terminal crossing her arms in front of her. "Still, doesn't it seem odd that it all worked out this way? It almost feels like we have been following a script."

The puzzle clicked together, like the last move in a mind game where all the pieces fall into place. Chloe unstrapped her gear and handed it to Meg. "Here, take this."

"Where are you going?"

"To get caught, of course." Chloe grinned.

"Wait, what?" the other said, suddenly becoming tense.

"Just trust me, and try to get a comm open to the Shade. Scot will explain everything to you as soon as I get him back online."

Without waiting for a response, Chloe stepped into the lift and closed the door, she had to get the neural link to James, everything had come together exactly as he had planned it and it was time to play the final move.

* * *

James sat back into his seat across from the young women who had been accused of being a stowaway.

Her cheeks were still red with tears, and though she tried to hide it, her body was still shaking. In the last few hours, her entire world had been turned on its head. Under different circumstances he would have felt bad for her, but at the moment he did not have time for such things.

Darith had been pacing the room for a while now, the stress of the situation was obvious in his bloodshot eyes and frazzled hair. Since coming on board, James had watched the large Drak'or descend from a self-important, overconfident starship captain into the disheveled mess he was now.

"No, I want all non-essential crew off this ship now!" Darith shouted into his comm. "Everyone else I want in breathers twenty minutes ago, you incompetent Norf."

"What about us?" The young woman asked, a fresh wave of panic washing over her.

Darith paused a moment as if the words hadn't even registered. "This room has a self-contained system, we will be fine."

"That's convenient." James said, holding back a grin.

"Very," Darith said sternly. "What the core are your men doing out there? How hard can it be to find one girl? Your men are the only things left on this whole ship! Can't you just run a life signs scan already!?"

Ever since Darith had Chloe escorted out of the room, James had been slowly driving the man mad, planting suggestions in his ear and carefully manipulating his crew into utter chaos. It hadn't been difficult. James had only needed to play along, pretend that he was willing to work with Darith until someone from the Shade made a move.

It had been easy enough to convince Darith that

the first report of an escaped prisoner was Meghnah. Darith must have access to their personnel files, so his imagination was able to do most of the hard work all on its own.

James only needed to suggest Meghnah's first target would be the life support and then continue to craft the narrative of incoming reports to match. Regardless of the reality, Darith's response would push the investigation in that direction, if you look hard enough for anything you will find it, real or imagined.

James knew that the Shade's crew would be working for their own freedom. By suggesting to Darith possible countermeasures to the incoming reports, he could not only manipulate the crew of the Dressick, but he could also use it as an opportunity to subtly pass instruction on to anyone of his own team who might be listening. Darith's current state was evidence of just how well the plan had worked.

There was a hard knock on the door, Darith pressed the intercom. "What in Vyanna's name do you want now!" He barked.

"Sir, we have captured one of the prisoners."

"It's about time, you inept amateurs; maybe now we will be able to put an end to this mess."

A loud hiss could be heard from the other side of the door as the decontamination area sealed itself and began its cleaning process. A moment later the door opened and two soldiers walked in, holding Chloe between them.

Darith stared for a moment, the gears turning in his mind. "What, in, the, nine, suns, Vinge's core, and all of Zaeith's prison, is she doing here!" The words were deliberate, slow, and to the point; it was more of a statement than a question.

"She turned herself in, sir." One of the guards offered.

Darith picked up the tea pot off the coffee table and chucked it at the soldier who spoke. "What the core is she doing outside of MY STATE ROOM!"

The soldiers ducked out of the way as the teapot smashed behind them, splashing brown stains on the door and walls.

James rose from his seat on the lavender sofa. "I believe she came to bring us something of vital importance to this operation, sir."

Darith turned his burning eyes to James, the blood vessels in his temples bulging as he tried to wrap his head around what was going on.

"She was carrying this," the second soldier offered, holding up a neural link.

James grabbed the link from the soldier before Darith had a chance to react, slipping it over his head.

"What are you doing? Stop him!" Darith shouted.

The soldiers grabbed their guns, releasing Chloe to point them at James. As soon the device was fitted into place, James began the activation sequence. Data flooded his mind like stars in the view field when you drop out of hyperspace. The neuron map was already complete, and he had previously sorted through the Shade's computer information. The only thing left to do was sort the new data Scot passed him.

Through the android, James was able to confirm the evacuation status of the Dressick's crew. In the time since Chloe had reactivated Scot, he had managed to contact the others; fortunately, there were all in one place, and confirmed that, as James had suspected, Travis had successfully gained access to the ship's primary computer.

Seph

James passed on his instructions, then closed the link. It took less than a second in real time.

Slowly, James removed the device and offered it back to the guard.

Darith clenched his jaw, cheeks bulging. "Would you care, Commander, to enlighten me as to what, exactly, is going on here?"

James nodded, meeting the drak'or's gaze straight on. "I am now prepared to discuss the terms of your surrender."

Darith's eyes grew wide, he lunged at James with both hands in an attempt to grab him. Stepping forward with his left leg, James extended his arm deflecting the large man's hand and using his own momentum to move his body around him, sending the drak'or toppling over the sofa and crashing into the coffee table.

The two soldiers looked at each other, guns still trained on James, apparently considering if they should shoot him now, or wait for the order.

"If you would, I would direct your attention to the viewing screen over there," James pointed to the far wall where there was now displayed an array of shuttles fleeing the ship.

The view field erupted with light as three cannon blasts shot out into the void, just missing the scattered envoy.

"My crew is now in complete control of this ship, you are of course free to look for them. But by the time you even trace them, your crew out there will have been destroyed, and your plasma shield will have been set to collapse on you. If you are not prepared to negotiate, you will die in exactly the same way I killed Gillian Maylis.

Every Descendant in the room's skin grew pale as the blood drained from their faces.

Catching on to the plot, Chloe quickly removed the soldiers' guns, who at this point were in no condition to put up much of a fight.

James took one of the guns from her and leveled its barrel between The captain's eyes. "Are you ready to talk?"

* * *

It had felt like an eternity waiting in the command node for Scot to contact them. Meghnah knew it had only been half an hour or so, but the silence had been unbearable. Just as Chloe had said though, Scot had contacted them, and his instructions were every bit as vague as Chloe's explanation.

He had told them to fire exactly three shots at very specific coordinates from the ship's primary plasma cannon. Fetu had tried to get some clarification as to what was going on, but Scot delivered his message then promptly cut the communication link.

"Now what?" Fetu asked, looking between Meghnah and Travis.

All Meghnah could do was shrug. Up until she had narrowly escaped getting shot by her best friend, Meghnah had thought she was on top of this situation. Now she was questioning whether she had any clue what was going on. And to top it off, Chloe, of all people, seemed to be the only person who was keeping up.

Not that Chloe wasn't smart, the opposite actually. She was brilliant; Chloe had mastered in months what had taken Meghnah years to get a handle on.

Seph

And how long had she been training with James, two weeks? But standing there, holding that gun, she had looked as if she had been born with it. The form had been perfect, her posture and breathing were steady, Meghnah had not been so terrified of someone holding a gun since the first time she had encountered James in a training simulator.

To say that Chloe was a prodigy was like saying space was a big place. Even still, while she was smart, she lacked experience. Yet somehow, she, out of all of them, had managed to make the most progress into getting off this ship. By the time Travis and Fetu had hacked into the computer, Chloe had already done most of the leg work for them, all they had needed to do was give it a push. As for herself, Meghnah hadn't even managed to accomplish the one task she had set out to do before getting swept away by the mechanism Chloe had already set in motion.

The room's comm link crackled with James's voice. "Meghnah, I need you to come to the atrium on the port side of the ship closest to the bow."

"How did you…"

"I will explain everything when you get here, oh, and bring a gun, just in case. Fetu and Travis, I need you to get all the guns somewhere they can't get to them, we should be okay for the next hour or so, but eventually someone is going to try to fight back."

Meg pulled up a map of the ship on one of the computer terminals, then traced it to the nearest tram which would take her to the designated coordinates. "Okay, I am on my way."

She could feel Travis and Fetu staring at her as she walked over to the lift. "Look, you guys know as much as I do."

Chapter 25

"This plague is completely out of control. If we do not cut off all access to and from the outer colonies, we will be putting every system in the galaxy at risk, in the ring as well as in the core. Who knows, we may already be too late." The panic in Councilor Halian's voice was palpable.

"Now, councilor," Governor Sylvinn interjected in that calm collected voice only she could manage at a time like this. "Where is your faith? Even now Director Xious is out there providing aid, and our missionary efforts have never been more successful. Here we are, on the brink of enlightenment, and you would have us pull back and abandon those who need us most?"

Trepidor could not help but smile to himself. The irony of the governor's words were lost to her. Yes, they were standing on the precipice of enlightenment, however, she would not be around to see it.

Seph

"Admiral," The governor interrupted his thoughts, "how has your investigation turned out? Do you have anything to report about the Vyrant, or its missing crew?"

The admiral sat forward in his chair, bringing himself just a little closer to the center of the room. "Unfortunately, I have confirmed that Gillian Maylis is in fact dead, along with the remainder of his crew. Captain Darith was able to get a recording from a radio probe they had launched just before activating their shield for the last time. Out of compassion, they had broken quarantine and Captain Maylis had allowed a few of his men to board the station to provide medical aid, by the time he realized his men had been infected it was too late, the only thing left to do was activate the shield and wait. The only survivors were those who were picked up by the Engineering Corps in the jump pods. May Vyanna keep their souls."

Sylvinn nodded solemnly. "Colonel Maylis will be sorely missed, he was the last of a great line, and his death will be felt by all for some time. When we are done here, I would very much like to see the report from the Dressick myself."

"But of course, your excellency." Trepidor bowed with his head. She would never see the report. Not only because it did not exist, but because only a few of the people seated around this table now would ever be leaving this room again, not alive anyway. Besides, it might as well be true; Darith had reported that he had traced Maylis to Dramia, where he had already captured the saboteurs. Soon Gillian Maylis would join his brother in the afterlife, may Vyanna keep their forsaken souls.

A heavy knock on the chamber doors interrupted the conversation around the table.

"Who dare disrupt this meeting?" Sylvinn demanded, rising from her chair as the door opened.

Empress Cathrin strode into the room, a long lavender train trailing behind like something from the ethereal realm, flowing about her shoulders like angelic wings.

Sylvinn flushed when she caught sight of her, "Empress, what causes you to intrude on the conference of the Divine Council?"

Everyone's eyes fixed on the image of Vyanna as the two guards stepped inside and pulled the doors closed.

"I have come to rid this council of your heresy. Director Xious has been informed of your treachery against Lady Vyanna and in his infinite wisdom declared me as the head of this council."

Gasps echoed through the room as the seated councilors tried to process the implications of what Cathrin had said.

Sylvinn narrowed her eyes, "You have no authority to do this." She hissed.

Trepidor stood, tossing his cloak behind his arms for dramatic effect. "She has every authority!" He affirmed. "Xious contacted me privately this morning to inform me of this. I believe he has also been in contact with several other members of this council who he deemed he could trust. Our governor has betrayed us, and it is the will of Vyanna that this council should be dissolved, and the heresy of the past be purged from among us."

Sylvinn clenched her fists into tight balls. "The Order will never stand for this."

"I am the Order now," Cathrin proclaimed, raising

up to stand on her toes in an attempt to rival the fingalin in height.

The two women locked eyes with each other, caught in a battle of iron wills. Finally, Sylvinn let out a sigh, her slender shoulders dropping as no one rose to her defense. "Alright, I know when I have been beat." She turned and began to leave.

She paused in the middle of the room and turned to face Cathrin again pointing her finger in her direction. "But know thi-" a bright flash filled the room along with the scent of charred flesh and oxidized atmosphere.

The horror-stricken counselors jumped to their feet, many of them clutching their cloaks to their bodies as if it would protect them.

Cathrin turned to address the congregation. "I stand before you as the avatar of Vyanna, as promised by the prophet Zymo, and Declared by the prophet Xious. I stand before you now to usher in the enlightenment as was promised to our ancestors, the Descended, when Vyanna anchored her throne to the sun. Who among you is worthy to stand with me as we now enter this great age of enlightenment?!"

A third of the counselors, including Trepidor, fell to one knee and bowed. This was expected, these were the members of the Enlightened who had sworn to bring an end to the age of eclipse. The remaining councilors looked to each other, confusion and uncertainty in their eyes, but one at a time they began to fall in line, until only Cathrin stood at the head of the table, her image reflected in the great mirror behind her, every bit the visage of a goddess.

* * *

Xious watched the churning pool of molten rock, which had once been the planet Corah'harin. The last holdout among the Coalition which had now officially dissolved and become part of the New Descendant Empire. It had taken centuries of planning, carefully laying the groundwork for the revolution which Xious had made a reality.

The Alliance had been unprepared for this, and there was no one left in the galaxy who could stop him. Not even Zaeith or Glayina, and the swirling mass of magma below was proof of that. Xious had learned all he could of the ancient arts of magic from Zaeith, always pressing him for more until he began to grasp at power which the mercenary was too afraid to tamper with. For years Xious had served as his first officer, though he had never discovered his true name. At one point Xious had hoped to take over from him when he retired, taking upon himself the name of the devil, soaring around the galaxy like some deranged vigilante.

The thought of it amused him now, he had been so childish back then. The man was a coward, and because of that, he would never understand what true power was. Glayina, however, was truly powerful, but she was also a fool. All Xious had to do was praise her, and her ego had done the rest. In her pride she had revealed to him all her secrets, laying before him the truth of the galaxy and opening up to him the power of the gods.

The power the witch had given him allowed him to rise in the ranks of the Descendants, and now he was revered as a prophet, a true visionary with the ability to call down the powers of Vyanna from heaven. He chuckled to himself; what a farce. Now with the full power of the Descendant military, and this battleship, which he had designed himself, even Glayina was only an insect compared to him.

The hardest part had been tolerating the Drak'or's absurd religion. Their declaration of all technology as witchcraft had blinded them. Ironically it was this same religion which had allowed Xious to unite the Coalition under the new Empire. Using the power he had gained, he had declared himself the Dark One, reincarnated in the flesh to once again fight for the justice of his people; what a joke. A hospital here, a new school there, and the Coalition had been begging for scraps at his feet even before he had brought about the new plague. Now he had been elevated to the status of a savior; the old governments hadn't stood a chance.

The destruction of Ulun'tess and Corah'haren had not been necessary to reign in the magistrates of the Coalition. They were more than satisfied with the eradication of the disease, from colonies who had pledged their devotion to Vyanna. And, of course, the fact that the plague always disappeared exactly three days after a colony had taken the oath had caused the people to petition the magistrates in droves.

No, this demonstration was for the benefit of the Federation. The Guilds were more organized than the factions of the Coalition had ever been, and far less superstitious. The only things they cared about were money and power, specifically their own power. But after this, no military force would dare challenge the Descendants again. Never had the galaxy seen the full might of a dragon-class cruiser. The fact that the Alliance had ever considered their own citadel ships comparable was laughable. And now the entire galaxy knew why.

Then again, the Zhemarah wasn't an ordinary dragon-class. It was the divine providence, the hand of mercy and hammer of justice, to the Goddess Vyanna. It, and its sister ship, had visited both of these worlds, and untold fortunes had been spent in an effort to save them from the plague. But despite the pleading of many of the people, the magistrates had demonstrated no faith. They had refused to take the oath, and declared Xious a charlatan. As a result, the disease had become so viscous even the plant life, and the planets themselves, had fallen victim to it.

For the sake of the galaxy, Corah'haren, at least, had to be eradicated. And so with great sorrow, Xious took upon himself the task of cleansing their world. At least, that is the story the rest of the galaxy would get. But the message would be clear, and the Federation would not resist.

Of course the Fingalin Empire had been behind the Enlightened from the beginning, this had been their idea. Many of the members of the royal family were both members of the divine council, and among the Enlightened.

The Empress would become the new face of sovereign power, and behind her the power of the Divine Council. It had taken the better part of the last millennium to empty the council of the original elders and replace them with representatives from the Empire, and now that Gillian Maylis was finally dead, there was no one left to deny them.

Of course Xious had his own plans, he had not spent the last twenty years developing this scheme only to share the throne with that spoiled brat of an empress and her divine council. While Xious had stood on the front lines working to see their plans to fruition, they had sat on their glass thrones fattening themselves on the suffering of the galaxy. But Xious had shown them miracles, and it was Xious who they were loyal to, not the Descendants, not the Divine Council, not Cathrin, and certainly not Vyanna. Xious was the living embodiment of the Divine, a prophet, and every word he spoke was doctrine.

"Sir, Grand Admiral Trepidor is waiting for you." One of his senior Chaplains interrupted his thoughts.

"Perfect." Xious turned and crossed the viewing platform, exiting the enormous glass dome which sat at the bottom of the southernmost point of the ship. "Inform the cardinal that I will be taking the call in his private conference chamber."

The conference chamber was a circular room made of carved onyx, with immense mirrors of poured obsidian on the wall, a blatant deviation from the standard Descendant aesthetic. A decision Xious had made for most of the executive portions of the ship. Reluctantly, he had let them build the more populated areas to the common design.

Xious summoned the projected control interface for the circular holo-emitter in the center of the room, then called up the pending call request to Trepidor's private quarters on A'un, Vinge's moon, and the Descendant council seat.

Trepidor's image appeared in the view field, pacing back and forth across the invisible office, while never leaving the center of the viewer.

"Good news I trust, Admiral," Xious asked, raising an eyebrow in mock amusement.

Trepidor turned to face the imaging device. Dark circles had formed under his eyes and his hair was ruffled as if he had been pulling on it for several minutes. "Well, it's not bad new… I mean, not necessarily."

Xious's face tightened. If this idiot had messed this up again, he would have his head. "What, exactly, do you mean by 'not necessarily?'"

Trepidor began squirming under the director's gaze. "The Dressick is late reporting in," he finally admitted.

"Isn't that the ship that was supposed to have taken care of that loose end we talked about?"

The admiral shrank, playing with his hands and avoiding eye contact. "W-well yes, but it doesn't necessarily mean that things are not tied up."

"O'rah cress meku seph re'kah." Xious muttered the spell under his breath. Trepidor's body became rigid as the curse forced him to look into the caster's eyes, and removed his ability to control his own body.

Xious leaned forward, almost touching the hologram with his nose. "Can you promise me that Gillian Maylis is dead?"

Cold sweat broke out on the admiral's face as he tried to resist the spell's effect, tried to work out some lie or half-truth that might convince Xious to spare his life. "N-n-no," his tongue tripped over the words as if he had gagged on some kind of small animal. "B-but i-n his last report, D-arith said he had caught up to the ship w-who had made c-ontact with the Vyrant, It was named th-e S-Shade. It's a small ship. Th-there is n-no way they could have escaped the Dressick,"

Xious felt the blood as it drained from his face and began to boil again. If Captain Darith had crossed paths with Zaeith, they would be lucky if there was enough left of him to bury.

"Fo'el ty'ell o'rah"

Seph

A dark red line of blood began to appear on the admiral's neck spreading across his throat. Trepidor let out a scream of agony,

"No please, I can fix this!" He yelled, panic welling up in his eyes.

Xious turned to leave.

"Please, It's not too late. Cathrin already has control of the council, even if he is alive, no one will believe him!"

Xious paused. "Meku."

There was a thud as the admiral collapsed to the floor and began gasping for breath. Xious turned to his pathetic bundle of a form, slouched on the ground and holding his neck. As much as he hated to admit it, he still needed the admiral. Someone had to hold Cathrin's leash, for now.

"I will take care of Maylis myself, in the meantime make sure our empress doesn't do anything foolish with her new-found power." He paused, turning away from the imaging device. "And Admiral."

"Y-yes?"

"You *will* not fail me again." Xious reached out with his mind, deactivating the holo-projector with a thought. He would come to regret this, but at the moment, there was not much of a choice. Maylis had to be dead, and Cathrin needed to be kept in check.

Returning to the holo-field, Xious called Cathrin's chambers. It was only a moment before her projection appeared. "Xious, how unexpected, has something come up?"

Xious bowed low, "I am afraid so, your eminence. It appears the forces of darkness have once again conspired to threaten your reign, and consume the divine plan."

Cathrin laughed. "After everything that has been done? Surely you must be mistaken, Director. I have been chosen by Vyanna herself, there is not a power in the galaxy which could stand in our way."

Xious suppressed a grimace, soon enough he would be rid of this pretentious child and the Divine Council, but for now, they were necessary. Once the other governments had been officially dissolved, and they had outlived their usefulness, he could be free of this charade.

Xious rose from the floor but did not meet the empress's eyes. "Even so you Highness, I have seen it in a vision, and I am afraid I must be delayed in my return to your side, for Vyanna has given me a task which I must see to with the utmost urgency."

"I am the avatar of Vyanna, how can she have commanded you to do something, and I not be aware of it?"

Now Xious did meet her gaze, setting his jaw into a face of stone. "You may be the image of Vyanna, but I am her voice, do not forget that unless you would like to be replaced."

Cathrin frowned but did not protest. "Very well, Trepidor can see to my preparations, but do not take too long, you will be required for the coronation ceremony."

Xious bowed at the waist, allowing his complexion to return to a humble demeanor. "Of course, your imperial majesty."

Cathrin cut the connection, and Xious had to suppress a fresh wave of irritation. No matter. Once he had settled things with his former master, not even Vyanna herself would be able to stand in his way.

Chapter 26

Kurt pulled up a chair and sat down. The man passed out across from him was old and disheveled, the reek of alcohol coming off his body, said he had drunk enough to knock out one of the massive euindas that lived in the oceans of Atlione. The crust which formed around his beard and mustache told a similar story.

"You Thrag?" Kurt half shouted at the man. He had spent several weeks tracking rumors which had eventually led him to this particular bar, which if he was being honest with himself made almost any religious version of damnation seem preferable. Though if the rumors were true, Thrag probably felt much the same way, as he tried to drown whatever remained of his life in booze, waiting for whichever god may still be paying attention to decide a fitting punishment and finally allow him to die.

It had been a bizarre and strange set of events which had led Kurt to this corner of the galaxy, which seemed to be a blind spot to both mortals and the divine alike. Ever since boarding the Shade, his life hadn't been the same. In only a few months, everything Kurt had believed about the world, and the universe at large, had been turned on its head, and he wanted answers.

An old colleague of his had been in the vicinity when he had transferred to the Engineering Core's cargo crane. Once news broke about the fate of that particular ship, Kurt had gone underground. Everyone was reporting it had an unfortunate accident, but after watching someone pull off not one, but two hyperspace folds which were only possible in the most abstract interpretation of the theory. The term coincidence had been removed from his vocabulary. No, what happened to that crane was no accident; the rescue of the Vyrant was an impossible mission, and now that it had been accomplished, someone was trying to cover it up.

After doing the best he could to erase himself from the world, Kurt had done a deep dive into conspiracy theories, sometimes spending days at a time following rumors of impossible encounters, only to discover the most mundane explanation at the end. The most intriguing, and substantial stories, not surprisingly, came from the outer colonies. The superstitious nature of the Drak'or religion provided a petri dish for fantastic stories and hallucinations.

However, as outlandish as many of the stories were, after weeks of digging a thread of truth began to emerge, stories which, like the Shade, left Kurt with more questions than answers, and at the end of his questions was Thrag.

Inexplicably, this pathetic excuse for a human being was the single common denominator in every story Kurt was able to substantiate.

Seph

He motioned to the bartender, then pointed to the empty mug in front of the passed out man across from him. A moment later, an identical mug was set on the table. Kurt tossed a coin to the bartender, then slid the mug over to his drunken companion. "I'll ask you again. Are you Thrag?"

The man rolled his head to one side, peering up at Kurt with a single bloodshot eye. "Depends, who's askin'?"

"Only a mad man, looking to justify his own insanity."

Thrag pushed himself up in his chair, resting most of his weight on his elbow, and took a swig of the offering Kurt had presented him with. "Aye I'm Thrag, but you'll find no justice 'ere."

"Maybe you can offer me something else."

Thrag tossed back the large mug, chugging so much of the beverage that Kurt wondered if he was attempting to drown himself in it. The mug dropped with a heavy thud on the table. "I've got nothin' nobody ought to want, mad or otherwise. Even if ya do, it ain't worth the price."

"I was prepared to accept my own damnation before I stepped through that door." Kurt nodded behind him.

Thrag began to laugh, at least Kurt thought it was supposed to be a laugh. In reality, it sounded more like a vacuum hose choking on a mud puddle. "Damnations goin' to be the least of your worries, walk away or you'll end up like old Thrag, if yer lucky."

"I am looking for the witches, can you, or can't you tell me where to find them?"

Thrag stared for a long moment, Kurt was beginning to worry that the man may have died on him, when he began to rise from his chair. "Ah no, I've got enough of you people's souls on my conscience. If you are that determined to lose your soul, find yourself another dealer."

Kurt learned across the table grabbing the old man's wrist before he could pull away. Reaching into his pocket, he slammed a handful of coins on the table. "All I need is a map, what I do with it is my own business."

Slowly Thrag slumped back into his seat staring at the money. "Fella, you ain't got no idea what you're asking for."

Kurt released the man's arm, sitting back in his own chair and tossing one of the coins across the table. "Then enlighten me."

"At first they'll give you everything you ever wanted; they appear as beautiful women, with long flowing hair and skin as fair as the evening sky. The'll make you feel like a man in ways no woman ever has before, but in return they will take from you everything that makes ya feel alive. Right in front of your eyes they'll change into hideous monsters, the bodies of hags, mixed with giant snakes. They will suck you dry until you're nothing more than a husk of flesh and bone, not alive but unable to die."

Kurt smirked. "If what you say is true, why are you here?"

Thrag let out a long wheezing sigh, "Because I thought I could outsmart them. If they let me go, I'd send the souls of a hundred men. But I was wrong."

Kurt slid another coin across the table. "So what went wrong?"

"Nothing, I got exactly what I asked for, they let me go, but they didn't set me free."

Seph

"You look free to me."

Thrag laughed so hard he began to cough and choke on his own tongue. Regaining his composure only after slamming his fist into his chest a few times and taking another long chug. "Free to live a life of pain. I haven't been able to taste a thing in almost fifty years. They're jealous beasts, if I try to touch a woman her skin might melt, or her hair might fall out. Any pleasure turns into pain. The only peace I have is when I pass out, seen how I can't even sleep 'less I'm drunk."

"I hate to suggest it, but why haven't you… put an end to it yet?"

Thrag grabbed one of the coins and tossed it at the bartender "Hey, get me another of these things!" he shouted. "Ya mean kill myself? Ya think I ain't tried that. They won't let me die, not as long as I know how to find 'em, and fools like you keep looken. Well, it ain't worth it."

Kurt slid a few more coins across the table as Thrag took the new mug from the bartender and began to drink. "Like I said, I only need a map."

Thrag let the mug slam into the table. "Thanks for the drinks, but I ain't going to help ya, least not while I have the brains to stop myself."

Kurt let out a sigh and stood, leaving the remaining few coins on the table. If Thrag was in as deep as he claimed, there might be another way to get what he was looking for. "I will find them, even if you won't help me." He moved to a table across the room and waited.

It took much longer than he had anticipated, Thrag had to drink enough liquor to float a ship in before he passed out, but eventually he did, and once he did Kurt found he was much more willing to talk. Quasar coordinates and other navigational data began to spew out of Thrag's mouth like some kind of AI readout. Kurt recorded the data on his pad, then left Thrag a final tip; if he was right, he wouldn't be needing money much longer.

Pulling his coat up around his face to protect him from Feshick's persistent dust storms, he stepped out into the red world possibly for the last time.

* * *

Shortly after entering the Dead Zone, the stars disappeared from his sensors; not only could light not escape the paradoxical area of space, but it couldn't get in either. Navigating was impossible. The inky blackness continued in every direction, and no matter how far Kurt tried to jump he couldn't escape, whether the witches were real hardly mattered to him. Once someone had been foolish enough to enter this section of space, there wasn't a way out of it.

After a week, by his guess, of strategic wandering, his food supplies had been drained. He found himself waiting for the escape of death to claim him.

"Now, now, why would someone have come all the way out here?" The female voice was soft, and had an amused ring to it, with an underlying bitterness like claws hiding beneath the surface.

"I am looking for you, I suppose." Kurt said, rising from his bed and looking around the small cabin.

"For me, you say? Why I am flattered, it is not very often that my meals deliver themselves so freely."

Kurt swallowed against the lump forming in his throat. "I have come to learn of the ancient magic."

There was a bright flash of light, and a young

woman appeared standing in the cabin. Long dark hair flowed over her shoulders and down her back, accentuating the curves of her pale skin which was clearly visible through the sheer gray dress which left just enough to his imagination. Kurt felt himself drawn to her, mesmerized by the vertical pupils in her bright yellow eyes.

"Why should I teach you about magic?" The alluring sound of her voice pulled him in like the aroma of incense.

"I seek to understand the nature of our universe. I am a scholar and a philosopher, nothing more."

The woman stepped forward, pressing her body against his, a long fingernail tracing the exposed skin on his arm, the warmth of her breath teasing the edge of his ear. She inhaled, and he felt as if a small portion of his essence had been stolen.

The woman recoiled her eyes narrowing into thin slits across the wrong axis. "You have had contact with the Hunter!" She hissed.

Kurt froze, feeling drained out of his arms and legs. "The Hunter?"

The obvious confusion on his face must have been enough to satisfy her as she soon relaxed, leaning over him once again, brushing his lips with her breath which smelled of jasmine. "Tell me Scholar, what is your name?"

"K-Kurt." He barely managed to stammer, tripping over his own tongue.

"Well Kurt," she said with a soft giggle that echoed in his mind, betrayed by her appearance. She twirled in a circle stepping away from him, the motion removing the need for his imagination. "I am Glayina, Queen of Erindite."

A dark shadow lifted from the view window, floating in the void was a gargantuan structure, fused together from the hulls of spacecraft from every age of the Alliance.

She grinned, exposing snake-like fangs beneath her crimson lips. "Welcome home."

Chapter 27

James found himself once again admiring the Descendant's craftsmanship as he walked the vast empty corridors of the Dressick. The eerie echo of his footsteps accentuating the sheer grandeur of it. It felt in many ways like wandering through an art exhibit. He wondered about the various stories represented in the elaborate stone carvings and elegant glass etching. Legends, frozen in time and retold generation after generation, a few embellishments here, a little twisting on occasion to fit the new political, social, and moral narratives of the changing times.

How would the people of these tales feel about the world they had left, and what their inheritors had done with it? A chill ran up his spine at the realization that a few of these pieces may have been carved by the very people they depicted. If the legends were true, some of the Descendant vessels dated back to the Alliance's first adventures into deep space.

It was strange to think about the fact that some of his ancestors may have once walked through this same hallway as they mapped the very first passageways through the stars. Of course the idea was little more than a fantasy, as James had no idea when or where this specific ship had been built, and it was difficult to see much of anything in a three-thousand-year-old ship remaining relevant today. So even if this had been one of the original vessels, it was unlikely it still retained any of its original parts, save for possibly the stone work itself.

A small robot darted under his feet, almost tripping him in the process. It was one of the small nids, or NID3's as they were formally designated. It stood for Non Independent Drone, and the Dressick had several thousand of them. Unlike automated custodial droids, or other AI controlled robots, nids required direct instruction for every task they performed, a feature which made them the most, and least, useful robots ever manufactured.

With a nearly unlimited number of possible attachments, and more being developed every day, nids could be used to assist in accomplishing almost anything. But their processing power limited them to only being able to perform exactly one thing at a time. They always performed whatever that one thing was precisely as instructed and would continue to do so until turned off, or instructed to do something else.

This combined with their easy to approach price tag, and the fact that, unlike AI controlled robots, they never decided that they knew how to do something better than you, had made them the most common droids in the galaxy. Finding use not only in commercial spaces, but also in many private homes.

Seph

They were kind of like a pet, except they always behaved themselves.

Besides that they were kind of cute, with square heads and two horizontal antennas on their small humanoid bodies. They resembled tiny Fetus, James thought with a chuckle.

A familiar cold sensation began to tingle at the tips of his fingers, it was as if a dark cloud was billowing down the corridor. The Captain approached from the direction of the hanger. The surprise of seeing him caught James off guard. Before he could stop himself, he snapped to a salute, coming to attention in the middle of the hall.

The Captain continued past him, ignoring the gesture. "Get the ship ready for departure, we are going to Atlione."

"The Shade, sir?" As far as James knew, Fetu had not yet been able to finish the repairs on the fold generator, having been kept busy trying to maintain order amongst the remaining crew of the Dressick, as well as account for the engineers who had not disembarked during their rendezvous with the crane.

Locking the Dressick's crew in their quarters had, so far, proven effective. Using the nids to patrol the hallways was making things easier, but the process was still time-consuming.

The Captain paused in the hallway, speaking over his shoulder. "No. We will take the Dressick." He resumed walking, making it clear the subject was not up for conversation.

James inhaled deeply, then let out a sigh. He had so many questions, not the least of which was, how had the Captain tracked them down and gotten on board so quickly.

A few paces behind the Captain, Nevarian appeared. He glanced at James with a half-smile that was equally sympathetic as it was judgmental. Brushing aside his concerns for the integrity of the space-time continuum at the moment, James decided to focus on the task he had been given.

Getting the Dressick to Atlione was not going to be any easy task, it simply was not meant to be managed by such a small crew. Sure there were enough of the ship's original crew left on board, but they could count on little more than passive compliance from them. Anyone from the Engineering Corps who had been considering an extended contract, was no longer interested, deciding to cut their losses and get as far away from the Shade as possible. Then again, between Fetu and Travis, they might be able to make it work.

James found Fetu installing something under the hull of the Shade. The round object was about two feet in diameter. Its center was a geodesic glass dome raised no more than half an inch from the object's edge. The matte black material lining the back of the dome made it appear to absorb light more than it reflected it. Though judging from the mass of wires Fetu was working with, the object served only as a cap for something much larger contained within the ship proper.

"Part of the fold generator?" James asked. That would be strange, the fold generator was located in the engine room, though the focusing lens was on the outside of the ship. If he remembered correctly, it was above the bridge.

"No, Scot's working on that. This is something The Captain asked me to install." Something sparked from inside the opening where the large man was working and a nid dropped from somewhere inside, falling on its head before flopping on the floor.

"Vyanna help me, if I could get this droid to work, I'd be done with it already." He ducked out of the hole wiping grease from his hands with the rag tucked into his belt.

James stifled a laugh as he pointed to the device attached below Fetu's ear. "That little gizmo is your whole problem." It was a neural transmitter, more rudimentary than the one James used. Only capable of sending instructions out and thus posed none of the risk of a true neural link. Rudimentary, however, did not mean easier to operate.

"What, this thing? I thought they were supposed to make it easier."

James shook his head. "Only if you're really good at it, and nids can be especially difficult to control. They need specific commands, our thoughts are usually too abstract for them to get an accurate picture. If you get distracted or your mind starts to wander it can be a bit of a mess. You would have more luck trying to use a kitten to knit a sweater."

The small robot righted itself then walked in an oblong circle before crashing into Fetu's leg and going limp on the floor.

"I suggest vocalizing the commands, as well as thinking them. It helps clear up the clutter which tends to get in the way."

Fetu bundled up his rag and tossed it at James, "Did you just come down here to give me a hard time?"

Expertly, James avoided the object, letting it sail over his shoulder. "I was hoping I could get you and Travis together on a project."

"Oh?" Fetu tilted his head, ears twitching. The nid

followed suit, the two did look a lot alike.

"The Captain said he wants us to take the Dressick to Atlione."

Fetu laughed. Throwing a thumb over his shoulder to point, "Fly this thing, with eight people? Not likely."

James nodded, inspecting the strange engravings around the outside of the object Fetu had been installing.

"I was afraid you would say that. But what if we used the nids?"

Fetu let out a snort. "To run a ship? Sure it is a lot of hands, but do you have any idea what kind of task management would be involved in that?"

James shrugged, turning to face his friend, "No, but what if we gave that job to Scot?"

Fetu shook his head. "Not a chance, he has quite a bit of extra processing for a SK01 unit, but there would need to be a buffer between him and the information that could somehow assign task priority."

"What if we only used half the nids to run the ship, and used the other half as the buffer."

Fetu inhaled, then let it out in a puff. "You don't know when to give up, do you? Anyone ever tell you, you are too smart for your own good." He scratched the back of his bald head. "Yeah, it's possible; it will require a lot of new code, but Travis can handle it. It's obvious you aren't an engineer though, cause otherwise you'd never have suggested it."

James laughed. "Not my job to make it happen, just to have the ideas." He shrugged, then nodded to the strange device hanging from the bottom of the ship. "When did The Captain come on board?"

Fetu shrugged, "No idea, I came down to check on how Scot was doing. He was just sort of here. I

Seph

wouldn't think about it too much though. You might hurt that pretty little head of yours, and we can't have that. Who would come up with these crazy schemes for the rest of us?"

James grinned. "Get us moving again, I need to go check in on Darith before *he* starts coming up with crazy schemes."

His concern over Darith had been unnecessary. As James approached the state room where Meghnah was keeping an eye on him, The Captain burst through the doors, the edges of his cloak drawing the air into his wake. James resisted the urge to salute, though there was nothing he could do about the reflexive stiffening of his muscles. The Captain stopped and faced him. He found himself forced to break eye contact with him. There was something ancient burning in his eyes, and for a second James thought it might be enough to singe him. It was as if there were a palpable hatred deep inside him. Like the embers of a fire smoldering deep within the ground, and someone had cracked open its cage.

"I want that man off my ship."

James nodded. "Y-yes sir." The words rolled off his tongue as if they were some heavy object he had been attempting to hoist over his shoulder, only to find he did not quite have the strength.

The Captain's gaze softened a little. He looked as if he were about to say something, then thought better of it. Turning he continued down the corridor. The pressure on James's chest lifted a little when he disappeared beyond the curve.

He wasn't sure what he was expecting to find when he entered the estate room, but whatever it had been, he was not prepared. Darith sat curled into a bundle on the floor rocking backwards and forwards muttering to himself. There was a large crack in one of the stone walls not far from him. Dark circles had formed under his eyes, he looked as if he had aged a decade or two since James had last seen him, and not slept in as long.

Meghnah stood off in the corner, a blank expression on her face which looked unnaturally timid for her. She held a black sword in her hand of a design James didn't recognize, unlike a Drak'or blade, the hilt had a full crossguard, both edges appeared to have been sharpened, and the blade itself was straight not curved.

"What happened here?"

Meghnah shook her head slowly, eyes remaining unfocused on something across the room. "I'm not sure... it happened so fast. I am still processing it, I think."

"Start from the beginning."

Meghnah inhaled breathing slowly. "Right, Darith here had been attempting to negotiate with me, though he isn't very good at it. He obviously isn't used to being on the losing side of things. The Captain blew through the doors like a solar flare. He slammed Darith into the wall over there." She pointed to the cracked stone. "After that, I'm not sure, I couldn't hear what The Captain was saying, but he was holding Darith by the throat. Darith kept trying to pry his hands off, The Captain pulled this sword out of nowhere and was about to run it through his neck. Darith started muttering the name 'Xious,' he just kept repeating it. I thought The Captain might kill him. But he tossed him on the floor there," she nodded in his direction. "And that's about it."

James took a moment to observe the room again.

Seph

Darith dragged his body across the floor, crawling on his hands, grasping at the hem of James's pants. "Please, Please." He gasped between sobs. "Keep him away from me, Please, let me off this ship."

James looked up at Meghnah, the bewilderment in her eyes becoming tangible.

* * *

Sleep did not come easily that night. After storming out of the state room, The Captain had systematically broken every piece of glass on the ship. It had always been strange that there were no mirrors on the Shade. Now James found himself wondering once again about the reason for it. It seemed unlikely that The Captain had felt the need to smash them all strictly out of anger, but it was difficult to come up with an explanation that didn't seem overly superstitious.

Unable to quiet his mind, James wandered the corridors of the empty ship. The custodial droids were attempting to clean up what was left of a glass etching. Carefully, James stepped over the pieces. Had he seen this one before The Captain smashed it? I didn't make much of a difference, it's not like he knew the stories behind the images.

Had The Captain's actions been motivated by the etchings themselves, perhaps? The Captain certainly gave the impression he had a distaste for the religion. Maybe using the name for the devil was some kind of revenge for a perceived slight against him. A sort of passive aggressive defiance.

The Captain had never come across as petty though. And it wasn't like he could take on the entire Order by himself. Though the way he had been acting, James half wondered if he would try. It was difficult to get a handle on what was going on in The Captain's mind. Spending any substantial amount of brain power thinking about it, made little difference in that regard. Besides, there were more important things than The Captain's disposition towards Descendant doctrine.

James did not have much time in the last day to stop and put things into perspective; now that he was taking the opportunity, the picture that was forming was anything but reassuring.

Darith had come to Dramia looking for Gillian. Not the Shade, not The Captain, but Colonel Gillian Mayles. Why? Darith had said Gillian was a traitor, which he supposed was technically true. But in reality, the only thing Gillian had done to 'help overthrow the Vyrant' was give his crew the option of survival. The Shade had more than come out on top during their battle, and from the onset the Colonel was only doing his job. At least that's the way it had looked.

What had that job been? If the Vyrant had not been directly involved in the DSI 3122 incident, and they really were just maintaining the quarantine, why did it matter if he had survived or not? The pit of his stomach sank, perhaps whoever was responsible for the station, had also been meant to eliminate Gillian. Perhaps he had been marked as dead even before his encounter with the Shade .

Since the Shade got involved, they had to make sure not only to eliminate Gillian, but also any witnesses. They had probably hoped that destroying the cargo crane, and making it look like an accident would be enough. But when the computer record showed the rendezvous with the Shade, they had to make sure all the loose ends were tied up.

Seph

So they had hired those two scumbags back on Dramia to check it out. Darith had been sure Gillian was with them, so it must have been included in their report. Briefly James wondered what would have happened had he not let them go. Based on the fact they had annihilated Ulun'tess, nothing good. Dramia would have made for a more noteworthy target, but an accident was still an accident.

Either way, by the time James had questioned the two it would have been too late. Had they failed to report, it would still have given them the confirmation they needed. Why would they go through so much trouble to get rid of one man? And who exactly was Xious? James had never heard the name before, but he seemed to have some kind of history with the Captain.

He might find answers to his questions on Atlione, though he was starting to think a more in depth conversation with Gillian might be in order.

A chill formed in his extremities, which brought James to a stop, the familiar tightness in his chest signaling The Captain 's presence. He turned to see his dark figure billowing towards him. He stopped, his bright red eyes looking James over like a customs droid searching for contraband.

James had been too preoccupied before he too noticed how tired The Captain looked. The scent of fire and smoke radiated off him, mud and ash caked to his clothing, skin, and hair, which appeared disheveled and ragged. The lower corner of his cloak had been singed, and there were several holes in his uniform which had not been there three days ago. The Captain looked like he had been through the core and back, references to the name aside.

"Sir, I didn't expect anyone else would still be

awake." James folded his hands behind his back, this time settling for an at ease position to combat his natural impulse to salute.

The Captain let out a long tired breath, his shoulders drooped and James thought for the first time, that the man looked... vulnerable.

"I doubt I could sleep if I wanted to, James." There was a sincere honesty in his eyes that for some reason made James feel uncomfortable.

"I do not mean to pry Captain, but is there anything I can do?"

The Captain let out a long sigh, leaning his back against the wall sliding into a sitting position. "Can I trust you?"

The question caught him off guard, what was that supposed to mean? But the Drak'or's eyes told him that he was serious.

"Of course, Captain." It was lame, and he knew it, but what was he supposed to say?

The Captain exhaled, running a hand up his forehead through his hair. "The world is changing James, and I don't think I can stop it. In fact, I feel like it is all I can do to keep up." He stared at the wall, eyes unfocused.

Pushing down the awkwardness of the situation, James sat down beside his captain. "In all fairness sir, I think you may be taking on too much responsibility."

The Captain let out a hollow laugh. "Perhaps so, perhaps not. Xious is someone I failed a long time ago. Had I been strong enough to do what I should have then, he would not have become what he is now."

"Which is?"

The Captain rolled his head to look at James. "A monster."

Seph

They stared at each other for a moment, James didn't want to break the silence, which felt almost... sacred.

"So what will you do now?" James asked when it became too unbearable.

"Stop him. No matter what it takes."

"Will we find something on Atlione to do that?"

"Maybe." Zaeith stood, brushing out the wrinkles in his uniform pants and straightening his cloak. "Here, take this." Reaching into his cape, he produced the white glove Chloe had taken from the Vyrant. "I believe you are ready for it now."

James took the glove, turning it over in his hands he noticed the gemstones had been removed.

"If you have any questions, I am sure Gillian can answer them." The Captain placed his hand on James's shoulder. His eyes burned with the kind of calm reassurance that grounded you, and promised that everything would work out in the end.

"Sir?"

"Don't worry about it." He said with a nod, then continued to walk. A few feet down the corridor The Captain paused. "Oh, and James." The drak'or turned, half facing him, he looked over his shoulder. "Thank you."

The warmth returned to his body as The Captain disappeared once more. And again, James found himself with more questions than answers.

Returning to the officers' deck, where they had each claimed a room for themselves, James paced the corridor wondering how offended Gillian would be if he barged in on him now. As he contemplated knocking on the door, Chloe stepped out of her room.

"James, I didn't expect anyone else to be up."

James laughed. "You and half the ship. Apparently

nobody is getting any rest tonight."

"I suppose that's to be expected." She said, not quite making eye contact.

James shrugged, "I mean, it's not every day you find out the most powerful military organization in the galaxy wants to kill you."

They both laughed at that but it was empty, the kind of laugh that you use because it takes too much energy to cry.

Silence filled the space, the awkward kind that happens when both of you have too much to say, but don't have any of the words you need to say it.

"What's that?" Chloe eventually asked, pointing to the glove.

"Oh this?" James handed it to her. "It's that glove you found on the Vyrant."

"Did you get it to work?"

James shook his head. "No, The Captain just gave it to me."

"Wait, The Captain had it?"

James nodded. "Not sure why though. Look, he took the gems out of it."

Chloe turned over the glove, then handed it back to him. "I wonder why he did that."

James shrugged. "I was hoping maybe Gillian could teach me how to use it."

Chloe brushed a strand of hair out of her face. "It seems a little late, don't you think?"

He let out a sigh stretching the glove between his hands. "Yes, of course you're right. I just can't stop thinking about it. It's like an itch that I can't get rid of. You know, these same symbols are etched into something Fetu was installing on the Shade earlier today. That makes three places now, which as far as I can tell are unrelated."

"Four places." Chloe said looking up at him.

"Wait what? The disks, the glove, and whatever that thing was Fetu was working on, where's the fourth?"

Chloe looked away rubbing the back of her calf with the top of her foot. "On the floor of the shuttle bay in the Vyrant."

James stared, had she mentioned this before, surely he would have remembered. "What, you mean like a mural?"

She shook her head. "No, more like… a circuit board, I don't know how to describe it. I haven't really been sure I even saw it to be honest. That's why I never said anything about it. But it wasn't there when we arrived, Zaeith carved it into the floor, and I am pretty sure it is the reason we were able to get back safely."

James stared at her for a moment as he tried to process the implications of this new information. "Here, come with me." He grabbed her hand leading her through the ship.

She hurried to catch up. "Sure, but where are we going?"

"To figure out what this thing is."

"Isn't that a little dangerous? I mean, what if we end up opening up a hyperspace envelope or something?"

"Do you think The Captain would have given it to me if it was that easy?"

"I don't know that he wouldn't." She shot back.

James paused, then continued walking, a little slower so she could catch up. He realized with a start they were still holding hands. He felt a rush of blood in his cheeks, but couldn't bring himself to let go. Her hand felt so small in his, and something about how soft and warm it was both made his heart beat faster and put him more at ease.

"Alright, I will be careful, but I don't think it works like that."

"How do you think it works?"

"You said Gillian told you it was like a neural link, right?"

Chloe nodded. "Like a predecessor or something."

"I think it is a control device."

Chloe's muscles tightened. "Like a key…"

James paused. "What?"

"Something Gillian said. He said it was used for some of the more 'unique technologies' like a key, well, I said that part."

James nodded, then continued walking. "I suppose if I am right, that would be one way to describe it, though I think it is less like a key, and more like a command interface."

He led Chloe into the hanger bay, not stopping until they were under the Shade.

"What are you going to do now?"

James let go of her hand and slid on the glove. "See if I can't solve two mysteries at once." He braced himself against the pinch in his wrist, then shook his head clearing out the humming sensation it created.

He held out his hand, placing it against the glass dome. He closed his eyes and concentrated as if wearing a neural link. Before, there had been an empty space at the back of his mind. Now there was something hard and tangible. With a thought, he grabbed onto it and flexed it like a muscle.

The glass dome rang with a clear crystalline sound, emitting a bright green light from somewhere in its core. Information rushed at James's mind. Instinct kicked in as he began to sort and compartmentalize it. Only, he didn't need to. Unlike the neural link, data didn't bombard his brain. Instead, it sort of floated in the air in front of him, just beyond the tips of his fingers, like lines of code displayed over a holographic interface. Not tangibly, more like he had developed a new sense which allowed him to peek into the inner-workings of the device, and interact with it on a more intuitive level.

Chloe stared in amazement, twisting her body to get a better look at the object.

James broke the connection, and both the light and sound stopped. "Core."

"What is it?" Chloe asked, straightening.

"A plasma shield."

She starred, frozen for a moment by the revelation. "Are you sure?"

He nodded. "Absolutely"

"And the glove?"

"Definitely a control device, though it isn't exactly like the neural link, it is similar."

"Can I try?"

His immediate thought was no, of course not. She had no experience with a neural link and it would most certainly fry her brain. But as he contemplated it a little more he realized his concerns over that were unnecessary... probably.

Carefully he removed the glove from his hand, letting out a sigh of relief as the pressure dissipated. "Okay, but be careful, I like you too much to have your brain turned to jelly on me."

She reached for the glove and paused. "Is that a possibility?"

James exhaled. "Probably not..."

Gingerly, she took the glove. "What can I do to

avoid it?"

"Well, preferably have taken a neural link preparation course, and run a prelink trial."

"Or?"

"Before you touch the shield generator, imagine an empty filing space in your mind, then connect that to a body part, like behind your shoulder blade, or your left ear lobe."

She gave him a rather skeptical look. "Really, it's that easy?"

James shrugged. "I'm not sure I would call it easy."

She smiled slightly and pulled on the glove." Ouch!" She yelped. "Does it always do that?"

He nodded. "It's part of the link."

"Right..." Taking a deep breath, Chloe held her hand up to the device and closed her eyes.

James held his breath as he watched. Her eyes opened wide and she stared for a moment. His stomach began to tighten.

Chloe laughed. "I always thought this would be a lot harder."

Blood rushed into his face, as if his ego had gone three rounds in a boxing arena. "Well, I mean, this isn't like a proper link..."

"Okay, but... why did you make it glow?"

"Make it glow?" James was startled to realize it wasn't.

As if to answer his question, the glass dome suddenly illuminated with a deep blue light, emitting the same clean note it had before. A moment later it was silent.

"How did you do that?"

Chloe shrugged. "It seemed natural, I guess."

James couldn't help but smile. His ego might have

been bruised, but he was humble enough to recognize when he was outclassed. And as long as it was Chloe, he supposed he didn't mind that much.

Chloe removed her hand from the glass and stepped back out from under the Shade. "What does it do if you aren't using it to control something else?"

James raised an eyebrow. "Explode?" He asked, recalling the time they had attempted to use it on the Shade.

Chloe opened her palm, squinting with one eye she began to concentrate. An electric tingle ran through his body as a small blue light appeared in her hand. Slowly it grew until an orb of flowing energy hovered above her palm.

"How did you do that?"

Chloe giggled. "I guess it needed a more feminine touch."

James shook his head, "Right… Here, let me try again."

The sphere vanished and Chloe removed the glove. She breathed a sigh of relief, "Does it always feel that good to take it off?"

James took the glove. "The longer it is on, the better it feels to get rid of it." Sliding it on his own hand once more he winced at the pain. "Okay, let's do this."

Chloe smiled softly, "Be gentle with it, don't try to be rough. Less like you are kicking a ball, and more like you are holding my hand."

His pride couldn't let the instruction slide without a sarcastic scowl, though when he really thought about it he was more than a little embarrassed to admit that she was right. Still being called out like that hurt.

Closing his eyes, he felt for the empty space. He took a deep breath, inhaling and exhaling to relax his muscles. When he felt ready he reached forward with his mind, and scooped up the emptiness like scooping a leaf from a river.

A wave of energy rushed through his body towards his open palm. James opened his eyes to find a tiny green orb floating in the air. He stared for a moment, not sure what to make of the experience. Code like lines stretched out in his consciousness somehow describing the structure of the universe. Concentrating, he relaxed his body into the flow of energy, increasing it in his mind. The sphere began to grow until it was about eight inches in diameter.

Chloe lightly clapped her hands. "See, that wasn't hard was it."

James snorted, giving her a half-smile. "Okay, but why is mine green?"

Chloe shrugged. "Your guess is as good as mine, it's not like I made it blue on purpose."

James huffed. Well, it was nice to know she hadn't left him completely behind. Though if he were being honest with himself it was little more than a consolation prize, not that it was a competition. Though if it were, he had definitely lost.

James pushed on the orb with his mind, it was soft and palpable, its shape pressing back against him; space, time, and energy felt like clay beneath his fingers as it slowly gave way to his thoughts. In response, ripples began to form in the swirling energy. Pushing a little harder, he found he was able to control the flow, bending and moving as if to circumvent some object he had put in its path, the same way water might without gravity.

Getting a little braver, James grabbed the energy, stretching and pulling on it until it formed a long thin blade.

Chloe stepped closer examining it. "How did you do that?"

The current had slowed now. It flowed more evenly like the elegant rings of a gas giant from thousands of miles away.

James smiled. "I just… sort of did."

Chloe slapped him lightly on the arm. "Don't give me that!"

"Okay, okay, once you have the sphere, it's pretty easy to make it whatever shape you want. Pretend it's like water, and give it something to hold it."

Chloe's head bounced a couple of times as she twisted the corner of her lip, that answer appeared to satisfy her at least.

"Alright, but is it useful?"

James shrugged. "It's intimidating?" He offered.

Chloe laughed. "Give me a second."

She wandered off, returning a moment later with a small cargo crate.

"Try it on that."

James shrugged, then slashed the blade at the crate, moving it in a diagonal line through one of the corners. The blade yanked on his energy, almost like tripping over your own shoe laces, but otherwise did nothing.

Chloe raised an eyebrow. "Anything?"

James shrugged. Fighting back a wave of drowsiness. "I feel tired?" He released his concentration, and the blade vanished.

Chloe inspected the crate, pressing on the corner, the whole thing separated on a perfect line where the blade had passed through it. There was a loud crash as Chloe dropped the corner piece in surprise.

"Well, I'd call that something." James picked up the fallen corner examining the cut edge. It was perfectly smooth as if the metal had been separated at a molecular level.

Chloe examined the edge on the crate. Briefly the two exchanged the same unsettled glance.

James huffed, "I think I'm done for the night."

Chloe nodded. "Yeah, it's late, we have work to do tomorrow."

They both laughed. James removed the glove, handling it more cautiously now than he had before. A wave of dizziness washed over him as a headache slammed into his temples like something out of hyperspace. He stumbled forward, barely maintaining his balance.

Chloe caught him, one hand pulling back on his shoulder while the other supported him at the waist. "You okay?"

James nodded, using his hand to apply pressure to his forehead, "Sure, just… tired."

"Maybe we should get you in bed." The concern in her voice was earnest.

He nodded, stepping forward and losing his balance once again.

"Here, let me help you." She said, putting her small frame under his arm for support.

James gave her a weak smile, "Thanks."

Chapter 28

A hollow feeling grew in Chloe's chest as she carefully closed the massive wooden door. Saying good night had been harder than she had anticipated. There were so many things she still wanted to say. Whenever she tried to speak, the words would get lost somewhere in the neurons between her brain and her tongue. It felt like she was always tripping over herself, and it hurt feeling like there was nothing she could do about it. So much had happened, and it was all tangled up in a giant knot in her stomach.

More than anything, she wanted to thank James. Thank him for the training which had gotten her through the day. Thank him for the jacket, which had now saved her life on more than one occasion. But, if she was being honest with herself, the thing she wanted most was to thank him for the date, which seemed to have taken place in an entirely different lifetime.

She tapped her forehead against the door to her own room before opening it. How could she even begin to approach that subject now? The lights from the city, the view from the balcony. The feeling of the rain as it sprinkled on her face, soaking through her clothing and sticking to her skin. That all felt so far away, vanishing like the wisps of a half remembered dream.

As she entered the room, its automated lights came on. Letting out a sigh, Chloe walked over to the vanity table, where she had left James's folded jacket. She brushed the fabric with her finger tips. At some point the material had reverted to its worn blue appearance, leaving behind no trace of the Chef's coat it had absorbed.

She had meant to give it back to James, she told herself the only reason she hadn't was because there had not been a good opportunity. It wasn't as if she had known she was going to run into him tonight. If she had, she certainly wouldn't have gone out in her pajamas.

She half-smiled to herself. That was a lie, sure she hadn't planned on meeting him in the corridor. But secretly, she had gone for a walk hoping she would. Her heart ached for the opportunity to be alone with him. To see him smile, to make him laugh. To feel the warmth of his hand wrapped around hers. It was foolish, and she knew it. She had so many other things she should be focusing on. The Descendants were hunting them, they had followed them from DSI 3122. Tracked down and destroyed the cargo crane they had rendezvoused with. After hiring those two men on Dramia, they intercepted them at the orbital station. Somehow, Chloe didn't think stealing one of their ships, and flying it halfway across the galaxy, was going to improve their disposition.

Taking a deep breath to collect her thoughts, Chloe inspected herself in the room's elaborate mirror. Somehow none of those things really mattered. She was tired, exhausted even. But she was happy, happier then she had ever imagined she could be. There was something tangible to this that she had never had before. Even the outfit she was wearing now, it was one of the first things she had ever been able to call her own.

Meg had helped her pick it out back on Dramia, Chloe had insisted on looking for a new set of sleepwear, Meg was convinced it was a waste of time, but she went along. In truth, Chloe had been embarrassed when James had bumped into her before. She must have looked like she was drowning in Meg's old t-shirt.

Looking at her reflection, Chloe's cheeks grew numb. How was there a mirror here? Zaeith had broken them all hours ago. Reaching forward, she touched the surface of the mirror. The glass rippled like water under her fingertips.

She gasped, pulling her hand back. As the image began to settle, her sky blue t-shirt, and lilac lounge pants were replaced by an elegant white dress with a lavender shawl wrapped around her shoulders, clasped with a silver brooch on her chest.

Chloe looked down at herself, she definitely had not changed clothes. Cautiously she stepped forward, squinting her eyes to examine the image. It was more like a hologram than a reflection. The girl resembled Chloe, with the same white skin, slightly pointed ears, and shared eyebrows and nose.

But the girl in the mirror was shorter than Chloe, and her hair was pure white, like freshly fallen snow on the lakeside, and the blue in her eyes was so vast it was as if entire oceans had been swallowed in their depths, like a single drop of rain.

"Who are you?" She didn't understand why she was talking to the image, which was probably nothing more than her exhausted brain finally caving in under the pressure.

The young woman held up her hand, and pressed it against the surface of the mirror. Silver ripples echoed out from her palm, like waves viewed from beneath. Chloe hesitated, then took another step forward, and tentatively placed her own hand over the girl's.

The stranger wrapped her fingers around Chloe's, the mirror parted around her body giving way and rippling outwards like the surface of a pool as she pulled her through.

Chloe stumbled forward, the ground beneath her feet was like liquid glass, as she gazed into it, it felt as if she could watch the passage of time, winding its way forward and backwards like currents in a river. From somewhere in the distance the sound of silver chimes carried on the wind, which smelled of apple blossoms in a mild summer breeze.

The young woman released Chloe's hand. Stumbling over her own feet, Chloe turned to find there was no sign of her room, or the Dressick, anywhere. The whole world appeared white, and the whiteness stretched on forever in every direction.

"Welcome Chloe, I am sure you have many questions." The woman's voice was soft and inviting, in the way that instantly puts you at ease.

Blinking back the absurdness of the situation, Chloe

swallowed and attempted to speak. "Uh huh," she nodded.

The girl smiled softly. "I cannot promise you satisfying answers, but I will try."

Regaining a vague sense of self awareness, the questions began to pile on top of one another, fighting for space in the spotlight. "Who… are you?" Chloe finally managed the question she felt was most important to establish first.

The girl looked down at her hands, finger folded against her lap, and inhaled. "I am myself, nothing more, and nothing less. But I assure you, I am quite real, you have not imagined me, and you are not going crazy."

Chloe starred, taking a moment to process. "That's… Not really what I meant…" Although she did appreciate the reassurance about her mental state, crazy or not, it was nice to think her hallucination thought she was sane.

"I suppose not. My apologies." She waved a hand and the ground began to reshape itself, swirling into a vortex that formed into a sort of bench, though it looked more like a wave frozen in time. "Please. Join me."

" At times it is difficult for me to navigate the line between the things we say, and the things that we mean." She folded her hand over her crossed knees. "My name is Vyanna."

Chloe's stomach dropped, as her legs all but melted out from underneath her, she sat on the bench. Did she say… Vyanna, as in Vyanna, Vyanna. Like "Our Lady Vyanna?" Vyanna as in God?

She sucked on her tongue swallowing against the sudden dryness in her mouth. "So your…"

Vyanna shook her head. "No, I am not god, nor am I a goddess. There are those who worship me as such, but I do not ask for their worship."

Chloe took a moment to look at her critically once again, sitting here with her like this, it was amazing how much she resembled herself, they could have passed themselves off as sisters if they had wanted to.

"If you are not god… What are you?"

Vyanna looked down at her hands, inhaling, she focused on something far in the distance before meeting Chloe's eyes. "I suppose from your perspective, that is a difficult thing to understand. Once, I was not much different than you are now. Though, from a certain point of view, I have always existed as you see me. But it is not as simple as being one thing, or not being another. Time and space exist differently here than the way that you see them. And I come from a world very different from the one that you know."

Chloe pressed on her temples with her index and middle fingers, then ran her hands through her hair pulling it back out of her face. As complicated as this whole thing was, it couldn't possibly be any more complicated than Vyanna's answers.

"Okay, so you are not god, where is this place?"

Vyanna reached out and brushed Chloe's hair with her finger tips, her skin was soft and gentle. "This is a gateway which exists between your world, and mine."

"Where is your world?"

Vyanna smiled sweetly. "I come from a place that is independent of dimensions of reality as you understand them. A plane that exists outside of the fabric of space and time."

Was that even possible? The hallucination theory was becoming more and more plausible. Did people who were hallucinating know they were hallucinating?

"Why did you come here?"

"Because the Descendants are my responsibility. I may not have asked them to worship me, but they have chosen to in spite of that, and if it were not for my mistakes they never would have existed. So in that way I bear the blame for whatever is to become of them."

Chloe sat back against the frozen time wave trying to open up her mind enough to process the information she was being given. "What do you mean, they never would have existed?"

Vyanna's eyes grew distant as if she were remembering a time, that time itself had forgotten. "I was there when the Alliance was formed. I chose to intervene in their war. I should have left them alone. I should have allowed them to decide their own fate. I had been warned what would happen if I stepped in, but I didn't listen. I couldn't stand to sit on the sidelines and watch them slaughter each other, and for what? They didn't even remember what they were fighting over."

Chloe looked down at the floor and gasped. The events Vyanna was describing were playing out in the liquid glass as if it were a window through time.

Vyanna continued. "Because of my arrogance, I ended up causing the very tragedy I was trying to prevent. And I will bear that burden for the rest of eternity."

Chloe watched the scene unfold, Humans, Fingalins, and Drak'or murdering each other. Huge machines of destruction rained fire down from the sky, laying waste to entire cities. But more terrifying than weapons were the people.

Men and women charged into battle wearing the

same kind of glove she had taken from the Vyrant. They used them to twist and reshape the fabric of reality. Creatures made from earth and stone rose from the ground, destroying the machines. Bolts of lightning and fire shot from their hands as if the elements themselves were at the mercy of their command. They opened great fissures in the planet's crust summoning lava from deep below its surface, they molded it to their wills and turned it on one another. Others cause the oceans themselves to rise, sending them crashing down on entire armies, only to have them turned back on them.

A mixture of wonder and horror welled up inside of her. She had been told the story of origin, everyone had. Though the characters involved sometimes differed, the key details remained the same. The three races had been at war with each other, in their hatred they had destroyed their homeworld. But all that was left now, was a husk of a planet artificially sustained but impossible to revive. In all the retellings of the story she had heard, Chloe had never imagined destruction on the scale that played out before her.

"By the time I realized my mistake, it was too late. I did what I could to save their world, which put an end to the war. And I gave them access to the stars. For that, a portion of them began to worship me. They took my words and wrote them into scripture. Then they named themselves prophets, creating more scripture to suit their own interpretation of my actions. Finally, they twisted and corrupted it, using my name to justify the atrocities they commit."

"Why don't you stop them?"

Vyanna wrapped her arms around Chloe, pulling her close. Pressing their foreheads together, she looked

341

deep into Chloe's eyes.

There was a sadness in Vyanna that reached out to Chloe deep within her soul.

"Because it would always end the same. They might listen for a short time, but within a generation their greed and ambition would return. And what then? Ought I to stand over their shoulders at all times, forcing my own will on them? No, I think not. If I were to do so, I would be no better. I would be a tyrant who could never be defied."

She leaned back, sliding her hand down Chloe's arm until she grabbed her hand and squeezed it. "You cannot gain affection through oppression. And love cannot control. For love, is at its essence, freedom of will, and guidance to succeed. Obedience for itself can only be compelled by fear. And where there is fear, there is no freedom. And the oppressor will find that they are bound by the same chains which hold the prisoner."

Chloe nodded slowly, feeling as if she had only understood the smallest portion of what the goddess had meant. "Why me, why now?"

Vyanna squeezed Chloe's hand then stood. Walking a few paces away, she spun, her simple white dress twirling about her ankles. "I need to ask of you a favor, and until now you have not been ready to accept it."

"What do you mean? What has changed?" Almost as soon as the words left her lips, Chloe wished she could resend them, of course she had changed, hadn't she been contemplating that very thing. For the first time in her life, she was happy. And not because she had a warm bed, or a place to call home, or because James had shown her some small measure of affection. But because for the first time in her life, she had accepted herself. She had embraced who she was, and she had chosen to become someone. The more she thought about it, the more she realized, that more than anything, what got her through this latest ordeal, was a belief that her life was worth living.

Vyanna laughed, it was a sweet laugh, the kind that carries on the wind and makes you want to listen to it a little longer. "My child, I suspect you have already found the answer to that question. But I will be frank with you, tonight is the first time you have been prepared to embrace your own destiny."

Chloe nodded, standing from the bench and straightening her pajamas. It was difficult to look dignified in leggings and a t-shirt, but she hoped she had done as good as could be expected. "Okay." She inhaled deeply. "What do you need me to do?"

The goddess stepped forward and the two looked into each other's eyes.

"I need you to become my Empress."

The world fell out from underneath her. Empress? She tried to speak, but the words caught in the back of her throat. Had she really said Empress? Chloe wondered which of the two of them was more crazy, maybe immortality had a way of putting you out of touch with reality.

The goddess's eyes softened. "I know it is a lot to ask, so believe me when I tell you, I did not reach this decision lightly. But if I am to be redeemed, I must make reparations for the damage I have caused. And for that, I need your help."

Chloe blinked, shaking herself back to the moment. "The freedom of will, with the guidance to succeed." She repeated.

Vyanna nodded, placing a hand on Chloe's shoulder.

Seph

"And Chloe."

"Yes?"

"Look after Zaeith for me. Soon he will face a battle which he cannot win, and when he does, I will need you to be there for him."

"What could I do to help him?"

Vyanna pulled Chloe into a tight embrace holding her for a long moment. "Be his friend."

Darkness began to cloud her vision, closing in around her as she grasped for the vanishing threads of light.

She awoke to find herself in her darkened bedroom. Throwing the blankets off, she ran to the mirror. In its place was an empty frame, broken shards scattered across the floor.

She blinked, holding a hand to her forehead as dizziness overwhelmed her. Had it been a dream?

Chapter 29

The Dressick shook with a deep rumble, which vibrated the air in the ship as if it were a hollow acoustic instrument. Tendrils of light flickered in brilliant arcs of energy as the hyperspace envelope opened and closed again, ejecting the ship back into normal space.

Through the port side view window, the shape of the midway station could barely be seen, distinguished from the surrounding stars by a thin silver line which stretched out indefinitely in both directions.

In reality, it was impossible to fully comprehend the size of the individual units which made up the border wall separating the circle from the rest of the galaxy. It was made up of multiple trillions of individual shield generators. In truth, the energy field they generated was barely a deterrent against illegally crossing the border. For one, it only extended a few hundred light years in either direction from the fence. But more than that, it was easy to penetrate. Once you compensated for the subspace distortion, any viable hyperspace sleeve would do the trick.

The real issue for people wanting to cross it unnoticed was the alarm. If a hyperspace envelope crossed through the barrier, the Alliance patrols would know about it; and because each of the units operated independently, they also knew exactly which unit was breached.

James had often speculated that many of the smugglers who tried it did so simply for the thrill of the attempt. Of course, there was also the occasional hot shot who was trying to show off to his friends.

The prevention of these things weren't what the fence was designed for, it just happened to be able to be used that way. No one knew why the fence had been built to begin with, and the air of mystery that surrounded it had attracted scholars to study it for millennia. The truth was that the fence was one of the oldest infrastructures in the galaxy. Like the midway stations themselves, it had been completed over two thousand years ago, and at the time, the entirety of the Alliance was contained inside of the fence.

Each unit was self-contained, and self-maintained by automated droids, which worked on a sort of hive mind system. That was largely speculation; James had never achieved a high enough security clearance to find anything out. He did know that only a small crew was allowed access. What they did in them was one of the best kept secrets in the galaxy.

Chloe pressed her face against the glass, watching the station grow larger as they approached. "It's strange to think that I spent my whole life on one of those, but this is the first time I am getting to see it."

"Didn't they show you pictures or anything?" James took his eyes off the station to look at Chloe. They had all changed into Descendant uniforms for the approach to avoid suspicion. If the Dressick had been reported as stolen, they were caught either way. But, they were better off not pushing their luck further than necessary.

Chloe looked surprisingly natural in the uniform though. The lavender accents provided a soft harmony to her blue eyes. The white jacket a clean backdrop for her natural beauty, and the gray undershirt, visible through the open collar, subtly elevating the whole thing.

"Yes and no." She gave him the sort of nostalgic half-smile one gets when telling a story that is secretly more of a confession.

"Most kids get to see pictures in school, they even have scale models so you can see where everything is. But I didn't get to go to school. The closest I ever got to being 'shown' a picture was the fragmented maps Sphiya would give me. But I may have snuck into a classroom or two to take a peak."

James smiled at the thought of a curious young Chloe sneaking into a school to get a peek at how the world looked.

Her eyes returned to the station, which now engulfed most of the window. It was composed of a central body which from this angle resembled an upside down teardrop, connected to a smaller sphere suspended above it. Four sweeping wing-like structures jutted out from the sides, like the gemstone setting on a ring. The whole thing was surrounded by three rotating hoops, which served as shuttle bays, and rooms while crews waited to be allowed through.

Seph

"Mostly I did it for the books. I rarely had a way to access the data in them, but I liked to hold them up to my chest and pretend I could hear their stories in my heart."

He couldn't help but stare, partly from amusement, but also from wonder. The more time he spent with Chloe, and the more layers of her he peeled back, the more he found he admired her. She had a kind of subtle strength he had never witnessed before, the kind that keeps pushing. Not the kind of strength that explodes outwards, but that trickles like a stream, invisible and unnoticed, but unstoppable.

His personal comlink pinged at the edge of his consciousness. "Yes?"

Fetu spoke. "We have clearance for one shuttle. And four rooms at the station, if you want to head over, get your things. Captain wants to be off within the hour."

"Acknowledged." James said back, closing the link.

James held out his hand, "The shuttle is waiting, shall we head over?"

* * *

The quarantine area was small but comfortable. One spacious furnished living area with a kitchen in one corner. There were four suites, each with two full-sized beds and their own bathroom. A broad viewing window looked out into the stars, which panned slowly as the ring in which the room was situated revolved around the station.

The quarantine process was mandatory for anyone entering the ring. Normally it only took two days of isolation, but ever since the Aberration had broken out in the outer colonies, things had been taking much longer. While in isolation, crews could access their assigned isolation rooms, and transfer back and forth between their ships. The rest of the station however was off limits.

That did not stop anyone from advertising to the visitors, however. Brochures for entertainment activities arrived regularly, accompanying various catalogs selling everything from food, to clothing, and even components and upgrades for your ship.

There was little you could not buy, then have delivered to your room. And once clearance was given, crews often had approximately twenty-four hours to wait, while their ship was queued for the gate. It was estimated that more money passed through one midway station in a single day than was transferred in the ring and outer colonies combined. It was difficult to calculate the transfer of funds within the circle, since most of the imperial worlds operated independent of traditional currency.

Instead, they had a complex caste and class system in which the basic needs of the imperial citizens were met by a social distribution exchange. Beyond that, an individual or organization was awarded an amount of social credit. The more one contributed into society, the more credit they received and by building credit, you could raise your rank within the system. Likewise, when there were substantiated reports of social detriment, credit was removed.

No one person owned anything within the Empire, and the profits from any sales outside of imperial worlds went directly to the royal family. If someone left the Empire and resigned their citizenship, they could cash out their social credit. The exchange rate was always fluctuating, so unless you were paying close attention, it was difficult to say how much they were worth. But it was often speculated that most Imperial citizens were valued about the same as any given system in the rest of the Alliance. A theory which was strongly supported by the fact that several of the recent immigrants had used their funds to terraform new worlds.

This of course meant anyone passing through the midway station either had a fortune to spend, or was spending somebody else's money. And so, came the endless supply of free samples and trial offers. All you had to do was place a call, and as soon as your quarantine was over they would send a cab to pick you up.

At this point James had become rather disillusioned with the whole thing. During his time with the Alliance, he had been back and forth across this border more times than he cared to remember. Though he considered himself lucky, most people in the Alliance military spent their entire careers guarding this border.

And so James sat quietly on the sofa, playing some new FPS that was apparently a big deal, the virtual reality device, provided courtesy of Lightdrive, the leading designer in virtual reality gaming technology.

Fetu flopped his massive body down beside him. Speaking through mouthfuls of food. "How is it?"

James shrugged, keeping his focus on the game. Someone was trying to sneak up on his last sniping post. "It's not bad, the mechanics are pretty smooth. But it would be nice to have a little more competition."

Meghanh glanced over her shoulder where she and Chloe sat scanning through product catalogs, and vacation brochures. "Ego doesn't suit you, James."

James triggered the remote detonator on the mine

he left. The building exploded outward. Shots erupted from automatic rifles, as the blue streak of a sting-rifle blanketed the field. Removing his nine millimeter rail pistol from its holster James aimed, and waited. After a moment the firing stopped and a few heads began to poke out from their hiding spots to investigate.

James got off three shots, adding three more kills to his score. He dropped through the hole he had made in the roof of his current post. Removing one of the two sniper rifles he was carrying, he set up a dummy gun in the window. In a few more seconds, someone would come to check this spot. The only obvious way out was the stairwell, and they would be watching that closely.

Returning to the opening James jumped, grabbing the loose boards on the roof and hoisting himself up, staying low to avoid being seen. Aiming his gun at the dummy post, so he remained invisible from the stairwell he waited.

In the meantime, he pulled up the game statistics display, projecting it so Fetu could read the score.

"Looks like he has a KD ratio of six point four this game. What mode are you on?"

James huffed. "It was supposed to be free style, but it has turned into one versus all pretty quick."

"How many players."

"Thirty"

Someone approached the abandoned gun in the window. James gave them a moment to look around, then squeezed the trigger. Rolling back, he pulled himself over the ledge of the roof, dropping the twelve feet, and landing on top of the storage shed behind the building. Planting another bomb, he slipped around the corner, then watched as the remaining enemies filled inside. Holstering his gun, James dashed across the street, sliding into an alleyway then crouched behind a dumpster.

From here he could barely make out the heads of his opponents as they peaked over the edge of the roof. Two of them disappeared and reappeared around the corner. He waited a moment before he triggered the mine. It exploded, sending shrapnel flying, catching the two gunmen off guard, and eliminating anyone following them. Equipping his gun once again, he fired off two shots, adding a total of five kills to the count.

The game timer hit zero, and a final leaderboard appeared. James's username, Zero Nine, tripling the nearest score.

"I don't know Meghnah, I think he has earned this one." Fetu laughed.

James powered down the game, tossed the glasses onto the coffee table. "They got a little better towards the end there."

Meghnah huffed. "You have to go easy on the kids, James."

He shrugged, it's not like he was going all out. In that last round he only used the one gun. He had run out of ammo twice, which had created the opening for two of the deaths he had. "I suppose, but if you go too easy on them, then you rob them of the satisfaction of winning, besides the game isn't any fun if you know your opponent is playing down to you."

Meghnah chuckled, "I will keep that in mind next time we spar." She grabbed a small object off the table and threw it at him. James snatched it out of the air. It was chocolate. He set it on the table, then stood stretching his arms and legs.

"What are you two up to anyway?" He crossed the room leaning with one arm on the back of Chloe's chair.

She leaned back, pressing her bare shoulder against his arm, her hair was soft and damp, and she smelled of fresh citrus.

She held up the brochure she was holding. It was for a holo-theater. "I have never seen this side of a station before, it's interesting to look at what everyone else was experiencing."

James wanted so bad to move his hand up to her shoulder, but something inside him kept him frozen in place, unwilling to break the contact he already had.

"Have you ever been to one before?"

She shook her head. "Not properly, we had an old headset we could watch VR versions on, but it was difficult to share between us. If I wanted to use it, I often had to sneak it away in the middle of the night."

James shifted his weight, which caused the skin exposed by her fingalin style blouse to come in contact with his.

"We should all go, once we get moved out of isolation. It will be awhile before they get the ship towed through the gate anyway."

Chloe shifted, turning her body towards him, and pulled her hair up, brushing it back with her fingers and pressing herself against him. "I would enjoy that."

Gingerly, James finally managed the nerve to place his hand on her shoulder. "It's a date then."

Meghanh glanced between the two of them. "You know James, we can trade rooms."

He felt the muscles in Chloe's back stiffen as her cheeks flushed red. He squeezed her shoulder.

"Thanks Meghnah, but I'm okay where I am at. I do

think I am going to turn in for the night though."

Meghnah shrugged. "Suit yourself, and let me know if you change your mind."

Chloe shot Meghnah a glare, and for a second James could have sworn he saw comet trails. He squeezed her shoulder one more time, then left for his room.

"You want the shower tonight, or in the morning?" He called to Fetu.

The large man shoved a fork full of food into his mouth. "Go for it, I will be up for a while anyway."

"Alright." James opened the door, hanging his jacket on the hook. It was going to be a long four days.

* * *

James keyed for orange juice on the control panel for the food synthesizer. It wasn't the same as the fresh squeezed stuff Travis tried to always keep on hand, but there was something comforting about its consistent and reliable quality.

The stars drifted slowly along with a smattering of ships. From here they almost looked like toys from a child's playset. In the darkness the window was almost hypnotic with the vastness of space displayed in full view.

"Ah, Commander James."

James turned to see Nevarian poking his head out from the room he and The Captain were sharing.

"Would you mind terribly getting me a bowl of plain rice? I would do it myself, of course, however at the moment I am quite in the middle of something."

"Sure, give me a second." It was a fairly normal request, Nevarian was always busy with something.

As the days had gone on, he had been spending more of his time with the rest of the crew. Though he still kept to himself, burying his nose in a datapad. He had shown himself to be quite capable in games of strategy. After the second day, he was the only one who would still play chess with James. To both of their satisfaction, they were evenly matched.

James was winning six to four. Though the first didn't really count. It was obvious that Nevarian had underestimated James at first. Nevarian had given him several openings, that were rather careless compared to the way he was playing now.

The synthesizer printed rice grains a few dozen at a time. Unlike many dishes where the bulk of the food was prepared somewhere inside the working of the machine and then dispensed, simple things like rice it printed and dropped into the waiting dish as it went. In under a minute, a fresh bowl of steamed rice was ready.

James knocked on the door with the back of his knuckles. Nevarian appeared a moment later, blocking most of the doorway with his body.

"Thank you."

James handed the fingalin the bowl. "No problem."

The Captain spoke from inside the room. "James. Come in for a moment."

A peculiar look flashed across the doctor's face, indignation perhaps? It was difficult to tell, but it was apparent that he was less than thrilled about The Captain inviting James in. Nonetheless, he stepped out of the way, opening the door.

The familiar tightness in his chest returned as James entered the room. It was much the same as the one he and Fetu were sharing. Light tan carpet, walls in a yellow cream color, and dark green doors. The biggest difference was that instead of having two beds, there was only one bed, and a sleeping pod.

The Captain sat on the edge of the bed; it was the first time James had ever seen him out of uniform. His torso was exposed, and he appeared to have several monitoring devices attached to his chest and head.

Nevarian handed The Captain the bowl of rice, then sat down at the makeshift workstation he had set up.

The Captain reached into the pocket of his uniform laid out next to him on the mattress, and pulled out a small data card. "I understand you intend to visit the station tomorrow when they release us."

James nodded. "Yes, that had been our plan, did you need us for something?"

The Captain held out the data card. "No, in fact if you can avoid the ship, at least until after it has been towed through the gate, I would appreciate it."

James took the data card. "What is this for?"

"I would like you to convert the funds on that card into Imperial credits. All the information you'll need is there."

"Yes, sir," James nodded, cupping the card in his hand and moving into an at ease position. "If you don't mind my asking sir, why do you not handle the exchange yourself?"

The monitor Nevarian was working on beeped a few times, and the fingalin doctor rapidly typed a few lines out on his datapad.

"I was planning on it, but something has come up and my attention is needed elsewhere."

James glanced at the various transmitting devices attached to The Captains body, then looked to the doctors monitoring equipment.

"If you would like sir, Fetu and I are capable of handling the crossing tomorrow."

Nevarian leered over his screen. "You would do well to do as you are told, and not ask too many questions."

The Captain shot a piercing glare at the doctor.

Nevarian sighed. "Look Commander, you seem to be a decent man, I could say I even like you, and on some level that would probably be true. You are clever and that is dangerous. You tend to ask the sort of questions people shouldn't know the answers to."

The Captain rose from the bed and patted the fingalin's shoulder. "Nevarian, everyone is not Xious. It is better to be betrayed by an ally, then to have only enemies."

"Even so sir, the current situation dictates a certain discretion."

The Captain returned to sitting. "I am aware of that my friend, and I trust every member of this crew with my life."

Nevarian snorted, "We trusted Xious, and how many people have died because we did?"

The Captain laid back on the bed exhaling into the room. "And that is a mistake for which I must now atone. But Xious made his own decisions, neither you nor I are responsible for that."

James coughed clearing his throat. "If I may sir, you mentioned Xious before. Who was he?"

"He was my first officer, before Fetu took the job. I had hoped to one day pass the ship to him."

"What happened?"

"He wanted something from me that I couldn't give him."

"What was that?"

The Captain sat up staring long and hard into

James's eyes. "I hope, for your sake, you never find out."

James folded his hands across his lap and bowed. "If it is alright, I will be taking my leave sir."

The Captain returned a nod of the head. "Thank you. And James, I am trusting you not to speak of tonight with anyone."

"Of course sir. Doctor," James gave a nod towards Nevarian, and left.

"You are getting careless again." He heard Nevarian say as the door closed behind him. Setting the data card on the table, he rubbed feeling back into his fingers. Even in a setting like this, The Captain's presence was intense. It hadn't been much of an issue, since he rarely left his room. But it was difficult to imagine the carefree attitude that had been pervasive over that last four days had The Captain decided to join them.

Perhaps that was why he always secluded himself from the rest of the crew. Certainly the more James got to know him, the less the effect seemed intentional. Maybe some people were just that way; maybe for every Chloe in the universe who make every room brighter the moment she enters, there had to be at least one person like The Captain to remind you how vast and lonely a place the universe was.

Or maybe he had just been awake too long, and this was his brain's way of telling him it was time to sleep. Scooping up the data card, he turned it over in his hands. It was stamped with a corporate ID code. It was probably worth a small fortune. James had never considered purchasing credit in the Empire himself. The cost was simply too high to be reasonable for anyone who didn't intend to become a full citizen.

Having some credit to their names was certainly

going to help smooth things out. Especially if it could be used to slow down the Descendants. Though in reality, that was unlikely. They were going to have to bank on the fact that by stealing the Dressick, they had not needed to file a flight plan with the station at Dramia. Which meant, in theory, there weren't any clues to their destination.

Of course now that they had registered as the Dressick at the midway station, if the Descendants were watching they now knew where they were. Hopefully they could get to Atlione and depart with the Shade before they could catch up.

James tried to push the thought of the Descendants out of his mind. That was a bridge they would have to cross when they came to it. For now, they could enjoy themselves. It had been weeks since the events that took place in the outer orbit of Dramia. And everyone was finally starting to settle down.

Tomorrow they would be inside the inner circle, and the rules of the game were about to change. If they played their cards right, they might be able to make it back out of this in one piece. For now, they needed to trust that whatever The Captain was looking for on Atlione was worth it.

* * *

The main dome opened up before them. This level of the station was said to have as much surface area as most of the moons around habitable worlds. The vast cityscape glowed, with enough lights to appear as daylight on any planet, surrounding the building in an ethereal haze. Stretching out beneath an invisible canopy, which was so high, aircraft reflected the light from the city below.

Crossing the glass bridge just past the station gate, the hyper rail was displayed, passing underneath and overhead, disappearing and reappearing from brightly lit portals at either end of the entry gate. It was the only artificial hyperspace sleeve in the galaxy. The technology which created it had been lost to the millennia since its construction. Now it stood as a monument to an era long forgotten. With it, it was possible to travel from one midway station to the next in a single day. A trip which even the best navigators struggled to make in a full week.

The midway stations predated the invention of the fusion core. Which meant they, like the Shade, were powered by antimatter drives, and the gravity was artificial so there was no horizon. Instead their view continued outward, ending abruptly at the edge of space.

James called up a map of the city on his datapad. "I need to go take care of something for The Captain, you guys go on ahead and I'll catch up with you at the theater in two hours."

Fetu slapped him on the back. "Good luck, see ya then!" He walked off into the crowd, and would have vanished if it weren't for his size.

Chloe shifted her weight from one foot to the other, avoiding eye contact. "Mind if I tag along?"

James smiled to himself, and hoped it didn't show too much to everyone else. He had wanted to ask her to accompany him, but didn't want to take her away from other activities she might like to pursue.

"Not at all, I would appreciate the company, if you don't mind missing out on the station."

Chloe shook her head, "I won't be missing out.

Don't forget, I grew up on one of these. I may not have participated in all the 'luxury' activities, but there isn't a lot here I haven't already seen."

His stomach began to churn and the tips of his ears grew hot. It was strange to have something not be new for Chloe. Everywhere they had gone so far, including the isolation room had been a first. Everything here was mundane and ordinary. It felt like someone had yanked a rug out from underneath him.

"I suppose you're right, I guess I got caught up in the excitement and forgot a little."

"It's okay. Besides, I think I would rather spend my time with you then explore the station."

The warm sensation in his ears erupted in his head, and James felt like he was going to float out of his shoes. "Right, we need to go to the exchange."

"Oh, I know where that is, it shouldn't take more than an hour to get there. Only a few minutes if we take a cab."

Meghanh nudged Chloe with her elbow, then made a fake gun with her hands and clicked her tongue pointing it at James. "You have fun, and if you happen to miss the show we won't wait up. Make sure you are at the shuttle when the crossing is finished. If I have to come find you in whatever hotel room you rented, you will never need any alone time again."

Chloe turned at least three different shades of red and purple. "It's not like, we aren't... Meg!"

Meghnah disappeared into the crowd with a wave of her hand.

"Don't worry about her, she is only teasing you. But it is nice to know we have her permission if we wanted it."

Chloe wrapped her arms around him, burying her

face in his chest. "Don't you start too, I don't think I can handle anymore of that, especially not in public."

Fighting the urge inside himself to hold onto her forever, run his fingers through her hair and disappear into eternity, James separated himself from the embrace and took her hand.

"I'm sorry, I didn't mean anything by it. Let's get this over with, shall we?"

Chloe nodded pointing to a nearby building. "There is a transit station over there, we can get a cab to the exchange. And maybe if we have any time left, visit the lower decks."

"Okay, if that is what you want." James had never heard of anyone wanting to visit the lower decks before. That was the part of the city that was kept hidden from visitors. Residential decks, office spaces, schools and all the other ordinary things people tried to ignore when on vacation. Then again, for Chloe, this wasn't a vacation.

As promised, it only took them a few minutes to get to the exchange. The building was large, made with alternating vertical segments of metal and glass that angled away from each other. Inside, tall metal sheets hung on the walls, each with a unique piece of abstract line art cut out of it. Androids of various humanoid and non-humanoid appearance mingled with the crowded lines of people waiting for their turn in the que, and attempting to address concerns and questions as they arose.

James had never been here before, and was surprised to find it packed. Most of the people wore business suits or uniforms belonging to one organization or another.

"Careful in the que." Chloe whispered as they found

a place in line.

"Have you done this before?" James raised an eyebrow, gripping her hand a little tighter.

"Yes and no." She kept her voice low, and it was easily drowned out by the bustling crowd. "We used to pick up a lot of our marks at the exchange. People with money to spare often gravitate towards it. As well as people with appetites that are… more difficult to satisfy."

James tried not to think too hard about what that last part might mean. "Okay, so don't talk to strangers? I don't think we look like a terribly appealing target." He spread out his hands to indicate the faded blue jacket, worn out work pants, and t-shirt he was wearing.

Chloe exhaled and rolled her eyes. "No, you look like you are trying too hard to look like you don't have anything. But you are in the line for the Imperial exchange. Nobody gets in this line without a lot of money in their pocket. You may not get solicited, but if you're not careful your pockets will be empty long before you make it to the front."

It hadn't really occurred to James that the classic nobody look would backfire on him in this instance. Though now that he thought about it, she was right. If he had been trying to lie low, he never would have been in a place like this to begin with. And had he tried to come here undercover, he certainly would have made more of an effort to blend in. It was too late now. Sure he could change the appearance of his jacket, and the crowd was such, that most people wouldn't notice; but if Chloe was right, which he did not doubt she was, it would only serve to make him that much more appealing to anyone who had already tagged him as a potential mark.

Keying up the command interface on his jacket, James had the nanites conceal the data card. At least that way, unless someone managed to take the jacket from him, no one would be stealing the card. And if they did manage to get the jacket, well they deserved it.

There were two close calls as they made their way to the front of the line, but both were avoided well before they could cause a scene. Chloe noticed the would-be-thieves, and a quick glance sent them off to their next mark.

Once at the front of the line, James summoned the data card and placed it on the desk. The fingalin looked at it, then at James, squinting critically. "And what am I supposed to do with this?"

"I would like to turn everything on that into Imperial credit."

He scoffed. "Young man, do you have any idea how much a credit is worth at the moment?"

James shrugged. "Not really."

"I am afraid if you are trying to impress your pathetic excuse for a girlfriend there, you are only going to embarrass yourself."

James restrained himself from pulling his stunblade and zapping him. "I think you should do your job, and let me decide whose company is worth my time."

The fingalin sighed. "Very well. But I warned you." He plugged in the card.

For a moment he studied his display in silence. His eyes went wide, and he glanced between James and the readout.

"Who did you say you were again?"

James leaned his elbow on the counter. "I don't

believe I did."

"To move this amount of money, I will need some sort of identification."

James exhaled, bracing himself for the worst. The last thing they needed was an arrest to add to their records. If The Captain had overlooked the security measures and missed something. He pulled out the modified Descendant ID card and passed it under the protective force field.

The man scanned the card. Glanced at the data, then keyed in a command. "Here is the transfer detail."

A projected display appeared in front of James:

Org: Dark Moon
Rep: Shon Javius
ISC purchased: 126.99
From: 13,367,884.11
Federal Notes
Rate: 105,258.93/1
Total ISC: 98,860.58

"Does this look correct, sir?"

James swallowed hard. "Uh, yeah, looks great."

The fingalin nodded and the display vanished. "Very well sir, thank you for using our services. Please enjoy your visit, and if you need anything be sure to contact the embassy." He passed the data card back to James.

James picked up the card and stowed it in his pocket. "Thanks, we will do that." He turned to Chloe, tossing his head towards the entrance. "Let's go."

When they were safely inside the cab, both James and Chloe released the air they had been holding in their lungs.

"Did you see how much money there was?" Chloe

was sitting on the edge of her seat.

James shook his head. "I saw, but I don't think I believe it."

"You two okay back there?" The driver asked, glancing over his shoulder.

"Yeah, we decided to check the exchange rate for Imperial credit."

The driver gave a knowing nod. "Absurd ain't it? You could almost buy a ship with half a dozen of those things. And to think, if you are born a citizen of the Empire you get three thousand of em'. Anyway, where are you headed now?"

"To the western lift." Chloe instructed.

A grin spread across the man's face. "It sure is nice to dream, ain't it." He turned his attention forward as the cab began to move along the mag rail.

Once at the lift, Chloe led James down several levels to a small sparsely furnished office space, with plain walls of uncoated sheet metal, and a single synthetic wooden desk at one end accompanied by various other pieces of office equipment.

The service woman looked up from her datapad as they entered. "Oh, I am so sorry, I wasn't expecting anyone today, I am terribly sorry if one of the children has caused you trouble. Is there anything I can do?"

Chloe shook her head, pulling a chair up to the desk. "Nothing like that. I would like to make a donation."

The women paused. Mouth hanging open slightly, she took a second look at Chloe in her traditional fingalin attire. "Why yes, yes of course, we would be happy to take anything you would offer, and of course any donation you make to the school you will be able to use as credit against any trade tax you might incur on the station."

Chloe smiled softly. "Thank you, but that won't be necessary, really," she removed a small data card from her bag. "Here take this."

The woman took the card and plugged it into her computer. She stared at the display, squinted to get a better look. She removed the card and offered it back to Chloe. "I am sorry miss, I think you may have given me the wrong card. There are over four thousand Federal notes here."

Chloe shook her head and closed the woman's hand around the card. "Just make sure the kids get some books for me."

Tears began to well up in the woman's eyes, and she nearly jumped across the desk to give Chloe a hug. "Thank you, thank you so much. You have no idea how much this will mean to the children."

Chloe patted the women's back, then stepped away. "Probably not." She agreed and turned to leave taking James by the hand.

"Can I at least get your name. To attach to the donation I mean." The women called after them.

Chloe turned to face her. "Just say that it was a gift from Vyanna."

Chapter 30

Everyone sat together in the officers' lounge at the very end of the ship's northern hemisphere. Everyone, except The Captain that was.

The biggest advantage of the system Fetu and Travis had rigged for being able to control the ship was that it was mostly automatic. When they first set out, Meghnah reviewed the navigation data which Scot had generated in conjunction with the AI, which effectively ran the Dressick already. Once it was approved, and sent into the system, the only manual maintenance it needed was for James or the Captain to do the occasional check in via their neural link.

This left everyone free to pursue whatever other activities they might be inclined towards. At this exact moment, that meant catching a glimpse of Atlione as the ship came out of hyperspace.

Colorful arcs of electricity danced across the window as the envelope opened. The rumbling of the ship as it tore through the fabric of space was exaggerated here on the outer edge, where they were furthest from the fusion core, though the room itself must have sat on some sort of float, which absorbed much of the movement.

They appeared to share a parallel orbit to the planet, not much further out from it than its second moon. Trailing just enough to cause a partial eclipse of the sun, which illuminated the blue sphere in a sapphire halo.

Wisps of clouds swirled around the planet's surface in great strips, unimpeded by mountains or landmasses. The occasional ring of small islands dotting its surface like tiny flecks in a precious stone.

"I had forgotten how beautiful it was." Gillian inhaled as if he could already smell the ocean air.

Chloe walked up to the window, placing both hands on it, and leaning forward as far as she could. "It does look a lot like a jewel."

James smiled inwardly. This was his first time visiting Atlione. Unless you were fingalin, most of the planet was inaccessible, And unless you were a citizen of the Empire, the rest was unaffordable. The planet was home to the largest liquid ocean in the known galaxy, water or otherwise. It hosted more species than any other world in the Alliance, which of course made the planet fascinating to biologists, and many of the artificial species which existed were a result of genome studies performed here.

Since everything that lived on Atlione had to be able to survive in the harsh ocean climate, they were also particularly adept at handling zero gravity environments. Something that had been necessary during the early days of space travel. Unfortunately, the species that evolved here were very particular about the kind of ocean they could survive in, and none of them had ever been successfully integrated into a new environment.

All these factors contributed to its nickname as the Jewel of the Empire. Their exclusive claim to Atlione, and its resources was considered one of the biggest blunders of the early Alliance. At first, nobody else really wanted the planet. There simply wasn't enough landmass. And with the vast amount of resources being put into space exploration, none of the other governments wanted to dump capital into exploring it. This would end up being the catalyst for the economic divide which now existed between the Empire and the Federation.

The door opened, and the temperature of the room dropped as if an icy breeze had blown in when the Captain entered.

James rose to attention with a salute.

The Captain took a moment to observe the floating planet, spinning silently in the view window. "Come, we don't have much time."

* * *

After so much time spent on the Dressick, it was strange to have everyone in their normal positions onboard the Shade. James pulled up his display; at least for now, the link would not be necessary.

The ship lifted from the floor of the hanger with ease. A moment later they had passed through the atmosphere shield and a detailed hologram of the system appeared in the viewfield. As the sensor scope zoomed in, the Shade grew from a tiny speck to a meter in length.

Approaching the planet in a shallow orbit, the Shade skimmed the atmosphere, its shield absorbing most of the impact, the effect was hardly felt on the inside. Meghnah fired the front plasma thrusters, the drag plate on the hull opened as the Shade began a rapid deceleration, falling in an arch towards Atlione.

The shielding on the Shade was more than sufficient to handle a high speed reentry, but there was no need to tax it more than necessary. The general idea was to establish gravity lock and then free fall until you crossed the flight barrier, bringing your relative speed as close to zero as possible.

The full detail projection of the world was breathtaking. As it spun in darkness below them, the Shade floated motionless on the thin wisps of cloud.

James's stomach lurched up into his chest as gravity vanished, and the ship began to accelerate once more.

Held to her chair only by safety straps, Meghnah adjusted the pitch on the drag plates, thrusting the ship forward along a curve which now perfectly mirrored their original approach. Gravity returned to normal.

The intercom beeped, and Fetu rattled off his diagnostic report. "Shield disabled. Antigravity polarization disabled. Antimatter coil disengaged. Ion drive, inactive. AMS active. Gravity at point nine three. Atmospheric pressure point zero six and climbing. Hull integrity normal. All systems clear."

As the curve of the planet rose up to meet them, the hologram projection began to flatten, waves beginning to take shape on the surface of the water below. A cluster of small islands appeared, and at its center one larger ring-shaped island, the remains of what was

Seph

once a volcano, that had long ago collapsed forming the sandy caldera, which was close to nine miles in diameter, and was the planet's only freshwater lake.

Meghnah maneuvered the ship over the beach on the outside edge of the island, rotating the thrusters, she set the ship gently on the sand.

The Captain released his safety restraints. "They have undoubtedly been watching us since we left the Dressick. If anyone comes asking, give them the new ID cards I gave you all. Remember, you are here to take some water samples for a project on Reicue 12. You are not familiar with the details of the project. Only that they need water samples as part of the ongoing terraforming efforts."

"Yes, sir." The crew said in near unison.

"Gillian and I should be back before sunrise. If we are not, do not wait for us." With that, the Captain disappeared down the shaft.

A moment later, Fetu stepped through the door from the engine room. "It's been a while since I have brought a ship down like that!"

Meghnah shot him a glare with a sideways smile. "The way I remember it, it's still been a while since 'you' brought a ship in."

Fetu snorted. "I helped. You know if I wasn't back there to switch over all that space stuff, we'd be fish bait."

Meghnah undid her belt and stretched her arms. "I have every confidence in Scot's ability to do that job."

Fetu sat down in the captain's chair. "Fine, alright, you win. Thank you for bringing us in one piece, all by yourself."

She powered down her terminal. "You're welcome."

Chloe removed herself from her seat and stood next

to the view field. "Guys, I think someone is coming." She pointed to a few moving dots near the edge of the projected zone.

James zoomed in on the area. A group of eight Imperial patrollers were making their way down the beach. "Well, ready to test our cover?"

"Right." Fetu droned. "Let's get everything set up."

Nevarian had most of the sciencey looking stuff set up by the time the rest of the crew managed to disembark. Meghnah had placed the ship only a few dozen feet above the tide line, so it was a short distance to haul most of the gear.

It was only a few minutes later when their visitors arrived, led by a fingalin women in a bright red dress, accompanied by seven other fingalins, each with their own warstaffs. The five women who were among them wore their hair in intricate braids, each one representing her own taste, and dyed in bright colors which complimented the various stripes and freckles on their skin.

All wore fingalin clothing, open at the back, with arm bands which started at the end of their shoulder caps, and ended at their elbow. With their pants ending below knees to allow for full use of their fins. Except for the woman in red, they appeared to be in some kind of uniform. Though each was a different color. They clung tightly to their bodies, designed to optimize movement while underwater, while exposing only their shoulders, backs and fins.

"Welcome to Caldera." The women in the dress spoke, placing her elbows at her waist and opening her arms. "We were not expecting any visitors tonight. What brings you to our planet?"

Fetu stepped forward returning the gesture and

bending at the waist. "My apologies, I did not contact you directly. I had hopped since we were landing so far from the city, it wouldn't be a problem."

She stepped forward a little, separating herself from her guards. "We have many citizens and tourists who spend a great deal of time enjoying our planet's natural beauty. So forgive us our intrusion, we merely came to address any needs you may have, to facilitate your stay of course."

"My name is Fetu. We are simply collecting water samples for a project on Reicue 12." He offered her his ID card.

She took the card then handed it to one of the guards behind her, not taking her eyes off the crew. "A pleasure. I am Duchess Railayia Naysiaria, of the Imperial royal family. May I assume, Fetu, that you are in charge of this operation?"

Fetu scratched the back of his head. "Well, I own the ship, but he is really in charge of this project." He pointed to Nevarian, who was occupying himself with the equipment.

"Are you a biologist then?" She raised her voice, looking past Fetu at the doctor.

Nevarian looked up from his datapad. "No, I think you will find I am a neurologist. Though I do have a basic enough grasp of the principles of biology for this particular assignment."

The guard handed the Duchess a datapad, along with Fetu's ID card. "I see you are with Dark Moon," her voice raised a little, sounding impressed. "It is not every day I have the opportunity to welcome such important visitors. If only I had known, we would have prepared more appropriate lodging for you." She returned the datapad to the guard and handed Fetu his ID.

He scratched his ear. "Oh, we will not be needing any accommodations, we should be out of here before sunrise."

"Oh, but I insist. I couldn't possibly allow someone with your standing to visit our fair world without extending our finest hospitality. Surely your work is not so time sensitive that you would refuse even the offer of a meal?"

Nevarian approached the congregation. "We are in quite a rush, you see, the work I am doing is specific to the microbes that thrive here at night. It is believed that the geological composition of the volcanic sublayer here, is similar to that of Reicue 12. It is possible that by studying the organisms that thrive in low radiation zones around these formations, we may be able to synthesize plant material that will aid in the atmospheric development of the moon, during the prolonged night periods."

"Well, we shall have to wait here until you are done. It will already take you five weeks to reach Reicue 12. A few more hours will hardly make a difference. Besides, if you would like, you are welcome to use our entanglement transmitter, which I am confident will get your results to their destination, much quicker than you could deliver them in person.

Fetu glanced back at James, he shrugged. All they could do at this point was play along, unless of course they wanted to cause a scene. But it was obvious that hospitality was not the Duchess's primary concern.

"Well I'm certainly not about to make you leave, it's getting late though, might get pretty cold."

Railayia smiled. "We will manage."

"Right…" Fetu returned to the group, where

Seph

Meghanh, Chloe, Travis, and James had formed a loose circle.

"Now what?"

James shook his head, "The only thing we can do is go with them. If they are here when The Captain and Gillian get back, we'll be in trouble."

Meghnah nodded. "I agree. Maybe if we play along long enough, they'll decide we were telling the truth and let us leave. But if we keep fighting her, she's only going to get more suspicious."

Fetu let out a huff. "Alright then. Let's wait a couple of hours though, and really try to sell this thing. You guys keep them company. I'll let the doc know what we are planning."

There was not much conversation after that, several of the Duchess's guards attempted to inquire with Nevarian more about his work, but he expertly brushed them off. They avoided Meghnah. James could hardly blame them, she could be rather intimidating when she wanted, and tonight apparently, she wanted to be.

Chloe was the most willing to entertain their attempts at conversations, and they had been delighted to discover she was familiar with several of their favorite card games. James had tried his hand at a few, but they soon decided his "beginner's luck" was too strong, and he was politely uninvited from participating in any capacity besides watching. And even that was questionable, since it made them second guess many of their own decisions.

After a couple of hours, Nevarian collected his things and approached the Duchess. "Alright, I have finished setting up. Now all that will be left to do is collect the data once the computer has finished processing. It will require my attention again in precisely seven hours, if I am not here at that time, many of the results may be ruined. If that happens, we will need to start from the beginning again tomorrow."

The Duchess curtsied. "That would certainly be unfortunate, but no need to worry, that is more than enough time to relax and enjoy yourselves."

The guards took up ranks around the crew, with four in the rear, and three up front in a sort of triangle formation around the Duchess. They led them along the beach until they came across a section of the crater's rim which had been carved out to form a path. A large arch of white sandstone denoted the entrance, carved at the top was a message James couldn't read, but it appeared to be written in the fingalin language. A long silver bridge led out from the gate to the primary landing dock. Waves crashed around its base held at bay by an invisible force field. The floor of the bridge was carved in an intricate rolling pattern, which resembled the water below.

Leading into the crater was a stone path of many multicolored paving stones, mostly in blues, greens, and reds, though a few, black, white, and yellow stones were scattered through the winding mosaic.

They only had to follow the path for a few minutes before it let out into a harbor on the inside of the caldera. Waiting at a silver dock, which resembled the bridge to the landing pad, was a long boat made of dark wood which appeared to hover a few inches above the water. The boat's elegant flowing construction had no obvious means of propulsion, and the deck was covered by nothing more than a brightly colored canopy of heavy cloth. The edges of the canopy were tasseled and looked like they were dancing in a slight breeze. The whole thing was an illusion of serenity and simplicity who's very nature was garish by design.

Underneath the plain exterior was more tech than some starships were equipped with. The floating effect was caused by the gravity drive hidden somewhere in the hull. And unseen to the naked eye was the powerful force field which would keep the vessel just as peaceful even in some of the worst hurricanes.

The mundaneness of it all was more a statement of technological power and advancement than putting it all on display would ever have been. It certainly added an air of magic to everything.

The boat sailed silently across the lake, leaving behind only tiny ripples where you would expect to see a wake. Moonlight reflected off the water's surface, and the air was sweet with the scent of salt and ocean.

Magnificent white towers rose out of the center of the lake, their sweeping architecture seeming to defy the laws of physics. The whole city glittered with the light from the moon. As they approached, thousands of lights could be seen below the water's dark surface, making the underwater city almost indistinguishable from the night sky above.

"Beautiful, isn't it?" Railayia broke the silence.

The crew all turned to look at her. She was smiling, the smug sort of smile that only people who care too much about the things they own can manage.

"It really is." Chloe was the first to speak up, she was kneeling on one of the outer benches leaning over the side, as she watched the underwater city.

"It's different than I imagined." Meghnah's voice was distant, she kept her eyes more on the Duchess than on the surroundings.

"Caldera represents the peak of civilization. Even

the Imperial capital on Celaria does not enjoy the perfect balance of harmony between nature, beauty, and the wonders of innovation. Of course, it is necessary that the capital is more suitable for outsiders so visiting dignitaries don't feel like we are keeping secrets. Here on Atlione, we do not concern ourselves so much with the opinions of others. It is our private sanctuary, a place where the concerns of the galaxy simply do not exist."

"Is Caldera the only city on Atlione?" Chloe asked.

The Duchess shook her head. "No, of course not. There are many cities beneath the waves, however the vast majority of them are inaccessible to most. They are hidden deep beneath the ocean, where the strong winds of the planet's surface do not affect them. That is what makes Caldera special. The crater protects the lake from the winds. Allowing us to build more easily above the surface. Also, the lake is rich in mineral deposits, left over from ancient volcanic activity."

The portion of the city which was above the water, stood on an immense platform, elevated a few feet above the lake. It was supported by a single twisting pillar which spread out to the platform's edge in six distinct arms, rising up to support several of the higher layers of the city. James imagined that from above it looked something like a flat urchin.

There were several almost identical boats at the city dock, which, other than being gold not silver, were identical to the pier. A ramp extended from somewhere inside the boat's hull as they approached.

Railayia rose, walking across the deck, then motioning for everyone to disembark as the vessel glided to a stop. "This way, please."

They were led through a maze of winding paths

even James was having a hard time keeping track of. None of the city's walkways ran in a straight line, and they moved up and down almost as much as they did side to side. Everything was either cast out of highly polished metal, like the supporting structure, or carved from white sandstone. Colorful curtains hung in the openings of the small stone structures which appeared to be either houses or shops, possibly both.

The most intriguing thing about the city was the complete absence of anything that could be considered a door. Instead, rectangular openings were cut into the stone, with a second wall sitting in somewhere between three and four feet back. Colorful cloths hung in square openings with matching awnings in place of proper windows.

Railayia led them up to a spacious veranda which overlooked the lake. In its center was a flat stone table, with shallow chairs designed more for lounging than for sitting. At the edge of the platform was a sizable infinity pool.

"Please, make yourselves comfortable, our chefs have prepared a light meal for you," she folded her hands over her lap and bowed. "If you need anything, simply ask one of my guards, they will see to it that your needs are met."

She disappeared, but the escort remained blocking the path leading down from the balcony.

Fetu coughed, "Well, I guess we don't have much choice then."

Nevarian scowled at the large man. "We have several hours before the samples will be ready for collection. We should enjoy the city while we wait."

Fetu's ears twitched. "Right, that's what I meant." He walked over to the edge, peering down at the city below and whistled. "Wow, that's a long ways down."

James, Nevarian and Meghnah all exchanged glances, the situation wasn't good, but it could be worse. At least for the moment, they had successfully distracted the Duchess from whatever The Captain and Gillian were up to. If they were lucky, The Captain would return before they did and have time to hide out on the ship. Assuming they had succeeded in convincing Railayia they were here to collect water samples. They could return at the designated time and leave.

James glanced at the guards, more likely that the Duchess was suspicious of them, and this was a sort of house arrest. Or worse still, Railayia was waiting for something herself.

A moment later, several fingalins in dark uniforms appeared. Like the other fingalins' dress, the servers' flowing uniforms left their backs and fins exposed. Each of the servers brought with them a tray of assorted foods which they laid out on the stone table. When they had deposited their trays, they all lined up, folded their hands over their laps and bowed, before departing back to wherever they had come from.

James sat sideways on one of the lounge chairs, so he could be upright and face the table. He plucked a small grape-like fruit from the tray and examined it closely. As far as he could tell, there was no puncture mark that would indicate it had been tampered with in any way.

"Is it safe?" Meghnah watched him, but kept one eye always on the guards.

James shrugged. "At least this one appears fine."

Nevarian laid on one of the chairs and grabbed a round purple fruit. He tossed it into the air, caught it, then sniffed at the skin before taking a small bite. "The food is fine, if you question it, you will make them more suspicious."

He was careful to keep his voice low, but James quietly wondered if it mattered. He wasn't as concerned about the food being poisoned, as he was with a listening device hiding nearby.

James plopped the small fruit he was holding into his mouth. It was more sour than he was expecting, with a sticky sweet juice, more like citrus than a grape. He grabbed another one and this time bit it in half. Beneath the purple red skin was a soft orange colored flesh.

Fetu sat down opposite James. He selected what appeared to be a small crustacean wrapped in a thin layer of meat and marinated in sauce. "Hey, this is pretty good."

Travis joined him, and in a moment they were exchanging detailed critiques of each dish as they sampled it.

Chloe sat beside James, sharing the chair with him, she laid her head on his lap. "This is nice."

James stared at her for a moment, watching the reflection of the sky in her eyes. He wished he could discern the thoughts beneath those bright blue irises, but they remained elusive. He imagined what it must be like to have grown up idolizing this kind of society. Wondered what the other children would think if they could see her here, as a guest to one of the Duchesses of the royal family. He brushed her long blonde hair with his hand.

She tried one of the small citrus fruits. "James. Do you ever think about the future?"

He paused, leaning back in the chair and letting out

a long breath. "Sometimes, I guess."

She shifted, nestling down into him a little more. "Do you think you could live this way?"

James glanced around. "You mean like here on Atlione?"

She shook her head. "No, not here specifically. With servants, people catering to your every need, never being able to do anything for yourself. Having someone there to watch you, all the time."

He poured two glasses of wine. "I suppose I never gave that much thought." It made his skin crawl, the fakeness, the pretense, the thinly veiled masks of artificial emotions. Years of training had taught him to watch his back, to suspect everyone, and read their intentions on their faces. His paranoia was bad enough when no one was trying to hide anything. Here it was like someone had pulled the ships fire alarm in his head. "What about you?"

She shrugged. "I spent my whole life imagining it, dreaming of some day being able to fit in with the others. It all seems so fickle now, I think my heart will always belong on the Shade, no matter where I end up."

James's chest tightened. "Why do you think you would go somewhere else?"

She sat up, wrapping her fingers around the edge of the seat, her hair bunching up a little at the top of her head, where he had been playing with it. "I don't know, people change I guess, things change. The whole galaxy is changing around us and it feels like nothing ever gets to stay the same."

She wasn't looking at him and even though their hands were touching, it was as if the expanse of space had come between them.

Seph

He took her hand and squeezed it. "I think we can make the future be anything we want it to be."

She smiled softly, brushing back her hair and taking a sip of wine. "What kind of a future would you choose?"

The question carried more weight than it implied. "I don't know. I guess, for now, one where we don't have to look over our shoulders anymore. Where we can go back to doing honest work and getting paid for it. What kind of future would you choose?"

She huffed in the ironic sort of way someone does when laughing at a private joke. "I don't know, James. Not so long ago I thought I did, but now I feel like I finally found what I spent my whole life looking for, and it isn't anything like I thought it would be. Now I am so afraid that if I let go I will lose it. I don't think I want anything to ever change, but that isn't the way things are, and I am scared that if I try to hold on too hard, I might lose myself and forget why it was important."

James wrapped his arm around her and pulled her close to himself, she was obviously having some deep thoughts tonight. "Where is this coming from?"

She leaned her head on his shoulder and shook it a couple of times. "It doesn't matter, I am just contemplating my place in the universe."

He rubbed her shoulder. "Whatever it is, I am sure you will make the right decision, because that's the kind of person you are. So I wouldn't worry about it too much."

She sat up nodding. "You're right, and I am probably overthinking things." She took a bite of a soft pear-like fruit. "Would you like to go for a swim?"

When they asked about it, the guards promptly

provided them with swimwear, and directed them to one of the small outbuildings to change. James had been hesitant at first, he wanted to stay prepared to leave at any moment, but a few exchanged glances with Nevarian told him it might be a good idea.

The water was warm, more like a hot spring than a pool. The perfectly smooth walls hid any sort of heating or pump mechanism, the gentle flow of water off the edge told James there was likely more gravity manipulation at work.

After they had been in for a few minutes, Meghnah decided to join them. It had taken some convincing on Chloe's part, but once she did, Meghnah began removing her uniform at the side of the pool. Which caused no small amount of embarrassment among the guards, who insisted she use the outbuilding. It had likely been the most effective thing any of them had tried to push them off balance.

Chloe was delighted by the water, she radiated a child-like glee that James had not seen since the night she had danced in the rain on Dramia. It was infectious, and appeared to melt even Meghnah's reservations.

After the two girls had made several attempts at drowning each other, then teamed up on James, they found themselves sitting together on the small bench overlooking the star-filled lake.

"What do you suppose the city is like down there?" Chloe asked.

Nevarian slipped his feet into the water beside them. "Not much different from here."

"Have you been there?" Meghnah asked.

"Many times. But that was a lifetime ago."

Chloe laid her head back against the stone. "Why

did you join the Shade?"

Nevarian's fins opened and closed, churning the water around his feet, "I had my own reasons, though they do not matter much anymore. It was so long ago, that it is little more than a distant memory."

They sat in silence for a moment. Eventually Fetu and Travis joined them.

"What now?" Fetu was the first to break the silence.

"We are not going to get out of here without a fight." Nevarian answered.

They had seen almost nothing of Railayia since she had led them here. As food disappeared, services arrived to replenish it. Otherwise, there had been almost no contact with anyone from the city.

James inhaled. "I agree, there is more going on here than the Duchess was letting on. I suspect when the time comes, only Nevarian will be allowed to return to the ship."

Fetu was floating on his back in the middle of the pool, "So, what do we do about it?"

Meghnah made a water spout with her hand a squirted Fetu, "We will need to keep playing along until an opportunity presents itself."

"I think we can make one." James slipped his arm over Chloe's shoulder and pulled her away from Meghnah.

Fetu turned in the water so he was standing on his feet. Sweeping his arm, he sent a wave crashing into Meghnah.

Chloe yelped, covering her face with her arms and curling up against James.

Nevarian, who also managed to catch a decent portion of the wave, closed his eyes, enjoying the water on his skin. He opened his fins into full fans.

James let go of Chloe's arm, and she slid back next to her best friend giggling. Fetu and Meghnah both burst into laughter.

James looked up at the sky, careful to make sure nothing he said would reflect off the water, or back at the guards. "The trickiest part will be the ferry. I am confident it was being controlled by a neural link the Duchess was wearing."

Nevarian nodded. "More than likely."

Fetu twisted his ears. "Travis and I can get around that."

Travis shook his head. "Sure, given enough time, but I doubt we would be able to bypass it before we got caught."

"What if we didn't bypass it?" James suggested.

"Did you bring your link?" Meghnah asked.

James shook his head. "No, but I did bring the glove."

Chloe shifted. "Will that work?"

Meg, Travis, and Fetu all turned to look at him. It was Fetu who spoke. "What glove?"

"The Hand of Vyanna, or whatever it is."

Nevarian grinned. "If it is the device I believe it is, not only will it work, but it should prevent anyone else from taking back control."

Meghnah pulled herself out of the water, sitting beside Nevarian. "And if it isn't?"

"Then we don't make it very far." James admitted. "But I think we can test it to be sure. I am assuming this pool uses similar technology?"

Nevarian and Travis both nodded.

"We might have a chance. But we will have to talk about it later."

James pulled himself out of the pool, then changed

back into his uniform. He returned to the veranda and approached the guards.

"Can I get a datapad? I need to check on some bets I placed earlier."

One of the guards disappeared. They returned a moment later handing James a pad. "Will this work?"

"Perfect," James said taking the pad and powering it on.

Chloe and Meghnah had both changed and were sitting together in one of the chairs at the table.

James leaned over placing a hand on Chloe's shoulder. "I think I am going to go take a nap."

With that James went to the largest of the outbuildings designated as a bunk room.

The building itself was much the same as the other he had seen. An open door that led into a hallway which connected to the interior of the building. Inside were five beds, and two sleeping pods, an indication that the Duchess had called ahead and had the room prepared for them. Each of the beds had its own privacy screen, which at the moment were deactivated.

Thankfully the others had understood his message, and within twenty minutes they were all together again.

James typed out a message on the datapad then handed it to Fetu, "Take a look at these odds, and tell me what you think."

The message read:

Jamming device.

He removed the folded up glove from his pocket and handed it to Chloe.

"Go check and make sure this will work."

Chloe nodded. Slipping it onto her hand, she winced against the pain and returned to the veranda.

A moment later, she came back and pulled the glove off her hand, holding it out to James. "It works."

James nodded, taking it. "Alright, good night."

The others appeared confused for a second, but caught on, echoing their own good nights.

A moment later, Fetu was finished with the datapad. "There you go."

"Is it working?" James asked.

Fetu nodded. "I got to hand it to you; that is a pretty brilliant stunt you just pulled."

James shrugged. "You can complement me all you want when we get out of this alive."

Meghnah sat next to Chloe on the bed across from him, "Right, so what's the plan?"

James glanced at Nevarian. "Are there any other docks, besides the one we landed on?"

The fingalin nodded. "There is one at all four of the cardinal directions. We came in at the north dock, I believe."

James nodded. "Okay, we will want to leave by either the western or eastern dock. If we do get out of here, they will expect us to go somewhere familiar. My guess is that when Nevarian goes to leave, they will assign at least two of the guards to go with him. The rest of us will have to stay here, but we are going to protest it."

Everyone nodded to indicate they were following so far.

"Once they are gone, we will make our move." James summoned the stunblade from inside his jacket and offered it to Meghnah. "I trust you know how to use this?"

She nodded, "But how did you get it in here?"

Seph

James grinned. "This isn't my uniform jacket. It is a military issue nano jacket."

Fetu barely suppressed a laugh. "You clever devil."

Meghnah took the knife. "Okay, so you want me to take out the guards?"

"Yes and no. First you will act as a distraction. To create an opening, get their eyes off this building for a moment, then you can start a fight. While she does that, I will sneak onto the roof of the changing room. Once the rest of you hear fighting, come out. By that point there should be one or two warstaffs available."

James looked at Nevarian. "Do you think you could explain well enough to get us to the dock?"

The doctor shook his head. "But don't worry, I will be able to double back and lead you there myself."

"You sure?"

He nodded. "Just don't keep me waiting."

"Okay, we will have to formulate the rest of the plan as we go. For now, get some rest. I am sure the guards will be changed before the time comes, so we want to be as fresh as possible."

* * *

It was near sunrise when they awoke, the eastern edge of the sky glowing with a dim purple halo around the edge of the caldera. The air was saturated with fine mist that was crisp on the skin, and smelled of the ocean.

As James had predicted, the guard had been changed. They sat chatting together at the back edge of the veranda. Most of their warstaffs were either leaning against their shoulders or laid on the ground.

James followed Nevarian out of the bunk room.

As they approached, the guards scrambled to pull themselves together, lining up in front of the path leading down into the city.

Nevarian stopped a few feet away. "I must go retrieve my samples now, the rest of the crew will join us shortly, then we will be leaving."

The guard closest to the center coughed. "I am afraid you will be retrieving the samples by yourself, the Duchess has requested that you remain on the planet for a few more days."

Nevarian frowned, "That will not be possible, we must return to Reicue 12 as quickly as is feasible."

The guard shook her head. "As of an hour ago, there is a ban on offworld travel. The Duchess expresses her deepest apologies for any inconvenience this may cause you. But as guests of the Empire, you will be extended every courtesy."

Nevarian's ears flicked, he scanned the group. "Very well."

He began walking and two of the guards broke off, following him. The remaining five spread out and blocked James's path.

James inhaled slowly then let the air out in a huff, before turning and crossing the veranda to the bunk house. The others all sat on the edges of the four beds waiting for him.

"So far they are following the script. Meghnah, you're up."

Meghnah rose from the bed, removed her uniform jacket to reveal the thin gray Descendant undershirt, and handed the jacket to Chloe. "Make sure I get that back."

James watched from the hall, careful to stay out of the guards' line of sight as much as possible.

Seph

Meghnah walked to the pool at the far end of the platform, knelt, and ran her hand through the water. She stood, and began to undo her pants. Immediately, two of the guards had run over to her, and began talking with her.

That was the cue James was waiting for. Returning to the bunk room, he pulled the cloth out of the window nearest the changing room, then tossed it on the bed. James pulled his body through the small opening, resting his weight on his waist. He flipped his hands so they were holding the inside lip, then rolled forward. Ducking his head against his chest, he unfolded his back against the wall keeping his knees up, then dropped to the ground.

The space between the two outbuildings was narrow, and he found himself standing very close to the edge of the platform. kicking off the changing room wall he grabbed the inside edge of the window. Pulling himself up, he put his foot on the bottom ledge, then pushed off, grabbed the roof of the changing room, and slid up onto his stomach.

Once on the roof, James rolled over, adjusting his body so he could see the guards. Reaching into his pocket, he pulled out the glove and slipped it on his hand, it pinched into his wrist. Exhaling, he let his mind sink into the emptiness it created. The air came to life, as it began to hum with energy.

He checked to see where Meghnah was on the balcony below. She was refastening her pants, the two guards turned their back to her and began to leave.

In a single fluid movement, Meghnah stabbed the closest guard with the stunblade, then spun to kick the second guard in the chest as he turned to respond. He hunched over as his lungs collapsed.

James pointed his index and middle finger at the guards near the ramp, focusing on the flow of energy he scooped it up, concentrating it with his mind, squeezing the grip like a gun between his remaining fingers.

The first guard collapsed as Meghanh slammed her shoulder into the second man, using his weight to rotate her body. Blue streaks of electricity flew across them striking the body of the second guard, Meghnah jumped back, allowing the force of the blast to toss the body back into the pool.

James felt for the sensation which functioned as the activation mechanism for the glove, then inhaled, forming a precise image of what he wanted in his mind. The energy became a single point at his fingertip.

A wave of electricity washed over him, as a bright green beam shot from the glove, striking one of the guards at the entrance in the shoulder. The man twisted and collapsed on the ground. Two of the remaining guards turned to fire at James, while the last one charged at Meghnah.

James ducked low, avoiding the shots by hiding behind the ledge of the roof. When he looked up again, Fetu and Travis were charging across the veranda. Meghnah had ducked behind the table, and tossed both of them warstaffs from the first two guards.

Travis caught the staff out of the air, spinning it and instantly activating the shield, as all three of the guards concentrated their fire on the group. As Fetu returned fire, one of the guards switched her staff to shield mode, sheltering the other two.

James lifted himself on his arm again, and fired. The

guard was prepared for it this time, and managed to catch the beam on his shield. Travis moved to the front of the table, while Fetu moved to the flank, drawing fire from their opponents.

Meghnah jumped on the table rounding off a handstand to build momentum, she flung herself into the air. Soaring across the veranda, she landed only a few feet away from the lead guard. She swung her staff at Meghnah, who drew her front leg back, side stepping the swing. Catching the staff, Meghnah jabbed the palm of her free hand into the guard's jaw, using the staff as a leaver to put her into a lock and drive her face-first into the stone floor.

James took the opportunity to fire off another shot. Both of the remaining guards jumped back, taking cover from James in the street.

Travis spun his staff switching it to firing mode, releasing two shots nearly simultaneously. Both of the remaining guards collapsed as the electricity pulsed through their bodies.

James dropped down from his position on the changing room's roof. Chloe came out of the bunk room a moment later. The crew gathered near the ramp. Meghnah and Chloe each grabbed one of the warstaffs. Chloe held hers awkwardly, and James found himself cursing the fact that up until now he had only trained her in firearms.

Travis stepped up beside her. "Here, like this." He repositioned her arms, then showed her his own stance. "The button there energizes the head, the one under it fires, and if you twist the grip like this. It becomes a shield."

She swung it experimentally, mimicking Travis's forum.

Nevarian reappeared from down the street motioning for them with a staff of his own.

"We don't have much time." He said as they approached.

James nodded. "You take point. Travis, you guard the rear. Meghnah, you're in charge of keeping the doctor alive. Fetu, stay on offense and keep your eyes sharp. Chloe, stay close to Meghnah and do as she says. I am going to break off and provide support."

James turned off into an alleyway, then used the same trick he had used before to climb on a nearby roof, keeping a close eye on his companions as they made their way through the city.

Most of the roof tops were low, single story buildings weaved together so that it was almost impossible to tell where you were. Layers of the city rose and fell, then wrapped back around each other maximizing the use of the overall area, while minimizing any shared space.

The sun was coming up now, and bright orange and red streaks scored the eastern horizon. People started coming out of the buildings, and opening up shops. They gave the group as much space as possible. But then gathered in clumps behind them.

James tried to keep himself as many levels above the rest of the group as possible, while keeping them in his line of sight. Jumping from rooftop to raised alleyway, then scaling buildings where necessary. At times, he was able to get as many as four levels up from them. But he was soon forced down closer if he didn't want to risk losing the group.

He caught glimpses of guards running through the street, but they had assumed they would go for the northern dock, and Nevarian was leading them west.

Seph

Suddenly, Nevarian came to a stop, and James jumped down to see what was going on, only to discover the road had been blocked by a force barrier.

"Great," Fetu said, powering up his warstaff and turning back the way they had come. "This means they know what we are trying to do."

Nevarian nodded, "Most likely. Master James, do you mind?" He swept one hand out to indicate the force barrier. James stared at it for a moment, not sure what the fingalin was getting at. He squeezed his gloved hand closed, then placed it palm open against the wall.

There was an immediate pressure on the edge of his mind. Taping it with a mental finger, it sprung open and a network of codes, diagrams, and information floated at the edge of his fingertips. Manipulating it the same way he would a neural link, James decoded the power switch, and with a twist of his wrist the barrier vanished.

Nevarian gave a shallow bow, "Thank you," then continued down the road.

James was beginning to get a feel for the city, and was able to move a few streets ahead. Soldiers were waiting for them at the dock. Not the guards they had encountered thus far, but military personnel in full suits of high carbon ceramic armor.

Hoping over roofs, James returned to the group. "We have trouble up ahead."

"More guards?" Meghnah asked.

He shook his head. "Military."

There was an explosion of stone as a bolt of energy struck the building next to them.

"Company!" Travis yelled as he caught several more shots on his shield.

Fetu began returning fire.

James imagined the energy in the glove forming into a shield. A bright green barrier erupted in front of him, and a wave of energy rushed through his body. Taking up a position beside Travis, he helped block the oncoming fire.

"We have to keep moving."

Nevarian nodded.

James and Travis took turns as the rear guard, while Fetu attempted to keep the soldiers behind them from getting any closer than the end of the last street. Sandstone exploded around them, and civilians screamed as they ran for cover.

Nevarian stopped again, James signaled to Fetu and Meghnah. Fetu took his place as a shield, while Meghnah took over suppressive fire.

"What's going on?" James moved to the front of the group. He didn't even need to wait for an answer, peering around the corner he could see the soldiers on the dock.

Nevarian glanced at James, "Any more bright ideas?"

James peered around the corner. There were about fifteen of them. With at least a dozen in the street behind them.

More sandstone exploded, filling the space between the buildings with dust. The soldiers on the dock opened fire as well, and James pulled himself back around the corner.

"You, Chloe, and I got shields. Meghnah fires forward from the center. Fetu and Travis bring up the rear, we form up into a triangle, and push them out to the sides.

Nevarian bounced his head side to side. "Not bad, but I think we can do better."

James raised an eyebrow. "Oh?"

The doctor bent down and picked up a handful of dust and sand. "Watch closely, you might learn something."

Turning on his shield, Nevarian stepped out of the alley. The soldiers opened fire. Nevarian threw the handful of dust into the air.

"Ty'ell vhen lavay zymo,"

As the sand caught the rays from the rising sun, it erupted into brilliant light scattering across the dock in a shower of colors.

The soldiers stepped back. Twirling the staff over his head, Nevarian used its momentum to shift it into offensive mode, then laid down a spray of fire catching three of the soldiers in the chest. Their armor absorbed most of the shock, and they fired back. When Nevarian reached the end of his sweep, he carried the staff into a second spin which activated the shield just in time to block the incoming shots.

"A'el O'rah laiem aphiss."

A small fire erupted on the dock behind the soldiers, who jumped away from it clearing the center.

James took the opportunity to join the doctor, a new idea forming in his mind on using the glove. One of the soldiers fired at him, James summoned the bright green shield, using it to catch electricity. Instead of letting it dissipate, it lurched trying to escape from him. Focusing his breathing, James closed his hand around it. Codes and images describing the energy unfolded in front of him, almost like deciphering a computer program.

It caught James so off guard that he lost his focus, the information vanished as a second shot caught him on the shoulder. A high-pitched ringing erupted in his ears, and his vision blurred as he was knocked off his feet. His jacket reverted to its worn blue as the nanites rushed to collect and disperse the energy.

Chloe activated her shield, running out to protect him from any more shots. "Are you okay!?"

Even though she was shouting, he could barely make out what she was saying.

Nevarian laid down another round of fire, getting close enough now that the final shot presented itself as a strike to the side of one of the soldier's heads.

James shook himself, as the ringing stopped, and the world started coming back into focus.

Nevarian, now with two wartaffs, stood with most of the soldiers lined up in front of him. He used one staff as a shield, while firing off shots with the other, at a much slower rate now than before.

"I'll be fine." James said, standing shakily on his feet, it took a moment to regain his balance, and he was only vaguely aware of Meghanh, Fetu, and Travis, now backing onto the dock while covering the onslaught from behind.

James took a deep breath, then nodded at Chloe. "Drop your shield." He generated his own shield again, stepping in front of her.

Chloe ducked behind him, rapidly firing at the exposed soldiers. Their armor absorbing most of the damage.

A shot connected with James's barrier. "Shield!" He yelled, switching places with Chloe again.

The codex of information appeared in front of him, wrestling the energy he reshaped it to his will, and amplified it. A wave flowed out of his body and into the glove.

Finishing his rotation, James came back around to

face the soldiers. He opened his hand and a burst of lighting erupted from his palm, it danced across the metal dock in hundreds of arks, enveloping the soldiers and dropping several of them to the floor.

"Go!" He yelled.

Chloe dashed to the nearest boat, while Nevarian kept the remaining soldiers occupied from the side.

James turned, firing a blast of energy at the soldiers behind them. "Meghnah, now!"

Meghnah twisted her staff, switching it into a shield, swapping places with James as she rushed forward.

Fetu and Travis followed suit, switching to offensive mode, and firing as James brought his shield back up, and used it to cover them, as they made their way to the boat.

Nevarian moved towards the center, closing the group behind James so that all the soldiers were now firing from the same direction.

Chloe, Meghnah, Fetu, and Travis all stood at the front of the vessel with their shields activated, creating a safe zone in the center of the deck. James placed his palm on the floor. Sweat dripped from his forehead, and he realized for the first time he was hyperventilating. His limbs felt like jello, and a fresh wave of dizziness and nausea washed over him.

He inhaled through his nose, getting a handle on his oxygen flow. The diagrams and interfaces for the vessel unfolded in his mind. First he activated the force field. The invisible barriers sprang into existence, catching the energy blast from the soldiers. Someone in their ranks started shouting orders, and they began boarding the other boats.

James kicked on the gravity drive and began

pushing the boat out onto the lake. Once it was moving at full speed, he brought it around in a curve until they were headed towards the opening in the crater's edge.

The rest of the crew powered down their weapons and collapsed on the deck. James forced himself to his feet. He realized, with a start, that the connection to the vessel remained intact. He wiggled his fingers, feeling the systems respond to him.

James turned to see several boats following them. Pushing himself, he reached out with his mind. Forcing the connection out beyond the edges of the boat.

As he brushed against the surface of the lake, new sequences began to open up. They were complicated, hundreds of thousands of them, mixing together and changing. He touched them with his mind, and realized whatever they were, somehow they were describing the water itself. He drew it into himself, as power rushed into his hand. Reaching out even further he found the systems of the approaching boats.

Wrapping his hand around their shield generators he clenched his fist, feeling them as they powered down. Closing his eyes, he focused on the energy he had stored from the lake. Then giving it shape with his mind, he thrust his hand forward, releasing it.

The surface of the water behind them began to roll, building energy as it went until it had formed into a massive wave, which crashed down over the top of the other ships.

James stumbled forwards as energy drained from his body like a bowling ball had slammed into his stomach. The whole world spun, he fell to the deck. Breathing deeply, fighting against the exhaustion,

Seph

James turned to sit. Looking at the rest of the crew, everyone but Nevarian looked stunned.

"What in Vyanna's name was that?" Fetu asked.

James shook his head. " I have no idea."

Nevarian moved over to him, checking his pupils, and feeling his pulse. "You should not have been able to do that." He said flatly.

"Do you know what it was?"

Nevarian nodded. "And you should never attempt something like that again, it very nearly killed you."

A few minutes passed in silence as the sun fully broke over the horizon. The oceanic air rejuvenating James's lungs as he lay on his back, breathing against the weight on his chest.

Meghnah shifted, "Where did you learn to fight like that?" she glanced at the doctor.

Nevarian sat back against the wall. "When you spend as much time with Master Zaeith as I have, you pick up a few things."

The pier was empty and deserted when they arrived. James had finally managed to clear his head, and get his feet under him again. And so, he walked with the others along the trail which led them back to their ship.

The sound of birds singing in the trees echoed off the ocean waves. Seeing it in the daylight like this was a new kind of breathtaking, and James felt a pain in his chest, at the fact that they would not get to see more of the planet's promised beauty, having destroyed their fair share of it only moments before.

As they approached the Shade, an uneasiness grew in the bottom of his stomach. James glanced around, his senses on high alert. Everything was exactly as they left it, and the ship appeared untouched.

Someone shouted from somewhere up the hill. The crew came to a stop as a line of soldiers marched out of the trees. Everyone powered up their staffs preparing for battle.

"That was quite the show you put on," Duchess Railayia Naysiaria stepped out from behind her soldiers, "but this is as far as you go."

James held out his hand concentrating power into his palm.

Nevarian glanced over at him, "No, don't!"

His stomach lurched back through his spine, like he had been dropped from the top of the lift barrier. He felt like he was falling thousands of feet before he hit the ground. The world spun in circles around him as sand filled his nose. It was all he could do to stare at the horizon. A small black dot appeared above the waves, growing larger. James squinted, trying to focus, but his vision only blurred as dark rings closed in around him. he fought with everything he had to stay awake, anything to remain conscious. In a moment, there was nothing but blackness around him. His weightless body floating in a starless sky.

Chapter 31

The Captain of the Shade was silent as they walked along the beach, the night air cold as it blew over the open ocean, waves crashing against the shore. The Captain insisted on walking below the tide line, where the sea washed away any trace of their passage.

What lay behind those burning eyes and cold expression? In the last two months, this man had turned his life upside down. Though, Gillian was sure it started long before The Captain became involved. It was difficult to tell at this point whether the mysterious Drak'or had saved him, or condemned him.

The quarantine assignment had been out of the ordinary, but routine none the less. Director Xious had reported that his resources were stretched to their limits. At least that was the story told by General Chellis. Sending Gillian had been Admiral Trepidor's idea. The Vyrant was available, and due to his lineage Gillian was a well-respected officer.

It was unorthodox for the Army to get involved with one of the Clergy's operations. But by making it a joint venture the council had hoped to strengthen the Order's over-all resolve, on the front lines of the battle against the Aberation. Sending someone familiar, like Gillian, would help to ease the tension between the two groups, by helping the Clergy not to feel slighted by the encroachment.

Gillian never would have guessed that Jasvlin would have been on that station, but the footage he had been shown was undeniable. And now the grand admiral had sent Captain Darith after him. True, allowing the Shade's crew onto the Vyrant and abandoning the ship had technically been treason. It wasn't as if Gillian had expected to get off easy, but the ferocity with which he had been pursued was of another order entirely. Combined with the thought that the destruction of the planet Ulun'tess had in fact not been an accident, it was too disturbing to ignore. Of course, even if it were true, no one would ever believe it.

Then again, should he ever think to tell anyone of the events of the last two months as a whole; the idea that there was an elaborate conspiracy against him and his family was far from the only thing which they would have trouble believing. Though the concept that one might fabricate such things was equally absurd.

This was the general tone of Gillian's thoughts during the journey of several hours before they reached the first landmark.

Cut into the side of the hill rising up away from the ocean were a series of small dwellings. Similar to other fingalin structures, these had no doors, only colorful curtains hung in the open windows. However, these buildings were laid out in seven even rows stepping up along the edge of the craters outer wall.

This had been where Gillian's family had stayed when they visited Atlione. These homes were reserved for individuals and families with a significant social standing, and unlike many of the facilities in the Empire, only private credit qualified.

It was a place where the important and powerful members of society could escape from the pressures and obligations that ruled their everyday lives. And as Gillian remembered it, staying here was one of the few times he and his brother had spent any quality time with their father. Though, in hindsight, there was little of that time Gillian could call quality.

The buildings were protected from the surf by the tiers of a stone wall, which held the ocean back like the edge of a pool. It rose up at a dozen different levels. Depending on the tide, it insured that the water's depths changed at a predictable rate.

Gillian pointed out across the open ocean. "We would swim straight out from here. If I remember correctly, it takes about two hours. There is a small community there. From that point we head south. It's less than a mile from the village."

The Captain stepped out to the next ledge, where the wall dropped another foot or so down into the water. The waves crashed around his knees as he stared out at the horizon.

"I will need your help." He said flatly.

Gillian glanced around. "Finding a boat?" Obviously he did not expect the drak'or to keep up with him underwater.

The Captain shook his head. "No, I do not want to risk anything so conspicuous."

Gillian started, "What might I ask was your

intention?"

The drak'or turned to face him, eyes burning like embers on the ocean waves. "You are going to do the swimming for both of us."

Gillian twisted his ears. "And how, exactly, did you envision that working?"

A gust of wind blew off the sea, catching The Captain's cloak and wrapping it around his body. As the cloth twisted, the wind began to pick up speed, droplets of water peeling off the tops of the waves as they were driven forward. Gillian had to cover his face with his arm, opening his fin as a shield.

A loud crack echoed into the open air, and The Captain let out a blood-curdling scream. Gillian glanced at where he had been standing, but the Captain was gone. Frantically, Gillian began searching the area. An electrical sensation erupted on his calf, as scales scraped across his leg he jumped back, turning to look at what had touched him.

Two solid red eyes, burning like fire appeared out of the black water, the serpent's sleek black body winding itself around his legs. Gillian swallowed hard as it worked its way up his body, wrapping several coils around his waist, then up over his shoulder. Its tongue flicked next to his ear.

Gillian stood frozen, motionless in the night air. Water lashing around his feet. Altogether the creature was as long as Gillian was tall, with a body as thick as his leg. If it wished, it could crush him, ending his life in an instant.

A sharp voice echoed in Gillian's mind, dripping with venom. "Go now, before we run out of time."

"Captain?"

The serpent nodded. "Yes," the voice hissed.

Seph

Gillian inhaled attempting to regain his composure. "Alright." Walking into the ocean until the waves began to lift him from off his feet, Gillian launched himself into the water using his hands to break the surface, then stoking hard, bringing his body down to the ocean floor. His fins flared out like giant fans, relishing in the feeling of the open ocean around him. He stiffened the spins, then launched through the water.

The snake's body stiffened and tightened around him, growing heavy and hard. Gillian felt as if he had tied a stone weight around his waist. He began to sink, but soon compensated for the shift.

The stone floor soon passed, replaced first by natural sand, until suddenly the ocean dropped into a steep slope. Gillian swam downward, along the mountain's rocky edge, using the currents around its crevices and canyons to pick up even more speed.

At first, the water was cold, but his body adjusted, and he found himself feeling more and more alive with every stroke of his fins. It had been years since he had let himself free like this, immersing himself in the underwater world.

He could hear the song of Atlione's massive aquatic mammals echoing through the water. Closing his eyes, he spun in a barrel roll, the melodious music washing over his soul. His race may have conquered space, but no matter what technological achievements they made, they would always belong to the sea.

Gillian lost track of time, letting his mind drift in the thrill of swimming, and in what felt like only a moment small lights began to shimmer in the distance. They came up on the small village, its twisting wave-like structure, blending in with the floor of the ocean.

Gillian swooped by in a long arch, hiding himself behind tall strands of seaweed, which grew around the edges of the alcove where the settlement had been built.

The sleeping city shimmered in the dim lights of its streets like something frozen in time. The stone buildings were cast in shades of blue and green, which were distorted through the lens of the surrounding ocean.

Gillian took a moment to reorient himself, then headed straight south. Huge volcanic rocks jutted out of the sea floor, rising towards the surface, their dark exteriors littered with pockets, and tunnels, teaming with life.

As he followed along the upward slope of the rock face, flashes of moonlight, and shadows of clouds, passed overhead, forming vague shapes around each other. The surface grew closer and stars began to appear, shimmering in the water.

Exerting a final push of momentum from his fins, Gillian launched himself from the water, soaring into the evening air. Water droplets formed around him, each reflecting the midnight world like its own tiny universe.

He twisted his body into a roll, holding his arms out, spreading his fins like wings. He moved through the air in an arch, twisting away from the small island formed by the jutting rocks.

At the last moment he clasped his hands over his head, diving back into the water, then pushing with his fins, sent himself soaring around the island's perimeter, skimming no more than a foot below the surface.

Using the wind driven waves to slow his momentum, Gillian approached from the leeward side of the rock. Using the pockets of stone for hand holds, he pulled himself from the water, climbing the last three feet from the surface, to the small outcropping he and his brother had discovered many years ago.

The evening light was bright after having spent so much time in the depths of the sea. Gillian blinked, letting his eyes adjust.

The snake's skin began to soften as it loosened its grip around him, slithering from his shoulder. Moving a few feet away, the serpent rose to the end of its tail. Wind wrapped around the protective rock, batting at Gillian, and once again he was forced to cover his face.

The air swirled around the small plateau, picking up sand and debris from the ground. It centered around the snake like a whirlwind. The creature shifted, and folded in the wind, twisting around itself. It's scales flattened, until they burst open unfolding into a cloak.

The Captain turned to face Gillian as the wind died down. The drak'or was dry, not even a drop of water on the ground.

"Where is this cave?"

Gillian pointed up the rock face ahead of them, "Hidden about fifteen feet further up."

The Captain followed Gillian's finger with his eyes. Staring up at the black monolith of rock. He shifted his foot back into a wide stance then sprinting forward, leaped into the air disappearing into the rock face.

Gillian stared after him, did he jump all the way up to the entrance? Was it even jumping still if it was three times your own height? At what point did a jump become indistinguishable from flight?

Inhaling, Gillian began climbing the heavily pitted cliffside. When he reached the opening, he could barely make out the outline of The Captain's shape in the darkness of the cave.

They walked in silence, the smell of algae and salt, almost acidic against the cold wet stone. Drops of water echoed in the cold space as the tunnel wound its way down through the rock.

Light from the surface soon vanished, Gillian slowed, trying to feel his way along the wall. He was unable to keep up with The Captain who seemed unfazed by the darkness. If he had brought a datapad, this wouldn't have been a problem. But he had not carried one with him when he had abandoned the Vyrant, nor had he ever borrowed one from the Shade.

"Hold up. I can't see." His voice echoed in the lava tube, bouncing off the twists and turns in the rock.

The hollow sound of boot fall came to a stop.

"Zymo ty'ell dreku."

The words reverberated in the darkness, sending a chill down Gillian's spine. A small glowing orb illuminated the space with warm yellow light.

Gillian blinked as his pupils dilated. He wasn't sure what surprised him more at this point. The light itself, or the fact that these things were still surprising him.

The cave continued down for two miles, narrowing at times to the point where they had to crawl through the small openings. And on occasion, opening into cavernous chambers.

After over an hour, the cave narrowed until it became impassable. The Captain held up his hand, and with a few flicks of his fingers moved the light around the chamber. Something flickered from the small opening, barely larger than Gillian's forearm.

The Captain motioned with his head, and Gillian reached into the opening, feeling around, his fingers

Seph

brushed against something cold and smooth. It had a round shape, like a puck, with small grooves in the face. Shoving his arm into the opening up to his shoulder, Gillian grabbed it and extracted it from the rock.

Examining the glass object in the light, it appeared to be a holobook. There was a data card tied to it by a small string.

Gillian glanced at The Captain. "I suppose this is what we came for?"

The Captain took the book from him, and removing the data card, held the small glass plate up to the light. A rainbow of colors refracted out of it, dancing around the room. A moment later he returned it to Gillian.

"I believe so. Let's go."

The return trip was every bit as quiet, and damp as the trip down had been. The Captain   lead, seeming to pass through the narrow openings as easily as their shadows traced the walls.

Gillian's mind turned to the small glass object in his pocket. Jeriell must have gone to extraordinary lengths to create it, and have it hidden here of all places. Holobooks like this were not particularly common, outside of historical libraries.

Considering the hiding place, it did make a certain amount of sense. The glass would be resistant to damage from the elements inside the cave. However, the data card attached to it would not. The data card, which he hoped contained the projection sequence that would allow the book to be read. Without that, coming here would have been pointless. Except to confirm that Jeriell had been trying to communicate with Gillian, and potentially knew something about why the Order hunted down and killed his daughter.

Standing at the edge of the rocky opening, Gillian looked out at the pale purple sky, indicating the sun was about to peak over the horizon, the ocean waves were rolling underneath, catching and reflecting the dancing rays across its surface.

Other than for the sounds of the sea, the world was quiet. The occasional bird could be heard calling out, its squawk informing others of food, or warning them to stay away. Gashwars now scuttled about, their dull grey outer feathers camouflaging them against the rock. Otherwise, the life of Atlione lay hidden deep beneath its watery crust, leaving its surface in a sort of serene tranquility replicated nowhere else in the galaxy.

The Captain stared out across the open world, his eyes distant and cold against the morning light. His expression was vacant, lost in contemplation over some hidden mystery masked by his dark complexion.

Gillian flexed his fins experimentally, the muscles which held them taught resisted, a tight burning sensation growing along his arms and back muscles. It had been a long time since he had undertaken any serious swimming like this.

He stretched his muscles as best he could. By the time they made it back to the caldera, he wouldn't be moving at all for a day or so.

"Shall we head back?"

The Captain gave a quick nod. "But we will not be swimming."

Gillian glanced around. There was the rock ledge, the small landing below them, and a planet full of open ocean. He twisted his ears. "Do you have another means of crossing the ocean?"

As if to answer his question, a gust of wind began to blow from deep inside the cavern. Gillian had to clench his fins tight to his body to keep the wind from catching beneath them.

The air current twisted around The Captain, his cloak, fluttering in the breeze. Stretching his arms out, the material fell from his shoulders, and billowed out like the wings of a giant bat.

The Captain's scream joined a chorus of snaps, as if every bone was being broken and mended back together. His shape began to blur as if he had been consumed by an unearthly shadow. It was difficult to distinguish where exactly his body began from where it ended.

The black fog twisted and turned in the wind until it began to condense around itself. Five long claw-like toes formed out of the inky black mass, gripping the edge of the rock. They were attached to two massive legs, like predatory birds, only covered in thick black hide.

The Captain 's clothing had melded into his body, replaced by black spines which made a mane around his shoulders and back. Its bat-like wings grew from his sides and arms, jutting outward from its wrists. His face had morphed to resemble a nocturnal demon, long horns and ears grown backwards from his head. Eyes glowing like fires, set against massive fangs in the creature's mouth.

Gillian stumbled back a step, the muscles in his body tensed. The snake had been one thing, but the monster standing beside him now had been pulled straight from children's nightmares.

"Prepare yourself."

The voice echoed in Gillian's mind, like a low growl from somewhere in the darkness. Before he had time to react, the creature grabbed him in one of its long arms, then launched itself into the air.

Releasing him, Gillian's stomach lurched as he fell, only to be caught again by one of the beast's clawed feet. The creature dipped to one side as it began to dive towards the water, its wings spreading open and catching the wind with a thunderous roar. Each stroke sounded like a drum, churning the water below them as they began to gain altitude.

They soared over the ocean waves, much faster than Gillian could have imagined. The jutting volcanic rocks disappearing behind them, absorbed by the horizon. Up ahead the towers of Caldera loomed over the skyline, glittering in the predawn sun.

* * *

Time slowed as James collapsed on the sand. The fingalin soldiers faced off with the crew of the Shade, warstaffs charged, nobody moved.

Nevarian powered down his staff, dropping it on the ground and holding his hands up and out to the sides in a show of peace. No one from the other line moved, and slowly the doctor hunched down over James. Without taking his eyes off the Duchess, he checked James's vitals.

Chloe held her breath, she didn't dare think about what he might find, the possibility that James might not have a pulse, might not be breathing. After everything they had been through today, there was no way it could simply end here, not when they were so close to the Shade.

"He will be fine," Nevarian announced, rising slowly to his feet.

Chloe exhaled in a sigh of relief.

Seph

Railayia nodded, "Good, It would be a shame if any of you died on me now, after all the work I have put into keeping you alive."

Fetu took a step forward. "You call that keeping-"

Nevarian cut him off with a wave of his hand.

Chloe glanced between Nevarian and his staff, if he went for it, the soldiers would shoot him without hesitation. As it was, neither Fetu, Meghnah, nor Chloe were in a position to shield him without exposing themselves. They had gotten carless, and now they were paying the consequences.

The Duchess huffed. "Don't think you can win, there is no way out of this for you."

Nevarian clenched his fists. "What do you want from us?"

Railayia shook her head. "Why doctor, the only thing I need from you is to come quietly back to the city with me. There is someone who is looking forward to meeting you all, and I do not intend to disappoint him."

A chill ran down Chloe's spine, someone was looking forward to meeting them? Here? Nobody should have even known they had come here. Whoever it was, she was sure, she had no desire to meet them.

Nevarian inhaled. "I do not know who you think we are, but as I told you before Duchess, we are here to collect water samples for a project on Reicue 12. They are very sensitive, and if I do not get to them soon our time here will have been wasted."

The Duchess laughed. "You never expected me to believe that, did you?" Her ears twisted. "Surely the crew that was able to hijack the Vyrant, destroy Ulun'tess, best Captain Darith in open combat, seize the Dressick, and sneak a stolen ship through a midway station, can come up with a better excuse than that."

Fetu scratched the back of his head, "Hold up, you don't believe we did all that… do you?"

The Duchess starred a moment, it was unclear whether the emotion on her face was puzzlement or amusement.

"Take them back to the city, make sure they are under heavy guard at all times," she motioned with her hand. "And this time, let them starve."

The soldiers slowly walked forward, beginning to form a circle around the crew.

A blood-curdling screech rang in the air, as a huge demonic creature flew over the Shade, coming around and diving towards the soldiers, it dropped something from between its claws, the white fingalin body, rolling on the beach a few meters away from the group.

Retraining their weapons, the soldiers began to fire on the beast, whose skin billowed with dark smoke, as flames appeared to dance across the surface of its wings.

Taking a few shots directly to the chest, the creature crashed into the sand between the two groups, erupting into a cloud of shadow and smoke.

The Captain rolled from the thick black fog, springing to his feet, tendrils of shadows leaving a trail behind him. Soldiers continued to fire. The darkness coalesced around him, forming a black sword of an unknown origin in his right hand. The Captain parried the bolts of lightning on the blade.

The Duchess stepped back, watching in horror, as he sliced through the first of her soldiers in a long diagonal stroke. The Soldier's warstaff split in two, sparks flying into the air, and showering down around him.

The next closest soldier charged at The Captain. Spinning his staff for momentum, he brought it down towards The Captain's head. The Captain used the flat edge of the sword to catch the neck of the staff, guiding it down his arm. He stepped forward with his left foot, planting it in the sand. Rotating his body, he caught the staff in his left hand, then kicked his left foot into the soldier's chest.

There was an explosive crack as the armor plating shattered, the soldier stumbled backwards, releasing the warstaff, eyes wide in shock before collapsing to the ground.

The Captain spun the staff with his left hand, catching several shots as they assailed him. Twirling the staff over his head, he laid out three rounds of electricity before dropping it.

The soldiers quickly reverted their weapons to defense, absorbing any damage The Captain's shots may have done.

He charged forward, moving at impossible speed, shadow collecting in his open hand to form a Drak'or battle axe. In the blink of an eye, he was on top of the soldiers. Bringing the sword down at an angle, sparks flew from the soldier's shield as the blade ripped through the energy barrier. The staff exploded into sparks, leaving scorch marks on the white armor plates. With a second swing the soldier collapsed, blood seeping into the sand.

The remaining soldiers scurried backwards. The Captain stalked towards them, one of them fired. The Captain caught the electricity with the edge of his sword, then turning in a full circle, he hurled the axe, planting it into the soldier's chest.

In what felt like a glitch in the universe, The Captain flickered, leaving only a shadow in his place; he was suddenly standing over the fallen soldier. Placing his boot on the soldier's waist to hold the body down, he removed the axe, bits of armor cracking away.

The Captain's expression was cold, his eyes burning like binary stars against the void of space. A gust of air blew out from him and an icy chill washed over her, the ends of her fingers growing numb with the pressure.

The Captain walked towards the remaining soldiers, taking slow menacing steps. They kept their shields raised backing into the ocean.

The sky began to darken as storm clouds gathered over the beach, wind throwing sand into the air. Zaeith came to a halt as the waves began to swell, pushing the soldiers back up the shore.

Twirling his sword, The Captain grinned. Lightning flashed in the sky above, its thunderous roar echoing off the rocky edge of the caldera.

The soldiers deactivated their weapons, diving into the surf and vanishing beneath the waves.

Chloe caught movement out of the corner of her eye, Railayia was fleeing towards the tree line. In a flash of shadow, The Captain was standing in front of her.

Railayia collapsed to her knees tears streaming down her face, "Please, please, don't kill me."

The sky continued to darken as rain began pouring onto the beach.

The Captain raised her chin with the point of his sword, glaring into her eyes. "Tell Xious to leave them out of this."

Seph

He removed his sword from her throat, and she curled up into a ball, rain soaking into her dress as she sobbed in the wet sand.

No one dared say anything as The Captain walked up the ramp to the Shade. Fetu helped Nevarian gather James from the beach. Chloe glanced at Meg, she had the same look of dread Chloe felt in herself.

A large hand wrapped itself around her shoulder, giving her a comforting squeeze. "Don't worry," Gillian said. "Everything is going to be alright."

Chapter 32

The Captain's quarters were dark, save for the light emitting from the holo-projector. The data card had contained the sequence necessary to read the holobook, and been sufficiently undamaged to be retrievable, something Gillian could assume was the result of divine intervention.

He flicked through the pages, there were hundreds of them. Individual notes and documents that on their own were next to meaningless. But compiled as they were, each hastily written note, or transfer record, painted a very disturbing image.

They hinted at a vast conspiracy to overthrow not only the Divine Council, but the whole of the Alliance. Resources allocated in a deliberate attempt at sabotaging key projects. Personnel changes to give a particularly advantaged individual status and prestige, or to take it away from another. The systematic removal and replacement of the elders by members of

Seph

the Imperial family over the last five hundred years.

Gillian's father had his hands in almost all of it, sitting in the shadows quietly manipulating everything around him to his advantage, right up until his death when he personally appointed Xious to replace him.

It wasn't only his father though, it went back even further than that; his grandfather, and his great grandfather had been involved in the scheme. Every head of the family leading all the way up to Jeriell for the last seven generations has been subtly working to dismantle the Order.

Now Gillian was scanning through journal entries, his father had known he was dying for some time, and feared that Jeriell would not uphold the traditions. Gillian himself had not been groomed for the position of elder, his father thought he was weak, and would be unable to withstand the other members of the council.

He wasn't wrong. Gillian had spent his entire life trying to please his father, never able to fully live up to his expectations, no matter how successful he was. Izarrius was a strict man who would expect nothing less than perfection from those around him, not even his own sons. As a result, Gillian had been taught to keep his head down and not ask too many questions. Even with an entire starship under his command, all he ever did was follow orders and adhere to protocols.

Still, it stung more than a little to find definitive evidence that his father had considered Xious, a Drak'or no less, a more worthy heir to his legacy than Gillian. If someone had told him that Izarrius had picked Xious, he would not have believed them. But here, in this database Jeriell had given up his life for, was a copy of the original document signed and sealed by his father, declaring that it was the irrefutable will of Vyanna, that Xious should take his place as director, and that he would be the voice of Vyanna to usher in the age of enlightenment.

Gillian let out a long hollow sigh. There was nothing here that directly implicated Izarrius in the plot to murder his progeny. Only to remove them from the council, and any claim they might lay on his seat. But it was not a stretch to assume that plot was laid out after the elder had passed away.

"What will you do?" The Captain's voice was calm and steady like a lighthouse in a storm.

Gillian shook his head slowly. "What would you do?"

He was silent for a long moment, the text from the display reflecting in his eyes. "This is not a decision I can make for you."

Gillian let out a sigh, exaggerated by throwing his arms out as he turned from the display, passing across the room. Of course that would be his answer. It's not like any of the options the Captain may have considered were achievable for Gillian. After witnessing what had happened on Atlione, if The Captain had found himself in Gillian's place, he would just kill everyone.

Even if Gillian could do that, it wouldn't solve anything. All he would have accomplished is creating a power vacuum.

Gillian turned back to face The Captain. "If I could, I would reclaim my father's seat on the council. If I could expose their hypocrisy to the Order, maybe we could have the council reseeded."

The Captain remained silent.

Gillian let out a sigh, "But that would be impossible, wouldn't it?"

Seph

More silence.

"If everything here is true, Xious controls the council. By now they would have had more than enough time to purge anyone who was not sympathetic to their cause. This whole incident in the outer colonies could have accelerated their plans by several decades at least. Coalition worlds are already pledging themselves to the Empress. And if the Empire is already under her control, not only would I have to get rid of Xious, but I also need to pacify the entire Fingalin Empire."

The Captain shifted. "Replace Cathrin."

Gillian stared. "Replace Cathrin? It isn't so easy to trade out the Empress. She is assigned by the council, trained for years to fill the roll. Even if Cathrin were to die suddenly, I am sure the council has someone else lined up."

"As Vyanna's voice, they would listen."

"Xious would never relinquish the seat to me. I am a traitor now, he is a prophet and a savior. I am a monster who has thrown in with the Devil."

"I will take care of Xious. Focus on finding your Empress."

The door opened, flooding the room with light. The Captain removed the book from the projector and handed it to Gillian. "I suspect she is closer than you think."

Gillian stepped through the lift shaft and onto the deserted bridge. It was odd to see it so vacant. For most of their journey up until now, the crew had worked on rotating shifts, so there were always at least three people manning the command center. Then again, nothing had been normal since they had been taken prisoner on board the Dressick.

Despite Gillian's protests, Nevarian had managed to keep him hidden on Dramia. As it turns out, a planet is a big place and it is easy to get lost on one. So long as you are okay with never being able to leave that is.

The room was dark and cold, the occasional beep or chirp interrupting the silence. The empty view field stared back at him like an ominous omen, like the quiet calm before a raging storm.

In reality, the emptiness was a facade. The Captain monitored every system through his neural link. The entire crew was on standby, and once James had woken up, The Captain put him on the neural link as well.

Whatever had happened to him back on the planet did not appear to be serious. Nevarian had given him an injection of some sort, and he had been awake again in minutes. The doctor's explanation contradicted itself at every turn. Apparently he had almost killed himself, but since he didn't he should be fully recovered after a good meal and a good night's rest.

Returning to the shaft, Gillian allowed himself to drift down to the lower deck. Gliding along the zero gravity corridor, he stumbled on the landing platform of the mess hall. The crew, excluding The Captain and the doctor, sat huddled around a table.

"Mind if I intrude?"

Fetu laughed, then stood and offered his chair. "You stopped being an intruder a long time ago, you're one of us now."

Gillian nodded in a shallow bow, sitting in the offered chair.

Fetu grabbed another from a nearby table, and turned it around to sit backwards on the seat.

Travis glanced at Gillian, ears twitching. "Did you find anything interesting in that glass?"

Seph

Gillian let out a sigh. "Proof that my family betrayed our religion long before I was born."

Everyone sat in silence for a moment, not quite making eye contact. A sort of vague heaviness in the air, a physical manifestation of the uneasiness they were all experiencing,

Fetu was the first one to break the spell. "So, now what?"

James shrugged. "The Captain said our next move was up to Gillian. It all came down to what was on the glass and how he decided to handle it."

Fetu slapped Gillian on the shoulder. "Okay boss man, now that you know, where do you want to go?"

A light smile broke at the corner of his lip. He hadn't realized it before, but these people had become his friends. Comrades in arms against a whole universe out to get them. Maybe that was a little dramatic, but it did seem that way. Everything he had ever known or believed had been stripped from him. All he had left were a few fragmented ideals and shattered ambitions.

He let out a long sigh. "I don't know. I don't feel like it matters anymore. No matter where we go, we can't hide from Xious forever. And even if I did run off to some far away colony and disappear, I wouldn't be able to live with myself knowing I had gotten you so tangled up in my family's problems."

Chloe sat down the steaming mug she had been sipping from, pressing it between her hands. "What do you think Vyanna would want you to do?"

All eyes turned to stare at the small girl, whose face began to redden as she sank into her chair. The air had become so still it was as if a pocket of pure vacuum had opened.

"What, did I say something weird?" She asked.

Meghnah shook her head. "Since when did you start advocating for Vyanna?"

"Well.. I.. uh," she was staring down into her mug, the tips of her ears turning bright red. Her embarrassment was so palpable Gillian could almost feel her heart fluttering.

Meghnah raised an eyebrow.

Chloe shifted uncomfortably in her seat. "Well... I mean, that's his religion, right? It is not any different from me asking you what Vhast teaches."

Meghnah shook her head, "No, it's different. Vhast is a philosophy, not a god. It doesn't have a will or opinions. You could have asked, 'what do you believe is the right thing to do?' Or 'what do the Descendants teach you should do?' But you asked specifically, 'What would Vyanna want you to do?' As if you believed their god might want him to do something contrary to the religion who invented her."

She fidgeted with her mug. "I only thought that maybe… Okay, while we were on the Dressick I was curious, so I did some research. It has a huge library. The Descendants aren't all bad. I mean the teachings make a lot of sense. And after everything else we have seen, is it so far-fetched to believe their version of the story of origin? Their doctrine isn't about control or power or subjugation. It's about peace, about tolerance for other people and their viewpoints. It's about knowledge and learning, that there is a lesson to be learned from everything around you, if you can open your mind to the universe and let go of hate and bigotry and bias. That each individual is as important as the whole, and there is more worth in a single person than in a thousand stars."

Fetu laughed. "I don't believe it, you have gone and

converted on us!"

Chloe took a deep breath and exhaled slowly. "No, it's not that. I just think that if you look deeper than what you see on the surface, there may be more there than you are giving them credit for."

Gillian sat back in his chair, watching the lines on Chloe's face, her soft cheeks framed by her long platinum hair. Her slightly pointed ears and deep blue eyes, evidence of her fingalin ancestry.

He imagined her in a white dress draped in a lavender cloak. Her calm demeanor, the bravery she had demonstrated over the last few months. He thought of the way she had interacted with the fingalin soldiers on Atlione. Her knowledge of the subtleties of political maneuverings. And in his mind, he compared her with the image of every other empress he could recall.

Decades of schooling had failed to produce girls even half as qualified, Gillian could not recall a more suitable candidate who had ever been proposed for taking on the role.

He rose from his seat, "If you will excuse me, there is something I must attend to."

Chloe looked up at him. "I'm sorry. I didn't offend you, did I?"

He shook his head, "Not at all Chloe, on the contrary, you have inspired me. There is much I wish to discuss with you. But first, I must inform The Captain of my decision."

James raised an eyebrow. "And what might that be?"

Gillian let a smile break on his lips. "We are going to Vinge."

He found The Captain meditating in the sanctuary on the ship's upper deck. The deep earthy incense infused the air with its sweet aroma.

The Captain looked up as he entered, tendrils of white smoke shifting around him casting shadows in the flickering candle light.

"Have you made your decision?"

Gillian nodded. "I am going to reclaim my father's seat on the council."

The Captain grinned.

Chapter 33

James activated his consoles view display, high-pitched beeps and chirps erupted throughout the sleeping command deck as its systems came to life. The view field flickered as a holographic projection of the Shade and its immediate surroundings sprang into existence.

The ship floated in a slow orbit around the Dressick which trailed Atlione at a distance not much further out than its furthest moon.

James took a deep breath, taking one last look at the tranquil image. He felt a tug on the edge of his mind, and the display screen attached to the neural link confirmed Meghnah had finished inputting the jump coordinates.

"Alright James, I sent you the calculations for the Dressick, you are clear to open a hyperspace envelope."

"Thanks, Meghnah."

James took the information and forwarded it on to Scot, along with the instructions to execute the command in the nid network.

If everything went as planned, the Dressick would make two jumps, one out towards Vinge on an intercept course that would arrive approximately forty-eight hours after the Shade did. Once it got about halfway it would drop out of hyperspace, and jump again. This time towards the outer colonies. The sleeve Meghnah had calculated would open up a couple of dozen lightyears past the wall, where the ship would then shut down and drift aimlessly through space.

With no additional destinations, it would be several weeks before it was found again, and discovered to be abandoned, at which point it would be too late to catch up to the Shade. Any trace they left would have dissipated into the void.

"Okay Meghnah, you have five minutes." Using the neural link, James created a countdown which superimposed over the view field on each of the other displays.

"Affirmative, syncing fold generator now."

The Captain summoned a display in front of his chair. "Chloe, go ahead."

The ship's sensors erupted with static as Chloe dumped random radio noise through the ship's sublight and deep space transmitters.

James tuned out the receivers, silencing the eruption which pelted his mind like thousands of tiny shards of glass.

The time passed agonizingly slow as the timer ticked down. Everyone waited in silence. This was possibly the most dangerous maneuver James had ever been a part of. The idea was to hide their own hyperspace fold under the much larger envelope generated by the Dressick. Scattering enough random radio signals would muddle the trace, further obscuring the envelope created for the Shade.

Of course, the amount of distortion was likely to raise questions. Hopefully the inherent risk of opening two hyperspace windows on top of each other would keep anyone from proposing it as a viable theory.

The problem had to do with the dimensional stress fundamental to a sleeves structure. Hyperspace sleeves existed as sub-dimensional tunnels which wound their way through the fabric of space-time like folds in a galactic six-dimensional cloth. As stars and planets rolled around the universe, they twisted and shifted in an intricate dance with matter and energy.

The very act of opening an envelope could create and destroy a thousand sleeves warping the fabric of reality and distorting the edges of space. The larger the envelope you were opening, the more distortion it caused; and the smaller the sleeve was, the more susceptible it became to the whims of gravity.

The theory to this particular jump was to try to separate one sleeve into two. As soon as the Dressick had an open envelope, they would attempt to open a second envelope into the same sleeve. By calculating the size of both folds, they could use the forces of the envelopes to split the sleeve. Plenty of simulation had been run proving the validity of the theory itself, but it was impossible to predict the end result. If they were lucky, the sleeve would split into two uniform paths running parallel to each other. If they were extremely unlucky, it would explode into millions of tiny sleeves and rip both ships apart by their molecular structure.

The timer hit zero, arcs of electricity began dancing across the invisible surface of space in front of the massive warship, waves of distorted gravity echoing outwards from the spot in which the energy coalesced into a glowing ring of lightning. Arcs of purple and blue light danced across the opening like millions of tiny insects.

Meghnah turned up the thrusters on the Shade's ion drive, adjusting their orbit around the larger ship. In an accelerated dive, the Shade launched over the top of the Dressick, sweeping over its bow in a long upward arc. There was a deep hum as the fold generator activated, the sparks of electricity at the envelope's event horizon, twisted around each other forming into a swirling vortex of lightning.

Bolts of energy lashed out at the Shade like titanic whips of glowing wrath, caching on the shield like fingers on a plasma globe. The ship dove through the eye of the storm.

The world folded inward on itself, and James's stomach lurched into the ceiling as a wave of nausea washed over him. Lights swam in the air around his vision as the whole ship rocked and bent.

As suddenly as the vertigo began it vanished again, the view field showed the chaos of sub dimensional space.

James exhaled, tension in his muscles released. Quietly he sat back in his chair checking the instruments and sensor arrays. The moment before crossing into the envelope, Chloe had shut off the radio scatter.

"Envelope closed." Meghnah confirmed.

The Captain relaxed back into his chair. "Sleeve integrity?"

"Stable, but only just. It is difficult to say, but it looks like we should come out within fifteen light-years of our original projection. "

Seph

"And the Dressick?"

"Unclear, I can't get a reading on a second sleeve, but it isn't in ours."

The Captain 's display vanished. "Very well, keep me informed." He rose from his chair, then disappeared into the center shaft.

James finished reviewing the system's data. Everything appeared to have survived the transitions, and while the shield itself showed a significant amount of power drain, it had held up to the exceptionally brutal event horizon, and the ship's hull had been left untarnished.

"How long until we return to normal space?"

Meghnah huffed, tossing her head back and forth, "About a week, but it is hard to say for sure, there is still a lot we don't know about this sleeve."

He let out a sigh. "Right, I'll see what I can do to get you some more data."

Using the neural link, James began scanning the dense layers of space around them, firing off tracer beams at regularly varied intervals. There were four major factors that contributed to how quickly you could traverse a given hyperspace sleeve. The length of the sleeve was the most important, and the easiest to get a handle on most of the time. Second was the shape of the sleeve, the way it twisted and turned through the dimensions of space. This was affected largely by the density of the sub-dimensional layers around the sleeve. Deeper tunnels tended to move faster, and tended to have fewer twists and turns along the way. This affected the energy flow, which was kind of like a hyperspace heartbeat; it was measured by the intervals in between gravitational waves. But more practically, it was the rate matter trapped between the subspace layers traveled along the edges of the sleeve.

Normally this would have been calculated long before a navigator would even consider opening an envelope. Using finely tuned sensors it was possible to probe the layers of subspace and return incredibly detailed readings on its overall structure. In this case, however, the sleeve didn't even exist until they were already inside it.

For reasons James didn't quite understand, it was more difficult to calculate from inside sub-dimensional space. It had something to do with the state in which matter and energy existed within the sleeve. Once you were in sub-dimensional space, you existed simultaneously at every point along it. Travel through hyperspace was therefore instantaneous, and the time you experienced passing was an illusion created by the elasticity of space springing back around you. But no matter how much fancy talk it was dressed up in, the passage of time in hyperspace felt real enough, and it always lined up with time in normal space, so it all seemed to be a matter of semantics.

The data collected by the tracers began to pour back in, and James forwarded it on to Meghnah. The computer would interpret it in a few minutes, but she had enough experience to have a general idea of what she was looking at raw.

Meghnah frowned. "We aren't very deep, we might need to make an extra fold."

James nodded as the computer started to display the information in more intelligible terms. "We were prepared for that possibility coming in."

Meghnah glanced up at him around the edge of her display. "Yes, because we had calculated that we might not end up where we intended to."

Seph

"You said we should be within fifteen light-years? That shouldn't be more than a few days or so."

Meghnah shook her head. "We will end up pretty close to where we wanted to be. The problem is, Vinge won't be there."

"Where will it be?"

Meghnah shrugged. "That I will have to calculate once we are on the other side."

* * *

James faced off across the mat from Chloe on the Shade's upper deck. Sweat dripped from his forehead, and he had to wipe it off with the back of his forearm to keep it from dripping into his eyes.

They weren't using the AVRG this time, and nothing was being simulated. James tightened his grip on the silicone training knife which had become smooth with the oils from his palm.

He twitched, making a move to step forward to attack; Chloe reacted instantly, subtly shifting her weight, preparing a counter James knew he couldn't beat. Her eyes stared cold and calculating, watching even the slightest movement of every muscle in his body, like a cat stalking its prey.

He relaxed his right arm, creating an opening. She brought her foot forward, closing the distance between them. James brought up his right arm, sliding it along the back of her forearm, and deflecting the thrust out away from his body.

She stepped through the attack, sweeping her left leg behind her. James mirrored the motion and the two found themselves facing off once again.

Not only had Chloe been training with James over

the last three days, but Meghnah had also joined them for many of their sessions. Chloe had picked up on her forms and breathing techniques and quickly adapted them for her own use, combining it with the focus and attention she had learned during firearms training.

He drew in a breath through his nose then exhaled slowly through his mouth, calming both his muscles and mind. She had been more apt at close-quarters combat than he expected when they started, but now she had become exceptional.

He loosened his muscles again feinting another opening, this time she didn't fall for it but drew back a little herself. James took the opening, stepping forward with his left foot and jabbing his fist forward.

Chloe pulled her left foot back, moving out of range of the punch. James followed through, slashing with the knife. Chloe dropped, rolling forward under his arm, and spinning on her heel as she stood.

James tossed the knife to his left hand, stepping across his right leg drawing his body out like a blade, so he no longer had his back to her.

She lunged forward with her knife, James brought his right foot forward again, catching her wrist on the outside with his empty hand and twisting her into a lock. As Chloe's body turned, she slammed her left elbow into his chest, bringing her fist up and into his lower jaw, at the same time she pulled her captured arm in towards her chest, breaking free from his grasp.

She swept back her foot, drawing away from him and gaining some distance. James rubbed his jaw where she had punched him. He was starting to get quite the collection of bruises now, and not only physical ones. Between Meghnah and Chloe, he had not managed to win a match all day, and somehow the fact that Meghnah remained undefeated against the entire crew didn't help much.

James resumed his battle position breathing deeply. He needed to focus, he was letting it get to him and making sloppy mistakes. He should have been ready for that punch, should have been able to anticipate it, but he hadn't.

The edges of his vision began to blur, and his gut lurched upward as the world folded inward on itself. He clutched his stomach fighting back the nausea and dizziness as the world spun around him.

Before his mind could fully register what was happening, the room sprang back to normal.

"What was that?" Chloe asked, looking unsteady for the first time in over an hour.

James shook his head, sucking in oxygen as he tried to reground himself. "We've dropped out of hyperspace."

James watched the kaleidoscope of thoughts twist around on Chloe's face. "But we still have four days."

James nodded. "Something pulled us out of the sleeve." He placed the training knife on its rack then grabbed his blue jacket. He had taken to wearing it most of the time since they left Dramia. Calling up the command interface, he began the process of transforming it to mimic his uniform. The nanites went to work, collecting the sweat from his skin and converting it into energy.

Chloe handed him her knife and began patting her skin with a towel. "Do you think it is Xious?"

James met her eyes for a long moment. "I doubt it could be anyone else."

Back on the command deck, James slid on his neural link then fired up his console. Fetu and The

Captain arrived a moment later.

The view field activated. Two ships unlike anything James had ever seen hung in the flickering hologram. The two Dragon-class carriers orbited each other like a binary star system, with several dozen Wyvern-class ships orbiting in extended rings around them.

The dragons each consisted of three separate core sections, two of which orbited the central one along an outer ring which circled the body of the ship near the front. The ship itself resembled a long tower laid on its side with flat wings coming out at three of its edges. At what would be the southern pole of the ship's body, towards the forward edge, were five rings which had a vague resemblance to a rib cage.

Meghnah emerged from the shaft, hair still dripping with water from the shower, which soaked through her uniform. "What's going on?"

"Two Dragon-class warships." Fetu said, taking up a position next to The Captain's chair and standing in the at-ease position.

"Core!" Meghnah cursed moving towards her station.

Chloe shifted towards the rest of the crew, "We're being hailed."

The Captain gave her a sharp nod.

The view field flickered and the image of the massive ships was replaced by a fingalin Descendant officer.

"I am Cardinal Lameres of the Zhemarah. By order of Director Xious, you are to surrender yourselves immediately. The Director has promised to show leniency if you turn over the traitor and submit yourselves to the will of Our Lady Vyanna."

The Captain stiffened in his chair, eyes set hard.

Seph

"Xious does not speak for Lady Vyanna, Gillian Mayles does."

Anger flashed over the officer's face. "What kind of blasphemy is this?! Not only are you harboring a known terrorist and a traitor, but put him above the Prophet Xious? You are not even worthy to be speaking his name!"

The Captain relaxed back into his chair. "Gillian Mayles will take his proper place on the council. Xious can either step down willingly, or be removed."

The officer's lips pulled into a tight line. "Do you honestly believe you-"

The hologram flickered, a figure in Descendant ceremonial armor appeared. Plated in white gold and trimmed with sterling silver. A long lavender cloak hung from his shoulders. He wore a glove on his right hand where five gemstones glowed from a sickly yellow to bright lavender.

A grin twisted his face, amusement swimming in his deep red eyes. "My old friend." He held his arms wide in greeting, then bowed at the waist. "It has been so long, yet I see you have not lost any of your edge in the last ten years."

The Captain rose from his chair stepping up to the hologram. "It doesn't have to end this way Xious, it isn't too late. We can still help each other."

Xious swung his arm in an outward slash. "You are wrong Captain, it is too late. You have nothing left to offer me. You had the whole galaxy at your fingertips, you could have brought an end to this years ago; but you chose to stand by and do nothing. You ignored the plight of the galaxy wallowing in your own self-pity. Cowering in the corner because you were too afraid to make a difference. You sat on the sidelines and watched, offering nothing more than your paltry condolences, as the Alliance fell apart around you."

He visibly relaxed, shoulders drooping as he slowly shook his head. "I am not like you, Captain. I could not stand idle as the people around me suffered." He held his hands out wide. "I have built an empire, and when I am finished I will lead the galaxy into a new age of peace and enlightenment, the like of which your insignificant imagination can't even begin to fathom."

The Captain clenched his fists. "You are wrong, Xious."

Xious scoffed. "What would you know? I am endowing the galaxy with faith!"

The Captain shook his head. "This isn't faith Xious, it's subjugation!"

Xious looked down at The Captain, who looked very small compared to the image. "If it brings peace to the galaxy, what's the difference?"

"Some things we must discover for ourselves, even if the whole galaxy has to burn around us first."

Xious laughed. "No my old friend, my name will be praised in every corner of the universe, every star system will hail me as their savior, and I shall herald in a new era of freedom and stability the likes of which have never been seen. I have succeeded where you failed, I have done what you were too afraid to do, and become more powerful than you have dreamed possible."

The Captain closed his eyes and let out a long sigh. "Glayina is not who you think she is."

"No, *I* am not who you think *I* am!" Xious shouted. "She is a fool, like you. Oh, but she told me about you. Told me how you hunted her and her daughters across the galaxy, slaughtering them, chasing them from their homes. If she is a monster now, it is because you made her that way. But I am aware of her tricks, of her schemes. How do you think I found her and lived? She is as narrow-minded and shallow as you are. I saw right through her plans, and I bested her in her own game. I studied the ancient knowledge of the Descendants alongside her children, and I deciphered the texts even she was unable to understand. I have become a god, Zaeith! She couldn't stop me, and neither can you."

The Captain's body relaxed, and his voice became distant and hollow. "You have made your choice."

Xious stiffened, "Who are you to judge me?! Bow before your God and I might consider letting you live."

The hologram vanished and the massive Dragon-class ships were once more displayed in the view field.

Everything was silent.

"What now?" James asked.

The Captain turned to face the crew, eyes burning like the core of Vinge itself. "I am going to finish this." The Captain began walking towards his quarters.

Fetu stepped aside. "What about us, sir?"

The Captain placed a hand on the larger man's shoulder, looking him in the eyes. "Stay alive."

chapter 34

The holographic image flickered silently in the view field, the two Dragon-class ships circling each other like the ancient beasts they were named after marking their hunting grounds. It had been over half an hour since The Captain left the bridge, and presumably the ship entirely, though there was no indication that was the case. James was beyond doubting The Captain's ability to come and go undetected.

Gillian stood, staring at the hologram, only a few feet away from the view field. "Magnificent, aren't they?" His words were empty, lacking any true emotion one would associate with awe and wonder.

Meghnah grunted. "If by magnificent, you mean terrifying."

Gillian's lips broke into a half-smile, "Well yes, I suppose they are that as well. It is somewhat surreal to be on this side of them. Though I doubt anyone on board has ever truly appreciated them the way we are experiencing them now."

James glanced away from his terminal. There was something beautiful about them, the way they danced with their envoys, the sweeping curves in their design. They had a certain elegance that contrasted the unimaginable destructive power they represented, in a way that made them almost as much philosophical art pieces, as they were physical ones.

He returned his attention to his console, as much fun as it would be to wait out their impending doom by discussing the finer point of Descendant architecture, he planned on saving that conversation for another day. He had been scanning the ships and pulling up whatever information he could from their registrations.

The two carriers were the Zhemarah and the Zhemseph, both built within the last three years. Each of them were potentially carrying two Drake-class dreadnoughts and a dozen Wyverns, along with a fleet of more than a thousand fighters. Each of the Drakes, if they were present, would add another three hundred fighters to that number. And each of the Wyverns could be carrying as many as sixty additional fighters for a total of four thousand six hundred and twenty individual fighters and drones.

Even if they could out maneuver the enormous plasma cannons of the larger ships, there was simply no way they could keep up with numbers like that. Even using the cloaking device was only good until they decided to blanket the area with lasers.

Sending the Dressick off as a decoy had been a good idea, but now that they found themselves in this situation, James missed the extra firepower.

A bright light flashed from one of the Dragons as

a warning blared on his display. The Zhemarah had opened fire. His readout showed a significant power drain as the plasma bolt impacted the shield.

Using the neural link, James found the control for the new plasma shield Fetu had installed and activated it. The Shade's image in the view field was enveloped in the small orange globe. And the Shade's power consumption skyrocketed, the plasma shield might be impenetrable, but the Shade's antimatter coil was simply not designed to handle this kind of output; at this rate it would only buy them a few minutes at best.

"Meghnah, get us moving."

"On it!"

The ship veered into a long arch, catching in the gravity well generated by the Descendant fleet and accelerating around behind them. Bright flashes of cannon fire erupted from the edges of both ships as the Wyverns began to circle into formation and follow after them. Small bright dots began to swarm for the Descendant warships, each indicating a fighter or drone.

"More ships incoming." Chloe shouted.

"I see them." James confirmed

Fetu leaned forward in the Captain 's chair, summoning his own display overlay. "Meghnah, reverse our orbit, and drop us underneath again. James, I need you to do something about our energy consumption."

"Right." James found his connection to Scot using the link, and sent him a message to help him modulate the plasma shield. Then as the Shade's forward momentum began to dissipate towards the top of its arch, James shut off the plasma shield and hit the cloak.

Seph

The Shade dropped inward towards the Zhemseph, and Meghnah nudged the ion drive so it would propel them between the two ships, and launch them back into orbit on the other side.

Cannon fire from the Wyverns ignited the area where the Shade had been and along its predicted trajectory ahead of the swarm of fighters.

James began pulling the data from the first plasma burst gathered from the deflector shield array, reconfiguring it and dumping it into the phase shield.

The hologram flashed and a bright orange sphere appeared around the cluster of ships.

"What is that?" Meghnah asked.

"A plasma shield." Fetu answered flatly. "Keep our orbit shallow and try to stay as far away from the fighters and that barrier as possible."

Chloe swiveled her chair to face Fetu and James. "Why would they activate the plasma shield with us inside it?"

"To keep us from leaving." Gillian answered.

"But can't you fold through a plasma shield?" She turned back to face the view field.

Gillian shook his head, "Not if you can't see where you are going."

The Shade reached the end of its dive and swooped back inward, narrowly missing one of the outer spheres orbiting the core of the Zhemseph. James dropped the cloak and opened fire on the back end of the nearest Wyvern. The flashes of plasma were absorbed by their energy shields, and the ships began rotating in place continuing on their orbital paths.

The swarm of fighters peeled off from the larger ships using their gravity wells as slingshots to launch them around the Shade .

James started the targeting sequence on the laser array. "We are going to need some way out of here, because tricks like that won't work long."

Cannon fire exploded from the fleet of Wyverns, passing through the Shade as if it were a holographic projection.

The lasers finished charging and fired, the nearest Wyvern's shield concentrated at a point where it connected with the sixteen separate beams of light. James reset the polarity on the plasma cannons, polarizing them to the laser output and fired.

An orange sphere sprang into existence around the ship, absorbing both the lasers and plasma blasts into its swirling vortex.

The Shade shot through the cluster of ships followed closely by the swarm of fighters, several of which got caught in the battleships' gravity wells. The majority made it through however, and began pelting them with energy bolts.

It wasn't long before the Descendants compensated for the phase shielding. Warning lights started flashing as several hundred shots made contact with the force field.

Orange globes appeared around the other Wyverns as the Shade continued in its long orbit, flying out past the edge of the Zhemarah in an elongated ellipse, before falling back around the other side of the massive Dragons.

James recalculated the plasma cannons, as well as the energy blasters and returned fire on the fighters. Hull fragments exploded outward turning into additional projectiles along their former paths, most of which were absorbed by the larger ships' plasma shields.

Seph

Using the neural link, he pulled Scot into the tactical panel and had him start calculating the fluctuation algorithm the fighters were using to break through the phase shield, then fired up the newly modulated plasma shield.

The shield formed as a series of revolving rings in a spherical grid around the ship taking only a third of the power it had before.

"Meghnah, drop the thrusters." Fetu ordered, "Bring us back through the center and head off the swarm from the front."

The background hum of the Shade's engine coil fell silent and it dropped once more between the two carriers, falling with barely enough forward acceleration to grab the edge of the Zhemseph's gravity well and sling shot them back around on an orbital path opposite to the one they had just left.

Scot finished the calculation and James dropped the plasma shield, pulling up the phase modulator and reactivating it.

The hum of the antimatter coil kicked in again as Meghnah fired the iron drive, adding directional momentum.

As they approached the oncoming horde, small orange lights erupted from the fighters, each activating its own plasma shield. The glowing orbs drifted closer to one another like tiny fireflies. The spheres began to meld together as if they were bubbles joining and growing around each other, until they formed a single massive wall of light.

"Get the plasma shield back up, and at full strength!" Fetu ordered.

"What are they doing?" Meghnah asked.

Gillian glanced over at her from the view field,

"They are going to try to incinerate us on the edge of that wall." His voice remained even and calm.

James snapped his head up to look at him through his display overlay. "Wait, plasma shields can be melded together like that?" Pulling back the modulation parameters, James activated their own shield.

"Yeah, but only if their polarities match. James, full output on the laser array at this frequency." Fetu said.

There was a chirp as the transmitted message came through on his display. James used the neural link to quickly input the data and begin charging the array.

The continuous beams connected with the oncoming inferno, which absorbed it into its swirling mass. A warning flashed indicating that the antimatter coil was exceeding its maximum output threshold.

A moment later, the Shade dove into the raging barrier. Its plasma shield peeled off like the skin of a fruit, opening into the vast cocoon generated by the enemy fleet. The lasers projected across the void, decimating any fighters which happened to cross their path, and connecting with the opposite side of the field.

The oncoming fighters rippled outward, like particles on the surface of water when they come in contact with soap. James glanced down at the energy read out, the warning light had vanished. Not only that, but the power flow had reversed. Energy was coming in through the plasma shield emitter, and being forced out through the other systems. In fact, there was so much energy coming in that without somewhere to put it, they now had the opposite problem they had before.

James dumped the extra power into the phase shift

Seph

modulator, then activated the distortion array cranking up its energy output to full.

Eight sensor clones of the Shade sprang into existence around it, shifting and merging to make it impossible to distinguish which was the real ship.

Thousands of tiny energy blasts erupted from the Descendant fighters, the vast majority of them failing to even come close to striking. The phase shield managed to mitigate most of the others. Warning lights flashed at the few dozen which managed to breach the force field, indicating severe damage to the hull's outer shielding.

"We've been hit!" James shouted.

"Acknowledged." Fetu mirrored the data on his own overlay. "Meghnah, give us a little spin. Everyone, once we pass through the other side go dark!"

The Shade began rotating counter clockwise, maintaining its orbital path. James adjusted the force field putting its output to the front of the ship, keeping it between them and the onslaught of energy bolts.

Massive beams erupted from the Wyverns as they passed through the cluster, narrowly missing themselves in the attempt to catch the Shade in the complex web of destruction they created.

James continued calculating the phase modulator algorithm based on the input received through the force field emitter, barely keeping up with fluctuations in the attack.

The Shade launched through the edge of the plasma barrier, pulling out its own bubble of shield. Instantly, the power consumption exploded again. James dropped out every other system as energy bolts were absorbed into its surface, stabilizing the energy flow.

The sound from the engine room died off as

Meghnah powered down the propulsion. The quality of the view field projection reduced to random flashes of light, and bright spots as Chloe shut down all but the most essential sensor arrays. Finally, James turned on the cloaking device, and dropped the plasma shield. Warning lights flashed as a few more energy bolts struck the ship's hull, the inertial dampeners absorbing the impact so nothing was felt by the crew.

Everyone held their breath; if the ploy had worked, every trace of the Shade would have just vanished from enemy sensors. After the barrage they had just taken, it should be impossible to tell if they had been destroyed. There shouldn't even be any shrapnel left to recover.

Minutes passed in silence as they continued their long orbit around the binary center of the battlefield. The enemy fleet disappeared behind the glowing masses of the two Dragon-class ships in the hologram.

There was a simultaneous sigh of relief as the tension in the room dissipated. At least until their orbital paths crossed again, the battle was over.

James sat back in his chair glancing at Fetu. "What's our next move? We won't survive another round of that."

Fetu shook his head. "I'm not sure we have many other options, at least not until The Captain gets back."

Chloe swiveled her chair to face the others. "Can we get outside of the plasma shield the same way we got through the fleets?"

"No." Fetu answered flatly. "You can't force the polarity of a plasma shield from the inside, and I don't like our odds for guessing."

James turned his own chair. "But if we had a ship on the outside we could?"

Fetu nodded. "Theoretically, but we don't. Besides,

even if we did, I am not ready to leave The Captain behind."

James swiveled back to his display overlay. Then using the neural link, searched for Scot's entanglement transmitter. As he suspected, it was running and maintaining a constant connection to The Captain.

"Meghnah, can you calculate where the Dressick ended up?"

She turned to look at him, then nodded slowly. "Yes, probably, but why? We can't contact it without giving ourselves away."

A grin tugged on the corner of his lip. "Maybe we can."

"What about Zaeith?" Chloe asked.

James shrugged. "He can take care of himself, besides, his last order was to stay alive, and I intend to follow it."

He keyed on the intercom, "Travis, I need you on the bridge ten minutes ago."

A moment later, Travis appeared in the shaft ears twisted. "What's up?"

"I need you to help me get a new program for the nids running." James stood, offering his chair to Travis.

The Fingalin's ears flicked, "Sure, but how do you intend to get to them?"

"I am going to be sending a transmission out on a private subspace communications line, so make sure the code is as compact as you can make it."

Travis grinned sitting in the chair. "You got it."

James focused on a point at the far wall, letting his vision blur as he dove into the telepathic connection with the ship. He opened the combat simulator he and Scot had been playing with over the last several months, then began redefining the AI parameters.

Meghnah interrupted his thoughts. "Okay I found it, I am sending you the information now."

"Thank you." James used the neural link to pull the information from the tactical terminal, then linked Scot into his connection. "Scot, I need you to terminate your connection with The Captain, and use your transmitter to contact the nids onboard the Dressick. Have them lunch the fold program with these parameters."

James felt a mental protest from the android. The telepathic equivalent to "I am afraid I cannot do that."

James thought back, "I am not asking, terminate your connection, and send the command."

The droid returned an error code indicating the task had failed due to a command code override. James removed the override and sent the command again. A moment later, the connection with The Captain was terminated and a link established with the nid network onboard the Dressick.

James grinned, and uploaded the new AI simulation protocols to the tactical terminal for Travis. "Here is what I need from the Dressick once it gets here."

Travis nodded, not looking up from the display as he typed furiously into the computer. "Ah yes, I see. Okay, that shouldn't be a problem. I can tweak this and once that is finished compiling, we can dump that into here without any issues."

James felt Scot tugging on the edge of his link. "What is it?" He thought.

"May I reconnect my link with The Captain now?"

"No, I need you to maintain a connection with the nids for a moment longer."

Travis pressed a final key on the keyboard with a dramatic flourish. "And it is finished."

Seph

James grabbed it from the terminal with his link and passed it to Scot. "Execute this program, then you can establish your link." James continued to monitor the line until the transmission was sent, then dropped Scot from his link.

He exhaled long and slow. "Now we wait."

* * *

Minutes seemed like hours as they waited for the plan James had come up with to come together. They orbited around the titanic Dragon-class ships, passing the fleet twice before it broke apart. The fighters returned to the hangers, and the Wyverns resumed defensive patrols around the larger carriers. A small contingent of fighters began a search pattern, looking for any positive signs one way or another that the Shade had in fact been eliminated.

James held his breath monitoring the communications line closely. When the Dressick arrived, the first thing it would do was begin broadcasting in an attempt to make contact with them. He prayed it would get here soon. If he were the one running the search, when he inevitably didn't find anything, he would use a laser grid to blanket the area for good measure.

James quietly reviewed the tactical data from the last battle. The auto repair system had come on, and tiny nanites had gone to work patching the holes in the armor plating. It was a nice feature to have in place. But it would take almost a week for the job to be finished.

As it was, all it would take was a lucky shot, and vital systems were bound to get damaged. With the sheer size of the barrage they had just been through, it didn't even need to be that lucky.

Their trip through the enemy plasma shield had helped significantly with their power drain issue. The antimatter coil had been able to catch up during that time, and they now hung around ninety-three percent of their total output, and that number was climbing.

They were in better shape than they had any right to be in, any other ship in the galaxy would have been torn to shreds. The Shade had once again managed to surpass its reputation, all thanks to the strange and unique modifications The Captain had made to it over the years.

But even with its enhanced force shield, phase modulator, cloaking device, and the distortion array, which as far as James was aware was a Shade exclusive, they would not be able to hold out forever. Not only did it require vast amounts of power to operate at full capacity, they were tricks which given enough time any skilled tactician would find a way to beat. With as many ships as they had, they had already demonstrated they could get around it simply by overwhelming their capabilities, no skill required.

Last time a few dozen shots got through. Next time it might be a hundred, if they survived long enough to go another round after that, it could be as many as a thousand, and that was being conservative. They had already cracked the phase algorithm twice.

The communications array erupted with static as the Dressick appeared out of hyperspace, hundreds of nids each spamming a different channel waiting for an input command. James plugged Scot in as the logic coordinator to the nid network and initiated the simulation program.

Seph

The Shade sprung to life as Meghnah reactivated the propulsion and engine system. James turned on the modulated plasma shield, dropping the cloak as the view field image reconstructed itself. Chloe patched in the sensor information being transmitted by the Dressick giving them a clear view of both sides of the plasma barrier.

The enemy fighters scrambled to respond, firing off energy blasts without taking time to aim them. James targeted the nearest Wyvern, queuing up the solid state missiles and fired. The projectiles spread out in a giant web and bypassed the enemy force fields, before they had time to activate their plasma shield, exploding on the battleships' hulls. The ship began falling in an uncontrolled spiral towards the body of the Zhemarah.

A bright flash of light soared past them as the Dragons took advantage of the opening, firing their lateral cannons. Meghnah expertly avoided the explosion of plasma, sending the Shade into a series of spins and using the plasma thrusters to dodge around their targeting paths.

The Dressick activated its plasma shield moments before the Zhemseph's canons enveloped it. The battlecruiser's forward laser array fired. A single massive beam connecting with the shield being generated from the two Dragon-class ships.

Both carriers began firing their lateral lasers, hundreds of tiny beams focusing a grid on the dreadnought's shield. Most likely they were trying to prevent it from matching shield polarity, but James had anticipated such a tactic and included it in the original specification he had given to Travis. The Dressick would respond by using the incoming polarity shift to calibrate its forward laser, mirroring the shift in the enemy shield.

Meghnah adjusted their orbit to bring them over the top of both ships' outer rings, and out of the range of the lateral laser arrays.

The fleet within the barrier reorganized, becoming a swarm once again, they approached along an intersecting orbit.

The plasma shields of the Dressick and of the massive Dragon-class ships collided. Cascading magnetic waves rippled outward, decimating force fields and tearing apart many of the small fighters. James took the opportunity to fire off another round of missiles on a precalculated trajectory.

The enemy Wyverns activated their plasma shields which disintegrated the incoming missiles on contact. On a whim James pulled up the system he knew contained the hyperspace warheads. He began calculating the trajectory, but the system required hundreds of parameters he did not understand. Undeterred he set them randomly and fired nine of the projectiles, each targeted at a different battleship.

The polarity of the clashing plasma shields matched each other and an opening appeared as the Dressick was absorbed into the battlefield. The lasers from the two Dragons traced long scars across the dreadnought's hull, but the warship was designed to take a beating, and with no living crew on board, bright lights began to coalesce in front of it as its main particle cannon began charging.

The hyperspace warheads collided with the orange orbs of the approaching ships' plasma shields, erupting into tiny electrical storms on their surface. Tiny hyperspace envelopes opened all over the battlefield tearing through any ship which happened to cross their path, and wreaking havoc on the enemy fleet.

Meghnah drove the Shade down, directly between the Zhemseph and the Dressick dragging the enemy fleet behind them, and preventing the larger carriers from firing, or risk hitting their own ships.

As the Shade dropped below the firing path, the Dressick's cannon unleashed a beam of accelerated particles, tearing through the edge of the Zhemseph and evaporating a chunk of the enemy fleet.

Enemy ships rerouted, abandoning their pursuit of the Shade and instead targeting the much larger warship. Pelting it with plasma and energy weapons.

Meghnah accelerated, pulling out of the gravity well at full speed, twisting the ship to skim under the belly of the Dressick towards the plasma shield.

James pulled the polarization data being transmitted by the Dressick and fed it into the plasma shield emitter. Once the polarities were matched, he turned on the force field and phase modulator, then cranked the plasma shield up to full power. The shield began to solidify, then disperse as their emitter joined in the effort of generating the outer barrier.

The Dressick began moving backwards at full speed, withdrawing from the enemy plasma shield and pulling the Shade out with it.

A moment passed in stunned silence as they sat isolated within the Dressick's shield.

A huge grin spread across James's face, and he looked around to see everyone else smiling as well, he couldn't help but let out a shout of excitement.

Fetu shouted, "I can't believe we pulled that off."

Chloe's face fell, and she stared distantly at the view field. "I have to get on the Zhemarah." She said matter of fact.

"Wait, what?" Meghnah asked looking up from her terminal.

"I have to get on that ship," She said more insistently.

"And how exactly do you plan on doing that?" Fetu asked.

James removed his neural link. "Let me worry about that, and focus on getting me an opening."

"Right…" Fetu drew out the word adding a sarcastic drawl. "Okay, Meghnah, bring us in to skim the edge of their shield, Travis you take over tactical, I will need you to keep the nids on top of that shield polarization, Gillian you can help."

"Thanks. Com'on, Chloe. Let's go."

Chapter 35

Zaeith knelt at the altar within the Shade's sanctuary, inhaling the deep earthy incense. Power surged through his veins as he attuned his mind and body to the flow of energy around him.

Time slowed as the edges of his senses became sharp and focused. The electrical fields of everything around him glowed in his mind's eye as they interacted with the surface of his skin.

Through the meditation he could see everything on board the Shade. The glow of the engine, every conduit and circuit in the ship down to the tiny servos which controlled the weapons array; the crew as they prepared for the inevitable battle ahead; Nevarian, Travis, and Gillian sitting around a table in the mess hall.

He could sense their life force, pulsing with energy which his body constantly drew into itself. It wasn't that he was unaware of the effect his presence had on those around him, but it was an inevitability, another inescapable part of the natural order of things.

This was the price he had paid for the power he now possessed. The magic he used had left his body and soul twisted and deformed, and now, he was little more than a hollow husk of the man he had once been.

"Dreku zymo seph Zhemarah," Zaeith spoke the prayer into the empty room, feeling the pulse of the universe. Closing his eyes, he could sense the folds and layers in the fabric of space and time.

Reaching out with his mind, he caught hold of the tiny ember glowing on the end of the incense. Filling his lungs with air, he drew in the energy from the flame. Life drained into him, leaving behind a trail of smoke and a pile of ash.

Rising, Zaeith crossed the room and dropped down the central shaft, landing easily on the platform below. Opening the door he crossed the threshold into his private room. There were no lights here, only darkness. But that didn't bother him. These days it had little effect on his vision, which in reality he had not relied on in a much longer time than was worth remembering.

Walking to one edge of the circular chamber, Zaeith held out his hand, and using his partially connected neural link summoned a hidden compartment from the floor. The box raised until it was just above waist height, then slid open at the top.

Inside was a collection of jewelry inscribed with the runes of god tongue, one of the few magical languages which had been all but forgotten after the destruction of Vinge. Artifacts like these now littered the galaxy; they were so popular with the upper ranks of society that a skilled counterfeiter could consider it a legitimate career.

As popular as they were, few people understood their significance. The ancient civilization of Vinge had been one of magic. Before its fall, spellcraft had infused every segment of their society. Bending and twisting the fabric of reality with little to no thought of the consequences. A civilization where mortals worshiped tangible gods, who walked side by side with them, sharing with them their power as they carried out their will.

Now technology had all but exceeded most of their accomplishments. And while their grand cities lay in ruins, the Alliance Vyanna created thrived, the pursuit of knowledge driving them further than those ancient inhabitants ever could have imagined.

But there were still some secrets kept by the ancient traditions of the past. And there were many organizations throughout the galaxy who pursued them, hidden in the shadows and tucked away from the watchful eyes of anyone who might be looking to steal their power, or taint their pursuit of knowledge.

Organizations like the Forgotten, who hid on abandoned planets which had been dismantled for use in terraforming more habitable worlds. They shunned any participation in society, abandoning both reason and sanity in an endless pursuit of the power of the now dead gods.

Glayina the Witch Queen was a result of their research. Going beyond what even they were willing to do, she experimented on herself, twisting herself into a monster barely recognizable as anything that could be passed off as living.

Her power was a dark necromantic sort like his own, which fed on the life force of other living beings, pushing the user beyond the confines of mortality at the cost of their humanity. She collected children, using them in parts of her experiments in an endless drive to resurrect the ancient god king and take his power for herself. Stealing unsuspecting men from their families to use as fuel in her pursuit of power.

The only real power that opposed her was the Creed. An organization as old as the Descendants, they considered themselves guardians of the ancient knowledge of magic; they sought only to preserve the ancient ways, and prevent a repeat of the cataclysm that destroyed Vinge.

Members of the Creed underwent a series of serious trials to prevent anyone from stealing the knowledge they guarded and taking it to the Forgotten, or otherwise abusing it.

Zaeith himself had a long history with the Creed, and had planned to have Xious initiated once he was ready. But the more powerful Xious became, the more he hungered for power, and the power which Zaeith and the Creed had to offer was simply not enough for him. He, like Glayina, had sought the power of now dead gods, and gone looking for the power which was forbidden among members of the Creed.

Publicly, they were an intermediary civil organization which helped to negotiate difficult disputes between conflicting parties.

Darkmoon was a faction within the Creed. A small community of mostly Drak'or who resided primarily in the inner circle, and practiced the true form of Vhast. Originally, Vhast had not been about the complete abandonment of magic, and by extension technology. It had been about learning to live in harmony and balance with the natural forces of the universe, abandoning spell weaving methods which relied on the bending and manipulation of the dimensions, and instead teaching magic which focused inward, submitting oneself as a conduit through which the natural magic of the world could flow freely.

The irony was that the practitioners of Vhast who went so far out of their way as to shun any non-mechanical technology still practiced this form of magic through meditation and breathing techniques.

Zaeith removed one of the black rings from the case and slid it on his finger. In reality, it was not a ring at all. It was a longsword forged before the collapse of Vinge. It had been crafted from darksteel, a metal that was only found on A'un, and had the unique property of being able to absorb magical energy, as well as sever magical bonds. Usefully this meant it was even able to cut through modern force fields, including the Descendant's plasma shield.

The ring was a result of a storage spell, used prolifically throughout the ancient world to move and transport important items. It was accomplished by engraving the spell into the surface of the item in one of the magical languages. With the technique having been lost to time, many of these artifacts were doomed to remain in their converted form, passed down from one generation to the next, never fully understanding what it was they possessed.

Removing a white ring, Zaeith slid it on the index finger of his left hand. This one was a battle axe, a predecessor of the Drak'or throwing axes. Made of mythril, it had the property of being able to channel and reflect magic. Though rare, the metal was easier to find in this day and age, if you knew where to look for it.

Both materials were difficult to cast the transformation spell on, because these properties had to be accounted for in the spell's construction, otherwise the spells could fail in ways which were often catastrophic.

The next thing he removed was a longbow, represented as a bracelet tied around his left arm, followed by a double ring connected by a steel bar placed on the middle and index fingers of his right hand. This larger ornament was a scythe, a much less practical weapon, whose value came from the imagery it invoked when seen, and not so much its usefulness.

Zaeith tied a string of silver beads to his belt, attaching them just above his right thigh, and towards the center of his back. This was a collection of double-bladed drak'or throwing knives, with curved serrated edges.

He closed the box, and it retracted into the floor. Inhaling deeply, he felt the pulse of the universe. He pulled his hood up over his head, the circuits of the neural link connecting. For a moment, Zaeith could feel the ship as if it were an extension of his own body.

He quickly tuned out the extra inputs. This was a secondary function of his link; the device's real purpose was to regulate the vast amount of power stored in his body. Long ago, he had done as much as Glayina, and traded his body for power. Blood no longer ran through his veins, and his heart had not beat in many years. He was more shadow than flesh, with the dimensional plains of darkness and reflection fused into his body and soul. He possessed no aura of his own, instead his body fed off the life force of those around him, like a black hole consuming all matter which ventures too close.

Seph

Locked in a constant battle for his sanity, against a raging storm of blood-lust and hatred which boiled inside of him, he had learned to control it, harness it to his will. But only if he carefully regulated his power, bleeding off just enough of the energy he collected from others to keep the rage from boiling over, but never use so much of it that the blood-lust would overtake and consume him.

His neural link was a device designed by Nevarian to mitigate both issues. It allowed him to dump excess energy back into the ship, using it as an extension of his own body. Via an entanglement link he maintained at all times with the ship's SK01 unit, both it and the doctor could keep a constant eye on his mental stability, and intervene if he ever got out of control.

Nevarian was regularly updating the software, and tuning it to more effectively perform this function. It also required regular maintenance; during periods of excessive use the amount of power could overwhelm the system.

The connection worked like an anesthetic. Calming the torrent in his mind, it further sharpened his senses providing a clarity that otherwise was unattainable without constant meditation.

Zaeith moved to the back of the circular room where a black cloth hung over the ship's one and only mirror. Aside from this one piece, large chunks of glass were prohibited on the Shade. Glass was the single most dangerous material in the universe. It was a conduit where the physical world and the plane of reflection crossed, through which high order magic could be channeled.

This had heavily influenced the Descendants aesthetic choices, with many of the designs heavily steeped in the ancient traditions of Vinge, and the material being required for the function of many of the technologies which Vyanna left.

But having full panes of glass, especially mirrors, was like having an open doorway to the entire galaxy, at least the part of it that still practiced the ancient ways, and Zaeith had no interest in inviting any of them onto his ship.

It had not surprised Zaeith to learn that Xious had joined the Descendants after abandoning his position as the Shade's first officer. Though the religion had fallen a long way since its inception, it was still the holder of the largest collection of magical artifacts in existence. And though they understood little of it, it was also a direct gateway to the only source of true power in the galaxy.

Magic was infused into every aspect of their technology, and they understood almost none of it. Someone like Xious who had unlocked the secrets of that technology could use it to unleash unimaginable destruction. Which is precisely what he had done, adding both Corah'haren and Ulun'tess to the casualties of Vinge's war.

He tore the cloth from over the mirror. Even in the dark, its reflective surface glowed to his heightened senses, reflecting back a hazy twisted version of himself that looked more like a shadow than a person.

Zaeith waved his hand over the glass surface. It rippled outward, flowing like liquid and scattering in tiny drops of silver to reveal the command deck of the Zhemarah. Summoning his scythe, Zaeith stepped through the portal.

Fear gripped the officers on the floor below the command platform, not a fear that was visible on their faces, but a deep instinctive kind of fear of an inevitable certainty. The hunger inside of Zaeith burned, he grabbed the fear with his mind feeding on it, enlarging it, forcing it to the surface.

The officers drew their sidearms, fingalin sting-guns, they obviously had not been prepared for the enemy to simply walk onto their bridge. He hoped the ensuing chaos would disorganize their offensive and give the Shade the advantage they needed to survive.

The soldiers on the floor began firing, bolts of blue lightning flying at him in slow motion. Zaeith twisted, dodging the first bolt; it scattered across the view screen behind him. Stepping sideways he ducked, another shot hurtling over his head, the smell of ionization thick on the air. Standing over the nearest soldier, the remaining shots colliding in the space he had been only moments before.

The man stumbled backwards tripping over his own feet and falling into his chair. Zaeith raised his scythe amplifying the fear of those in the room even further. Now the officers on the command platform had caught on to the commotion.

He grabbed the console in his left hand and tore it from the floor, tossing it into the view screen and shattering it. The man in front of him fainted, passing out from the overwhelming fear. More lightning arched across the room.

Zaeith held out his left hand, a vortex of shadow appearing in his palm. He caught the energy bolts, absorbing them into his arm, then thrusting his hand forward amplifying and releasing the energy back at the ones who had shot at him.

Lightning scattered from his fingertips, electrocuting not only the officers, but also destroying their computer terminals.

Zaeith crossed the room in an instant, slashing with his scythe and cutting through the next soldier who was still standing, then turned to face the soldiers on the other side of the room. They switched their guns to rail mode, and fired.

Moving as quickly as he was, it was easy for Zaeith to trace the bullets with his eyes. He calculated the trajectory, then launched himself into the air, twisting to avoid the second round of fire.

Pulling his arms and legs in, Zaeith threw his body into a forward flip landing effortlessly on the command platform where two senior officers backed away in fear, shielding themselves with their arms.

The door at the back of the room opened, soldiers armed with sting-rifles entering onto the platform. He paused, letting their fear ferment as he waited for their next attack. The sting-rifles fired in unison; raising his hand to the side, Zaeith caught the lightning and pulled on its energy. The rifles let out a high-pitched scream as their output frequencies shot upwards, overloading their power coils and exploding in the soldiers' hands.

Forcing it with his mind, Zaeith deconstructed the structure of the energy and forged it into a whip, lashing out with it at the two senior officers.

The electric tendrils wrapped around them like fingers. They seized as the energy pulsed through their bodies unable to stop it. They collapsed to the floor little more than charred husks.

Zaeith leapt up onto the handrail around the outside of the command platform. Looking down at the handful of officers huddled against the far wall, he grinned. He could taste their fear on his tongue, and it made him feel alive again.

Bullets traced silently across the space between them, Zaeith took the energy he had been storing and reached out with it towards the small projectiles, grabbing them with his mind. He turned them away from himself, and accelerated them into several of the remaining computer stations. Feeling the folds in the surrounding space, he took a step slipping between dimensions.

He rematerialized a few feet in front of the soldiers, burying his scythe into the last remaining computer. Sparks exploded outwards, showering down around him and burning into his flesh. Zaeith ignored the pain, as his body began regenerating.

The soldiers dropped their guns drawing stunblades from around their waists. Screaming, they charged. Zaeith stepped sideways, spinning around the first soldier, catching the second soldier's arm. He twisted it, the ligaments snapped as their shoulder tore apart. He tossed them into the next officer, sending them both toppling to the floor.

Another officer closed in, lunging forward with his knife. Zaeith folded again, unfolding behind them, and summoning his bow. Drawing the string, he poured energy into the weapon, a long thin shadow forming an arrow.

Exhaling, he released the string. The arrow flew through the air, impaling one of the soldiers in the back. The remaining officers scrambled to regroup. Zaeith released one shot after another until everyone on the command deck was dead.

The neural link kicked in, siphoning off the extra power, and cooling the rage. With a thought he reverted the bow into a bracelet, then jumped back to the command platform. Leaving the scythe behind. It had served its purpose. Zaeith stopped to consider the carnage.

Something inside of him told him he should feel something. He had spent so much time on the battlefield, faced death so many times. All he felt was empty, a void which only more destruction could fill.

Breathing slowly, he suppressed the urge to go on a rampage, and focused on the task at hand; he needed to find Xious, that was the reason he had come here.

Stepping into the hallway, Zaeith used the energy he had gathered from the officers to harden his skin.

More soldiers rushed around the corner, this time in full body armor. The front line knelt to give the soldiers behind them a clear shot. Explosions rang out as the combustion rifles propelled their projectiles forward.

Zaeith walked forward as the bullets ricocheted off his body, deflecting into the glass etchings and shattering them all over the floor.

Glass crunching under his feet, the front line dropped behind, running back down the hallway to gain distance. Taking up new positions, the remaining soldiers dashed to the edges of the hallway. The center line cleared, the rear line began firing covering for the others as they regrouped.

Zaeith summoned his sword and axe continuing his slow march, terror rising in his opponents. Concentrating that fear, he used it to grasp the shards of glass with his mind, lifting them into the air in a sphere around him. He concentrated power into the glass, charging it with magical energy. They glowed with blue light as Zaeith propelled them forward, driving them into the soldiers. They exploded, tossing the bodies aside.

A new unit of soldiers arrived, two dropped down stabilizing rocket launchers on their shoulders. Two others setting up a laser turret.

The missiles fired. Zaeith used his sword to parry the first one. Unsummoning the axe, he caught the second missile in his hand. Using its momentum he spun on his heel and channeled energy into hurtling it toward the laser. It exploded, chunks of stone, falling from the marble walls as soldiers scattered out of the way.

Zaeith charged forward, coming down on top of the enemies before the smoke cleared. Spinning the longsword over his head, he summoned the axe again. He brought the sword down on the closest soldier, slicing through the joints in their high carbon ceramic armor. Each swing dispatched another soldier, blood staining the pristine floors of the Zhemarah's corridors.

A moment later, Zaeith stood alone in the hallway surrounded by the bodies of fallen Descendants. Once again the safeguards activated, calming his mind. He breathed in through his nose exhaling long and slow out his mouth as chemicals flooded his brain. Reaching out with his mind, he searched the ship for any evidence of Xious.

Concentrating on his breathing, he pushed his senses outwards, feeling the life force of everyone onboard. Hunger began welling up inside of him, and it was all he could do to suppress it.

A shiver ran through his body, aching, begging him to release his power and consume them. He hated how much he craved it, needed it. How alive it made him feel, if he admitted to himself that he enjoyed it, would he completely lose control?

The neural link brought him back from the brink of madness. Helping him to contain the impulsive nature of his power. Continuing his search, he found the aura of his old first officer. It had changed since they had last met, grown and twisted, becoming grotesque. Where once it pulsed with energy and life, now it thrashed against itself, like two predators fighting for the same prey.

The aura was emanating from the assembly hall. Xious was waiting for him, and he had no doubt planned a grand execution. Not wanting to push his appetite any further than necessary, Zaeith searched out the folds in the fabric of space, finding one which led to the chamber, he stepped through appearing outside the assembly hall's main doors.

The doors were carved of empress wood, but the carvings and inlays were new. Instead of depicting the nine suns, or the solar system of Vinge, they depicted Xious, standing above a world, with people of every race represented by a different color of glass bowing before him. The hand of Vyanna on his right hand, with images of planets and stars pouring out of it.

Zaeith grimaced, he had been naive to think he could have saved this man, pride had consumed him. He thought himself a god, he believed he could take the legacy of Vyanna and mold it into his own. The power of the gods was not so easily mastered or controlled.

Zaeith pushed open the door, revealing the chamber beyond. The room was dark, with only the faintest of light illuminating the white stone floor, the walls were covered in etchings of black glass. Lavender tapestries hung from the ceiling. And a long lavender carpet ran from the door to a raised dais on the opposite side of the room. At the top of the dais, Xious sat in full ceremonial armor upon an ornate throne carved from black glass which matched the artwork on the walls.

Zaeith entered the room and the door slammed closed behind him. Two massive men each at least eight feet tall stepped out of the shadows behind the throne.

Xious laughed. "I was beginning to worry you were not going to make it. You have caused quite the commotion, you know?"

"Stop this Xious, there has been enough blood shed."

Xious sat forward on his throne. "No!" He shouted, anger filling his eyes. "It has not been enough, it will never be enough. Not until the galaxy is kneeling before me. Not until you are begging for my mercy!"

Zaeith met his eyes, sensing the hatred buried beneath them, radiating outward and connecting him to the two men, who emitted no life force of their own. Zaeith cringed as he explored them with his mind, realizing what they were. Golems created from the flesh of the dead, and animated with the magic the Creed had rejected.

Xious sat back in his throne. "Make him suffer." He said with a smile forming at his lips.

The twisted creatures lumbered down the stairs of the dais, skin twisting unnaturally where it had been stitched together. The reek of death and decay emanating from their bodies. Their clumsy footsteps echoed with a heavy thud each time they hit the ground, sending vibrations through the floor which caused the entire room to shake.

Zaeith had not anticipated Xious would have

the power to create monsters such as these. The construction of golems was a difficult process which both required high level magic, and mastery of over eight of the ten planes of reality. They were ruthless beasts immune to the sensation of pain, and enhanced by the flow of magic to make them nearly indestructible. Even magical attacks had little effect on them.

Zaeith spun his longsword, stepping forward with his left foot he held his axe out in front of him, raising the sword so it angled behind his back. This fight would not be as easy as the last.

In an unexpected burst of speed, the monstrosity on the left lurched forward, the sound of bones cracking under its own weight as it moved. Raising its arm high and outward from its body it swung its massive fist towards Zaeith's head.

Using his axe, Zaeith parried the blow pushing the hand outward with the brunt of the blade, and turning his whole body, he stepped forward with his right foot slashing the sword across the golem's grotesque torso.

The magical barriers which would have been enough to deflect even bullets peeled away from the darksteel blade as it pierced the creature's skin, cutting a huge gash into the flesh which failed to produce any blood, only the stench of rotting flesh.

Zaeith used the momentum of his spin to continue under the creature's arm, burying the axe into its gut as it fell forward across its center of gravity. He yanked the weapon back, returning to his stance as he now faced the second monstrosity.

The golem leapt into the air, both fists raised together.

Zaeith reached out, sensing the flow of space around

him. He swept his left foot back, turning his back on his attacker, he dove forward folding between the layers of reality. In a flash of light he reappeared above the golem's head. Maintaining the energy from his spin, he brought his right foot around to kick the back of its skull. Its neck snapped forward as the creature lost its balance, stumbling to catch itself.

Zaeith landed in a crouch, cloak flared out around him as mist from the inter-dimensional travel evaporated off the surface of his body and clothes.

A loud ringing erupted in his ear. His vision blurred, nausea threatened to overwhelm him. Breathing against the pain in his temple, Zaeith reverted his sword back to a ring and pressed the heel of his hand against his head. The life energy on the surrounding decks began to burn itself into his mind, as a deep primal hunger swelled inside him. The subspace link was gone, rage and hatred were boiling beneath his skin, devouring what was left of his humanity.

The two golems regrouped, turning to face Zaeith again. He could see them only as hazy forms surrounded by dark red rings in his vision. The sound of millions of hearts beating around him hammered his consciousness, his body began to shake, pleading with him to succumb to the addiction. Inhaling, he began to draw on the life force of the Zhemarah's crew. Feeling their power surge through his veins, his vision began to clear as the pain in his head subsided.

The doors at the back of the room burst open as a line of soldiers flooded in. Zaeith could feel Xious's hubris growing, turning like meat roasted on a spit. Saliva began to build up around his tongue at the thought of consuming it. But it wasn't time yet, he wasn't ready. Hubris was a marinade to soak his meat in before broiling it under the fire of fear!

Soldiers took up positions at the back of the room. Reverting his battle axe, Zaeith smiled. Bolts of lightning sprang from their sting-rifles, catching the golems in their path; the electricity danced across the bodies, healing their wounds and reinvigorating them. That didn't matter, in fact Zaeith preferred it this way, devouring them would be that much more satisfying if he got to play with them first.

Zaeith's body became wreathed in shadow as the bolts of energy connected. A black hurricane of darkness and lightning swirled around him. Reaching down, he yanked two of the beads from the string at his belt.

The golem he had kicked in the head, charged forward bringing his fist down hard for a crushing blow.

Zaeith caught the monster's arm with his left hand, holding it in place. No matter how the creature pushed or pulled it could not break free of Zaeith's grasp.

The golem let out a scream as Zaeith twisted the arm inward, the sound of muscle, tendons, ligaments, and bone snapping under the pressure. He tore the arm free from the golems shoulder, tossing it aside as if it had been a paper doll.

Moving forward in what would have been no more than a flash of shadow, Zaeith thrust his hand into the golem's rib cage, grabbing the glass sphere which served as its core and yanking it from the creature's chest.

Squeezing it in his palm and channeling magic into it, dark fissures appear on the outside of the sphere until it shattered into a thousand pieces. The golem's body spasmed and collapsed into a heap on the floor.

Seph

As Zaeith stepped over the corpse, he felt the fear of the soldiers growing into abject terror. Xious's pride shifted into amused curiosity.

The remaining golem moved in from the right holding both arms out to the side, it swung them inward trying to crush Zaeith between its fists.

Holding his hand out, a burst of plasma erupted from his palm, incinerating the entire body section of the creature, leaving only its arms and legs intact, meted off at the elbows and knees.

Another round of lighting scattered through the room. Zaeith conjured his axe, catching the electricity on the weapon's edge. It began to spark as arcs of energy jumped across the blade. Activating the two beads in his right hand, twin throwing knives appeared. Squeezing them between his first and second, and second and third fingers, and balancing them on the heel of his thumb, he pulled his arm back over his shoulder. Bringing it forward at the elbow and flicking with his wrist as he reached the end of the draw, he flung the two blades into the air. They spun like boomerangs, flying in elongated arches they crossed the room, each slitting the throat of a separate soldier before clanking to the floor.

The fear boiled over in the soldiers, paralyzing them where they stood. Unable to move or react, their eyes grew wide as Zaeith continued forward. Reaching out with his mind, Zaeith found the scythe he had left on the bridge and with a thought reverted it back into the double rings, which appeared on his fingers.

Releasing the spell, he called forth the scythe into his open hand. Shadows sheathing his body. Feeling the life force of the soldiers, tendrils of darkness reached out grasping at them with shadowy fingers.

Zaeith breathed in their essence.

It filled his lungs, pulsing in his chest, like the heartbeat he no longer had. The soldiers began to age, growing old in front of him, until their last heartbeats slowly died, leaving behind only the echo of life in crumpled corpses.

Zaeith turned to face Xious sitting upon his throne, feeling his energy, the fear he had hoped for wasn't there, not yet. Closing his eyes, he searched the ship. Skipping over the tiny heartbeats of its crew, he found the smooth steady pulse of its main fusion core.

Meeting Xious's eyes, Zaeith grinned, bearing his fangs. Grasping the pulse of the engine core, he began to drink. Absorbing its power for himself.

A blunt force pounded itself into the side of his head, like a brick flying at the speed of light, as his neural link reengaged. Powerful sedatives flooded into his body as the system attempted to catch up. Zaeith felt the rage and anger drain away, leaving him deflated and lethargic.

Xious began clapping slowly as he rose from his throne. "Well done, a spectacular presentation indeed. But I am afraid I have wasted enough time on you, and my empire is waiting."

Zaeith let the scythe return to a ring, beginning a meditative breathing cycle.

A glowing lavender blade appeared in Xious's hand, generated by the arah'a'el zymo he wore. "With the footage from today, I will be able to prove beyond a shadow of a doubt that you are exactly who you claim to be. And after defeating you, there will be no one left to challenge me! The galaxy will worship me as their god. And not even Vyanna herself would be able to stop me."

Seph

Zaeith shook his head slowly, not saying a word.

Xious laughed. "Your silence betrays your fear. Zhemeku, A'elrek'ah, Mek'o'rah, Ve'o'ku." In a flash of light, Xious folded between the layers of space, appearing an instant later in front of Zaeith. He swung the lavender sword in a horizontal strike.

Zaeith conjured his axe, blocking the blow on the edge of the weapon. Parrying it over his head, he summoned the longsword thrusting it forwards. An energy barrier appeared around Xious. The dark steel blade tore through it, puncturing his armor below his left rib.

"Zhemeku, A'elrek'ah, Mek'o'rah, Ve'o'ku." In a flash of light Xious folded backwards, pressing his hand to his side and letting out a low hiss. "How dare you defy your god!" When he removed his hand, the wound was healed, blood still staining the white gold plating of his armor.

"O'vhen o'gaeus ty'ell kay'atur." At incredible speed, Xious came forward and slashed downward with the energy blade.

"Vehn gaeus ty'ell kay'url o'rah," a curved Drak'or short sword appeared in Xious's left hand.

Zaeith once again parried with the battle axe.

Xious twisted to his right. Avoiding the possibility of another lunge from Zaeith, he reversed the short sword, jabbing it towards Zaeith.

Zaeith caught the blade with his long sword, reaching it over his shoulder and behind his back, then spinning on his heel, slashing horizontally with the axe.

Xious reforged his energy blade into a shield, catching the axe mid swing, then pulled back putting a few feet of distance between them.

The two warriors paced in a loose circle, each maintaining distance from the other. Xious's energy had sharpened, gone was the arrogance of before, replaced by the finely honed instinct of a killer.

Zaeith widened his stance drawing his legs out into a vertical line across his body, holding the longsword straight out as an extension of his arm, forward, then reversed the axe so its neck ran along the edge of his forearm.

Xious charged, darting side to side, his movements were difficult to trace as each step blurred into the next. He slashed upward on a diagonal curve.

Bringing his right foot back across the length of his torso, and rotating his body, the blade swept past, just missing his tunic by less than an inch. Sweeping his sword down, Zaeith brought the blade behind the energy sword as if to parry.

As their edges met, the dark steel blade slid through the lavender glow, absorbing it into its black surface. In the same motion, Zaeith slashed forward with the axe directing it towards Xious's throat.

The Director's eyes went wide, fear radiated from the man who had proclaimed himself god.

"Seph!" At the invocation of the abbreviated spell, Xious vanished in a flash of light, reappearing across the room, steam rising from his armor. He began focusing his breathing. "You surprise me Zaeith, it appears you still had a few tricks I was not aware of."

Zaeith adjusted his stance, keeping the axe protectively in front of his face, longsword extended up from a position back and out from his waist.

Xious began laughing. "No matter, I tire of playing your little game. It is time to end this." He pulled his right hand back, elbow bent at a sharp angle two fingers extended over his left palm. "O'aphiss ty'ell buru," a fire ball formed over his left palm. Opening his right hand, he thrust it forward propelling the inferno towards Zaeith.

Spinning the axe to hold it properly again, Zaeith caught the fire ball on its edge. Continuing the rotation in his wrist, he generated a wheel of flames.

"Zhem aphiss," he whispered, adding power to the spell, flames jetted out across the floor in a sixty-foot blanket.

Xious held his gloved hand out in front of him, ducking behind it for cover. "O'finn cress hor'ock."

A wall of ice formed from the water molecules in the air. Shielding him from the flames. The barrier melted slowly under the intense heat, sustained by the magic Xious poured into it. When the flames dissipated, a thin transparent barrier remained.

Xious screamed, letting out a tortured cry of deranged madness. Glowering at Zaeith, his eyes burned red with hatred, glowing in the darkness like tiny fires in the night. "I've mo!" he yelled, thrusting his hand forward, fingers outstretched like the talons of a raptor.

Blue burst of pure magic shot forth from his fingers, flying towards Zaeith in high arcs through the air.

Zaeith held up his arm, generating a magical barrier around himself. The missiles of energy collided with it, splashing and dissipating on its surface.

"Zhem Zek!" Xious shouted, the words barely intelligible through his rage. A single bolt of lighting struck out from his hand thunder echoing throughout the ship.

Zaeith parried the lighting with his longsword, absorbing the magic into the blade.

"Aphiss, Aphiss!" Xious screamed. Small fire bolts, leaping from his hands.

Stepping forward with his left foot, Zaeith spun, deflecting the first flare with his axe, then continuing to rotate, blocking the second with the sword.

Xious breathed deeply, a hint of insanity gleaming in his eye and began to laugh. "I underestimated you! I thought you knew nothing more than cheap parlor tricks. But now I understand. It's not that you were afraid of power! No, no, no, no, no. You went looking for it too. Didn't you?!" He laughed again. "No, it wasn't that you were afraid, it was that you were weak! You couldn't handle it, so you ran away!" His laughing devolved into a hoarse cackle.

He bent over, placing his hands on his knees to catch his breath. When he looked up, he was smiling. "That's why you have been hiding all this time, afraid that if you came out into the light you would have to see your own shadow!"

Holding his hands out he shouted, "Meku buru, Kay'url meku!"

Xious began floating in the air, as Zaeith found himself falling to the ceiling, gravity in the room had reversed, Xious had cast a levitation spell on himself, to prevent him from falling.

Rotating his body and recalling his sword, Zaeith managed to catch himself, one hand on the ground with his right knee, standing on his left foot. Looking up he fixed his gaze on Xious's position. Casting a spell of his own, he launched into the air. He flew towards Xious, channeling magic into his axe, flames igniting around the head.

Xious vanished in a flash of light as Zaeith flew through the space he had occupied only a moment before, twisting, Zaeith caught himself on the wall, landing again on one knee, using magic to hold himself in place.

Xious waved his hand in large circles from his hips out, locking his left behind his right by the thumbs when they came together in front of his chest.

A beam of light fired from his palm. Zaeith barely had time to deflect it with his axe, sending it at an odd angle towards what used to be the floor. The stone tiles where the beam hit disintegrated into nothing.

Xious pushed his hands forward heels pressed together, fingers cupped to the sides. "Lavay zymo!" he yelled. A beam of bright white light erupted from his hands burning with the intensity of a sun.

Zaeith pushed off from the wall soaring above Xious in the air.

Xious snapped his finger and gravity reversed again. Unable to react, Zaeith found himself laying on his back on the cold stone floor.

Xious floated down slowly, laughing as Zaeith scrambled to his feet.

"Zhem O'laith laiem dreku, kay'url zayek ve'fo'el."

The shadows in the room began to coalesce at its center, twisting and folding around themselves.

Flames erupted in the darkness, glowing like the eyes of a great beast, as a deep growl began to echo off the walls.

A large foot covered in black scales stepped out of the swirling shadows, claws like talons at the ends of its toes. Pulling free from the shadows, the black head rose from the floor, dark smoke streaming from its nostrils, fangs protruding from beneath its lips. The remaining shadows pulled back into wings, revealing the rest of the dragon's massive body.

As the beast charged him, Zaeith summoned his dark steel sword, drawing his arm back and holding it horizontal to his body.

The dragon's mouth gaped, bearing down on him with ink black fangs.

Zaeith reached out with his mind, the life force pulsed inside of Xious. Twisted and mangled around itself, it glowed with pride and arrogance. Overflowed with confidence and ambition. And as the dragon's jaws closed around him, Zaeith smiled.

Slashing forward with his sword, Zaeith cut through the throat of the dragon. It's jaws snapped shut, passing through him as if he were nothing more than an illusion of the shadows.

The creature reeled back, roaring in pain.

Zaeith grabbed the creature's head with his mind then pointed the blade of his sword downwards. An invisible force thrust the creature's head into the ground. Reverting the axe to jewelry he placed a hand on the dragon's nose, then inhaled deeply, absorbing the magic that created it into himself.

Rage and blood-lust boiled inside of him, the neural link struggling to keep up with the surge of energy.

Zaeith turned to Xious. The smile left the Descendants face, his eyes growing hard and dark. Clenching his jaw, Xious held out his hand once more. "O'atur laith dreku zayek ve'o."

A dark shadow rushed forward, slamming into Zaeith's body and dissipating into nothingness.

The confidence and arrogance in Xious melted into terror, his eyes growing wide as an uncontrollable panic took hold of him. "What are you?"

Zaeith grinned as the echoing pulse of his life pleaded with him to devour it. The curse of darkness

Seph

Xious had used, was one of the deadliest spells ever written. It had a single purpose, to kill everything in its path. Nothing that was living could escape its power unfazed.

"O'atur laith dreku zayek ve'o," he repeated stepping backwards. The phantom image formed again, launching itself at Zaeith.

He walked forward, shadows gathering around him. The image vanishing with no effect.

In a flash of shadow, Zaeith appeared in front of him. "I am darkness," he whispered.

Xious fell to the floor tripping over his own feet.

Zaeith vanished into the darkness, emerging behind Xious. "I am shadow," he said, leaning over to whisper it into his ear as the scrambling man backed into his legs.

Xious looked up, panic gripping his throat, unable to speak. Crawling on his hands and knees he tried to get away.

Zaeith melted into the floor as a shadow, then moved in front of the man once again. Rising out of the floor, rage burning inside of him, Zaeith looked down at the man whose life force swelled with true terror and despair.

"I am death."

The dark emotions inside Xious boiled over, finally ripened by the sting of conquest snatched away at the moment of victory. Zaeith grabbed the pathetic man by the neck raising him into the air and bearing his fangs he hissed. "I am Zaeith."

Wrapping his mind around Xious's pulse, Zaeith began to drink, Xious began to age, as power surged through Zaeith's veins.

A bright flash of light appeared at the edge of his

periphery.

Somewhere someone was screaming, calling out to him.

Dropping the Descendant's limp body to the floor, Zaeith turned.

A young woman stood near the Dais, pale hair draped around her shoulders, blue eyes piercing through the darkness.

She was calling his name.

There was something familiar about her, something that dug into his skin, burning itself into his soul.

"Guin?"

He tried to focus on her, the rage that had consumed him beginning to dissipate.

"Guin?" He asked again, stepping forwards.

She smiled softly. No, not Guin. Her hair was white, not silver, and she wore the black and red of the Shade. Guin always wore white.

The energy drained from his body, nausea and dizziness replacing the blood-lust in his mind.

"Zaeith!" Chloe cried, tears streaming down her face.

Pain tore through his stomach.

"No!" James yelled.

Time slowed, as Zaeith looked down. The smell of burning flesh filling his nose and throat.

His vision blurred and began to blacken as the glowing lavender blade retracted from his abdomen.

Chapter 36

Feeling the glove mold to his hand, James winced as the familiar pain stabbed into the underside of his wrist. Flexing his hand, James inhaled slowly. "Are you ready for this?"

Chloe nodded.

They had taken a few minutes to arm themselves, Chloe now had his railgun slung over her shoulder, and James was carrying his sting-rifle. James took a moment to himself to admire her. Here they were preparing to make an impossible unshielded hyperspace jump onto the most powerful warship in the galaxy, yet there was no hesitation behind her eyes.

Gone was the insecure little girl who had hid behind meaningless conversation, and used loudness as a cover up for the broken pieces she was hiding inside. The child who hid herself away behind pale makeup and false faces. She had been replaced by a woman who was secure in her place in the universe, confident and driven.

Only a few months ago he had found her to be annoying and petty. But that wasn't Chloe, not the real Chloe. There was still a lot he didn't know about her, but he wanted to. She had shown him a side of the world he hadn't known existed, and she loved life with a passion and a wonder that was intoxicating in its effervescence.

He removed one of the black disks from the wall, examining the text inlaid into its surface. Even now, they were unremarkable. A tremor of anticipation shook his arms and legs, and he closed his eyes, taking a deep breath to calm his nerves.

"You okay?" Chloe asked.

James nodded. "Yeah, it's just kind of a big deal."

Chloe smiled weakly. "I watched you use that thing to create a small tsunami, how much harder can this be?"

The pressure James felt bearing down on his shoulders loosened a little. "I guess we are about to find out."

He placed the disk on the floor, then taking Chloe's hand stood over it. Reaching out through the glove he felt the shape of it in his mind. It was like a vast dark spot in a sea of light. Everything around it buzzed with energy, data about its structure unfolding in front of him at the slightest touch of consciousness. But the disk was different, the more he examined it, the more of a mystery it became.

James shifted his focus instead to the engravings. The gold leaf came alive as his thoughts touched it. The words began to come together, and James felt as if he could almost read them, like the hazy images on the back of your eyelids as you drift on the edge of wakefulness and dreams.

Still, there didn't seem to be anything remarkable about the object. As far as he could tell it possessed no mysterious electrical components, no computer code or software. No mirror, no glass. Nothing you would expect to find in a fold generator.

James pushed his mind deeper into the layers of space around the disk. The glove worked as a sort of universal neural link. As an interface to activate technology that had no obvious means of functioning. Like the plasma shield generator, or the ferry boats on Atlione. But it wasn't limited to that.

When he had created the wave, sinking the fingalin ships, it hadn't been with the help of any existing technology. The glove had allowed him to manipulate the water itself. Warping its structure to his will, like editing the base code of the universe.

Tiny folds extended from the edges of the disk, rippling through space like traces of light burned as after images into your eyes.

"It's not a fold generator."

Chloe looked up at him scrunching her nose and lip, "It's not?"

James shook his head. "I should have realized it sooner, The Captain was never using this as a fold generator."

"What is it?"

James looked up at her, the idea still forming in his head, "It's a tether, he used it to make sure he ended up back where he wanted to go. It could have been anything from this room, as long as it was part of the room, the book was just convenient and easy to carry."

Chloe let out a small sigh. "So, we can't use it to get to the Zhemarah?"

James shook his head. "No, but that might be a good thing."

"How?"

James smiled. "It's difficult to explain, but when I use the glove to control technology, I have to have a certain understanding of how the tech works. If this was a fold generator, it really couldn't be operating on any of the principles I understand about it. But when I moved the water on Atlione, I didn't need to understand how it happened, I only needed to know what I wanted it to do. I wasn't controlling a piece of equipment, I was manipulating the elements themselves."

Chloe nodded slowly. "So if Zaeith wasn't using the disk to open an envelope, then he must have been using magic. And if he was using magic that means, all you need to do is understand the basics, and you can use the glove to do it."

James smiled. "Right. If I can use the glove to find the right hyperspace sleeve, it shouldn't matter if I know how to fold or not, the simple fact that I can fold, should be enough to get us there."

Chloe paused for a moment looking away, eyes growing distant.

It was not without its risks, in fact if James thought about it, the fold not working was probably close to a best case scenario, imagining that there was a high probability that not fully understanding the process could transform them into sub-dimensional goo.

Chloe looked back at him and nodded. "Okay, let's do it."

James took a deep breath, feeling along the edges of space with his thoughts, he carefully examined the folds and bends as they flowed around him. Straining to reach outward following along their paths his view expanded. James tried to imagine the inside of the Zhemarah. Using the corridors from the Dressick as reference.

The images in his mind twisted and turned, winding around themselves, uncurling into strands like tiny glass hairs.

James thought about the space surrounding the Zhemarah, recalling images from the battle only a few minutes ago. The thoughts clarified the other images he was seeing, and he could feel the shape of the titanic warship in his mind. Thousands of tiny folds surrounded it, wrapping themselves in and out of the gravity well generated by its fusion cores. James imagined grabbing the strands between his fingers, the ones near the Zhemarah in his left, and the ones near himself in his right, then gently brushing them outward, letting any unconnected strings fall away.

The remaining sleeves he traced with his eyes, finding their endpoints and eliminating any that fell outside of the ship's hull. Sifting through what was left, James found one that glowed with energy, as if he were looking at the end of a fiber optic cable.

He took a deep breath. "Ready?"

"Ready." Chloe confirmed squeezing his hand.

Focusing in on the single fold in space and time, James used the glove to decode its structure. Holding the sleeve with his consciousness, James opened the end of it and stepped through.

The whole world began to spin in a different direction as James's vision faded to black, his body becoming weightless. He found himself flouting in a sea of empty white, voices half whispered in unfamiliar languages clawing at his mind. Time stood still seconds stretching on into eternity as the space between his heartbeat expanded like the pulsing of a distant star.

Thoughts began slipping away, his consciousness fading into the nothing that surrounded him. Something soft squeezed his hand, sending memories flooding back into his mind. He caught the scent of apple blossoms, as if drifting on a breeze.

The pit of his stomach lurched as the Zhemarah's audience chamber unfolded. James blinked, a wave of dizziness flowing over his mind.

His muscles felt tired, his head ached as if someone were pounding a drum behind his eyes.

"Zaeith!" Chloe's shout rang and echoed in his ears with a high-pitched squeal that emanated from everywhere and nowhere all at the same time.

A dark shadow moved across his vision, two red dots leaving trails of fire in the darkness as they moved in tandem with each other.

James blinked fighting back the sensation of drowning, and steadied himself.

His vision began to clear. Shadow tendrils trailed off The Captain like smoke rising from a fire. He looked at them, eyes burning with a rage older than time itself. His mouth moving, the sound falling short of James's ears.

"Zaeith!" Chloe shouted again, there was a slight croak to her voice, she was crying.

A limp figure behind Zaeith moved, light reflected off its shimmering white and silver armor. James focused; Xious becoming clearer. Gripping his gun he stepped forward.

Lavender light flashed, a blade appearing in the Descendants hand.

Seph

James tried to scream, but the sound caught in his throat, and burned like desert sand.

Xious thrust the blade through The Captain's back, its purple glow piercing through his stomach and protruding from the other side.

Adrenalin surged into James's body, clearing his mind, and freeing his muscles.

James stepped forward, concentrating his remaining energy into the glove he imagined a sword forming in his hand.

With a bright green flash, the blade extended slicing through the darkness of the room.

Xious turned to him and smiled.

The Captain began falling, stumbling, he caught himself, holding his palm over the hole in his abdomen.

Turning to face Xious he hissed, exposing long fangs under his upper lip.

Blood drained from Xious's face, his skin going from a smooth charcoal to a thin ash.

The Captain straightened, removing his hand from his stomach. The wound had healed, closing around itself, not even leaving a scar, only a singed hole in his uniform remained.

Xious stepped backwards. "H-how are you... still alive?"

James looked between the two men, holding his blade out in front of him and making a triangle with his feet.

Zaeith stepped towards Xious, his sword vanished from his hand. He reached out, grabbing Xious by the throat and throwing him across the room.

Xious slammed into one of the massive glass etchings, black shards shattering around him as he fell to the floor. He pulled himself out of the debris, brushing glittering dust off his armor. The spines on his helmet bent, crushing into one side of his face.

Letting out a scream, Xious tore the head piece off, tossing it aside. His eyes blazed with hatred, hair disheveled and glistening with sweat. "Why, won't, you die?!" He seethed between clenched teeth. Thrusting his hand out with a talon-like finger, saliva flung from his mouth as he shouted, "Zayek O'rah!"

James let out a scream as every bone in his body shattered into a thousand pieces. Collapsing on the ground, his muscles began to spasm as the pain overwhelmed his consciousness.

* * *

"O'atur laith dreku zayek ve'o," Xious spat as a shadowy phantom rushed towards James' crumpled up body.

Chloe's heart lurched, her chest tightening as the air escaped from her lungs. She couldn't scream, couldn't think. Everything was moving in slow motion as her gut clenched around itself.

Xious turned to Zaeith laughing, a twisted glee flickering in his eyes.

Chloe squeezed the grip of her railgun, and leveled it with her eyes, pulling back tears, she exhaled, and squeezed.

Xious lurched backwards as the bullet penetrated his skull, twisting unnaturally as he fell.

Nausea filled Chloe's stomach, and her arms began to shake as the world began turning again. She dropped the gun, tossing it away from herself, and clutching at her shoulders she dropped to her knees beside James and began to cry.

Zaeith stepped in front of her, kneeling down and placing a hand on her shoulder. "I'm sorry." He whispered.

Folding her arms over her knees she looked over at James's body. His arms and legs were twisted at strange angles, blood was soaking through his clothing, and where his skin was visible dark bruises had formed. His eyes were vacant, and unfocused. There was no need to check for a pulse.

James was dead.

* * *

Zaeith stared down at James's broken body. As powerful as he was, healing magic was one of the few things that were beyond his grasp.

Chloe laid her head on James's chest, tears streaming down her cheeks as she buried her face in his jacket.

"You know, I could still save him." A hideous snake-like voice hissed from somewhere in the darkness.

Zaeith looked over his shoulder, Glayina's voice echoed in his ears. Rising to his feet, he faced the witch as she stepped out of the shadows behind the black throne.

"What are you doing here?"

Glayina clicked her tongue. Crossing the room to stand over Xious. "Come now, Dark Hunter, I am hurt. After all this time, I thought you might be happy to see me alive. I suppose I am a lot harder to kill than either of us thought. Are you disappointed?"

Zaeith raised an eyebrow, "Would you like to test that theory?"

The enchantress laughed. "Oh my dear Dark Hunter, you and I both know that I am no match for *the* God Slayer. I only came to watch." She nudged the Descendant's body with her toe. "Well, and to collect what is mine." She looked up at Zaeith, yellow eyes blinking sideways. "Xious was a promising pupil, had he not been so power hungry, he might have made something of himself. Unfortunately, he was as stubborn as you are. And I was going to have to dispose of him eventually. Mostly I wondered if you still cared enough to stop him yourself."

Zaeith pulled one of the beads from his belt, hurling the knife at the witch.

She vanished in a flash of light and smoke, rematerializing a moment later as the blade clanked harmlessly to the ground.

Glayina produced a small glass orb from out of the air. A glowing green mist swirled inside of it. "Now, now, I came prepared to bargain. The life of the boy, for the body of Xious, you let me leave here; alive, and with my apprentice, and I give you back yours. Otherwise, I take him with me."

Zaeith locked eyes with Glayina, he would be better of killing her now, even if it meant losing James, but when he saw the hurt in Chloe's eyes something inside of him moved. It was warm and soft, different from the emotions he had grown used to, and reminded him of life he had lost in the age before memories began.

"Very well, take him and leave." Zaeith said.

Glayina folded her hands in front of her lap and bowed. In a flash of light, both her and Xious were gone, and the glass sphere fell towards the ground.

Focusing his energy Zaeith sprang forward, catching the orb moments before it shattered on the stone tiles.

Returning to James, Zaeith straightened his body, placing the sphere between his hand, folded over his chest.

Kneeling beside him, Zaeith prayed. "Zymo dreku seph zhemarah."

"Light and darkness reflect divine providence." Chloe whispered, echoing the words of the prayer.

Zaeith looked into her bright blue eyes, as she tried to dry the tears, her platinum hair falling over her shoulders.

The faint sound of breathing escaped between James's lips.

Chloe coughed, looking down at him and wiping tears from her eyes she let out a sorrowful laugh.

"Thank you." She whispered.

Chapter 37

James flexed his arm experimentally. The exobrace made a faint buzzing sound as the motors kicked in, helping with the motion.

It had been almost a week since he had apparently died while on board the Zhemarah. He had woken up four days ago with little memory of the events, Nevarian took little time in assuring him that if it were not for the anesthetics in his system he would have been in excruciating pain.

Every bone in his body had been shattered. By the time he had been placed on the medical bed, they had been reduced to little more than grains of sand. Nevarian had injected him with nanites, who had replaced his old bones with new ones, a process which had taken approximately three days.

When he had first become conscious, he was paralyzed from the neck down. The doctor had explained it was because the new bones couldn't hold up to the pressure exerted by his muscles, and they would need more time to harden. Even now, four days later if it were not for the nanites reinforcing them, the simple act of moving could do a significant amount of damage.

The tiny shards of bone fragments also shredded his muscles, leaving them severely weakened. Nevarian had warned him that it was a very real possibility he would be dependent on the nanites for the rest of his life.

Chloe smiled, squeezing his hand. She had been sitting in the chair beside him most of the morning.

"We are about to unfold over Vinge. Do you want to see it?"

James glanced over at Nevarian who gave a short nod, "But be careful in the shaft, and bring him back here immediately after."

Chloe smiled softly, brushing her hair back behind her ear. "Of course."

She helped him to his feet, blood rushed downward as he stood for the first time, his muscles strained under his own weight, but the exobrace helped to relieve the pressure and keep him balanced.

Chloe stepped off the landing platform backwards, holding both of his hands as she floated into the corridor.

James stepped out into the air, becoming weightless as the pressure was taken off his muscles. The zero gravity was a relief on his body, his new skeleton not having to support the weight of his organs and muscle tissue.

"Doing okay?" Chloe asked.

James nodded. "Great actually."

"Okay, we will take it slow, alright?"

James smiled. "Sounds good."

Holding his hands, Chloe used her other hand to pull them across the hall to the lift shaft. Guiding him forward, she allowed him to grab the ladder.

With Chloe keeping him from drifting too far to one side or the other, James pulled himself along the ladder one rung at a time. The tube was somehow longer now than it ever had been before, not being able to simply jump to the next platform.

Arriving at the bridge, James waited for Chloe to float up next to him, letting himself drift to one side of the chute. Chloe landed on the platform, then pulled James out behind her.

His knees gave out under the sudden increase in gravity, and he would have collapsed if it were not for the exobrace compensating for his lack of strength.

Fetu swiveled in the tactician's chair, facing the shaft. "Good to see you moving around again." He grinned.

James chuckled. "Aren't you supposed to be off duty now?"

He laughed. "Someone needs to pick up your slack." Turning back to face the view field he continued, "Seriously though, I wasn't about to miss this."

"Hyperspace envelope opening now," Meghnah said.

The view field flashed, lighting scattering around the Shade's shield, and the projection of Vinge materialized in the hologram.

"Envelope closed," Meghnah confirmed.

There was a collective gasp as the crew caught sight of the planet of origin for the first time. Nothing could have prepared them for what they saw. The stories of Vinge's destruction had been passed down from generation to generation, sparking in the minds of children more questions than it ever provided answers.

Questions like, why don't we terraform it again, or how come we don't use pieces of other planets to fix it. Questions that parents had no good ways to answer, and by the time most children grew to adulthood, the story was one of those strange realities they learned to accept.

Looking at the planet now, there were no such questions. James had expected to find a barren rock, with deep fissures and canyons cut into its surface, dried ocean beds, and artificial atmosphere domes around the last remaining populated locations, kept intact only for their historical or political significance.

But Vinge was not a desolate world. Vinge was a destroyed world. Spinning on a perfectly vertical axis, what was left of the planet trailed its sun in the shadow of the moon. Unlike any other world in the galaxy, Vinge did not orbit its sun, rather it was dragged through the galaxy like the trail of a comet, stretching out as an asteroid field for millions of miles.

Directly behind the planet's moon were the most recognizable chunks, where four loose tectonic plates floated loosely around the world's glowing core. A force field took the place of an atmosphere reflecting the light from the molten core back down towards the floating continents in a perpetually underlit twilight.

The devastation of the ancient homeworld extended far beyond the confines of the planet itself. Looking at the map of the star system projected in the view field, it became apparent how much effort had gone into preserving the world.

Every other planet in the solar system, fourteen in total, had been reorganized into perfectly circular orbits, extending out from the sun in a cone around the corpse of Vinge. Sorted by size, the largest planets were farthest from the sun, and created a unique gravity well which held the world locked in its position.

After a long pause, Chloe squeezed his hand.

"We should get you downstairs."

James nodded. "Okay."

"Chloe." The Captain called out as she helped James into the shaft.

Chloe turned to face the Captain, "Yes?"

"When you have finished, get changed and meet me by the main hatch."

Chloe gave a quick salute. "Yes, sir."

Once they arrived at the medical bay, Chloe helped James back into the bed, then leaned over and gently kissed his cheek.

James smiled. "What was that for?"

Chloe shrugged as her earlobes began to redden. "I guess I am about to become an empress, I don't know how things are going to change after that."

She started backing away from the bed and James grabbed her arm. "No wait."

She paused. "What is it?"

Over the last few days, Chloe had told him of the Captain and Gillian's plan, how they had been preparing her to take over the role of empress and visage of Vyanna. But right now, in this moment, she was just Chloe, the girl whose eyes had lit up in wonder of Dramia, the girl who had danced under the moonlight, drenched by the rain. The girl who had laid beside him dripping wet in the observation dome of an ion lift. The girl he loved.

Pulling himself upright in the bed. "Don't go yet." He whispered.

Seph

Tears began to build under her lower eyelids. "I wish I didn't have to." She whispered back.

Pulling her closer, James pressed his lips to hers. She wrapped her arms around his neck, pulling him up and kissing him back. They remained that way for a long moment, each wishing they could make that instant last forever.

Eventually Chloe pulled away, James stared into her bright blue eyes. There were tears there, but she was strong, and didn't let them fall.

She smiled softly.

James gave her a quick nod, settling back into the bed. She turned away, not saying a word. When she left the landing platform, the doors closed behind her without a sound.

* * *

Chloe leaned back against the med bay door, tears streaming down her cheeks as she floated in the corridor.

"I love you." She whispered the words, she didn't have the courage to say to his face, hoping that maybe if she spoke her feelings aloud to the universe just this once, maybe they could be real.

Composing herself, Chloe returned to her bunk where she retrieved the long white dress she had purchased for her date with James. Sliding out of her uniform she exchanged it for the dress, then removing the lavender sash she had received from Gillian clasped it around her shoulders with a white gold brooch in the shape of a crescent moon.

Once dressed, Chloe made her way to the cargo hold where Zaeith and Gillian were waiting.

Zaeith's eyes softened when he saw her, and he smiled sympathetically.

Gillian glanced between the two, his ears twisting.

A moment passed in silence as the solemnity of what they were about to do sank in.

"This is really happening, isn't it?" Chloe said, it was more of a statement then a question.

Gillian nodded. "Yes. Are you ready to rule the galaxy?"

Chloe let out a half giggle. There really wasn't anything funny about it, but laughing was the only thing that held her together.

She shook her head. "No, you?"

Gillian huffed. "No, I suppose not."

Zaeith opened the door, revealing the docking tube with the Descendant shuttle.

* * *

"How could you let this happen?" Cathrin yelled.

Trepidor pressed the air out of his lungs slowly. Setting Xious's ruined helmet on the table he turned to face the Empress. "What was I supposed to do, refuse him?"

"Kill him!" She shouted.

Calmly the admiral wiped spit off his cheek. "He is a respected officer who holds a claim to the director's seat on the council."

Cathrin slapped Trepidor across the cheek. "Who we can brand as a traitor!" Turning away from him, she stormed across the room sitting in the tall glass throne. "We killed the rest of them, what are you so afraid of now?"

"The rest of the Order, Cathrin. Without Xious, we

are done for. And with the evidence they have against us, the followers will have our heads before the week is over."

"Xious, Xious, Xious, all anybody ever cares about is that crock. We never needed Xious, and we don't need him now. I am the Empress and I will not let some impostor who calls himself the Devil take away everything I have worked for."

"With all due respect, Xious was the voice of Vyanna, everything we have accomplished in the last ten years is because of him. And now he is gone, and Gillian Mayles is in possession of a document claiming that as he ascended into heaven, he declared Gillian his successor. And as far as Zaeith goes, he destroyed the Vyrant, hijacked the Dressick, and defeated both the Zhemseph and the Zhemarah in combat. I suggest you do not underestimate him."

"Lies, you and I both know Xious would never have chosen Gillian. If we deny it, the Order will have no reason to believe it either."

"Once the document Jeriell hid becomes public, they will have even less reason to believe us. Remember, Cathrin, both our names show up in Izarrius's journals. Xious did not. They can just as easily frame us for his murder as we can pin it on them, at least that story sounds plausible!" He couldn't help but raise his voice a little towards the end. He took a deep breath before continuing. "I am sorry Cathrin, but whether or not he is who he claims, we cannot win this one."

Cathrin shot up from her throne flaring her lavender dress out behind her like the wings of a dragon. "I do not care if it were Vyanna herself. No one is taking this away from me!" She yelled.

A knock sounded on the door. Grand Admiral Trepidor locked eyes with Cathrin, setting his jaw.

"Enter." Following along with the Empress had been fine when it came with the promise of imperial power, but with Xious out of the picture, he was not about to risk his life for her.

"How dare you!" She screamed.

Trepidor stepped up to her, rising to his full height. "I would remind you, Empress, that with the director gone I currently control two-thirds of our military power. If I say this is over, it is over."

Two guards escorted Mayles and his delegates into the room. Gillian wore a pristine uniform, cut for fingalins. It exposed his fins majestically as if he were intentionally putting them on display.

He was followed by a young woman in a white dress, with a lavender sash tied around her shoulders. Her platinum hair was put up in an elaborate fingalin style, with interwoven braids running down below her shoulders.

Trepidor sighed, shaking his head in defeat. With Gillian's lineage on display, and the literal visage of Vyanna by his side, the enlightened had set up their own defeat. Based on their own doctrine, no one would ever be able to challenge their claim to the Descendant throne.

The last man to enter was a Drak'or dressed in black, Trepidor wondered if this was the infamous Zaeith of the Shade, who had caused so much trouble for the enlightened, or simply a bodyguard Mayles had acquired along the journey. It didn't matter either way.

Mayles spread his arms wide, elbows at his waist and bowed. "I am Elder Gillian Mayles, Voice of Vyanna."

Seph

Trepidor returned the gesture. "Welcome, Elder Mayles. Come, let us discuss your future with the council."

Cathrin pushed past Trepidor jabbing a finger into Mayles's face, "I will never allow you to have a seat at this council!" Cathrin yelled.

Trepidor grabbed her shoulder and squeezed hard, then pulled her back. "What the Empress means is, we do have some conditions we would like to discuss with you."

"You will not speak for me, you toad!" Cathrin hissed through clenched teeth.

"Silence!" Trepidor said raising his voice and inflating it with as much force as he could. "You will be quiet, or I will have you removed."

Cathrin sunk back, doing as she was told.

"Now," Trepidor said, once again addressing Mayles, "I am prepared to turn over complete control of the council to you, I only ask that when you go public with Izarrius's journals you omit the name of the Empress and myself."

Mayles glanced back at the darkly clad figure who followed him. There was a period of silence before he spoke again.

"I don't suppose you would mind enlightening me as to precisely why you think I should do that, you are not in a position to deny my claim."

Trepidor bowed his head. "Of course you are correct, but I can assure you, things will be a lot easier for you with *my* cooperation."

The fingalins ears flattened as he narrowed his eyes. "Are you threatening me, Admiral?"

Trepidor shook his head, "Nothing of the sort your excellency, I am merely playing the last chip I have on the table."

Mayles visibly relaxed. "If I agree, how will you help me?"

"We will publicly denounce the rest of the council, then validate your claim that Director Xious's final wish before ascending to the throne of Vyanna was that you take his place as Vyanna's voice. We will hang around long enough to be convincing, and to establish this lovely young woman you have brought as the new empress, and then we shall step down from the council. And submit ourselves to exile on one of the smaller private worlds of the imperial family."

"NO!" Cathrin yelled, pointing to Trepidor she faced the two escorts. "Kill them, they are traitors, all of them. Kill them now!"

The two soldiers tensed, glancing between Cathrin and Trepidor.

Trepidor shook his head, and both relaxed. Ignoring Cathrin's order.

Cathrin looked around the room frantically, turning first to Mayles, then to the guards, and finally to Trepidor.

Slamming her body into his side, she pushed him over, grabbing his sidearm from its holster and turning to point it at Gillian.

A bright flash of light lit the room as the scent of oxidation filled the air.

Cathrin collapsed to the ground unconscious, as one of the escorts lowered his rifle.

Trepidor straightened his uniform, taking a deep breath. "She will come around, I promise."

Chapter 38

The scrying room was dark and cold, not unlike the rest of Erindite. It was one of the few rooms in the city that was made of natural stone, not welded together from the hulls of scavenged freighters.

Strange letters were carved into a ring around the room's circular perimeter. While he still could not read them, he had learned they were from the runic script, a derivative sister language to god tongue. It could be identified by its blocky square shapes which were a stark contrast to god tongue's more flowing curves for what were essentially the same characters.

The centerpiece of the room was the scrying pool, a large stone cauldron with straight sides that curved on the bottom, set on top of three circular stone slabs, each narrower and taller than the one beneath it.

He shared the room with three young girls, the only one he had met before was Sphex. Sphex was about eight years old, and had bright red hair, and beautiful green eyes, and a laughter which Kurt found to be contagious. She was bright for a kid her age, and Glayina often left her to teach him the lessons she was studying herself. Curiously, she had two blue feathers growing from behind her left ear, and one that grew from her right. Kurt had never had the courage to ask about them.

The other two girls were older, the eldest being about ten. They both had dark black hair, but it was silky smooth and well maintained. As far as he could tell they were totally ordinary, but as they watched him Kurt felt the same uneasy feeling he got when he looked at the Witch Queen's eyes.

Outside of a few other young girls, the only other people he had met in Erindite were adult women. Much like Glayina they had pale skin and yellow eyes, with oily black hair. They never spoke to him except to review his lessons at the direct request of the queen. Otherwise, they went about whatever work they were doing, pretending he did not exist.

Kurt had used the scrying room under the supervision of Glayina, or one of the sisters, but only to observe faraway places and gain insight into their historical significance. Today, however, Glayina had instructed him to use it to observe the battle between Xious and the Dark Hunter.

The Dark Hunter was an ancient enemy of Glayina, who was said to hoard power for himself. According to the witches, he was the one who had slayed the ancient gods.

Xious had demonstrated incredible power through the battle, out matching the Dark Hunter at every turn. Up until the last moments when everything flipped.

Seph

Even still, if the others had not arrived, he wondered if Xious might have won in the end.

The heavy wooden door opened and Glayina entered, closing it tight behind her. "Now my children, what did we learn today?"

The oldest of the girls raised her hand.

"Yes, Fleriel?"

The girl stood from the stone bench. "That no matter how powerful you are, arrogance makes you lose."

Glayina smiled showing her fangs. "Very good. Anyone else?"

The other dark haired girl raised her hand.

"Go ahead, Visha."

"That you shouldn't play with your food, or else it might get away?"

Glayina turned her head to the side, eyes blinking sideways. "And what makes you say that, my dear?"

Visha looked down at her feet fiddling her thumbs. "Well, If Xious had started off with his most powerful spells, he might have been able to win. But he wasted a lot of magic on smaller spells that didn't do any good, while his opponent didn't need to use any magic at all until the very end."

Glayina nodded. "Very observant of you, my dear, but it is more complicated than that. The real lesson you should learn from this is not to waste magic unnecessarily. It is okay to play with your food, but you have to be smart about it. If you are spending more energy than your prey, then you are the one being hunted."

All three girls let out a simultaneous, "Oh."

"What about you Kurt, what did you see?" Glayina

asked.

Kurt shrugged. "It seemed to me like the only reason Xious lost was because he let his guard down when that girl arrived."

Glayina frowned. "Then I am afraid you were not paying enough attention. Xious never stood a chance against the Dark Hunter, he was foolish to challenge him." She returned her gaze to the children, "and you will be too if you ever do the same."

"Then have we already lost?" Kurt asked.

Glayina grinned. "Not at all, taking over the Alliance was Xious's objective, not ours."

A chill ran down his spine. "What is our objective then?"

Glayina stepped forward, looking into the pool. "The power of the gods, of course."

Epilogue

Zaeith stared out over the horizon, the perpetual eclipse of A'un over Lavay in the sky above. Vinge's molten core glowing with amber light, in contrast to the long purple shadows cast by the edges of its floating islands.

"I trust them." Guinevere said, her voice was hauntingly beautiful like the first sunrise of spring.

"How long do you plan on doing this?" Zaeith turned to face her, staring into the endless blue of her eyes.

She walked out to join him on the ledge overlooking the ruined city of Tru'all below. "As long as it takes."

He held her gaze for a long moment, then looked away. "We are not gods, Guin."

She stared out towards the horizon. Playing with the white gold brooch around her neck. "No, we killed god."

"Ah'trell wasn't god." His words hung in the air like shattered glass.

"Maybe not," Guinevere finally admitted, "but if not us, and not him, then who?"

The ancient friends stood together in silence, staring out across the broken landscape, remembering a time when it had once been whole. Remembering a time when it had once been home.

Zaeith's voice was far away and distant. "I don't know, Guin."

Ash filled the air as the fractured planet heaved under its own weight.

"They will do a good job." Guinevere said into the silence.

Zaeith nodded. "You chose well." He chuckled lightly. "She is a lot like you."

She laughed, it was like tiny wildflowers falling in a soft summer's breeze. "And he is nothing like you."

The two immortals laughed together, the sound echoing into the silence of the night, shattering the stillness of the long dead world as they reminisced about a time history had forgotten.

Eventually Guinevere grew more serious. "It has been so long Zaeith, why do you still call me Guin?"

For a long time, Zaeith stared into the eternal ocean of her eyes, wondering if he might get lost in their depths. "Because someone has to remember."

She reached out her hand, small beads of eternity floating off her bracelet. "Goodbye Zaeith, we will see each other again."

"When?" Zaeith asked as a shimmering silver portal formed in front of her.

"Soon." She promised, as her silver hair faded to white.

Seph

He nodded, wishing for this moment to last a little longer, and eternity to be a little shorter. How long was soon when you were immortal? "Soon then."

He watched as Vyanna vanished into the portal.

"I will always remember."

Aknowledgments

Now it's time for all those boring thank you's at the end of the book that very few of you will probably ever really take the time to read, though I hope that isn't the case. Just like with the credits at the end of a movie, a lot of people were involved in getting this book out of my head and into your hands, and they deserve to be recognized for their contribution. (Especially since I went and splashed my name all over the cover.) Unfortunately I can't give you a cool after credit scene, or a special spoiler that you have to read the credits to get to, that doesn't really work with print the same way it does with video. However, I can thank you for taking the time, not only to read my book, but to appreciate along with me all of the hard work that went into making it a reality.

The first person I need to thank is my wife, who has tirelessly stood by me, and supported me throughout my writing. She encouraged me, and provided a wall to bounce ideas off of as I tried to work through the intricacies of characters arcs, and filling in plot holes as they popped up. She is also my number one proofreader, she read each chapter as it was written through every draft. Then she helped me scan the completed draft for any errors we missed along the way. And if that wasn't enough, she also took over most of the marketing and community outreach of this project, helping to make sure the book landed in as many hands as possible.

Next I need to thank my brother Jonathan, if it were not for him, the universe and legacy of Ving would never have existed. It was Jon who drew out the first maps of Ving, helping me to create races, character, and locations as we laid under the trampoline in our backyard. Or when we used the playground as a spaceship to explore the galaxy. Not only was he a huge part in building the foundation for what ultimately became this book, he and his wife Anya were also heavily involved in the review and editing process of the book's second draft. They provided feedback, and helped to smooth out the rough edges.

The cover design was provided by Michael Brewster who worked diligently to capture in a single image so many complicated ideas, and my imagination. Jacob Jessop provided the illustrations for the hard cover, bringing the worlds of the Alliance and their inhabitants to life.

I owe a big thank you to Chance Settelmire who performed the final editing on the manuscript, ensuring that all of the little details that had fallen through the cracks got cleaned up. It turns out then when you write over one hundred thousand words, there are a lot of cracks for things to fall through, at least when I am writing it.

There is an entire list of people who deserve to be mentioned here for their various contributions, from proofreading, to content editing, to moral support. Some family, and some close personal friends. For the sake of saving paper I will not name all of them, because this doesn't have to be exactly like movie credits, and they know who they are. This is my thank you to every single one of you no matter how small your contribution may have seemed. It was and is a big deal to me.

And finally I want to thank you reader for taking a chance on me and picking up this book. Wherever our journey takes us from here, it is all because of you, and the faith you put in me when you decided of all the books you could have picked up to read, you chose this one. Keep up to date on future releases and extra content at https://esandborn.com/

God Tongue

God Tongue and its sister language Runic are complicated in the fact that neither of them are complete languages. Originally God Tongue had no written components, and Runic had no verbal components, however eventually the two were combined to be complimentary.

However, they can still be difficult to decipher in either form since many of the phrases and glyphs used represent complex ideas more then a single word. Further both the glyphs and the phonetics can be combined together changing their meaning based on how they are merged.

An inexperienced observer may find it difficult to decipher the intent of the combination. While the complete system includes hundreds of individual glyphs I have provided a small sample of a few of the more important words that show up throughout the story.

The Glyphs shown are drawn in their God Tongue variation as they might appear on the Arah'a'el or in Zaeith's books.

	Aphiss: Roughly translates to Fire/Flame. It more accurately represents the concept of combustion, and thermal energy.
	Arah: Most commonly translated as Providence. This glyph actually represents the concept of Clairvoyance, Foresight, Knowledge and Interpretations of Future Events. It came to represent protection to The Descendent's as a reference to the ideology that such knowledge should only be used to defend life, and never to take it.
	A'un: This glyph is most commonly used to represent The Moon, and the natural moon of Vinge is named after it. Though its true meaning has to do with gravity and the interaction between matter.

Cress: Translated as Ice, Frost, or Cold, this glyph represents the transfer or despersal of energy.

Dreku: Directly translated this glyph represents Darkness. However, it does not refer to darkness in the traditional sense. Instead it refers to the absence of both energy and dimensionality, and was commonly used as a symbol for the Abyss by the civilization of Vinge.

Lavay: Literaly means The Sun at the heart of the Vinge system. It is somtimes used as a general refrence to nuclear energy, though historically a combination between the Aphiss and A'un glyphs would have been used.

O'rah: Represents the shape or form of matter. It is used by the Drak'or to mean the substance of self.

Rek'ah: Means Thought, or more specificaly the energy and demensionality of consciousness. The Drak'or use the word to represent the mind, though it has lost its association to the glyph in their culture.

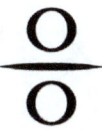

Seph: The single word that best discribes this glyph is Reflection. Though its meaning is more complex then what you see in the mirror. It represets the duality of matter, space, and energy.

Vay: Represents The Stars, it also represents the ambient energy contained within the universe. It was used as a symbol for navigators and map makers. Towards the end of Vinge's civilization it was more broadly used by anyone seeking to disseminate knowledge for the benefit of others.

Zhem: Represents the concept of Divinity. Often is used to refer to deitys in the same way the we might use the words God, or Gods.

Zymo: Illumination or Light, it refers specificaly to energy which exsits within the visual spectrum.

www.ingramcontent.com/pod-product-compliance
Lightning Source LLC
Chambersburg PA
CBHW060259100726
47907CB00002B/212